TEMPTED

Quentin drew Rachel into his embrace and she went willingly. She wanted him, if only for a short while. Though they could spend the rest of their lives together, she was far from sure that would come to pass. Even so, her yearning for him must be sated.

Their mouths fused in a series of kisses that began softly and tentatively but swiftly became heady and urgent.

"Rachel, Rachel," he murmured against her lips. "I want you."

"I want you, too, Quentin," she responded, almost breathless with raging desire and exquisite pleasure, not daring to ask herself if she was risking too much . . . everything— anything— for love.

Taylor—made Romance From Zebra Books

WHISPERED KISSES (3830, $4.99/5.99)
Beautiful Texas heiress Laura Leigh Webster never imagined that her biggest worry on her African safari would be the handsome Jace Elliot, her tour guide. Laura's guardian, Lord Chadwick Hamilton, warns her of Jace's dangerous past; she simply cannot resist the lure of his strong arms and the passion of his *Whispered Kisses*.

KISS OF THE NIGHT WIND (3831, $4.99/$5.99)
Carrie Sue Strover thought she was leaving trouble behind her when she deserted her brother's outlaw gang to live her life as schoolmarm Carolyn Starns. On her journey, her stagecoach was attacked and she was rescued by handsome T.J. Rogue. T.J. plots to have Carrie lead him to her brother's cohorts who murdered his family. T.J., however, soon succumbs to the beautiful runaway's charms and loving caresses.

FORTUNE'S FLAMES (3825, $4.99/$5.99)
Impatient to begin her journey back home to New Orleans, beautiful Maren James was furious when Captain Hawk delayed the voyage by searching for stowaways. Impatience gave way to uncontrollable desire once the handsome captain searched *her* cabin. He was looking for illegal passengers; what he found was wild passion with a woman he knew was unlike all those he had known before!

PASSIONS WILD AND FREE (3828, $4.99/$5.99)
After seeing her family and home destroyed by the cruel and hateful Epson gang, Randee Hollis swore revenge. She knew she found the perfect man to help her—gunslinger Marsh Logan. Not only strong and brave, Marsh had the ebony hair and light blue eyes to make Randee forget her hate and seek the love and passion that only he could give her.

Available wherever paperbacks are sold, or order direct from the Publisher. Send cover price plus 50¢ per copy for mailing and handling to Penguin USA, P.O. Box 999, c/o Dept. 17109, Bergenfield, NJ 07621. Residents of New York and Tennessee must include sales tax. DO NOT SEND CASH.

JANELLE TAYLOR

ANYTHING FOR LOVE

ZEBRA BOOKS
KENSINGTON PUBLISHING CORP.

ZEBRA BOOKS are published by

Kensington Publishing Corp.
850 Third Avenue
New York, NY 10022

First Printing: July, 1995

Printed in the United States of America

Dedicated to:
Sheila Taylor,
with thanks for research help on Augusta.
Laurie McRae,
for help with interior decorating descriptions.
Sharon Daniels, Tim Moore,
Susan Grimsley, Sarah Jones, India Taylor, and
Terry Toole for research facts about
Colquitt and peanuts.
Mike Berardino,
sports columnist for the Augusta
Chronicle/Herald for football facts.
Michael Taylor,
for visiting and collecting research in
Colquitt and in Augusta.
Scott, Lauren Ashley, Alice, and Jack Redmond,
special friends and new family members.
and,
Troy Aikman, Emmitt Smith,
and the super Dallas Cowboys.

One

Rebecca Cooper looked at Jennifer Brimsford, laughed and said, "Of course she'll go to the high school reunion with us. Rach can't possibly say no to her two best friends, or we'll strangle her."

"But I'm not one of your classmates, Becky," Rachel Gaines protested.

"That doesn't matter. You went to the tenth and fifteenth reunions. We didn't have a twentieth, and the thirtieth is special. We'll have loads of fun. You'll see old friends and make new ones. You have to go."

"But I didn't attend Richmond Academy, and I went to those other reunions with Daniel. He's gone now. I would feel out of place."

"Don't be silly," Becky teased, "you know most of our old gang. Besides, everyone will want to hear and see how you're doing."

"You can tell all the out-of-towners I'm doing fine. I've been a widow for fifteen years, so I've had time to adjust. I don't want to answer questions about Daniel all evening, or make excuses why I'm not remarried, or thwart attempts to set me up with their friends and brothers."

all of our finances and problems. If he died, I wouldn't have the vaguest idea about how to manage my affairs. You'll recall that the entire estate of our friend Mrs. Parson was wiped out by mismanagement and fraud. The dear woman is living on Social Security and government aid. I can't imagine losing everything and being poor."

"When I was learning my way through that maze, there were plenty of scary moments, but with God's help and guidance, good friends, an honest and patient lawyer and banker, I made it just fine. Before much longer, you two should sit down with Scott and Adam and get educated; one never knows when a tragedy could strike. There are unscrupulous people out there who will take advantage of a widow's lack of knowledge about money and investments. I was lucky that Daniel kept his records and accounts in excellent shape. Cliff was so kind to come over all those evenings to teach me that complicated computer program Daniel used and how to do my budget and monthly bills." Rachel didn't add, but thought, *He's such a nice man; too bad he has such a terrible wife in Janet.* "Daniel had set up savings accounts for the girls' educations, which was helpful."

"You must miss Karen the most; Evelyn's been gone for years."

"I'm glad Karen chose MCG so she could live at home while she was in school and doing her internship. It's one of the best medical schools in the country. Pediatrics is perfect for her, be-

mothers and grandmothers would come out of
the woodwork to run me out of town, tar and
feather me, *and* brand me with a scarlet letter."

The women laughed before Becky protested,
"For heaven's sake, Rach, times and people have
changed; in case you haven't heard, women are
free now to do as we please. A little hanky-panky
never harmed anyone, and you of all people certainly need and deserve a little diversion."

Jen added her opinion, "A little pleasure, too.
Right, Becky?"

Becky fluffed her short blond hair. "Positively."

Rachel laughed but refuted, "Times and people may have changed in other areas, but this
is a small southern town; that old double standard and tight morals still exist in Georgia. Do
I care what people say and think about me? Yes,
I do, because that's how I was reared. If I began
acting wild, I'd be ruined for life."

Becky moved a couch pillow out of her way.
"Phooey to stick-in-the-muds! You can't live your
life by others' dictates or you'll be miserable and
miss out on too much. You proved you're strong
and brave by rearing two preteen girls and making all of the family and financial decisions after
Daniel was killed, so take a few risks for yourself."

"Becky's right, Rachel; do it while you have
the time and health and plenty of money. No
one knows better than you that life can be cut
short. Look at what happened to Daniel and
think about the people you help with your vol-

unteer work. Death, illness, and disabilities can strike one low without warning or mercy."

Rachel admitted to herself that both friends made excellent points, but she wasn't ready to give in. "Get real, you two; I'm a mother of grown daughters, a grandmother. I have a reputation to protect; playing the merry widow isn't for me."

"It's called discretion, Rachel. You could have plenty of dates if you wanted to. Get a little romance in your life."

"She needs more than romance, Jen; the other side of her bed has been empty for fifteen years. It's past time to have it occupied once in a while."

"Taking your advice isn't as simple as it sounds."

"It can be. With the girls and grandchildren gone for a year, take advantage of your privacy. Kick up your heels and have fun. For heaven's sake, Rach, you're barely forty-seven, and you look more like you're thirty-five. Use those great looks and fabulous figure to snare yourself a new man," Becky urged as her affectionate gaze took in Rachel's lovely green eyes, shiny brown hair, near-perfect features, and flawless complexion.

Rachel teased her best friends, who were both slender and attractive, "Are you two suffering from hot pants today or an itch you dare not scratch? Are you hungry for vicarious adventures you think I can provide?"

"Who, us?" the two women asked simultaneously, as they looked at each other and giggled like mischievous teenagers.

"I wonder what your husbands would say if Scott and Adam knew what kind of wanton thoughts race through those two pretty heads."

Becky's blue eyes sparkled again with mirth. "Scott wouldn't trade my sexy thoughts and body for anybody else's. He doesn't care where I get my appetite as long as I eat at home."

Jen laughed and agreed, "Adam is the same way. Wasn't Daniel?"

"Daniel never talked much about sex; it was a private matter to him." *If I had known more about it at eighteen, I wouldn't have gotten into trouble with him. Lordy, I was so naive and didn't know it! At least I made certain my girls were well informed on sex and its consequences.*

"It's a good thing sex is in the open now so southern women can enjoy it like men always have. It's no longer our submissive duty; it's our right to say yes or no and to get as much satisfaction out of it as they do."

Rachel knew from talks and observations that Becky and Scott, and Jen and Adam, had good marriages, long and happy ones, which she felt were getting rarer in a time when divorce and extramarital affairs were commonplace. Her own marriage had lasted only thirteen years before Daniel died. She hadn't found a second husband because she wouldn't settle for just a replacement as so many frightened women did, no matter if everybody thought she was staying single too long. Still, she mused, glorious love and fiery passion would be welcomed if Quentin—

"Seriously, Rachel, will you come with us?" the brunette urged.

"I don't know, Jen." Rachel hedged. "It sounds like fun and I'd like to see Daniel's old friends, but . . ."

"No buts, Rach. She'll come willingly, Jen, or we'll drag her there; Scott and Adam will gladly help us succeed. It's only ten days away, so we'll shop tomorrow for smashing outfits. We want to look absolutely fantastic because this is the one reunion where people will look the most changed, look older. Thank goodness we have appointments with Dawn Friday morning; we'll need the works: shampoo and set, roots touched up, facial, manicure, pedicure. Anything, everything," Becky added amidst laughter.

"You two have nothing to worry about," Rachel said, "you both look marvelous. That new cut and lighter color are perfect for you, Becky."

Becky fluffed her blond bob again. "Thanks, Rach. I've just about gotten used to having so little hair, but it's a quick and easy style. My roots need touching up every two or three weeks, but it's worth the extra time and money. Scott loves it short and loose; he likes playing in it without me begging him not to muss my hairdo."

Jen fingered her dark and straight tresses. "You were brave to chop off your long hair; I get nervous every time scissors come near mine even for a trim; it took me years to get my mop this length, so I'm keeping it like this until I die."

"Long hair suits you, Jen, but mine was dragging down my face, and my dull shade of blond made my skin look sallow."

"You do look younger and sexier. The short length and platinum color flatters your skin tone and makes your features more noticeable. And the way you're doing your eyes now brings them out more."

"Thanks, Rach. It was past time to stop being heavy-handed with eye shadow and liner and to change to modern colors. Dawn also chose an excellent style for you; I'm glad you took her advice. It's soft and romantic, and your natural color suits you."

Rachel touched the swept-back bangs that left a wispy fringe across her forehead, then toyed with the silky locks that halted just above the shoulder. "Goldwell came out with the ideal shade for covering my gray and leaving me golden brown. With this bodywave, it stays fixed all week unless I help Henry in the yard or spend time in the pool."

"You lucky devil. I have to wash and blow-dry mine every morning, but I've gotten fast at it . . . Rach, the four of us are having dinner at the country club Friday night. How about dressing up fit-to-kill and joining us?"

Rachel noticed the swift change of subject and knew it was suspicious. "Thanks, but you don't need a fifth wheel along every time you four go out for the evening. Besides, I have scads of errands to run that day."

"You wouldn't be a fifth wheel if you had a date. There's someone Scott and I want you to meet; he's a new lawyer in Newton's firm. They went to law school together at UGA and were fraternity brothers. Newton told Scott he's long divorced and has two marvelous children who live in Macon with his ex-wife and her husband. I met Keith at the club Sunday. He's well mannered and has a terrific personality. He's into boating, golf, and tennis. He's forty-nine, has green eyes, brown hair, and a good physique. He's tall and good-looking and has money. His family in Macon, the Haywoods, are very prominent. Scott said he purchased one of the new condos and is joining the country club. He's only been here three and a half weeks, so nobody has latched on to him yet and he didn't leave a girlfriend behind. Sounds like a great catch, Rach. I'm sure he'd be delighted to join us for dinner."

"What did you do, interrogate him for hours to learn so much?"

"I had to find out if he would be a good choice for you, and he is."

"Stop playing cupid, Rebecca Cooper. You promised."

"Somebody has to since you won't venture forth on your own. Keith Haywood sounds and looks perfect for you. At least meet him and give him a try before the stampede starts and another woman grabs him. We want you to find a special man and get married again, be happy like we are."

Back to that old typical southern belief that a woman must have a man in her life to be happy, successful, and complete. That's true only if he's the right man. "I love you both for worrying about me, but I'm not miserable; and I'm not against men and remarrying. I've had plenty of dates since Daniel died; none were husband material, at least for me. Isn't it better to stay single and a little lonely than to marry just anybody?"

"Yes, but it's still a couple's world. At least find a steady companion so you can get out more frequently."

"I grab a man when an escort is necessary for the opera, symphony, dinners, or dances."

"But you dump them afterward."

"Not exactly, not rudely anyway; I just don't date many of them again. It would be easier to continue seeing some of them if they didn't become so serious or persistent after one or two dates."

"Can you blame them? You're quite a catch, Rachel Gaines, but you underestimate yourself. You're beautiful and sexy. You're an intelligent, polite, church-going woman, the wealthy widow of a well-liked man from a respected old family. You're interesting and fun, generous, kind, and considerate. What more could a smart man desire? But you let every prospect escape or shove him away after one date, two at the most."

"They don't give me any choice, Becky; most think a widow must be horny and so eager—

even desperate— to capture a man that they're all over me the minute I lower my guard."

"Surely you miss and need affection after being so long without Daniel? I couldn't go fifteen years without a good loving on occasion."

I haven't, but that's my secret. "If sex enters the picture, it has to mean something special to me and to him; there has to be some kind of commitment, a serious relationship, between us first. I can't just leap into bed for a one-night-stand with a friend or with a near-stranger." *Not again anyway.* "Besides, there are plenty of dangers lurking out there if one isn't careful and discriminating. You know the old saying about when you sleep with someone, you're sleeping with everybody he's slept with, and so on."

"That's what condoms and blood tests are for, Rach."

"They won't protect me from nuts and liars." *Or from faulty condoms. Even if I can't get pregnant again, if another one burst, I could catch a terrible disease. No sex is worth that risk, except maybe with Quentin . . . Oh, Lordy, if you two only knew what I did years ago during that cruise, you would be shocked speechless! I still am.* "You wouldn't believe how many men swear they haven't had sex since their divorces or wives' deaths to convince you they're no risk. I know for a fact that two of them were jumping into any available bed. And we all heard the juicy details from Janet about where the woman got pregnant and infected with VD because her date only pretended to put on a condom. When it comes to sex, some men will say or do anything to get into your panties."

"Don't be discouraged, Rach; there's a perfect man somewhere out there for you. But you can't find him if you aren't looking or you stay cooped up in this house."

"They haven't all been bad prospects, have they?" Jen asked.

That brief, passionate, and secret affair of twelve years ago danced through Rachel's mind. She pushed it aside before she gave herself away. "If all I wanted was just a husband, no. But I didn't want a bad stepfather for my two girls when they were young and vulnerable, and I don't want a terrible choice for myself this late in life. I'll admit it was tough and scary rearing two children alone and taking over for Daniel, but a hasty and difficult marriage would have been much worse for me and the girls." Rachel took a deep breath. "Let's see, a fourth of the men just want sex and a good time, so they pressure and entice me like crazy to give in. Another fourth wants me for my social status and Daniel's large estate, especially the ones without money or with financial troubles. Another fourth wants just any woman to fill the rank of wife and mother, usually to his bratty children from another nasty marriage or two. Some of the men in those three categories also wanted their own children. Even if I hadn't had that hysterectomy years ago, I wouldn't want to begin a new family at this point in my life. Even if I could have children, at my age, I might not be around to see them graduate from college or marry."

Rachel pushed aside memories of her two miscarriages and the two-month-old son who had died from SIDS in '76. A hysterectomy following her last miscarriage in '78— the only one her friends, acquaintances, and husband's parents knew about— had resulted in preventing one possibly promising marriage proposal when the man learned she couldn't give him children of his own; in particular, a son. It seemed that most men wanted their own heirs, as if that made them immortal or bound you to them. "I know the so-called respectable and expected thing to do is to remarry, but I'm not taking that step until Mr. Right comes along, corny as that sounds. I'm too old and set in my ways to invite such problems into my life."

"But you must get lonely and horny sometimes, Rach."

"Not enough to make a rash decision." *Again.* "My life has been busy and happy, so why make myself miserable just to have a man in the house when I've learned how to take care of myself since Daniel's death? I don't need a man to support me or handle my affairs or protect me."

"But the girls are grown and gone now, Rach. Evelyn lives in Ohio, and Karen might not live in Augusta after she returns to the States next year. You don't want to spend your Golden Years alone in this big house."

"I know, but most men are in too much of a hurry these days; it's 'jump into bed before the night's over or so long, baby.' Or 'why don't we move in together so we can see if this . . . "thing" works out between us?' That translates to: 'I'll just grab my suitcases and be back in a flash so you can wait on me hand and foot in and out of bed while we live off of your money because I have one or two ex-wives and families to support.' Some of them even talk about getting married after only a few dates. I do believe that love at first sight exists, but there's more to marriage than love and physical attraction; you have to be compatible. The last fourth were good men, but I didn't find one among them who suited me; there were always too many differences between us to overlook. And frankly, none of them turned me on. Call me old-fashioned or dreamy-eyed, but I want love, passion, rapport, equality, romance, friendship, and respect."

Rachel sighed. "Some of my worst experiences, if you two will recall, were with men who came from up North or the Midwest. They just don't seem to understand southerners; they can be so arrogant and condescending. They think our slow speech and easy-going ways mean we're stupid and slow, or easy prey for them. Some of them think we should take diction lessons to 'learn how to speak correctly.' I actually overheard Charles, you know he's from the upper Midwest, tell his ex-wife if his daughter said 'yes, sir or no, sir' to him one more time, he was going to give her speech lessons so she would stop using 'another one of those stupid southern customs.' Then, he expects this southern lady," Rachel scoffed as she tapped her chest, "to not only go out with him and be grateful for doing so but to also go to bed with him. Fat chance! Hell hasn't frozen over yet and never will." Rachel exhaled a heavy sigh. "Whatever happened to romancing, wooing, and getting to know each other? Who knows better than you two that friends make the best husbands?"

Becky and Jen nodded agreement before she continued, "So much has changed for southern women since we were born, and some of those changes have terrible repercussions, especially for the younger generation; yet, most thoughts and feelings about morals have remained the same. In the old days, a southern woman was expected to find a proper man in her own class, get married, do her conjugal duty, have babies, take care of the home and family, and always put others' needs first. A good wife was involved in church, charities, and clubs; and was a social asset to her husband. For our age group and circle, that's still true to a great extent."

"You're right, Rach." Becky sighed. "In our mothers' and grandmothers' times, no southern gentleman with real class left his wife, children, and marriage for any reason, even if he had a mistress on the side. And heaven forbid if a woman was caught having an affair, married or single. When a female needed something, if manners and charm failed to obtain it, her husband's or family's name didn't. We were So-and-So's wife, daughter, or mother; we were introduced with our maiden names; there was no Ms. in the South and few career women. My mother and grandmother can tell real pearls from fakes and even the quality of real ones. They can tell if china, crystal, and silver are inherited or purchased. They can rattle off just about anybody's bloodline who's important. A husband was always right, always the boss."

Becky rolled her eyes. "It was always be a lady, no matter what. My grandmother told me, 'It isn't the impression you make when you enter a room or meet someone, it's the impression you leave behind that matters.' Southern belles were known for hospitality, manners, breeding, and resilience. They didn't 'air dirty linen in public' or expose personal matters; problems stayed within a family circle. Now, people blab anything on TV or to those tabloids. It's marry well, or certainly divorce well. If you get knocked down or tossed aside, don't stay there. It's be tough and smart like Scarlett and do whatever's necessary to survive and succeed."

Rachel knew that most of Becky's words referred to members of their social class, positions to which Rebecca Hartly and Jennifer Davis and their maternal ancestors had been born, one which she had achieved through marriage to a man with the Gaines blue-blooded pedigree. "Now, we're also expected to do more, to be superwomen in every area; at least, the younger generation of women are. That's so much pressure for them to bear; so is the sexual revolution and its health risks."

Becky slid forward on the hand-tufted Chesterfield sofa covered in sumptuous cognac leather. She tapped her nails on the row of decorative brass tacking along its curved arm as she spoke. "Actually, Rach, a man isn't necessary these days to take care of a woman's physical needs, not if she knows where to shop and has the courage to make the needed purchases."

"Rebecca Cooper, what a naughty mind you have."

"It's the truth, Rach. At least it's a clean, safe, and private way to satisfy your needs until you find Mr. Right to take care of them." Becky grinned and settled back again in Daniel's old home-office, now Rachel's.

"It's still not as good as having a man," Jen remarked.

"Just how do you know that for certain?" Becky teased.

Jen stuck out her tongue, grinned, and quipped, "The same way you do, Miss Smarty Pants. Adam does take long business or hunting trips on occasion. If men can unclog their pipes as needed, so can we."

Rachel glanced at the closed door and cautioned, "If we don't quiet down or clean up our talk, Martha will hear us and be shocked."

"You're right, Rach, we'll behave ourselves. I wouldn't want your housekeeper to think you have trashy friends who are leading you astray. And your in-laws would have conniptions if we talked you into scandalous behavior. Have you heard from the Gaineses lately?"

soon as they received an invitation and visited the place, Richard and Dorothy seized the opportunity to buy in there. They sold their real estate business and car dealerships and opened new ones in Charleston, and they're doing nicely from what I was told. They left managers in charge of their other companies. Their daughters loved the idea of relocating to the Coast, and their two sons-in-law seemed happy to go along with it all."

"I guess it was agree or find new jobs, and maybe risk offending the Gaineses and being disinherited," Becky said with a laugh. "Nobody wants to be cut out of a will that big. Besides, everyone knows that few people ever won a battle against the Gaineses in business, politics, or a social situation."

"Except for Daniel; from what I saw and heard, he was the only person who stood up to them, and he usually won the argument. I remember when Adam was trying to update their insurance policies and they disagreed on the coverage amounts and types needed. Daniel debated the issue until they conceded. When Jeff tried to get the Gaineses to invest in that shopping strip on the south side of town, Daniel stopped them. If he hadn't, they would have lost a lot of money when it went under less than a year later."

Rachel nodded. "You're right, Jen, Daniel would argue when and if it was necessary. Daniel had this philosophy about not sweating the small stuff. If something wasn't life-threatening, he always said to compromise or give in. Then, when something important was at stake, people would listen. That method worked for him." *Too bad it didn't work for me where they're concerned. No matter how hard I tried or how well I did in their world, it was never enough for them. Daniel's death gave them the chance to almost close the door against me and the girls and they grabbed it.* Rachel continued, "Of course, in some cases, that method gives a control freak the idea he or she can run over you because you're too polite or kind to argue or refuse."

"I believe we know at least one person like that," Becky hinted.

Rachel and Jen laughed and said, "Janet Hollis."

"Positively, the little witch. Is Martha still working for her?"

Rachel shook her head. "She couldn't take Janet for more than two weeks after Lizzy left her. Janet was lucky Martha agreed to even give it a try. Housekeepers don't come any better than Martha. I don't know what I'll do when she retires; she's been with me for twenty years now."

"Is she thinking of retiring? How old is she?"

"She's sixty-five, but still going strong, thank heavens. Sometimes I think she has more strength and stamina than I do."

"You're lucky her son does your yard work and pool maintenance. He's one of the best in both businesses."

"Neighbors keep trying to lure him away with bigger salaries, but he's loyal to me." Rachel

all of our finances and problems. If he died, I wouldn't have the vaguest idea about how to manage my affairs. You'll recall that the entire estate of our friend Mrs. Parson was wiped out by mismanagement and fraud. The dear woman is living on Social Security and government aid. I can't imagine losing everything and being poor."

"When I was learning my way through that maze, there were plenty of scary moments, but with God's help and guidance, good friends, an honest and patient lawyer and banker, I made it just fine. Before much longer, you two should sit down with Scott and Adam and get educated; one never knows when a tragedy could strike. There are unscrupulous people out there who will take advantage of a widow's lack of knowledge about money and investments. I was lucky that Daniel kept his records and accounts in excellent shape. Cliff was so kind to come over all those evenings to teach me that complicated computer program Daniel used and how to do my budget and monthly bills." Rachel didn't add, but thought, *He's such a nice man; too bad he has such a terrible wife in Janet.* "Daniel had set up savings accounts for the girls' educations, which was helpful."

"You must miss Karen the most; Evelyn's been gone for years."

"I'm glad Karen chose MCG so she could live at home while she was in school and doing her internship. It's one of the best medical schools in the country. Pediatrics is perfect for her, be-

The three women nodded and took seats in the breakfast area where a glass top covered a picket-fence pedestal with a flower garden painted atop it. Green placemats matched the wood on the floral-cushioned chairs, which in turn blended with the wallpaper pattern of vivid blues, greens, and tans on a white background. As the women adjusted their positions, the chair legs made noise against large rose bisque Florida tiles.

Martha served big, juicy tomatoes filled with tuna salad, hot croissants, a fresh-fruit cup, and iced tea. "When you're done, leave the dishes for me to gather and wash later. Just visit with your friends while I do your bedroom and bathroom. Call me if you need anything else."

"Thank you, Martha; this looks wonderful."

"Thank you, Martha," the other two women echoed.

The housekeeper smiled, left the room, and went upstairs.

"She's a jewel, Rachel. If Myrtle ever leaves me, I want her."

"I don't know if she has any extra days, Jen; her schedule is always full. In fact, she has a waiting list, so she can be choosy."

"I'm easy to work for, unless the employee is totally incompetent. A good maid is harder to find than Master's Golf tickets."

"Jen's right, Rach; it's hell to lose and try to replace a good one."

"If Martha retired, I'd have to move to a condo. I could never manage this house alone.

I love my home but it seems so large with every-one gone except me. I'd be exhausted if I didn't have Martha to help keep it clean, and she's ir-replaceable."

Rachel saw Becky and Jen glance at each other. Before she took another bite of tomato with tuna salad atop it, she said, "I know, you two never had to do housework or cook when you were young, but I did. I taught my girls how to take care of a house and meals, too. One can't always have a maid."

"You were lucky and so are they. When we went off to college, we didn't know how to do anything. You should have seen me the first time I tried to press a blouse; it was ruined. And Jen," Becky added amidst laughter, "she de-stroyed an entire load of laundry *and* the ma-chine. As for cooking, we burned everything or it tasted horrible."

"Don't forget when the housemother tried to teach us how to make our beds and vacuum our rooms; she thought we were dumb and spoiled."

Rachel laughed at Jen's comical expression and tone. "You didn't have to labor long because you moved into a fancy apartment and hired a maid; you told me so. Even now, when your housekeepers are sick or on vacation, you hire cleaning services to fill in for them."

Becky held up her hands, laughed, and quipped, "These nails would cease to exist if they did housework or laundry. Besides, why do household labor when you don't have to? Even with the children away in college, I stay busy.

At least it gives me more time and energy for Scott and other pleasures. As for you, Rach, you have plenty of time on your hands to do exciting things besides helping Martha and doing volunteer work. Okay, I'll hush up about looking for love and romance . . . for today. How are the girls doing?"

Rachel finished chewing her roll and took a sip of tea before answering. "They're fine and happy. Both phoned me this week. Karen should be reaching their first port soon, and Evelyn loves Japan."

"A year in Japan would be marvelous, Rachel, but we're glad you didn't go with them. We would miss you terribly."

"Since Eddie's mother is traveling with them, it would have been too crowded and hectic for me to tag along. I'm glad she's there to help Evelyn with the children. Two little ones under four can be a handful, especially in a foreign country and with Eddie staying so busy at Honda."

"From what you've told us, it seems to be working out fine for Barbara living with them since Marvin's death."

"It does, Jen. Barbara adores Evelyn and the children, and they adore her. Evelyn's lucky Eddie has such a wonderful mother. The situation hasn't been a problem for any of them and I hope it remains that way."

"I'm sure it helps that Barbara has a mother-in-law suite attached to their home by a breezeway so everybody has privacy. Do you think they'll ever move back to Augusta?"

"I doubt it, Becky, not as long as Eddie works in the automotive industry. I miss my girls and grandchildren already. I only wish their trips hadn't come at the same time; it's lonely with all of them gone."

"A year will pass before you know it. Look how fast our forty-eight years have flown by. I forgot, forty-seven for you, Rach."

"What's a year matter?" Rachel quipped.

"That's what I meant; one goes by like a streak of lightning. Heavens, before we know it, we'll be collecting our Social Security and getting senior citizen's discounts. At least Scott will be retired so we can travel." Jen's expression was serious as she asked Rachel, "Are you worried about Karen working in those third-world countries for a year?"

"Yes, but I didn't try to change her mind about going. So many children in those countries need special medical treatment and their ship is loaded with the best equipment and medicines not to mention skilled doctors."

"You must be so proud of her for becoming a pediatrician."

"I am, Jen. She worked hard for her medical degree and physician's license. Karen was always independent, kindhearted, and determined. She was thrilled about being chosen for that medical team and humanitarian tour. But there's so much unrest and violence in those areas."

"She'll be safe. The world would rise up

against anybody who attacked a ship of doctors on a mercy mission." Jen reached for her roll.

"I hope you're right. Still, I'll worry until she's home next June. At least she won't be too lonesome; she has her fiancé with her. They're going into practice together after they return and get married."

"Does she want a big wedding like Evelyn's? That was one of the most beautiful and romantic I've attended. The reception was fantastic. People are still talking about it and trying to outdo it. You're a genius, Rach."

Rachel smiled in pleasure and gratitude. "I can't take all of the credit or even much of it; I had a magician handling almost everything for me. I basically told him what we wanted and he took care of all the details and added some great ideas of his own." As the two women talked about her youngest daughter's splendid wedding, Rachel mused, *I wish I could have had at least a small and special ceremony in church, but foolish me— If it hadn't been for that miscarriage, everyone in town would know why we eloped.*

"I bet the Gaineses will go all out when Karen gets married. I'm sure they'll throw a huge and lavish party for her like they did for Evelyn."

They only did it for show, my friend, not out of love.

Becky continued, "You should be proud of yourself, Rach; you did a wonderful job rearing those two girls alone after Daniel's death. I don't know what I would do without Scott; he handles

all of our finances and problems. If he died, I wouldn't have the vaguest idea about how to manage my affairs. You'll recall that the entire estate of our friend Mrs. Parson was wiped out by mismanagement and fraud. The dear woman is living on Social Security and government aid. I can't imagine losing everything and being poor."

"When I was learning my way through that maze, there were plenty of scary moments, but with God's help and guidance, good friends, an honest and patient lawyer and banker, I made it just fine. Before much longer, you two should sit down with Scott and Adam and get educated; one never knows when a tragedy could strike. There are unscrupulous people out there who will take advantage of a widow's lack of knowledge about money and investments. I was lucky that Daniel kept his records and accounts in excellent shape. Cliff was so kind to come over all those evenings to teach me that complicated computer program Daniel used and how to do my budget and monthly bills." Rachel didn't add, but thought, *He's such a nice man; too bad he has such a terrible wife in Janet.* "Daniel had set up savings accounts for the girls' educations, which was helpful."

"You must miss Karen the most; Evelyn's been gone for years."

"I'm glad Karen chose MCG so she could live at home while she was in school and doing her internship. It's one of the best medical schools in the country. Pediatrics is perfect for her, be-

cause she loves children and is very good with them. She'll be an excellent mother one day."

"She had an excellent teacher and example, Rach, so take credit where it's due. There have been times when my kids almost drove me nuts. Thank God my son finally realized the dangers of drug and alcohol abuse. He's clean now and doing great at Princeton."

"I'm happy for you and him. He'll make a good lawyer. Actually, all of us have been fortunate with our children. It's so easy for them to get in with the wrong crowd and make mistakes. They have so many temptations to deal with these days. The world and people are changing too fast and it's confusing for them. Confusing for us, too."

Becky and Jen agreed. Rachel poured them more tea, then all were silent for a time as they finished their lunch.

"Don't forget our arts council meeting was changed to July twenty-first because of the reunion next Friday," Jen reminded. "We're supposed to discuss sponsoring a show for two budding local artists."

"And don't forget my pool party on the sixteenth," Becky added. "I would have made it on the Fourth, but you know Scott's parents always have a big to-do on Independence Day. We can't break a family tradition, and it *is* loads of fun. I haven't finished my guest list and sent out invitations, so is there anybody you want me to include, Rach?"

Rachel sent her a playful scowl and teased,

"Don't you dare say to bring a date or you'll have one there waiting for me, like Keith Haywood."

"There may be a few single men present, but by coincidence, and probably with dates. I haven't decided about inviting Keith yet."

"That's fine; just don't shove anyone on me. Promise?"

"I'll try my best to behave," Becky quipped.

"How is the novel coming along?" Jen asked, changing the subject.

"That Sandhills Writers Conference at Augusta College last month helped me a lot. There's far more to writing books and getting published than I imagined. In the beginning, I just wanted to put my stories down on paper, then have people read them and enjoy them. I never realized how complicated the business is. As soon as I finish the manuscript, I need to find an agent to represent me. There's so much I don't know about literary contracts, advances, royalties, and such, so I have plenty to study and learn. Even after a publisher buys a manuscript, it takes one to two years to edit, prepare, and print it; then twelve to eighteen months to get paid royalties on sales, *if* you make enough to earn out your advance."

"Then, my dear Rach, it's lucky you don't need the money for support and darn lucky you attended that conference. It sounds like a difficult business, but don't worry; you're smart and determined, so you'll make it. Won't she, Jen?"

"We're positive. I bet you become the next Mary Higgins Clark."

"Thanks, you two. Of course, the others don't know I went to the conference, so don't tell them. The last time my secret slipped out, I was teased without mercy. I can't help it if I like to read and want to write soft horror and child-in-jeopardy novels; some of our friends consider them taste-less and think I have a hidden crazy streak. Some think this is a whim or a hobby, but I'm serious about writing and getting published."

"I'm sorry Janet overheard us and blabbed to everyone. *We* think it's a fantastic idea. You put it on hold for a long time after getting married and having children. Your duties are over now, so why not indulge yourself? If this is what you want to do, don't let anyone talk you out of it. Just be sure to dedicate the first novel to me and Jen as you promised."

"After the way Janet and Dianne carried on, are you certain you two won't be embarrassed to have your names in such a book?"

"Heavens, no; it will be a thrill and an honor. Right, Jen?"

"It will for me. I just finished reading the latest by Mary Higgins Clark and it kept me on the edge of my seat. Thanks for the suggestion. Next, I'm catching up on V. C. Andrews's old series."

"If you aren't careful, Jen, you'll be reading Stephen King next," Rachel teased.

"I will, if he's as good as they are. Speaking of Dianne, we ran into her at the club yesterday after tennis. She's planning to nominate you as the chairwoman for our new woman's club project. I think it's going to be a combination bake, crafts, and garage sale at the Civic Center in August."

"She won't have any luck there because I have enough jobs to do if they're going to be done right. I'm on too many boards, committees, and councils now. If I'm going to have time to write, I need to trim down my schedule and outside responsibilities; at least, not take on new ones. Some of those women think I have abundant free time because I don't have a husband or small children to occupy it. Dianne is one of those people, but I'm just as busy as she is."

"Probably busier, because she has a full-time nanny for her kids and a live-in housekeeper and cook," Jen said.

"And don't forget that part-time secretary who does her committee work and runs her errands," Becky added. "She loves to dole out jobs to others but not do any work herself, just claim the credit and glory."

Jen looked at Rachel and almost whispered her news, "You know Dianne recently had a face-lift; so did Betty, and Louise just returned from a diet spa. They all want to look twenty at the reunion, and Louise wants to look fabulous at her daughter's wedding in August."

"Dianne sneaked off to Atlanta to have hers done under the pretense of a shopping trip, but Betty let the news slip when she was telling us about hers," Becky related. "Betty looks terrific, but Dianne is a mess. She didn't trust any local plastic surgeon to work on her, but she should have. When we saw her yesterday, we couldn't believe our eyes; her face is as tight as a balloon filled with too much water. She looks stern, Rach, and her eyes and mouth are shaped funny now. If that were me, I'd fly my tail back to Atlanta and demand an immediate corrective procedure. She shouldn't have waited until so close to the reunion to improve her looks. For heaven's sake, we all have wrinkles and sags we want gone."

"Are you thinking of having one, too?" Rachel asked.

"Maybe in a few years; I'm holding my own pretty well. So are you, Rach; your skin is like a baby's and you have no wrinkles anywhere."

"Thanks. I suppose I inherited good skin from my mother; and those new creams work wonders."

The women chatted for a while longer before Becky ended their visit.

"It's getting late; we need to be going. Scott's coming home early today. Are you sure you won't join us Friday night?"

Rachel walked them down the hall and to the front door. "No, but thanks for the invitation," she said. "You all have fun."

As they approached Becky's car, the blonde turned to Rachel. "We'll pick you up at ten to-morrow for shopping and lunch."

"I'll be ready."

"That means you'll go with us next weekend?"

"As you said, Becky, I can't say no to you two and survive."

They laughed, then embraced. Rachel watched

Becky back out of her driveway and head down
the street to travel three blocks to where the two
women lived next door to each other. Becky and
Jennifer had been friends since childhood and
she was glad they had drawn her into their genial
duo years ago. The two women had filled many
voids in her life.

Rachel looked at her gardener when he
rounded the house. "You've done a superb job
this spring, Henry; everything is beautiful."

"Thanks, Mrs. Gaines. The pool's done and
I'm almost finished out here, so I'll be going
soon. I'll see you next week."

"Thanks, Henry."

Rachel went to speak with Martha before she
ran errands. She told herself, if she hurried, she
could get in a few hours of writing later. Since
she had a busy day tomorrow, she couldn't stay
up late working on the manuscript as she had
done for many nights after Karen left weeks ago.
She refused to think about failure and tried not
to imagine how she and her life would change
if she succeeded. If she couldn't find a good
man to curl up with and enjoy, a word processor
could be a substitute for a while. Maybe, she
mused with a grin, she should write wonderful
romance novels. Sort of like the song says, "I
can dream about you, if I can't hold you tonight."

*Maybe I should write a fictional sequel with a
happy ending to our brief story, Mr. Quentin Rawls.
I doubt you remember me from twelve years ago, but
I haven't forgotten you and our reckless affair. What*

would happen if we ran into each other again? Fat chance of that happening after so many years without contact and living worlds apart! Oh, well, I'll just have to be content to dream about you.

Two

As Rachel, Becky, and Jen left a mall boutique the next day, they met Janet Hollis and Dianne Blackwell who were also on a shopping spree. With everyone's hands burdened with packages, the usual embraces and cheek kisses between "close friends" weren't possible when the five women halted to chat.

After social pleasantries were exchanged, Dianne said, "It's fortunate we ran into each other today, Rachel; I intended to phone you later to ask you to be in charge of the new fund-raising project for our women's club. It's going to be a big and exciting affair at the Civic Center on August sixth from ten to five; that's a Saturday. It's a combination crafts, artwork, bake sale, and rummage sale. We're asking club members to check their closets, garages, and attics for things to donate to the event. You can also convince local merchants to contribute items. Of course, our members will have to bring their baked goods down that morning at nine to give you time to set up that booth. We'll sell refreshments, have entertainment on the hour, and at least five prize drawings. One of the radio stations will broadcast live from start to finish, and all three television stations have agreed to do coverage; so has the local newspaper and *Augusta Today* magazine. That will give you about six to seven weeks to collect everything from our members and the merchants, get the items tagged with prices and boxed by category; I'm sure that's ample time. You can store the boxes in your garage; we'll hire someone to transport them to the Civic Center. Louise is handling the publicity and entertainment. We'll let a caterer do the refreshments and divide the profits. You can assign members to work the booths. Make sure you select the best donations for the prize drawings."

Rachel tried not to stare at Dianne's bad surgical results as the woman talked on and on without giving her time to speak. She smiled to soften her refusal. "I'm afraid I can't do it; I'm on too many committees and projects now, so it's impossible for me to take on another one." As Dianne first looked astonished and then annoyed, Rachel attempted a polite explanation. "I'm in charge of the church bake sale on July thirtieth for the new homeless shelter, and collecting pledges for the Heart Fund and helping to plan their fall gala. I have to gather items for that celebrity auction on September third for the library extension, help out with a show on August second for a local new artist, and make collections for the abused children and wives' crisis center. I also have things to do for the community outreach program for the handicapped, and this is my six-month period to visit our church's shut-ins and take our senior citizens on errands. Plus, I have work to complete on a few other projects." *My writing for one.*

"But I'm sure you can fit in one more little job for such a good cause," Dianne protested. "You do these things so well, and we depend upon you."

"Thanks," Rachel said, "but I can't."

Janet— the vice president— added, "You really should say yes, Rachel. This sale is very important to our club and its members. You heard what Dianne said about the media, it will generate a lot of publicity and enhance our image. You simply *must* say yes; no excuses will be accepted."

Is that a fact? "I'll help out with phone calls and collections but I can't be in charge of such a big undertaking. My other responsibilities and projects would suffer, and I wouldn't have any free time for myself and my friends. Besides, six weeks is not enough time for anybody to do so much work."

"We all have to make sacrifices for worthy causes, and that's the only Saturday the Civic Center is available before Christmas. It's a great way to meet people. You'll have to call on plenty of men for donations. You are our only single member at this time, so that task is perfect for you."

Rachel tried to keep her fury from showing as she responded to Janet's snide remark. "Have Susan, Norma, and Rose gotten married since last month?"

"I meant, our only single member without

small children to take up your time, and you're still young enough to do the leg work required."

"Thanks for the compliment, but I can't take on anything else." She watched her banker's wife and nearby neighbor frown. "Besides, with all of the other collections I'm doing, I wouldn't be able to fit my car in the garage if I added another one; and everything would get mixed up."

"Where is your thinking cap today, Rachel? That's what Magic Markers and boxes are for, to keep things identified and separated."

Rachel forced out a phony smile just as Janet had done. "Trying to keep different things for several groups separated in an overloaded room would be difficult and time consuming. Why don't you two select another location and a later date? If you do it after the first of the year, I'll accept the job."

"It has to be held at the Civic Center to be impressive and to get free promotion," Janet snipped, "that's how to draw in the common crowd. Besides, the event is going to be too big to hold anywhere else."

"That's why I can't take charge; I don't have the time or space right now. It's an enormous task and a tight schedule. I doubt many of the members want to give up so much of their summer helping out whomever does it. Why don't you wait until you present this idea at our next meeting?"

"We're already committed; Dianne and I and the board have that authority, you know. I thought you would jump at the chance to contribute to a cause your daughter would love. In the board meeting, we decided the profits would go to buying clothes, food, and medicine for children from third-world countries. And toys for Christmas; that's why it has to be done in August, and that's the only open date the Civic Center has. How can you possibly refuse to head up this important project and sleep at night?"

You little bitch, you saved that coercive news for last, didn't you? "That *is* an excellent cause, Janet, though I personally would rather see us aid unfortunate American children. So many organizations and people help foreign children, but our country's poor and abused are often overlooked. That's why our local organizations are so important to me and why I'm scheduled so heavily with prior commitments to them."

"The board has made its decision. Surely knowing the charity involved will change your mind. I don't see how it could do otherwise."

Rachel caught Janet's domineering tone. There was no reasoning with the woman, so it was relent and be sorry and overworked or stand her ground and take the brunt of Janet's anger. "As I said, I'll help out but not take control. Maybe next year, Dianne, when my schedule is lighter."

"You must do this for us, Rachel," Dianne urged. "Please."

"I've already told you why I can't do it." *You two are not taking advantage of me again. I've let*

*you work me to death in the past; no more! I hardly
have time to write as it is now.*

Dianne frowned. "Well, I suppose we can ask
Betty Burke. She's busy, too, but I'm sure she
won't refuse such a worthy cause."

"Perhaps you can loan Betty your personal
secretary for a few days to help her get the lists,
calls, and mailouts done," Becky suggested.

"I'm afraid I can't spare her," Dianne replied,
"she isn't there enough as it is to handle all of
my chores. I certainly can't add more to her duties."

Becky shifted her packages and smiled. "As
Janet said, 'We all have to make sacrifices for
worthy causes.' Surely you can loan out your secretary for a few hours a week until the project
is underway."

Dianne glanced at the tall clock near the es-
calator. "That's impossible. You're really putting
us in a bind, Rachel, with your shocking refusal."

"I'm sorry, Dianne, but it can't be helped. A
person has only so much time and energy, and
mine are committed elsewhere until after
Christmas. It isn't as if I haven't done my fair
share for the club; I've handled three out of the
last five projects and assisted on the other two.
As large as our club is, surely there's somebody
else who can do this one if Betty can't accept."

"The timing seemed perfect for you, Rachel,"
Janet said, "with your family gone and without
a husband underfoot."

"That's why I agreed to do the other projects.

I gave them my word, so I can't let them down by giving our club first priority for six weeks."

Jen tried to help Rachel. "Why can't the club hire a temp for Betty like Adam does when extra help is needed or somebody's sick in his office?"

Janet exhaled loudly. "Jennifer dear, our budget doesn't need unnecessary expenses right now. We have to finance our annual ball that's coming up in October. Our treasury would suffer fiercely if we splurged on this charity event."

"Why can't we deduct secretarial fees from the sale's profits?" Rachel asked. "Surely that's a legal expense; we could ask Newton. It is an awful lot of extra work for any member." *Getting help from them will be nearly impossible during the summer, so the chairwoman will do most of it.*

"Some members don't mind being generous with their time and energies," Janet scoffed. "Thank heaven for unselfish and loyal people."

Jen forced an innocent expression and tone, and faked enthusiasm as she suggested, "Why don't you and Dianne head up the project? You two have more help at home than the rest of us. You could take your wonderful idea and do a fabulous job for the club."

Rachel watched Janet look at Jennifer as if Jen had lost her wits.

"Jen dear, wherever would Dianne and I find time to do it?"

Becky laughed, "In the same place Betty or Rachel or one of us would, by stealing it from other sources."

"That isn't amusing, Rebecca Hartly Cooper.

And you shouldn't joke about it, either, Jennifer Davis Brimsford. If Rachel can't do this tiny favor for the club, I'm certain Betty Sims Burke will be delighted to do so."

Good grief! Rachel thought, *she's pulling out those maiden names with bloodlines a mile long to put them in their places and point out I have no such pedigree! What a hateful snob you are, Janet Rayburn Hollis!*

"Not to change the subject, Rachel, but what lipstick is that?"

What now, Janet? Sharpening your clever knife to stick in my back? "Soft Carnation by Elizabeth Arden." She didn't ask why. From experience, she knew the woman would tell her.

"You really shouldn't wear that shade; it's too harsh for your pale skin and dark hair. It makes you look washed out and downright . . . deathly."

As expected, Rachel watched Janet smile as if she were being helpful. For once, she almost laughed in the woman's face!

An annoyed Becky spoke before thinking, "No, it doesn't; it's fabulous on her. It looks so good, Jen and I bought the same color this morning."

Janet glared at Becky. "Surely not, you two know better. Maybe it's Rachel's loud outfit that's clashing with it. Or that shade of brown on her hair. Dianne's honey-brown color would suit her better."

Let's see if two can play at your game, Mrs. Hollis. In a phony sweet tone, Rachel said, "This is my natural hair color, Janet; I haven't changed it since you've known me, so I don't know why it looks different today. As for this 'loud' pants suit, it's also listed as soft carnation. They seemed to match perfectly to me when I purchased them. Do they really clash?" She saw Janet gaze at her as if trying to decide if she were being challenged.

"Oh, well, maybe my eyesight is off today or maybe it's the lighting in here. If it isn't, I'll give you the name of a color and cosmetic specialist I used last year when I seemed to be making wrong choices for myself. He's a wonder with problem cases. You would love him and he'll be worth every dollar he charges. I'm sure you won't mind that he's gay since you used one of *those* to do Evelyn's wedding. I'll phone you later with his address and number."

"That's kind of you, Janet, but unnecessary; we all had our colors done last year. This is supposed to be one of my best."

"The girl must have made an error. If I were you, I'd have them done again. You wouldn't want to make another bad impression in public."

"We really must go, Janet, or we'll be late," Dianne said.

"You're right, Dianne. We'll see you all at church on Sunday. 'Bye, ladies. Jen, Becky, don't forget the class reunion next week."

Rachel was relieved neither Becky nor Jen slowed Janet's departure by mentioning they were bringing her along. As soon as the two women were out of hearing distance, whispering and glancing back as they left the area, she sighed and said, "I'm glad that's finished. They were determined I wasn't going to say no to them. Who in the world could do so much work in six weeks without becoming completely exhausted? If those two ever did any of the labor themselves instead of just dishing out orders, they'd realize how much time, energy, and sacrifice is involved in such enormous projects and why six weeks will leave the chairwoman and committee no breathing space. It's a good cause, but I hope Betty and everyone else refuse the job. It would serve them right to either be forced to call off the sale or postpone it or to take on the work themselves."

"Can you envision Janet Hollis and Dianne Blackwell making collections, tagging items, packing them, and all the rest?" Becky jested. "Can you picture them dusty and sweaty, nails chipped and dirty, surrounded by boxes, hair a wreck, and no makeup?"

"That would be the highlight of my summer, if not my year."

"Mine, too, Rachel," Jen concurred.

"Janet can act so conceited and hateful at times, so childish and ill-mannered," Becky fumed. "If she wasn't Clifford Hollis's wife and the Raburns' daughter, no one would put up with her snide remarks and cruel digs. You'd think someone with her education, breeding, and social position would have more class. The only reason Dianne pals around with her is to keep Janet from picking on her, and she's about the only person who will hang out with that bitch; they're only using each other. Dianne had better run fast and hide if she ever gets on Janet's blacklist because Janet will shred her to pieces with delight."

"Janet thinks by smiling and cooing, she can say anything nasty she pleases and her victim won't tell her off," Rachel added. "If anyone dares to call her on an insult, she plays the innocent and makes the accuser look like a fool. She has her dirty strategy down pat. But, if you've noticed, she mostly does it to women," *women from outside her birth clique, like me,* "and in situations where her target won't want to create a scene. Or she does it to men she considers wimps. I've overheard her say some really risqué things just to embarrass or fluster a person."

"She was certainly after you today, Rach," Becky noted. "I wonder why."

"When I was at the bank Monday doing business with Cliff, Janet came in with her brother to pick up Cliff for lunch. Her brother is divorced again and on the prowl. He asked me out and I politely refused; Janet took it as an insult to her. You both know her temper can be as fiery as her hair when she doesn't get her way. Now, she couldn't force that position on me. I suppose I'm on her blacklist."

"I'm surprised Cliff doesn't put a stop to her rudeness. He can't be so blind that he doesn't notice her offensive conduct. Scott would have a fit if I behaved like that to his friends or clients. One day," Becky predicted, "she'll get her comeuppance."

"I hope I'm around to witness it." Rachel murmured, "You know, Cliff probably stays silent to keep the family peace. You can imagine what Janet would do if he tried to correct her. He's been wonderful to me and I don't want to cause trouble for him, so I'll endure her as long as I can. But I'll tell both of you that her spiteful antics are wearing thin on me. I'm starved. Let's have lunch and forget about Janet and Dianne."

"Excellent idea; right, Jen?"

"I fully agree. Let's go before we lose our appetites."

Friday evening, Rachel put away the groceries, did her exercises, and ate her supper. Afterward, she sat down at her desk to write letters to her daughters and to wrap packages with small gifts for her grandchildren so she could mail them the next morning. Before beginning those tasks, she looked through a family album as she sipped raspberry tea and relaxed. There were pictures of special events, holidays, and various activities involving Karen and Evelyn that lessened her loneliness. She looked at pictures that included Daniel and his family and remembered the days they had been taken. How tragic, she thought, that he hadn't lived to see his children grown, to share in their successes and joys, and to hold his grandchildren.

After Daniel's death, two years following those of her parents, her only goal for a while was just living day to day and taking care of her children. When they were both in school, she filled her remaining schedule with social and volunteer activities which only partially fulfilled her. Now that her girls were grown and had their own lives, why shouldn't she feel restless? She was still young and energetic. One solitary night she had taken out an old dream that got stored away, dusted it off, and now was trying to complete it. She told herself she shouldn't be afraid of the unknown, should try to conquer it. With help from God, her friends, and her daughters, she had gotten past depression, many fears, and any self-pity. She had come to believe she had work to do, a new life to live. She didn't want to just amble along; she wanted to run, jump, enhance her existence and improve herself. She had to forget the past and her mistakes, except for what she had learned from them. She had been a good wife and mother; she tried to be a good grandmother. Now she needed a new challenge, her writing.

Rachel felt fortunate she had become best friends with Rebecca Cooper and Jennifer Brimsford, as both had helped her in many ways over the years. She wished she could confide her remaining secrets to them but had decided they were too personal. She knew they wanted her to be happy, and true southern happiness included being married. The general opinion was, as soon as a woman lost a husband to death or divorce, especially if she was young and had children, she found a replacement as promptly as possible. She suspected most people wondered what was wrong with her since she had never remarried. Being single did present disadvantages in certain situations, but she could not settle for just any man. She wanted a wonderful man; next time, one with an equally wonderful family.

Rachel scooted down in the chair and leaned her head back. She closed her eyes and reminisced about the birthday cruise she had taken twelve years ago. She had not confessed the story of her passionate shipboard romance with "James Rawlings from Texas" to her friends or to her daughters. Perhaps because he had been much younger than she and she feared they would think her wanton to have carried on with a stranger for two weeks on a ship and in foreign ports. Maybe she had needed to "feel alive," feel safe and desirable in a man's arms. She had been a widow for over two years; she'd had children to rear alone; she'd had in-laws who disliked her. Maybe a wild and rebellious streak had attacked her, weakened her.

She would never forget that night in November seven and a half years ago when she discovered "James"'s identity. She had been doing needlepoint when she heard his voice on the television, the same one that had whispered tantalizing pillow talk into her ear in a mellow tone that made her hot and willing to surrender. Thank goodness the girls had both been out on dates when she was enlightened by that commercial Quentin Rawls did for that cola company. At first, she had been stunned and angered; then, realized she had no right to feel that way considering they had made no promises or commitments to each other four and a half years earlier, only shared a wonderful vacation.

A smile lifted the corners of Rachel's lips as her mind visualized him. That night, she had become a closet football fan just to watch him, when he wasn't sidelined with disabilities or denied the starting position. From what the announcers and commentators said recently, he was getting too old at thirty-eight to play, and his virile body was weakened by several injuries. It sounded as if Quentin Rawls's "golden arm" was rapidly tarnishing and that was sad, even if he had duped her about his identity long ago. Maybe, she mused, he had a good reason for deceiving her, as she had done with him. After all, she was the one who bolted like lightning without saying good-bye or giving him the chance to exchange addresses and phone numbers.

Get him and what might have been off of your mind, Rachel, or you'll keep comparing all of your dates with him. You'll never see him again, and it's been too long since you last saw him to try to contact him. Besides, he's too young; mercy, you were having babies when he was a kid! He's been married and divorced twice, so he must not be good husband material. The tabloids paint him as a playboy, and you aren't looking for just another brief affair. He's a sports jock; you have nothing in common with him. Don't let him and silly dreams haunt you. If you want a man, check out Keith Haywood as Becky suggested; he sounds more suited to you and your lifestyle. No,

*if you do and it doesn't work out, you may have a
hell of a time discouraging him without creating hard
feelings with him and mutual friends.*

Rachel opened her eyes, straightened in the
chair, and changed her line of thought. She
glanced at a framed picture on the desk, one of
her parents, and wished they were still alive, but
was glad their lives had been full and happy
until their seventies. Perhaps she had inherited
female problems from her beloved mother, because she herself had been born when her
mother was forty and after suffering several miscarriages which had denied Rachel siblings. It
would have been wonderful to have had a sister
who was a close friend and confidante, someone
to whom she could tell anything and from whom
she could get advice on things she could not
discuss with her friends. She knew she was lucky
to have come from a close family and to have
been blessed with special parents. On Father's
Day, she had driven to Athens to place flowers
on her father's grave and to make certain it was
being tended properly. She had mailed a card
to Richard Gaines, but had not heard from him
and doubted it meant anything to the man.

Howard Tims and Daniel Gaines had been excellent fathers, so good memories made their
losses bearable. Daniel had been a good husband; and their marriage a pleasant one, except
for his parents' resentment of her. She had
loved him and he had loved her, but the grand
and glorious passion in her life had come from
a man she hardly knew and could never forget.

Don't start thinking about Quentin again!

Rachel looked at the remaining pictures in the album, ones from recent years. She closed it, put it away, and smiled. She had so many things to be thankful for, so many blessings and so few problems. Yet, a curious restlessness consumed her. She needed new adventures and successes of her own. Perhaps while the children were away, she could spread her wings and travel new and exciting roads. But if a man as irresistible as Quentin Rawls came along, she decided, she would be ready and willing to go after him.

The following Friday night, Rachel arrived at the Julian Smith Casino with Becky and Scott Cooper and Jennifer and Adam Brimsford. The lot was crowded with cars, trucks, and a few jeeps, so the women were let out at the entrance while the men went to find a parking space. Music from the sixties was playing inside the oblong building, constructed of big rocks with smaller end sections made of pine logs. A large stone gazebo with a windows-enclosed center and narrow outside walkway rose high above the tall roof. After being closed off for years, it was being repaired and cleaned so it could be opened to guests the following year.

As they waited under the porch's overhang, Jen apologized again for making them tardy due to a problem with one of Adam's insurance clients.

"Don't worry about it," Becky told her, "we aren't late; we just aren't early. I'm sure people will straggle in for the next hour. We'll have plenty of time to party before one o'clock."

Jen smiled in gratitude. "You look terrific, Rachel. The old gang will be delighted to see you. We're so glad you came with us."

"Thanks. I think Dawn did a fantastic job on all of us today."

"Our new duds look good, too," Becky remarked. "At least it's not too hot and humid tonight after those horrible storms during the past week. I wish they had voted to air-condition this old place sooner than next year. Open windows and doors and huge floor fans don't cool it in summer, not in Augusta. At least the dress is casual, though, so we can be comfortable."

"We couldn't hold the reunion anywhere else," Jen said firmly. "This is our place. It has atmosphere and history. Forget we graduated thirty years ago; pretend we're young again and don't notice the weather and pesty insects."

"You're such an optimist, Jen. I can hardly wait to see everybody. Here come the boys now. Let's shake a leg and have fun."

As the five entered a round foyer via double doors, they saw a banner over a rock arch into the adjoining room. It read: *Welcome ARC Class of '64.* The men collected their keepsake booklets and name badges from classmates working the registration table; the cards inside plastic holders with elastic cords to suspend around their necks prevented pins from picking women's blouses. On the classmates' cards were copies of their senior pictures, which evoked laughter and jokes and recollections of old days.

Adam and Jen were guided away from the registration table to a video camera set up on a tripod. Billy Bates was interviewing everyone who arrived for a souvenir tape which was for sale. He did the same with Becky and Scott, then wheedled Rachel into speaking for a minute about Daniel, herself, and their children.

As more classmates arrived, hugs and kisses and gleeful words were exchanged. Questions were asked and answers were given about what they had been doing since the last reunion in 1979, one Rachel had attended with Daniel only a few months before he was killed in the plane crash. The foyer became crowded as more people entered or hung around to chat.

"Let's check inside, see who all's here and get something to drink," Adam coaxed and headed that way.

"I don't believe it; they're finally remodeling the place," Becky said. "Look, they have a built-in bar and they're adding a kitchen. It's past time; serving food was always difficult here without one."

Rachel glanced at the L-shaped bar in the back right corner and into the unfinished kitchen beyond a serving counter in the front right corner. Soft drinks, coolers with ice, cups, small plates, napkins, bottles of red and white wine, and a variety of hors d'oeuvres and snacks were available. Beside the bar and on the floor were several beer kegs that were being used frequently. Straight ahead were double doors with glass-paned tops which opened onto a stone patio that overlooked Lake Olmstead and was partly shaded by giant oak trees. People enjoyed the lovely view and fresh air as they chatted and drank and waved aside insects, mostly yellowjackets drawn by the scents of beer and wine and colas.

Rachel glanced to her right at an arch which led to a tiled hallway where the restrooms were located. In the anteroom, she noticed purple-and-gold streamers and balloons that swayed in breezes created by enormous floor fans and fresh air blowing through tall opened windows. Huge posters with pictures from the *Rainbow* annual were placed here and there on sturdy easels, and groups gathered around them to reminisce.

Rachel looked to her left through three stone arches where tables and chairs were positioned on both sides of the room near the windows to allow ample space for dancing. The wood floor shined from a recent waxing and buffing. The ceiling was high and open with its rafters in view, from which abundant decorations were suspended. Music would be provided by a live band playing from eight to one. Until that hour arrived and during the musicians' breaks, a juke-box loaded with fifties and sixties tunes would fill in for them. At present, the Newbeats were belting out "Bread And Butter" followed by the Beach Boys with "I Get Around." Near the crowded easels, busy bar, droning fans, and jukebox, the combination of noises was loud. Becky almost had to shout to be heard over the mixture, "I can hardly believe their improvements; this is wonderful. With air-conditioning being added and the gazebo opened soon, our next reunion will be super."

Everyone nodded agreement.

Scott bunched them together and said, "Let's get away from this chaos. Let's sit near the stage so we can see and hear the action later."

"That's a good idea," Adam said. "Let's hustle, I see an empty table."

After they took their seats to claim them for the evening, the women waited and chatted while the men fetched their first drinks.

While Becky and Jen were engrossed in catch-up talk with an old friend, Rachel's eyes drifted around the room as she looked for familiar faces. The record changed on the jukebox to the Beatles' "A Hard Day's Night." Halfway down the other side, her gaze came to an abrupt halt. *It can't be! Move!* her frantic mind ordered the couple who blocked her view for a moment. After they walked away and her line of vision was unobstructed, Rachel stared at the tall, muscular, handsome man. Her green gaze took in his black hair and even features. She knew his eyes were blue, an incredible shade of it. She even knew how he looked without clothes. *Stars above, it is him! What are you doing in Augusta? At this reunion? With Carrie Simmons, rumored to be the 1964 class "bad girl"?*

Rachel yanked her gaze from the intimidating sight and tried to settle her nerves and slow her rapid heartbeat. She took the cup Scott handed to her and sipped wine as she pretended to listen to Adam as he related a conversation at the bar with an old friend. She wondered if Quentin Rawls had forgotten her; surely so, she reasoned, after the long string of women he had known and conquered since, if the tabloids could be trusted to report the truth on occasion. She wondered if she had been included in locker-room jokes, if she— "Rachel Tims" to him— would be mentioned one day in a tell-all book. What would her friends think about her if they read such a revealing story? What would she say to him tonight, as avoiding him in the same room seemed an impossible feat? What would she say to her friends if he mentioned that cruise to them? Should she get out of there before she was embarrassed or stay and pretend she didn't know him? She looked at him again. *Oh, no, he's glancing this way! He sees me!*

It seemed to Rachel as if Quentin made deliberate eye contact with her. And why not, she fumed in dismay, since she was gaping at him in what must appear to be obvious disbelief and heart-pounding panic? For a crazy instant, she hoped she looked better to him tonight than she had the last time he had seen her, naked in her cabin and his arms, the night before she had sneaked from the ship without even saying good-bye! She saw him grin, give his head a slight nod, and return his attention to Carrie.

Rachel almost squirmed in her metal seat as she realized she had been recognized. Since Beatlemania had been sweeping the country and world in 1964, another one of the fab four's old hits began to play: "She Loves You." The words "Yeah, yeah, yeah" seemed to taunt her and to increase her tension. *Heaven help me ignore and avoid him and don't let me be twice tempted by him. If given the chance, I can't weaken and surrender again!*

Three

Two hours passed without an embarrassing incident, but Rachel could not relax while knowing Quentin was in the same room with her. Twice they had been only fifteen feet or less apart, but neither had made any attempt to acknowledge the other. By now, everyone present knew the famous sports hero was in the room, and most had made a point of meeting him. Scott and Adam talked to him, then reported how polite and interesting he was. She was relieved Quentin had been kept busy and away from her; yet, she was a little surprised and even disappointed he hadn't approached her or even seemed to notice her a second time.

She had spoken with many of Daniel's old friends from out of town, with local friends, and danced with several of the men, including Scott and Adam twice each. While dancing with Adam to "Chapel of Love" by the Dixie Cups, they had discussed Wednesday's meeting for the Community Outreach Program for the Handicapped and the devastating flood that had struck central and southwestern Georgia earlier that week. Just this morning, she and others had taken donations of clothing, food, bottled water, and toiletries to a pickup point to be transported to the disaster area. After attending church on Sunday, she had worked for three days on her novel, writing by hand since terrible lightning storms also were attacking Augusta and she dared not turn on her computer.

She had eaten unwanted snacks to get food into her stomach to prevent the wine from dazing her wits. On the sly, she watched Quentin dance with Carrie and with others. She knew what it was like to be held in those strong arms and pressed against that virile frame while having fun on a dance floor on a ship, in exotic nightclubs, and on romantic beaches. She knew how it felt to have his cheek touching her head, to have his warm breath against her ear when he spoke to her, and to have his long fingers curled around hers while his other hand drifted along her spine. She recalled how she tingled and warmed when he nuzzled her neck or brushed kisses over her face. She recalled how they laughed, talked for hours, strolled in Caribbean towns in seven ports-of-call, ran barefoot in the sand, swam and snorkeled in tranquil waters in secluded coves, rode horseback on a moonlit beach, gambled in the ship's casino, sipped tropical drinks, shopped, and visited Granada before its turmoil. She remembered a bus ride through the Venezuelan jungle near Caracas to a glass-blowing factory where they had purchased keepsakes she still held precious. She hadn't forgotten a single event or moment she had shared with him years ago. She knew what a skilled and generous lover he was, and how her inhibitions had been washed away in a flood of ecstasy with him. He had been wonderful on the cruise, but was he still that same man today? Had he changed while running in the limelight? Or had he duped her like a con man years ago?

At one point, Rachel escaped to the ladies' room to keep from going outside with her friends for fresh air and quiet talk because Quentin and Carrie were there, and he was the center of attention.

As she prepared to leave the stall, Rachel heard Janet, Dianne, and another woman enter the oblong restroom. Only one had to use the commode, and she chose the first stall far from Rachel.

"Next time they're taking our picture before we get sweaty and mussed! You know everybody studies it like crazy afterward. Hellfire, my foundation is sliding off, my eyeshadow is smeared, and my hair is damp. I feel as if this sundress is clinging to every inch of my wet body. God, I need some quick repairs before this room gets crowded."

"You look perfect, Janet; you always do, so don't worry."

"Thanks, Dianne, but I looked better on arrival. This lighting is atrocious, and the noise and heat out there are unbearable. We should move this event to the Civic Center or Sheraton or Sacred Heart Cultural Center. I would be willing to pay more to have a nicer site and conditions, at least some damn A/C. I mean, we aren't kids anymore. Maybe some of those women will dress better in another place; such tacky outfits tonight. Maybe we should hold a class to teach those other creatures how to dress properly."

As she straightened hair mussed from dancing, Dianne scoffed, "Did you see what Carrie Simmons is wearing? Yuck! It looks as if it came from a bargain department. Can you believe she had the nerve to show up tonight? I wonder how she latched on to Quentin Rawls. Greg said he's rich and famous, one of the greatest quarterbacks of all time. He's a hunk, too."

Rachel stayed quiet and hoped they didn't notice her presence in the last stall as they gossiped about Carrie Simmons and her celebrity date. She also had an itch to see if they mentioned her.

Janet tossed a used lipstick into her purse and began to comb her red hair. "He told Jim he was old friends with Carrie's brother, another football jock. I heard he's practically a has-been; at least Donnie was smart enough to retire years ago when he got past his prime. Some of the boys said he's lost his touch and will probably be kicked out before this season starts."

"If he knew Carrie was the class tramp, he wouldn't have come with her and tarnished his image. Or maybe that's why he did; maybe she's still an easy lay."

"You know they're shacked up together in a hotel," Janet said. "Carrie couldn't stop her carryings-on after that party incident. She probably still can't."

The stranger— wife of a classmate— joined them and asked, "What happened with her years ago? Ollie said she was from a prominent family."

Rachel heard sheer delight in Janet's tone as the redhead revealed, "She was, but she got drunk or stoned at a party and screwed countless boys. A chaperon caught her half naked and sprawled on the backseat of a car in the school parking lot, putting out for anybody who wanted it. The boys saw him coming and scattered, so none of them got caught. There's no telling how many boys sneaked outside and took a piece of her. She was lucky she didn't get pregnant because she wouldn't have the vaguest idea who the bastard's father was. Of course, she swore she hadn't done anything wrong, that somebody must have slipped something in her drinks. Nobody would hang around with her after that; at least, not anyone who was anybody. She became *really* promiscuous and made things worse for herself by screwing half of the boys in the junior and senior classes. Her family moved after her graduation; they couldn't stay here after such a scandal."

"I met her earlier and she seems nice," the stranger remarked. "Maybe she's changed. That happened thirty years ago."

"Considering how much therapy she's probably had since then, she *should* have improved," Janet said, "she certainly couldn't sink any lower."

"Do you think she and Quentin Rawls are a twosome?"

"They could be, Dianne; with his list of ex-wives and countless affairs, he sounds as horny as she is. Bob said his brother is even worse, into drugs and other bad habits; he's been in jail and created plenty of bad publicity for Quentin, when Quentin wasn't doing it for himself. You know what they say, trash attracts trash, and Carrie rotted long ago. Now let's go get our picture taken; the photographer is setting up the camera. I want . . ."

Janet's voice trailed off when the door closed. As Rachel left the far-end stall, she decided the women hadn't realized she was there, though her presence probably would not have stopped Janet or Dianne from running their mouths. She could imagine what they would say about her if they learned she knew Quentin, and how well. As always, Janet was eager and ready to pounce on anybody she considered inferior to her, which was most people; and sycophant Dianne followed suite. Rachel believed that their treatment of Carrie was cruel; after all, the girl had made a terrible mistake and paid dearly for it, and possibly *had* been drugged or intoxicated against her will. Perhaps Carrie had been so desperate for friends that she sought them in the wrong way. Rachel wondered if the boys who took advantage of Carrie at that party ever felt guilty and sorry. Back then, they probably boasted about their participation. Long ago, it was only a girl's reputation that suffered from such tragic incidents. Today, Rachel fumed, what happened would be called "gang rape."

While she was washing her hands, dabbing away perspiration from the heat and humidity, touching up her makeup and brushing her hair, other women rushed into the ladies' room to repair their faces. They chatted among themselves and with Rachel. It was clear they were all having fun at the event.

As Rachel reentered the large oblong room, classmates were being positioned on portable bleachers to have a commemorative picture taken. Since her group's table was pushed aside for a while, Rachel remained near the easels, out of the way. She watched everyone laugh and joke as they waited for the instructions to smile and yell *Cheese*. From the corner of her eyes, she saw Quentin conversing with husbands of classmates while their wives and Carrie were busy with other people. He glanced her way twice but she pretended her attention was focused on the reproductions of annual pictures on the posters. For a wild moment, she feared he would join her but also *hoped* he would. At least that would give her the chance to learn if he was going to mention the cruise. Surely he was still a gentleman and wouldn't divulge their intimate secret in front of others, but it would be natural to say something about how and when and where they met.

Maybe he doesn't remember you, Rachel, and he's just toying with you because you keep staring at him and he finds your interest amusing. Even with a date

on his arm, some females were flirting openly
with him. She decided that a man with
Quentin's looks and fame must be familiar with
women's attention. Most of the men seemed excited and pleased to meet him, but celebrities
usually were treated that way to their faces. Of
course, Janet and Dianne were snubbing both
Carrie and Quentin, as if the couple was beneath them. She almost smiled as she thought
about how lucky he was to be avoided by them.

After the picture was taken, Carrie Simmons
rejoined Quentin. Rachel noticed they didn't act
cozy or romantic, but more like friends. She
headed for her group and reached it as their
table and chairs were replaced.

The head of the reunion committee took the
stage and stood behind a podium. "Let's quiet
down for a minute, folks, and take care of business. We have some awards to present. First, I
want to give the names of the reunion committee and thank them for a super job."

Rachel listened to the list, then helped ap-
plaud their work. She observed as printed
awards were handed out to the person who had
come the longest distance, to the person who
had changed the least and the one who had
changed the most, to the class sweethearts who
had been married the longest, to the couple
with the most children, and so forth.

The speaker continued his portion of the program by reflecting at length on top events of
1964 and the years that followed. At first, the
crowd seemed to enjoy the trip down memory

lane, but as the speech dragged on, everyone grew restless.

The man on the stage must have sensed it because he laughed and said, "I guess it's time to shut up and party. Have a great time and we'll see you again at the next reunion in 2004. Our theme will be 'Forty In 04,' so keep in touch with the committee and be here."

The audience clapped. Some whooped and yelled. Some hurried to the restrooms. Others swarmed the bar for drinks and snacks. A few called it an evening and departed after hugs, kisses, farewells, and handshakes. Old cliques gathered for more reminiscing and made plans to get together sooner than the next reunion. The band returned and began playing the Beach Boys' "Help Me Rhonda." Many couples rushed to the center of the room and began to skag or jitterbug.

"Let's tear up that dance floor, baby," Adam jested to Jen.

"I'm ready," she replied as she pushed back her chair and joined him.

The couple left to enjoy themselves, as did Becky and Scott.

Rachel chatted with Betty Burke for a while before the woman's husband claimed her for a dance. As she began listening to one of her favorite groups— the Righteous Brothers— singing "You've Lost That Loving Feeling," she almost dropped her cup of Diet Coke when Quentin tapped her on the shoulder and spoke to her from behind, his voice unmistakable.

"Would you care to dance with me?"

Rachel turned sideways in the chair, looked up at him, and nodded. She accepted the hand Quentin extended to her, rose, and walked a short distance before he pulled her into his unforgotten embrace. She hoped he didn't detect her trembling and anxiety, evoked by his stimulating touch and her tension. She noticed he kept a safe distance between them and other couples. For privacy? she mused.

"It's been a long time, Rachel, twelve years."

So, he hasn't forgotten me. "Yes, it has, Quentin." *Lordy, you still have a mellow and enticing voice and intoxicating aura! Please don't work your magic on me again.*

"Were you surprised to see me here tonight?"

"Shocked is more like it. You've really done well for yourself."

"I suppose so, but— as they say— glory is fickled and fleeting. Carrie told me you were married to one of her classmates and old friends."

You two have been discussing me? Let him know you weren't married when you met him! "Does she know Daniel was killed in a plane crash fifteen years ago, on his way to a Georgia football game?"

"One of the others told her the bad news earlier this evening. I take it from your name badge, you haven't remarried."

"No, I haven't."

"Why not? You're a young and beautiful woman."

Rachel stopped glancing around to avoid meeting his potent gaze. "I'm forty-seven," *nine years older than you,* "but thanks for the compliment."

"You evaded my question," Quentin teased. "Why haven't you remarried? Fifteen years is a long time for an attractive woman to remain a widow."

Rachel tried to sound playful. "Probably for the same reasons you're single; good choices are few and far between."

Quentin grinned and chuckled. "You're right. I guess that also means you're familiar with my marital history and two mistakes."

"You have made the news frequently over the years."

"I've been in those sleazy tabloids more times than in reputable newspapers."

"Ah, the price of fame. May I ask a favor of you?" she whispered.

Quentin slightly tightened his grasp on her hand. "Why not?"

"Would you mind not telling anybody here that we've met before?" She watched him study her tense expression for a moment before responding.

"I understand; a southern lady has to protect her image."

Rachel made sure no one could overhear them. "It may sound corny and old-fashioned, but yes, I do. These are my friends and acquaintances. I have children and grandchildren. What I did years ago was unusual for me and reckless, and I don't want it to come back to haunt me."

"I catch your meaning, but you were and still

are a real lady. Don't be nervous with me, and consider these lips sealed."

"Thank you for being a real *gentleman,*" she said, coaxing a smile from him. She liked the way his black hair was cut and combed, soft and full and swept back from his handsome face. A fringe of it played across his forehead and the length grazed his collar. She remembered how it used to blow around on the windswept deck of the ship. His eyes were as dark and shiny as expensive sapphires and— she knew from experience— his potent gaze could draw a woman into their depths without trying. His full lips were sexy, and she knew with quivering delight how they kissed. His body was firm and muscular, and she knew how it made love: slowly and deliberately or swiftly and urgently, but always with generosity and talent. Lordy, he was magnificent, and she was falling under his spell! "Did you tell Carrie you knew me?" she asked to distract herself from her crazy emotions.

"No, I only asked her who you were. I guess I was a mite devious."

Did you think I had lied about my name years ago, as you did? "She doesn't know me; she left Augusta before I moved here."

"Carrie said that everybody in town knows who the Gaineses are."

"Perhaps, but I'm a Gaines by marriage and I'm not a local."

"Carrie asked another woman who the lady was sitting beside Rebecca Hartly and Jennifer Brimsford, then told me."

"Did she ask why you were interested in me or get jealous?"

"No, I'm just a friend of her brother Donnie. I'm doing her a favor by escorting her tonight. I'm sure you know why she didn't want to come alone."

"I've heard one-sided rumors, but I don't know the facts, and it isn't any of my business. It took a lot of courage and I hope she's having a good time, but why did she come? You don't have to answer if that's personal."

"Donnie told me Carrie's had a tough life, here and after she moved. He didn't go into the details but reading between his words wasn't difficult. He said she's worked hard to get herself straight. She wanted to confront her past and conquer the bad parts so she can get on with her life."

"That's very brave and admirable. I hope she succeeds. Tell her not to let any of the snobs here hurt her feelings or treat her badly."

"That's nice of you to say, but you always were a nice person."

Rachel wondered if his voice had an odd tone to it during the last part of his sentence. It was hard to tell what he was thinking. One thing was certain, he still possessed that winning ability to put a person at ease. "How long will you and Carrie be in town?" she asked.

"She's leaving Sunday. I'm on vacation, so I'll be around for a while."

"Vacation? Here? Isn't this an odd place to select for pleasure?"

Quentin knew he couldn't tell her why he was

really there, not yet. She would find out soon
enough, so would the rest of the town. "Are you
saying Augusta has nothing to offer a kind
stranger?"

*I don't like that secretive gleam in your eye, and I
sense you aren't being honest with me, again.*
"Augusta has plenty to offer; it just doesn't seem
to be your type of place."

"Because I like cruises and exotic places and
special people?"

Rachel lowered her gaze and licked her lips.
Was he toying with her or trying to rekindle an
old flame or just being genial? Lordy, it was exhilarating to be in his arms again. Had he decided to stay for a while before or after seeing
her tonight? *Please don't ask why I left without saying good-bye, which should have been obvious to an
intelligent man like you, or try to talk about our past
together, not here, not when my wits are dazed.* "I
meant, big cities or secluded resorts."

"I get enough of big cities and crowds when
I'm on the road with the team. As for secluded
resorts, I haven't visited one of those yet. Maybe
that's an idea I should keep in mind when I
need peace and quiet."

The band hardly paused before playing another slow and romantic song, and Quentin did
not release her from his embrace. To Rachel, it
was almost like a trick by fate to keep her
trapped there. She couldn't decide if that was
good or bad, not with the way she was feeling.
The male singer was crooning words of a Paul
Davis hit, "You know when I look in your eyes,

I go crazy," which just about described her re-action to Quentin years ago and tonight. A slight sheen of perspiration glistened on his face and she felt the dampness of his shirt from his pre-vious exertions and from the heat, despite the cooling fans and slight evening breeze: as Au-gusta was known for its high humidity.

"You're mighty quiet, Rachel. Do I make you uncomfortable? If so, I don't mean to. We are old friends. We had a wonderful time together. You don't have to be nervous around me. What's worrying you?"

"I suppose I feel a little out of place since this isn't my class reunion; I'm sure Carrie told you that. My friends insisted I come so I could speak with Daniel's old friends, and they thought I would have a good time."

"Everybody needs a fun and relaxing evening out once in a while. Privacy and true friends can be hard to find and keep. Right?"

Surely you don't expect me to touch your hints even with a ten-foot pole, not here, not this soon, not after what happened between us. Yet, since he was being considerate and polite, she told herself to relax and enjoy his company, but to dig for clues about his feelings. "I doubt a big celebrity like you gets much of that, privacy, I mean. I'm sure your many fans deluge you with attention and pleas for autographs and for pictures. Being a superstar must be demanding."

"You're right; it gets frustrating at times. When I became a pro quarterback, I didn't re-alize I'd be on public display most of the time.

I admit, in the beginning, it was exhilarating to have a crowd cheering my name and to have the media painting me as a sports giant. But if one isn't careful and smart, it can become just as addicting and destructive as a drug. There's nothing as entrapping as believing your own publicity and thinking the great times will go on forever. The people who put you on the top and the ones you passed getting there are the same ones who will help take you down fast if you make a mistake or weaken. There's always somebody ready, willing, and praying— even plotting— to take your place."

"We Americans are bad about trying to immortalize our stars and heroes, then suffocating them with adoration and attention. Too many of us want to know every detail— good or bad— about their lives. That's why those tabloids are so popular. But I wonder how much a star really owes his fans," Rachel mused.

"Most think we're like their property; they believe, if it weren't for their support, we could kiss our careers good-bye, no matter how much talent we have or how much pleasure we give them for years. After the media tells the world your salary— even though they don't tell that half of it goes to all kinds of taxes— people want you to give them money for every kind of reason or cause that's known; they expect you to say yes and berate you if you don't. They want you to give speeches and make personal appearances and provide souvenirs or auction items for all sorts of things. I'm all for worthy causes, but everybody thinks their cause is a worthy one. I prefer dealing with those involving children or senior citizens. But I can't do those things without creating a media circus that smacks of self-interest publicity. Privacy becomes a coveted rarity, Rachel. Total strangers want to become our bosom buddies so they can brag about knowing us. But do or say something wrong and they'll turn on you in a flash, especially those tabloids. People you hardly know come out of the woodwork to sell them scoops they swear are true about you, and sometimes you can't prove otherwise. They'll print anything about you, fiction or fact; they have no conscience or mercy when it comes to destructive coverage if it makes money and headlines for them."

Rachel noticed how his eyes brightened and his voice softened when he spoke of helping children and elders; that pleased her. She also noted the signs of irritation and frustration when he related those other facts. "That's a shame, Quentin; but I suppose it's a dark facet to human nature. We want and expect our heroes to retain their golden images. The public forgets you're only human, too. I remember reading an article about Emmitt Smith. The writer said Emmitt was an ordinary person who happens to be an extraordinary athlete and that the spotlight follows his every action. Emmitt was quoted as saying sometimes he feels as if he's an animal on display. That piece stuck in my mind because it was so enlightening and poignant and well written."

You've been reading about football and the Dallas Cowboys? I wonder why I don't remember you mentioning an interest in sports . . . "Emmitt's the tops in his field, and a good man; I've played with him for years; he deserves his fame and fortune, and his privacy. Too many of us are put on demanding pedestals too many times. But when your fifteen minutes of fame are over, watch out, because it's open season on you. All I wanted to do was play football, not become a celebrity. But on the other hand, if one isn't a success, he isn't in demand."

Rachel decided not to mention his reported injuries and precarious rank on the Dallas Cowboys football team. "From the number of endorsements you've done, you're certainly in big demand. I've seen you in television commercials and in magazine ads many times since over the years."

So, that's how you discovered who I am. Or was it? And just how much study have you given me? "The pay is good, but some of the ads or commercials are silly, embarrassing. Take that underwear series. I felt stupid throwing passes in colored briefs. The receivers catching them in full gear had to struggle not to chuckle or shout jokes during the tapings."

She laughed. "So why did you do it? For the money and publicity?"

"Nope. Well, not exactly, not like you mean. The offer was a big one and I wanted the money to buy my parents a peanut farm. Contrary to what most believe, players didn't make that much before free agency started in '93. Those at the top depended on endorsements and on investments, when we could afford them, to supplement our incomes."

"A peanut farm?" Rachel was amazed. "Where?"

"Right here in the peanut state, down near Colquitt, the only town in Miller County. It's in the southwest section of the state."

Rachel had heard the town's name but didn't know where it was because Georgia was such a big state, the largest east of the Mississippi. She was confused by his choices. "Why did you select Georgia and peanuts?"

"I didn't; my family did. That's where I was born and reared."

She stared at him. "You didn't tell me you were a Georgia boy."

"The subject never came up; we didn't have much time together to get to know each other's history." *We were busy doing other things and busy keeping secrets, just like we are tonight.* "I played football for the Colquitt Pirates. We were a small school and our record wasn't the best, so I didn't grab the big boys' attention. But Coach Calhoun convinced me I was good enough for college and pro ball, and I loved quarterbacking. Georgia, Florida, and Alabama weren't interested in me, a nobody; so I did a walk-on try-out for Barry Switzer at the University of Oklahoma. That was Coach Calhoun's idea and it worked like a charm when Switzer saw me play. After graduation and with two national championships under my belt, I was drafted by the San Francisco 49ers and stayed with them for seven years behind Joe Montana. I was traded to the Dallas Cowboys as a backup and I've been with them for nine years. Switzer's even coaching me again." *Or will be if I make the cut, which looks doubtful from where I stand.*

Rachel was glad he didn't brag about his many awards or the number of Superbowls and Pro Bowls he had played in, and didn't complain about his problems, which were serious. She knew he had injuries to his left shoulder and right knee, though he danced with graceful fluidness. According to the news, he was trying to make a comeback this year; if he failed, he would either be traded or cut or forced to retire. That had to be a resented and perhaps embarrassing predicament because it was obvious he loved the game and wasn't ready to stop playing. So, she mused, why wasn't he in physical therapy or at preseason practice? What was he really doing in Augusta? "I don't know much about football; I never had . . . any sons to play. About the only team I noticed much"— *before knowing you*— "was the Georgia Bulldogs."

"Did you go to UGA?"

"For a couple of years."

"You didn't like college life or didn't like being away from home?"

Yes, let's fill in a few blanks for each other. "I loved it, but I got married in my sophomore year and quit to have children. After my husband graduated, we moved to Augusta, his hometown. Carrie may have told you the Gaineses owned several local businesses, so Daniel went to work for them. My parents, the Timses," *see, I used my real name and hometown on the ship, unlike you, "James Rawlings of Texas,"* "they owned a small farm near Athens and sold vegetables to the farmer's market for local restaurants. They're deceased now. I was a late and only child. I don't have any living relatives, but I do have two wonderful grown daughters, a fine son-in-law, and two delightful grandchildren." A parent of adults, a mother-in-law, and a grandmother, Heavens, she fretted, that must make her sound old and dull to him! She tried to prevent a slight blush from staining her cheeks as she scolded, *Whyever are you babbling on and on about yourself? What are you trying to do? Prove to him you would have been a better choice for a wife than his first two were? I wonder what would have happened between us if we had met under different circumstances and in a different location? Would something powerful have taken place? Would we still be together? Would I have prevented you from marrying those other two women? Or was I nothing more than a fiery summer shipboard romance, a good time?* Yet, he had remembered her face and name, and he was being a gentleman despite their past intimacy and her abrupt escape. But was he only seeking a second tryst during his visit there?

"We've both come a long way from our rural backgrounds."

His voice jerked Rachel back to reality, and she was sure he noticed her lapse in attention. "Yes, we have, Quentin, especially you."

"You'd never know you have grown children; you've changed little. You're still one of the most enjoyable people I've met anywhere. Not too many people can be themselves around me; fame seems to be a blinder or an intimidator, but you don't put on airs or freeze up. That allows me to be myself, which is nice and relaxing, and appreciated."

Rachel laughed to calm her tension as she wondered if he was being smooth or honest. Either way, she was being disarmed again by his appealing demeanor and stunning looks. "I see your parents taught you well about manners and southern charm. Thank you for the compliments."

After seeming to go on and on, the music halted and Quentin released her with noticeable reluctance. "It's nice to see you again, but you'd better rejoin your date before she gets lonely over there; she needs your support tonight. Thank you for the dances and pleasant conversation."

"Thank you, Rachel; I enjoyed them, too."

"Goodnight, Quentin. I hope you also enjoy your visit here."

I fully intend to do just that and more. "Good night, Rachel Gaines."

"Good night." Rachel left him to join her friends as couples filled the floor to do the twist to Chubby's old hit. She sat down and sipped wine to wet her dry throat. She saw her four friends smiling at her.

"Somebody we know caught a superstar's eye," Scott teased.

Rachel poked his arm. "He was just being nice and having fun."

"From what I've seen, you're the only one *he's* asked to dance, and I can't blame him."

"Maybe I'm the only single woman here besides his date."

"That isn't true and you know it. We're loaded with divorcees."

"Let me change it to, I'm about the only one without an escort."

"Watch out for passes from the 'Man with the Golden Arm'; true or not, he has quite a wild reputation with the ladies."

"Behave, Scott Cooper; we only shared a dance and a few words."

"But the evening isn't over yet," the contractor hinted with a grin.

"It's a shame he's about to be cut or traded," Adam said. "I don't see how the Cowboys' owner and coaching staff can do otherwise. They have three excellent quarterbacks in Aikman and Garrett and with their pick-up of Peete. When they trim down their roster to fifty-three after preseason, I doubt he'll be on it. From what I hear and read, they're all healthy, and Quentin Rawls isn't. He's been having trouble with his famous throwing shoulder since that injury in Superbowl Sixteen in January of '82."

"January of '82," Rachel's mind echoed, right before their cruise . . . Perhaps he had been escaping a cruel spotlight while recovering. Did he remember her because she helped him

through a rough period when he needed comfort and distraction?

Adam continued, "For Pete's sake, he's thirty-eight, one of the oldest players in the NFL. Despite his past history with Switzer, the man won't be able to keep him around if he can't play. This is Switzer's first year there, so he'll be out to prove himself. So will the Cowboys; they're coming off of back-to-back Superbowl victories and they want to 'threepeat'. Quentin should call it quits before embarrassing himself by being dumped. Poor guy also has a bum knee from Superbowl Nineteen; he played the last quarter in agony, and won an award. Lordy, that was an exciting game; he won fifty bucks for me that day. I bet his house is loaded with trophies; I know he's raked them in over the years, even while playing backup to top quarterbacks. I surely do hate to see a man like that go down in smoke. With his personality and knowledge, he'd be a superb sports commentator. I've seen him do it a few times when he was on the injured list; he's good at it. Surely one of the networks is trying to grab him."

Scott grinned. "He's got so much money he won't need to work after he retires. Backup or not, he signed for big bucks. Add that salary to incentives and commercials and he has to be rolling in cash."

"If he has any left over every month after paying off his ex-wives and from living so high on the hog," Adam amended. "Besides, he can't be making as much as he used to or could if he was in top-notch condition and was a starter.

You can't remain or be a star when you're warming the bench more than you're playing. I think his golden era is about over. His commercial value has fallen close to zero in the last two years. I don't see him in ads anymore."

"Adam's right, Rachel; he could be after you for your money," Scott teased. "Yesiree, can't be too careful around hungry sports jocks."

"Look who's talking. If memory serves me right, you two were sports jocks in school," Becky pointed out playfully. "Musketeers through and through. Both of you had cheerleaders lined up around the field to go out with you."

"We had to do all we could to keep from breaking their hearts, baby."

"Ha, both of you broke plenty," the blonde playfully accused.

"Ah, but not the two that mattered," Scott murmured to his wife.

"It had better stay that way if you don't want John Bobbitt being the only male to make history in a certain area."

Scott made a comical frown. "Ouch! That smarted, woman."

"You'll smart even more if you look up any of those old flames who are divorced and giving you the eye tonight," she joked.

Scott caressed Becky's cheek. "How could I possibly want another woman when I have a perfect one like you, my sweet thing?"

"How indeed?" she teased, followed by a brief kiss.

The group laughed and changed the subject to

former classmates' activities since graduation and the last reunion; they talked over the mellow strains and evocative lyrics of "Under The Boardwalk" by the Drifters.

As the others chatted, Rachel thought about how nice Quentin was. They had had so much fun and so many kinds of pleasure during that cruise. She was glad she had their initial encounter behind her, and it had been pleasant. She could relax now, as he probably wouldn't approach her again.

She danced with Scott, Adam, and other friends to past hits such as "The Little Old Lady From Pasadena" and "Leader of the Pack." Yet, she found herself feeling disappointed that Quentin didn't ask for another dance; but he had a date who needed his attention and support. He was gallant and kind to help out Carrie Simmons.

Her friends left the table to dance to "Proud Mary" and "Joy to the World," traditional end-of-night tunes, which were loud and long.

If he does phone you later, Rachel mused, *should you lean toward him or run like spilled water? You two live in different worlds and have different needs. He'll want a family, his own children, and you're beyond that point in life. Quentin Rawls can have his choice of women, young women, celebrities like himself. If you got serious with him, your daughters and son-in-law would think you've gone off the deep end. Your friends will think you've lost your mind and rush you off to a psychiatrist. People who know you will think you're robbing the cradle. Janet and*

Dianne would have a field day at your expense. The Gaineses would finally have the chance to say they were right about you all along! Besides, with all of his current troubles and past marriages, a serious romance is probably the last thing on his mind. Don't even think of having another brief affair with him, no matter how tempting the thought. After he's gone, your reputation will be in shreds and you'll be an outcast like Carrie Simmons; Janet will make certain of that, the spiteful bitch. Please, Rachel, don't get crazy and horny at your age and screw up your life.

"Rachel Gaines, for heaven's sake, woman, where are you?" Becky asked as she shook her friend's arm from behind. "I've been trying to get your attention; I asked you a question twice."

Rachel looked upward, forced a laugh, and said, "I'm sorry, Becky; I was thinking about the girls and other things. What did you say?"

"I asked if you're ready to leave. It's after one and the band's packing up. Most people are gone. We have the family picnic tomorrow, so we'd better get some sleep or we'll have bags and dark circles under our eyes."

"That suits me; I'm tired and sleepy and my ears are ringing, but I did have fun as you promised. Thanks for forcing me to come tonight. Last night," she corrected with another laugh.

"We're ready, honey," Becky said to Scott.

"Let's mount up and ride out," he said in a comical western accent. "Adam and I will fetch the car; you ladies wait for us at the door."

On their way out, Rachel glanced around the room as casually as possible, but she noticed that Quentin and Carrie weren't in sight.

"He left while you were daydreaming," Becky whispered.

Rachel looked at her friend with a quizzical expression. "Who?"

Becky almost giggled as she nudged Rachel and teased, "You know who I mean, your famous dance partner."

"Get real, Becky; I'm too old and dull for a man like that."

"You are not. You should have flirted with him; he seemed interested. Too bad he doesn't live here," Jen said, and gave a dramatic sigh.

Rachel joked with her two best friends in a low voice before they neared others. "If he did, I'd probably embarrass all of us by chasing him down and attacking him, so it's a good thing he isn't a local."

"Would you really?" Jen asked.

They stopped to speak to old friends, preventing any playful replies, and walked outside with them. Adam opened the car door and assisted them into the vehicle. About twenty minutes later, they pulled into Rachel's driveway. Adam helped her out, walked her to the door, and waited while she turned off the burglar alarm and stepped inside the house.

"Good night, Adam, and thanks." She waved to the others and closed the door. She rearmed the system, turned off the downstairs lights, and went to her bedroom. *What a night, Rachel, one*

you weren't expecting. Should you go to the picnic
tomorrow and risk seeing him again?

As she undressed and donned a blue silk
gown, she mumbled, "Quentin Rawls, why do
you have such a powerful effect on me? If we
were anywhere except Augusta, I might be sleeping with you tonight or soon; that's how crazy
you've made me. Get a grip, Rachel, don't act
foolish; you aren't a teenager. If I'm not careful
tomorrow I'll wind up making a complete fool
of myself. Lord, help me stay clearheaded."

Four

Rachel was disappointed, but not surprised, that Quentin and Carrie did not make an appearance at the family picnic which was held the following afternoon at the Savannah Rapids Pavillion. She decided, in the event she and others encountered him somewhere while he was in town, it was best to tell Becky and Jen they had met years ago. Before Quentin was thrust into her life a second time, she hadn't felt guilty about keeping that secret from them. After all, she had become best friends with the women just three years ago, long after the affair was over. But she didn't want her friends to learn the truth some other way and think she hadn't trusted them enough to confide in them. Even so, she was not ready to tell them she and Quentin had been lovers, not yet anyway.

"This is incredible, Rach; you two actually know each other. Don't you just love it when Fate and Cupid are good to us?"

"Honestly, I didn't think he'd remember me from being his tablemate on that two-week cruise. As I told you, I met him as James Rawlings; he must have been traveling incognito for privacy. Most of the guests weren't Americans, so I doubt many of them—if any—recognized him, and we didn't visit the usual tourist stops. I didn't see him being pestered for autographs or pictures, but that cruise was before he became a big star. By the same token, since I used my birth certificate for identification to enter foreign ports, I went by my maiden name on the ship to avoid confusion. I didn't recognize him, either; but how much do I know about football?" she said lightly to protect her own privacy. She loved and trusted her friends, but that episode seemed too personal to reveal, as if casual talk about the intimate affair would cheapen it, tarnish her golden memories. Perhaps she would confess the extent of their past relationship another day.

"You didn't even give us a tiny hint that you knew him, you sneak."

Rachel laughed. "And have Scott and Adam tease me like crazy and have you two start playing cupid during the reunion? No thanks. Besides, I was shocked to see him there."

"Well, it's obvious he remembered you; that's a promising sign."

Rachel eyed Becky in confusion. "Of what?"

"That you made a strong and special impression on him, silly. Come on, Rach, he meets thousands of women; but you stuck in his mind, stuck like Super Glue for twelve years, after only two weeks together."

"There were a lot of people aboard and there were many excursions to keep everybody busy.

He didn't spend much time on the ship after we anchored at our stops." *Neither did I.* "Sue and Bonnie, you knew them before they moved away from Augusta, they talked me into taking that trip for my thirty-fifth birthday and even got Martha to stay at the house to watch the girls for me. Bad weather delayed my friends' flight out of Denver—they were coming from a convention there with their husbands—and they missed the ship's sailing. I flew to San Juan alone and was supposed to meet them aboard. If I had been told they didn't arrive and had gotten off the *Carla Costa* before we were out of port, Quentin and I wouldn't have met. I assumed we were assigned to the same table because we were traveling alone. Most of the other singles had brought companions with them."

"It was the hand of fate at work, Rach, back then and now, sheer destiny. How romantic! I bet he's thrilled he ran into you again; that could be why he's staying in town longer."

Rachel's heart fluttered in excitement for a moment. "No way. I'm too old for him and we live in different worlds. For goodness' sake, he's a big celebrity and I'm a small-town girl. My daughters are grown and one has children, when he's probably just getting ready to settle down and start a family. I wouldn't interest him. He was just being nice and having a good time last night."

"Love is blind, Rach; it doesn't see age, differences, or obstacles. Go after him, woman; he's a fine catch. You could find out where he's staying, phone him, and guide him around town. That would be showing real southern hospitality to a visitor. For heaven's sake, Rach, he's not a stranger, so it won't appear forward of you."

"If I dated a man nine years younger than I am, everyone in our social circle would laugh their heads off and gossip something fierce about me. Besides, if he was interested in me, he would be here today trying to pique *my* interest."

"He couldn't come without Carrie," Jen said, "I'm sure last night was an ordeal for her, so why put herself through another one today? I feel bad about what happened to her in school; Carrie wasn't a drinker and didn't use drugs, so what she said about being tricked might have been true. We were young and foolish and cruel, Rachel, cowards not to give her the benefit of the doubt, to forgive her and stand up for her; after all, she was our friend. It's just that we were afraid of being ostracized, too; and we didn't want the boys to think we were sluts for hanging out with her, especially after she made more mistakes."

Becky agreed with Jen. "That could have been one of us."

"From what I saw, everybody was polite to her last night," Rachel said, "perhaps because she was with a sports star and they didn't want to look bad to him. It was smart of Carrie to bring him with her for support."

"Surely you noticed those hateful looks Janet and Dianne sent her?"

"I've seen her throw those daggers in my direction plenty of times; more accurately, into my body with the intent of drawing blood. I hate for anybody to be her target. And frankly, I hate the way she makes me feel like a coward and unjustly embarrassed when she's after me and I can't fight back. Well, let's forget about her or we're going to spoil our outing."

"What are you going to say if Mr. Rawls asks for a date? Do you think he and Carrie are a twosome? It didn't appear as if they are."

"Back to that subject, are we?" Rachel watched Becky grin and nod her head. "I don't think they're . . . a couple, and I don't know my reply to a date offer; I'd have to think it through what I'd say. I wouldn't want any friendly overtures from me to look like a green light to my bed."

"He looks like a perfect traffic stopper to me."

"Behave yourself, Becky Cooper."

"If he calls, let us know immediately," Jen coaxed.

"I will, but I doubt he'll phone or that I'll see him again."

"I bet he does, Rach."

"So do I," Jen concurred. "We saw how he looked at you last night; now we know why. His sexy smile could light up the darkest room, and his physique is splendid. Don't you just swoon over tall, dark-haired men with incredible blue eyes and the face of Adonis?"

"You two are hopeless romantics, little cupids through and through."

"Well, he seems perfect for you. The boys would take him into our group in a flash. We wouldn't press you if we didn't love you so much."

"I know, Jen, and I appreciate your concern. Now, let's go eat before the food is gone. The guys are signaling for us to join them."

After church on Sunday morning, Rachel skipped lunch at the country club with her friends because it was storming and she wanted to get out of the bad weather. She changed into shorts and a T-shirt, then wrote letters to her daughters, adding a page with cartoonish drawings for each grandchild with Evelyn's. Afterward, she relaxed for an hour with a mystery book she wanted to finish. Later, she planned to work on her manuscript, but it would have to be by hand since lightning was attacking the house again and the electricity had flickered off and on several times.

As soon as she laid the novel aside, her gaze touched on family albums nearby. Rachel retrieved them, piled them beside her on the sitting-room sofa, and began to peruse them. She halted for a few minutes when she came to pictures featuring her and Daniel's college days. She had been compelled to quit in her sophomore year after becoming pregnant when a condom failed during a reckless rendezvous. She had not returned to classes because she became pregnant again at Daniel's persuasion; perhaps he had needed to cement their relationship before they moved to Augusta and his parents attempted to free him from his "mistake." She had been forced to put aside her dream of becoming a writer, as a career after marriage to someone in Daniel's class was either frowned upon or impossible by the Gaineses. She had not worked at a job outside the home since the summer after her freshman year at college. By doing everything that was expected of Mrs. Daniel Gaines she had kept busy over the years, and most of the time with worthy charity causes. Even now, she did not have to work, as Daniel had left her financially secure with insurance, investments, savings, and real estate holdings.

Joining his family had required a big adjustment for her. She had gone from being single to being a wife and mother, from living in a frame house to residing in a large mansion, from an existence as the daughter of struggling farmers to a life of wealth and high status. She had gone from attending college activities and small-town diversions to being involved with bridge clubs, charities, committees, volunteer work, evenings at the country club and symphony and opera, and more. It had been hard learning to fit into a strange world of blue bloods with old money and social prominence, but most of them, she admitted, were good people. She was glad not many of them were like her in-laws with noses in the air.

The Gaineses— who had earned as much money as they inherited— owned rental properties that included houses and apartments and shopping strips, a local savings and loan business, a national candy company, a huge car dealership, a large real estate firm, hundreds of acres of raw land, and major parts of other local companies. Rachel knew how upset they were about giving Daniel shares in several of their companies, shares she had inherited and had refused to give or to sell back to them for a cheap price; that action was based on the advice of her lawyer and banker, done in confidence so Cliff and Newton could avoid conflicts with the Gaineses who were clients elsewhere. It had taken strength and courage and much prayer to hold on to what she believed rightfully belonged to Daniel's children and grandchildren. To prevent a scandal, the Gaineses had pretended in public to accept her decision, though they made their displeasure obvious to her in private.

Rachel recalled how, shortly after Daniel's death, she had tried to get involved with the businesses, go to board meetings, and take over Daniel's place; the Gaineses had stopped her cold, said it wasn't "a woman's place," and practically ordered her to stay home and take care of the children. Daniel's two sisters and his brother-in-laws had not dared come to her defense and risk being disinherited. Rachel knew what it boiled down to was that they couldn't seem to endure the thought that *she* had her hands on Gaines money and holdings. No doubt, she mused, the situation would be different if she had a son to take his place, one in Daniel's image, one they could control.

Rachel recalled how shocked and displeased the Gaineses had been to discover their only son had wed a "nobody," an almost poor country girl without an acceptable lineage. She was never one of "them," and was always considered from "the other side of the tracks." At family gatherings, the Gaineses had made her feel like an outsider, feel unworthy and beneath them. Even while Daniel was alive, she and her girls had been viewed and treated differently from the Gaines's daughters, Cynthia and Suzannah, son-in-laws, and the children of those couples. The tragic part was that Karen and Evelyn noticed the slights and they prevented any real closeness with their paternal grandparents, so unlike the loving relationships the girls had had with her parents before their deaths. Since the move to Charleston two years ago, the Gaines rarely even phoned and never invited them to visit.

On the last two Christmases, following no contact at Thanksgiving, they only asked them to Charleston for a few hours or the day, but never to sleep over. As for gifts, they seemed to be given with reluctance and with little care about their choices and without affection. It appeared to Rachel as if Daniel's death gave his parents the opportunity to shove Rachel and the girls out of their lives. Perhaps it was because Karen and Evelyn favored her and her family, not Daniel or his side.

Maybe, Rachel admitted, she was partly to blame for the gulf between them. She had gotten pregnant by mistake, and while unwed which was a terrible thing in the old days. In 1966, horror tales of botched or lethal abortions in dark back rooms and under humiliating and unsanitary conditions were enough in most cases to persuade girls to remain virgins. She had allowed Daniel to convince her that sex was all right between people who loved each other and planned to get married one day. It amazed her to realize how little she had known about sex and passion when she was eighteen. Of course, at that age, girls thought they knew everything about it. She had weakened one night and gotten trapped, a mistake she was certain the Gaineses had guessed. She had married Daniel before meeting Dorothy and Richard, she had breached their rules of etiquette and breeding, and she had married above her class, dared to snare their son. But she was not to blame for losing an infant son to SIDS, a male fetus to a miscarriage, and a young husband to a tragic plane crash during a storm, though her in-laws tried to make her feel guilty about all those tragic incidents.

She tried not to let the Gaineses' resentment trouble her, but it did; not so much for herself, but for the sake of her children.

Rachel closed the last album and put them away. She went to the kitchen to boil water for raspberry tea, in need of its soothing effect.

* * *

At seven, after the weather cleared and she was keying up the computer to edit the last chapter she had written to get into the mental creation mode for the next one, the phone rang.

"Rachel, this is Quentin Rawls. I hope I'm not disturbing you."

Her gaze widened, her hand shook, and she almost dropped the receiver at the sound of his voice. "Not really. I was just working on one of my projects."

From your tone of voice, I caught you by surprise a second time. "I wanted to tell you how good it was to see you again, and to say what a wonderful time I had at the reunion. Everybody was nice and I had fun."

"For the most part, they're a great group of people and the committee did a superb job. I'm glad you enjoyed yourself and I hope Carrie did, too. I'm sure having you at her side made a difficult evening easier for her."

"Thanks. I have to say, everybody was polite and pleasant to her. She said she had a nice time, and it seemed a good idea for her to confront her past to get certain things behind her. That's what friends are for, to help us survive bad times and to share good ones. Right?"

"I know I couldn't do without mine. Has she gone home?"

"Yes, she changed her reservations to Saturday afternoon and flew out about three o'clock. She achieved her goal but didn't want to push herself— and others— by going to the picnic yesterday, not without her kids."

"She has children?"

"Several, from a marriage that didn't last. She's been seeing a man for quite a while who Donnie and I know and he's asked her to marry him. She thought she'd have a better chance of marital success this time if she got rid of some demons from here. Donnie asked me to be her escort," *after I told him I was coming to Augusta to visit,* "so I agreed. She didn't want her boyfriend Fred coming with her in case things went badly with her old friends. She must have been satisfied because she left smiling. She's probably said yes by now."

"That's wonderful, Quentin. Congratulate her for me."

Now that you know we weren't lovers, let's get on to step one of my two plans. "I was also calling to ask you a favor. I hope you don't mind. If so, I'll understand and won't press you."

Rachel went to full alert. "A favor? What is it?"

"Would you be interested in exchanging lunch at the restaurant of your choice for acting as my tour guide around town until I get my bearings? I know you're a busy lady and this is short notice, but if you'll agree, I promise I won't take up more than a few hours of your schedule."

Rachel wondered if this was a sly way to ask for a date or if he was letting her know it was to be a noncommittal arrangement between old friends, or like a business luncheon. Should she set things straight in advance? *No,* she decided, *wait and see how things go between us because he won't be around very long and probably doesn't have anything romantic in mind.* "That sounds all right to me. I'll be glad to help out. When?"

"How about starting in the morning at nine and going through lunch?"

As Rachel's body warmed and her flesh tingled, she fretted, *Are you getting hooked this easily and quickly by him again?* "That suits me. Do you want me to pick you up, or you pick me up, or meet somewhere?"

"I have a rental car, so why don't I pick you up at nine? I doubt I'll get lost because I'm staying at the Bradberry Suites on Claussen Road. The guard at the country club gate can give me directions to your house."

He was staying only a few miles and minutes away from her home and knew where she . . . "How do you know where I live?"

"I looked it up in Carrie's reunion booklet; it had the names and addresses and pertinent facts about her classmates. Daniel's name was included, along with a note about his death."

So, he had planned to see her before Carrie left yesterday. What had he done on Saturday and today? Surely not sit around in his suite and twiddle his thumbs; at least not on Saturday, which had been a lovely day. So, why did he need a tour guide, her in particular? *Because, silly, you're the only person in town he knows.* "I'll tell the guard at the gate I'm expecting you and to point you in my direction. Since you're so close, you should be able to find me easily."

More easily than when I tried to locate you years ago after you sneaked off the ship. Quentin thought. *Maybe I could have avoided a lot of problems if you hadn't dumped me like that. No matter, it's only second down and ten yards to go and there's still ample playing time left on the clock. I won't worry until it's fourth-and-one, my lovely and skittish Rachel Tims Gaines. Just help me work out my business proposal here, then maybe we'll get personal. All I need is a few days' study before I reveal it to anyone, including you.*

"Are you there, Quentin?"

"Sorry, Rachel. I'll let you get back to work on your project so you can have tomorrow morning free. Good-bye and thanks. I'll see you at nine sharp."

"I'll be ready, Quentin. Good-bye." *Whatever were you thinking about moments ago? Mercy, Rachel, you're crazy to get tangled up with him again. Nothing can come of this except a broken heart and perhaps a scandal.* But Lordy, she would love to have things be like they were between them years ago! They had seemed so compatible, but a lot of water had flowed under their bridges. *Quentin Rawls might like you and enjoy you in and out of bed, but he'd never ask you to marry him. Marry? Why on earth would you think along that wild line? Besides all the differences between us, he's twice burned and surely wary. He only wants a tour guide and maybe a little recreation. Can you have a good time with him and for only a short time without risk-*

ing injury? She gave that query serious consideration and sighed deeply. *How can you possibly spend time with him and not fall for his charms, maybe fall harder this go-around? You only spent two weeks with him twelve years ago and he's still in your system. How will you get him out after he leaves, which he will. How will any man suit you after being twice tempted and twice surrendering to him? Mercy woman, you're going to get hurt if you fall into this golden trap.*

Get real, Rachel Gaines! He only wants some friendly assistance. Surely you can control yourself for a few hours. You can enjoy his company without falling into bed with him, unless you want to. If you do, that's nobody's business except your own, as long as you're discreet. Well, old girl, you wanted adventure, challenges, excitement, and here's your chance to grab them. Just keep alert and be careful.

Rachel clicked open a file in her computer, the one with records about Augusta, the one she and her old hospitality committee used to help introduce newcomers to town. She printed out the pages she needed, then made notes on them. She took tourist brochures from the Chamber of Commerce and visitor's center from a file in the desk drawer and added them to the pile. She did the same with city and county maps, after plotting out their route for tomorrow using a highlighter. Of course, they couldn't cover all those in a few hours, but maybe that would entice him to ask for another tour. She slipped the items into a large yellow envelope, then shut down her computer, as writing was impossible

tonight in her distracted state. She went upstairs
to select an outfit for the stimulating adventure,
warning herself not to get her hopes too high
or have unrealistic dreams about a new relationship. Quentin Rawls for a second husband? she
mused. That could never come to pass, she decided.

Monday at nine, Quentin arrived at Rachel's
house. He eyed her with an appreciative gaze
and smiled. "You look lovely this morning.
Ready to begin our little journey?"

"Thanks, just let me lock up and set the
alarm." As they walked to the car, she decided
he liked her choice of outfit: a fashionable yet
comfortable Dana Buchman silk crepe tunic and
pants. The top, which featured a row of small
and shiny black buttons down the center, was in
red and black paisley designs and halted just
below her firm buttocks; the flowing red pants
accentuated her slim legs. For easy walking, she
wore Chanel black flats; and she carried a
matching camera-style purse with a gold-tone
chain shoulder strap. Her jewelry consisted of
gold earrings, a herringbone bracelet, watch,
and two rings. One was a two-carat emerald soli-
taire, a gift from Daniel on their tenth anniversary, and the other a cluster of diamonds around
a two-carat center stone. She had given her wedding rings to Evelyn when she married— with
Karen's approval as the eldest daughter— a set
once belonging to Daniel's grandmother. Of

course, Dorothy Gaines would give her eyeteeth to have those rings back, and had given them to her in the first place only because Daniel insisted as was the custom.

After Quentin retrieved his sunglasses from the dash and slipped them on, he backed from her driveway while glancing over his left shoulder. As she donned her glasses, she noticed he was dressed in dark-blue slacks, black shoes, and a golf shirt in red, navy, and white stripes. He looked handsome, well groomed, and relaxed. No, she corrected, he was downright disarming. She told him in which direction to drive then said, "I'll point out the sites, then you can decide if there are places you want to visit later at your leisure. I have maps and brochures in this packet for you to use if you want more information."

Quentin glanced at her for a moment, but he could tell despite her sunglasses that her green gaze was focused on the road. She appeared poised, but he detected controlled anxiety beneath her calm facade. She looked beautiful and was still utterly fascinating and charming. She had appealing poise and a sunny personality, especially when she relaxed, which he hoped she did soon. He liked the way she was wearing her sleek brown hair; the causal yet sophisticated style suited her to perfection. She had a lovely oval-shaped face and delicate yet sensual features: full lips, slim nose, large green eyes, high cheekbones. Her complexion was a natural light olive shade; her skin, well toned and firm.

There was a rosy hint on her cheeks, either from blush or nervousness or both, and her size eight to ten figure was stunning. Most females, he concluded, would give anything to age as well as Rachel. He hadn't gotten over the way she had dumped him years ago, since they had been so close and she hadn't seemed to be an insensitive person. He forced his eyes from her face and said, "I really appreciate you taking the time to do this favor for me. I thought it would be more fun to have you along today. I'm glad you agreed to come."

Rachel knew he had been studying her from the corners of his eyes. His blue gaze was potent and arousing, so he wasn't making self-control easy for her. "Thanks, and I'm sure I'll enjoy it. I was on a hospitality committee for one of my clubs last year and showed newcomers around, so you didn't hire a novice for your guide," she said with a laugh to dispel her tension.

He chuckled and glanced her way again. "That's fortunate for me."

Rachel motioned to their right. "That's the famous Augusta National Golf Course where the Master's Golf Tournament is held. The grounds are beautiful and well kept. Maybe you can pull some strings and get to play it, but the course is closed even to members from mid-May to mid-October."

Quentin didn't tell her that he already had an invitation from a club member to return and play later. His time here was limited because of preseason practice and games soon, so he had to learn as much as possible about this area and fast. Until he made his furtive study and decision, she had to be kept in the dark about his motives for being there, as did everyone else. And, there was the personal matter between them to be resolved . . .

A few minutes later, Rachel said, "To our left is Lake Olmstead and Julian Smith Casino and park where we had the class reunion. At this intersection, Washington Road becomes Broad Street, the main street downtown." As they continued along, she pointed out other sites and told him a little about them. First came Harris House. "It was built in the late seventeen hundreds by a tobacco merchant who founded this area. Plans are underway to make it part of a block-long park to serve as a tourist center and a way station for people using the Augusta Canal nearby. I worked on the historical society committee to help renovate and preserve the site." Next was the old Confederate Powder Works which— along with army uniform and supply mills— played an important role in the Civil War. "Augusta was spared devastation because Sherman decided to march from Atlanta to Savannah instead of coming here," she explained. "Besides, he had already destroyed the rail lines." She related facts about the 1840's canal system which wound through certain areas of town, and still provided power for two mills. She guided him to the riverfront and suggested he park so she could point out interesting places there.

They strolled along a lovely section of River-walk as she explained about past floods that had spilled damaging water into the town until the tall levy and strong gates were built long ago. She nodded toward the blue expanse ahead. "That's the Savannah River; it separates Georgia from South Carolina. It was used heavily in past times for transporting tobacco, cotton, mill goods, and other products. Cotton Row and the Exchange are down the street from here. The new marina is down farther, between Fifth and Sixth streets. Near it, there's a church located on the site of old Fort Cornwallis and Fort Augusta. This area is called Port Royal; it has some expensive and luxurious condos, and the Discovery Center for the National Science Center is set to open in that building next year. It should be a big drawing factor for tourists."

"What's the population of Augusta and the surrounding area?" He sounded genuinely interested.

"Augusta is just under fifty thousand and Richmond County is around one hundred and ninety thousand. There are a lot of small towns and counties nearby so together they're called the Central Savannah River Area, the CSRA; you'll see and hear that mentioned in many places. Columbia County, where I live, is about sixty-seven thousand."

As they strolled along the landscaped walkway, he said, "I see several long bridges and a train line. What's across the river?"

Rachel exchanged smiles with an elderly couple who were holding hands on a bench in the shade of tall oaks. "North Augusta and Aiken County; old and tough competitors for river trade long ago. A small but very pretty town. Best I remember, the county is about one hundred and twenty thousand." When they reached the steps, she said, "Let's get the car and continue; you still have a lot to see."

Quentin tallied up the numbers she had given him for the CSRA: the surrounding areas were comprised of just under five hundred and seventy thousand. *Good, a large population for supporting the venture, if it works out.* His keen mind left business thoughts behind as he watched her shapely hips sway as she descended the steep steps. He noticed how neat the nails were on a hand resting atop her purse, how soft her flesh looked. He remembered how it had felt to his touch long ago. He kept catching whiffs of a perfume he recognized as *Passion;* his mother loved that scent and he had purchased it often for her. A breeze lifted wisps of her brown hair but did not muss the neat style. She moved and carried herself with ease, gracefulness, and vitality. It was apparent that she exercised regularly, was in good health, and ate right to keep her waist slim, her stomach flat, and the rest of her in stunning condition.

But, Quentin decided, she possessed more than appealing physical traits. She had a sunny smile and disposition. She was interesting and he enjoyed her company. She was a good conversationalist, neither too quiet and shy nor too chatty and overt. She had manners and intelligence. Yep, she exuded breeding and style. That had been his same impression long ago, the reason why he had been taken with her as they dined side by side on the ship and why he had spent so much time with her. She didn't seem to be a coward or cold-hearted, so why had she dumped him like that after getting so close to him? By damn, he deserved an explanation and would get one before his departure! After the things Carrie had told him about the snobby and formal Gaineses, he wondered what Rachel's husband had been like and why she had married into a family so different from her. Before he left town, he would get some answers.

At the vehicle, he suggested, "Why don't you drive so I can look at the sites you point out?"

"That's a good idea," she agreed as she went around to the driver's side. She had sensed that potent gaze on her for a long time and it unsettled her. By the time she had the engine started, her seat belt fastened, and put the car in gear, she had calmed her rush of nerves.

Rachel headed down Fifth Street and slowed at Greene to show him the Signer's Monument, under which two signers of the Declaration of Independence were buried, the city/county building, Old Town where restoration was flourishing, and Ware's Folly which now housed the Gertrude Herbert Institute of Art. She turned right onto Telfair where the Augusta-Richmond County Museum, Garden Center in the old Medical College of Georgia building, and Bell

Auditorium were located. She pointed out the Civic Center and Old First Baptist Church where the Southern Baptist Convention was born. She suggested he visit the award-winning Morris Museum of Art and the new city museum, and mentioned her volunteer work helping to promote local artists. On Greene Street, she gave him a history of the Sacred Heart Cultural Center, a historic church and architectural wonder. While heading down Fifteenth Street, she mentioned the birthplace locations of well-known people: George Walton, Woodrow Wilson, Jessye Norman, the almost infamous Ty Cobb, and others.

He grinned and chuckled. "You weren't exaggerating; you really do know a lot about this town." *That's a big help to me.*

"You should see it in spring when the dogwoods, azaleas, daffodils, and more are in full bloom; you'd see why it's called the Garden City. Around Greene Street is considered one of the prettiest areas." She pointed straight ahead. "Over there is the Medical College of Georgia, dental school, and research complex: MCG for short. That's where my oldest daughter attended medical school and did her internship; she's a pediatrician." Rachel turned onto Laney Walker. "We also have a technical school and a black college here, Paine; It's ahead of us now." After veering right onto Central and traveling a few blocks, she said, "This divided strip is another one of our loveliest areas in spring."

A few minutes and one turn later, she stopped

at a red light, and while they waited for it to change, said, "If you continue down a few blocks on Milledge, you'll find the Augusta Country Club; then, a few blocks farther, you're back at Julian Smith Casino on Washington Road. To our left, up the street, is Augusta College; it's part of the UGA system and has famous items on its grounds from the Civil War. This section is called The Hill; it's where the wealthy lived and vacationed long ago. When flooding and insect infestation became a problem in the low-lands, the rich moved up here to escape those problems. There's a lot of old money and blue bloods and Old South traditions in this town." Rachel turned right onto Walton Way. "Also, in-land plantation owners came during off-seasons and for recreation. That big building on the left used to be called the BonAir Hotel; the rich and famous stayed there to escape northern winters. Ours are shorter and milder. Snow is rare, but we get an occasional white blanket and ice storms. Needless to say, being unaccustomed and unprepared for them, they wreak havoc on us, which amuses our northern inhabitants and visitors."

Rachel parked the car at the Partridge Inn. "How about eating lunch here? They have good food and service, and it's lovely and quiet in-side." *And hopefully private since it isn't a regular daytime haunt of my circle.*

Quentin unfastened his seat belt. "Suites me fine. I'm ready to eat."

Outside the car, Rachel told him, "ARC, the

Academy of Richmond County, Carrie's old school, is two blocks down the hill from us."

They entered the restaurant and were seated. Tables were covered with white cloths and napkins were folded in fanned designs. The chairs were cushiony and comfortable, the furniture good quality. Greenery and flowers were placed at the best locations to beautify the room, as were white columns. The area was clean; the music was low; the lighting was perfect; and no friends or acquaintances were present.

"I see what you mean, Rachel; it's very nice and pretty."

A waitress brought them menus; a server, ice water.

"The inn is old and historic; it was renovated years ago. There's a good view from the penthouse porch and it's an excellent small-party location."

After their selections were made and orders were given, Quentin asked, "You said one of your daughters is a doctor, a pediatrician?"

"Yes, Karen, my oldest; she's twenty-seven." *Eleven years younger than you are.* "She's on a medical mercy ship that's giving aid to sick and injured children in third-world countries. She left a few weeks ago and will be gone until next June. She's getting married and setting up a practice with her fiancé after they return; he's also a doctor and on the same ship."

They ceased talking for a few minutes while they were served bread and butter and their drinks.

"Will they be living and practicing here?"

"I hope so, but they haven't decided yet."

"You must be very proud of her."

Rachel smiled. "I am; she's a good daughter and a good doctor."

Quentin sipped iced tea before asking, "You have another daughter, right?" He studied her expressions and tones each time she talked. Once more, he saw her green eyes glow with love, pride, and happiness. He heard them in her voice. A loving mother and a happy family, he concluded, which didn't fit the Gaines family image that Carrie had described.

"Evelyn, she's twenty-five. She's married to an automotive engineer. She has two children, a boy one and a girl three. She and Eddie are in Japan until next April. He's . . ." Rachel fell silent for a moment and moved aside for the waitress to set down her salad, then watched the woman serve Quentin.

After she left, Quentin coaxed, "Go on. He's what?"

"He's with Honda in Raymond, Ohio, in their research, design, and development center. Almost ninety percent of their Accords and Civics are made in America, their top two sellers here. He'll be studying and working over there with their engineers for a year. I can hardly wait for them to return to the States; I don't like them being so far away. Letters just aren't the same. At least when they're in Ohio, frequent visits and calls will be possible."

They finished their salads just as the waitress

brought their entrees. She asked if they needed anything else and when they declined, she collected the used dishes, poured fresh tea, and brought hot rolls.

"You were right," Quentin affirmed, "the food and service here are great."

They dined and drank in silence for a short while, each keenly aware of the other, each recalling past times together. The waitress checked on them once more and then gave them privacy.

"You didn't want to visit the Orient with your daughter and family?"

Rachel finished chewing her roasted chicken before she replied, "Eddie's mother went to Japan with them to help Evelyn with the children and with cooking and cleaning in the guest house; Barbara has lived with them in Ohio since her husband died. She's a wonderful woman and they all get along well, so I'm glad she's there to keep my daughter company in a foreign country. If I had gone, too, I believe it would have been a little crowded. I might visit before they return home next year, maybe over the holidays."

Quentin sliced off another bite of roast beef. "What about your family?"

"My parents died in '77, a few months apart. I was a late child, born when my mother was forty; they were both seventy when they died. It's sad but merciful not to leave a loved one behind for very long at that age."

He noticed she qualified her last statement with a time period. From what he had learned,

Daniel had been dead for over two years when they met, and she hadn't seemed a grieving widow aboard the ship. "What about Daniel's family? Are you still close to them?" He saw her tense and watched her smile fade before she tried to appear relaxed and forced a smile.

"They relocated to a retirement complex outside of Charleston two years ago; their two daughters and their families also moved there."

Quentin waited for her to continue, but she didn't. He detected major gaps in her response and an odd look in her eyes, a dulling of their previous sparkle. *Trouble there?* he mused.

"What about you and your family?" Rachel inquired.

"I'll tell you about them another time. We need to finish eating so I can get you home on time as I promised." He sent her a smile and added, "Maybe you'll be willing to do this again before I leave town. It's been fun."

Before thinking, Rachel responded, "I've enjoyed our outing today, too, so I'm for hire again."

"Good; you did an excellent job."

Later, as he drove along Stevens Creek Road, Rachel said, "I'll leave this packet of maps and brochures with you. I've included a list of restaurants with their addresses and ratings. If you have any questions, you can ask the desk clerk or call me; you have my number."

As he pulled into her driveway, he said, "Thanks, Rachel, you've been a big help and, as always, good company." He released his seat belt and opened the door. He paused to glance over at her. "How about showing me more sites tomorrow, say the areas outside of town? If you can make a day of it, I'll reward you with lunch and dinner. Or I'll make a contribution to your favorite local charity; it's your choice."

Rachel was surprised and pleased, and intrigued by his suggestion. She responded after he opened the door for her and she stepped out of the car. "Tomorrow is fine. I can work on my project another day. Do you want to start at nine again or later?"

Quentin shut the door and grasped her elbow to walk her to the door. "Same time is perfect for me; I'm an early riser and my schedule is clear."

"You get up early even when you're on vacation?" she asked as they walked to her front porch along a brick pathway.

"I guess old habits are hard to break," he replied with a grin, and she nodded agreement. As she probed her purse for her keys, his gaze slipped over a healthy and lush lawn, neatly trimmed shrubs of various sizes and types, and colorful flowers either near the large home or in scattered beds around hardwood or decorative trees. Her lot was spacious, a good distance away from large houses on either side of her creamy stucco one. He had noticed a tall and thick brick wall enclosing the backyard for privacy. He heard lawn mowers cutting grass on other lots, smelled the scent of their labors, and heard birds singing. It was a beautiful and serene setting, an expensive one, telling him that Rachel Tims Gaines had plenty of money and was indeed a member of the upper class, as Carrie had informed him.

"You have a skilled gardener; your yard is lovely."

"Henry is a wonder; he's been with me for years. He also does my pool maintenance. His mother Martha keeps house for me once a week. They're fine people, and I'm fortunate to have them." She switched off the alarm system and unlocked the door. She turned to him and smiled, having decided not to invite him inside. "Good-bye, Quentin. I'll see you in the morning."

He ordered himself not to make her nervous by staring at her, which was hard. "Good-bye, Rachel; I'm looking forward to it. Thanks again."

She watched him return to the rental car, wave, and leave. She took a deep breath and went to change into casual clothes.

"You handled that well. Now, let's see if you can do it again," she murmured.

Five

Tuesday morning, they set off to see Thurmond Lake at Quentin's request. This time, he drove. It was a pleasant trip and Rachel was proud to show off the popular recreation spot. They looked at the large dam and one of many parks which was located in the area while they made genial conversation, with each noticing that the other avoided delving into their mutual past or into personal details. Afterward, they drove along Bobby Jones Freeway to the Gordon Highway because Quentin wanted to see Fort Gordon, a large and important military reservation a few miles away. After obtaining a post map and information, they toured open areas and chatted about the site.

"How many soldiers are stationed here?" Quentin asked.

"I don't know, but it's a large number. Many of them— and especially the officers— return after retirement to live and work here. I think some of them like being near a base with a PX, hospital, and such so they can use their benefits. We also have a large veterans hospital in town."

"I would imagine there are lots of businesses that cater to soldiers."

"Yes, and particularly entertainment like lounges and such. I'm sure having Fort Gordon nearby helps out the local economy. There's a nice dinner theater on the post that's open to the public. I've only been to one play there, but it was well done and the meal was good."

"Does it create many traffic problems for the area?"

"I don't think so. We have heavy traffic at certain times of the day and on certain highways during work-commute hours but nothing like big cities experience. It does increase when special events are in town, like the Master's Golf Tournament in April. I have to say the city and county law enforcements do a splendid job of controlling it; they post helpful signs for weeks before the tournament so visitors know where to go; that prevents jams. If you recall from the map, Augusta is bordered by the river on the east. The main thoroughfares spread out from town in a five-prong fan shape; they intersect with Bobby Jones or I-20, so getting around is fairly quick and easy."

"I imagine this county is growing rapidly these days."

"It is. Because of the river, expansion is always westward, especially toward and into Columbia County. Augusta merges into Martinez which merges into Evans along Washington Road. Many new subdivisions are going in beyond this bypass because there's still plenty of large land tracts available. Of course, their prices are rising fast."

"Demand always increases something's value." *Like a quarterback everybody wants when he's on the top.* "It certainly seems as if your highway system is sufficient for taking care of heavy traffic and expansion." *Thank goodness or this town would be worthless to us.* "What about airports?"

Rachel thought that query odd since he knew Carrie had flown in for the reunion. "We have two. There's a small city airport, Daniel Field on Highland Avenue, and the main airport that Carrie used. The largest carrier is Delta; their big jets come in at Bush Field. Also smaller connector flights and private jets use it. Pull in there and we'll eat lunch at Applebee's."

Quentin chuckled. "So, an empty stomach wins out over a charitable heart, eh?"

Rachel smiled. "Today, I'm afraid so. The crowd has thinned, so it shouldn't take long to get service; then, we can continue our tour."

"I was hoping you weren't going to starve me for a donation. Thanks."

"How could I allow myself to mistreat a celebrity guest like you?" she quipped, then wished she hadn't used those words in light of her actions years ago when she had panicked and skipped out on him. If Quentin noticed her mistake, he didn't react to it, and she was relieved. Again today, he seemed relaxed and in a good mood.

At their table, he said, "There are plenty of hotels and restaurants to select from around here; that's good for both tourists and locals. Do you have the same advantages in shopping, schools, and industries?"

While the waitress prepared their table with water, rolls, and menus, Rachel pondered his unusual interest in every facet of the Augusta area. Was he only making small talk or was there more to it? Was he trying to discover everything about her surroundings that might affect her personality and lifestyle? If so, why? If there was another reason for his intrigue and study, what could it be? She placed her order, listened to Quentin give his, then watched the waitress leave. Mercy, he looked handsome and his smile was tantalizing; and she was certainly susceptible.

"You were saying?" he prompted her for a response. *Concentrate on her words, not on how lovely she looks or how appealing she is.*

"We have two large shopping malls and numerous small centers and the downtown section of stores and shops, plus free-standing ones. If you want to shop, I suggest Augusta Mall on Wrightsboro Road beside Bobby Jones Expressway; it's closest to where you're staying and easy to find. Or Washington Road is overflowing with almost anything you might need and you can't get lost so close to home. As for schools, we have plenty of them at all levels, including the colleges and MCG which I showed you yesterday. Many of the eating places on the list I gave you are located on Washington Road in either direction from your hotel. There might be a list of industries in one of those Chamber of Commerce folders in your packet."

The waitress brought their food and drinks, then left again.

Quentin studied her on the sly. She was wearing a long ivory tunic with elbow-length sleeves that was accented with thick ebony chenille cording on the neckline and cuffs and ran downward along both sides, the center front, and from shoulders to cuffs. Paired with tailored black pants and flats, the outfit was a striking contrast of casual elegance. Pearl earrings were worn in her pierced ears, revealed by her hairstyle. A gold bracelet of hearts banded her right wrist, and she had on the same watch and two rings from yesterday. Between bites, he said, "You mentioned the Fort Gordon dinner theater. What other types of arts and cultural offerings and entertainment do you have?"

Rachel finished chewing and sipped a diet cola. "Let's see. . . . We have the symphony, opera, Augusta College theater, Augusta Players, Sacred Heart Cultural Center, Bell Auditorium, Civic Center, Gertrude Herbert Institute of Art, Morris Museum." She took a deep breath before continuing. "Riverwalk Amphitheater, riverboat dinner-dancing cruises, National Science Center, comedy clubs, plenty of nightspots, scads of movie theaters. Then there's the Exchange Club Fair in October, bowling, upscale poolhalls, rollerskating rinks, and many kinds of festivals and craft shows. Plus, Atlanta, Savannah, Columbia, Charleston, and beaches and mountains, are within a few hours of us. Of course, being from Colquitt, you know those things. I keep forgetting you're a Georgia boy, or were one." *I think of you as a Texan.*

"That's amazing for this size town. What about sports?" He grinned.

"We have ample offerings of golf, fishing, watersports, and camping. Tennis is popular here; we have a large city complex and courts at Westlake County Club, so we draw in big tournaments at both. We have a national futurity at the Civic Center, horse-racing in Aiken across the river, car racing not far away, biking and hiking. International regattas and speedboat races are held on Lake Olmstead and the Savannah River. There are all kinds of youth leagues and county teams. Columbia County has a huge sports complex on Columbia Road called Patriots Park; the Dixie Championship for softball was held there this year and drew a huge crowd. We have the Green Jackets semipro baseball team at Heaton Stadium. You may have read that the Olympic boxing tryouts will be held here." Rachel paused to sip her drink, and he waited for her to continue.

"As to your major field of interest, we had a semipro football team called the Augusta Eagles, but it didn't last too long. Best I remember, its failure was due more to being too far off the beaten path than from a lack of finances or local support. The players were featured in Burt Reynolds's mid-seventies movie *The Longest Yard.* We do have the Georgia Thrashers that play here; but I don't know much about them, either. If you're interested in checking them out, the Chamber of Commerce or Greater Augusta Sports Council might be of assistance. Naturally all of the schools have their sports programs; some of the football teams have big and long-time rivalries, like Butler and ARC. Then, there's the UGA Bulldogs in Athens, and the Atlanta Falcons and Atlanta Braves not far away. Across the river, there are the Clemson Tigers and South Carolina Gamecocks. I'm sure you've played the Falcons."

"Yep, and beat 'em. Sorry about that." He grinned and chuckled.

Rachel laughed. "I doubt that's true, but thanks for the sympathy. If I were a football addict, I wouldn't be fraternizing with the competition."

Quentin leaned back in the booth, gazed at her, and murmured, "I don't know if it's good or bad you aren't one, considering my line of work."

Rachel noted his mellow mood and sexy smile. Despite avoiding certain subjects, they conversed easily, like years ago. They seemed to have a natural rapport, were drawn to each other. She wondered if his impression matched hers. "I— "

A young man stopped at their table and asked, "Excuse me, but aren't you Quentin Rawls of the Dallas Cowboys?"

Quentin hesitated a moment before admitting the truth.

"I knew it was you!" He thrust a piece of paper and a pen toward the football player. "Would you give me your autograph for my son?"

"What's his name?" Quentin asked as he took the items.

"You don't have to put his name; you can just sign it."

Quentin's blue gaze scanned the man's flushed face. "I prefer to make it out to him. What's his name?"

"It's . . . Jeffery."

Rachel glanced at the nervous man and concluded from his expression and tone that he was lying, and knew they knew it. She waited while Quentin wrote a short message, signed it, and returned the slip of paper.

"Thanks, he'll treasure it."

The moment the man was gone, Quentin frowned and scoffed, "No, he won't. Old Jeff there was pulling a fast one; he just wanted an autograph he could sell to a collector and make a few bucks."

"Do people do that often, get autographs and pictures just to sell?"

"More than you can imagine and it's annoying as . . . That one won't be of any value to him."

"Why not? You're a big celebrity, one of the greatest quarterbacks to play the game, according to the media."

"Thanks for the compliment. I ran my name into the message so he wouldn't have a clear signature. That's what he gets for lying to me.

He—" Quentin went silent as several others crowded near their table. *Blast it!*

"Mr. Rawls, can we have your autograph, too?"

Quentin said, "Sure, why not?"

Another asked, "Do you have any paper and a pen to use?"

"Nope, afraid not. I just came in for a quick lunch and quiet talk."

"You can sign on a napkin."

"Sorry, but it's too difficult and looks messy."

"We'll go get some paper from the waitress. We'll be back in a minute."

"Best hurry because we have a tight schedule and we're leaving."

Rachel watched the young men rush off while Quentin took a deep breath of annoyance. "Let's go before more people pester you. We can't relax or eat this way. If we get hungry, we'll stop later for a snack."

"Thanks, Rachel; you're very considerate." He stood, collected the check, and was about to guide her to the cashier when the fans almost raced back to their table. He bent over and scrawled his name on the papers, without messages this time.

One handed his back and said, "Date it, too."

"What is the date?" Quentin asked without smiling.

"July twelfth, I think. That's close enough."

When the rude man tried to delay him with questions afterward, Quentin forced a smile. "Like I said, we're in a rush. Sorry, you guys."

"This won't take but a minute. Will you be staying with the Cow— "

"Gotta go, boys; we're running late as is." Quentin grasped Rachel's elbow and walked to the cashier.

While he was paying the bill, the bold man joined them. Rachel blocked his path to Quentin. "Mr. Rawls is trying to be polite, sir, but we are in a hurry and his mind is on our business meeting later."

"I just want to ask him some questions. It won't take but a minute."

"I know, but he doesn't have time to chat right now."

"Troy Aikman would take the time to talk to his fans."

Anger chewed at her. "Not when he's busy and late. Sorry. 'Bye."

They left the restaurant with the man scowling and muttering as his friends joined him.

In the car, Quentin said, "That's the problem with signing one; as soon as others see you do it, they swarm you for autographs, too. It's hard to go anywhere and have privacy. You can't eat out or shop or attend any function without being interrupted or without having at least one person shadow you to try to overhear everything you say. I've actually had strangers plop down in a chair at my table and start chatting without asking permission to join me. Some of them can be rude and real pushy. Some even want you to sign lots of autographs, supposedly for their friends and families. I've had people ask for things I had used or was wearing as souvenirs, jerseys and footballs in particular. A few will steal them if you turn your back. After a few years, it makes the spotlight something to avoid and dislike. I love my fans and I need their support, but I deserve privacy on occasion."

"You handled that situation well, Quentin; you were polite to them and patient, even when that one man became rude and pushy."

"Being or staying polite gets hard sometimes. The minute you answer one innocent question, they think they can ask you anything. It's as if they think we don't have feelings." As he cranked the engine, he asked, "What is this SRS I read and hear about?"

Rachel realized he was dropping the touchy subject, as if he didn't like coming across as a complainer. "The Savannah River Site, across the river in South Carolina, not far away. It's part of the Department of Energy, a nuclear energy plant. Many of the people who work there live in Augusta and in Columbia County. It's huge, and you can't enter it without special permission. It used to be a bomb plant during the war. Now they handle plutonium and store spent fuel rods there. We can drive over there, but that's all; we can't get inside."

Before he left the parking space, he suggested, "Can you show me a few of the nearest towns across the river?"

"That's an easy request to fill," she said as she directed him to the bridge.

For the remainder of the afternoon, they

toured North Augusta, Bellvedere, Graniteville, Aiken, Bath, Clearwater, and Beech Island. He asked many of the same questions about those towns as he had about the ones in Georgia; some she could answer, most she could not.

"There's a visitor's center on I-20 across the river from your hotel if you want to pick up brochures on South Carolina. Or you can ride over to North Augusta on another day and speak with the staff there. My hospitality duties didn't include this area, so I'm not that familiar with it."

"You did fine; I only wanted to know a little about the surrounding locations" *since they pull in visitors and workers to Augusta. Seeing if I can obtain enough money will be my next goal. There are some people I need to meet, and maybe you can help with introductions and names, but later, because after I gather the needed facts, I won't have an excuse to stay.* "What about dinner? Where shall we eat? Something very nice and quiet."

"Michael's should be a perfect place; it's on Washington Road, just before we reach I-20. It's six, so you'll get a peek at the going-home traffic on one of our busiest roads." Rachel realized that restaurant was on the route home for her neighborhood and friends and acquaintances. It was possible people she knew would eat there tonight, but if she was seen with him, she mused, so what? They weren't on an actual date, just friends eating together. Yet, would it appear that way to others? *Stop being foolish and tense, Rachel, and enjoy the evening and Quentin.*

He drove to the restaurant as he made observations and light talk. He noticed her distraction and deduced she was worried about gossip, worried because she didn't trust him completely to keep their affair a secret. Maybe she was wondering why he hadn't mentioned their past connection or was fretting over when and if he would bring it up. He would, but after they spent more time together and she was at ease.

They were seated at a table in Michael's near the back of a cozy room, had ordered glasses of blush wine, and studied their menus.

Rachel watched him sip his drink; then she glanced around the room; only a few people were dining this early, but none close to them. He had taken a chair which placed his back to the couples, no doubt to guard his privacy. As they talked about the class reunion, people who had attended, the town, and current events, she again had the suspicion he was unusually interested in the CSRA. But, she wondered, why?

After they gave their orders and chatted a while, Quentin asked, "Do you have a career, work outside the home?"

Rachel lowered her glass. "For years I stayed busy being a wife and mother, and handling social obligations. After Daniel was killed I concentrated on rearing my daughters, taking care of our household, and doing charity work." She knew that was a little misleading, but she wasn't ready to mention her writing to him, not yet, not after the unfavorable reaction that news received from her social circle. "Now that my girls are grown and gone, I'll need to do things other than volunteer work. Currently I'm involved in several big projects for the arts, my clubs, and my church. As soon as they're finished, I'll have free time. Since I didn't finish college, I never studied for a particular career. And what about you; do you plan to continue playing football? Any idea what you'll do after you retire?" *That should focus talk and attention on you, off me for a while.*

"I'm one of the oldest quarterbacks in the game, so my years are numbered. I've had a little bad luck in the past, injured my throwing shoulder and one of my knees; that sort of decreases my value. Coach Switzer will be making cuts on the roster during and after the preseason games; I might be one of them. We have three top quarterbacks, so four aren't needed. In the '93-94 season, thirty-nine quarterbacks made moves. Kosar and Beuerlein left us in '93 and '94. I've been with the Cowboys for nine years and those guys are some of my best friends; we're trying to win the NFL Championship and Superbowl for the third time in a row; that's a sorry time to be released from my contract or to retire. What pro in his right mind wants to miss that kind of challenge and excitement?" he said with a chuckle. "If you play as long as I have, football is a major part of your life; it's in my blood."

"I'm sorry you might be forced to give up something you obviously love so much and do so well. I'm sure you'll be just as good at your next career choice. Anything in mind?"

A waiter arrived with their entrées, as neither had ordered an appetizer or a salad, so Quentin didn't answer her question. Instead he inhaled, smiled, and said, "Smells great and looks good."

"I've never had a bad meal here," Rachel remarked as she buttered and seasoned her baked potato and broccoli. She didn't eat red meat often, but had chosen a small filet mignon tonight.

"My steak is delicious, aged and cooked perfectly," Quentin noted with pleasure. "How's yours?"

"Delicious," she replied as soon as she had swallowed.

As they ate in silence, Rachel noted his excellent table manners and refined bearing. She concluded he came from a good family, as she'd thought years ago. Soft music filtered into the room, and conversation from other tables was almost inaudible. The lights were low and candles burned on the cloth-covered tables. The decor was lovely; a romantic aura seemed to float around the room.

"This is pleasant and relaxing, Rachel; thanks. It's nice to unwind with good food and a good friend in a peaceful setting."

Rachel smiled warmly. "I'm glad you like it."

"Do you eat out often?"

"Besides Sunday lunch at the club after church and a day out each week with friends, it comes in spurts, usually social gatherings or dinner parties. Cookouts are popular here during

the summer months. Sometimes club or committee meetings include lunch. What about you?"

"Too much. It comes with the territory of being on the road during preseason or playing season, having social obligations, being too busy or
tired to shop and cook after practice. Sometimes
my housekeeper cooks meals and leaves them
for me, but my schedule can be unpredictable."

*No girlfriend to come over or live-in lover to cook
for you I take it* . . . "Can you shop and cook?"
she asked with a mischievous grin.

"I'm okay with simple meals and I'm excellent
with a grill."

"I might just test that claim one night, if you
want to come over to my house and prove it,"
she half jested as her gaze fused with his blue
one.

"What about tomorrow night? Say, my famous
pork chops? That is, if you don't already have
plans for the evening." He drank the last sip of
wine.

"I'll be finished with my duties by five-thirty.
What about six o'clock? I'll even do the shopping if you tell me what you need."

"It's a deal. Now, back to tonight, what about
dessert and coffee?"

Rachel shook her head. "I'm full, but you can
order them."

He grinned. "Have to be careful with that
nice figure of yours, eh?"

The seductive glow in his blue eyes and mellow tone of his voice kindled her smoldering
desires into wild flames. She hoped she wasn't

blushing. "At my age, it's a constant battle. I doubt you have to worry about calories since you burn off so many playing ball."

"I still have to watch what I eat and have to exercise regularly. I don't play around all year, only during certain seasons when I have special goals to achieve or to maintain."

Those provocative words could be taken several ways, Mr. Rawls. "Here comes our waiter to check on dessert." *Lordy, you're the only treat I crave. Right about now, I could eat you with a spoon and savor every morsel. You're just too tempting. I wonder why you didn't answer my earlier question and why you haven't mentioned anything about our affair years ago. You asked about me but you cunningly sidestep queries about you. Any flirting you've done has been subtle. What's going on inside that handsome head? Are you leading me on for spite, testing the waters for another affair, or only after friendship this time? I can't put my finger on it, but there's a mysterious air about you, as if you have an unknown motive for being here.*

Quentin finished speaking with the waiter, who left to compile their bill. "That was a fine meal, Rachel, but wait until you taste my offering."

"I can hardly wait. Don't forget to give me your shopping list."

"That won't be necessary; I'll take care of everything tomorrow night, even wash the dishes. It's the least I can do to repay your hospitality."

"In that case, there's a grocery store up the road. Surprise me."

"I hope I will. Ready?" he asked after the waiter returned with his change. Quentin left a tip and assisted her with her chair.

Do you always pay with cash to avoid using a credit card and revealing your identity? Don't you know your face is well known from television and magazine ads? She thanked him as he opened the car door for her.

As he fastened his seat belt, he remarked in a casual tone, "Maybe you can show me those nightspots before I leave town."

Rachel laughed. "I'm not much into them but I'll try to help out. I'll check with one of my friends to see which places are the best."

He watched for an opening in the flow of traffic, then pulled into the center turning lane. "More the country club set, huh?"

"When I go out, I guess so. I know the people there and I usually accompany friends; being a single, it makes for a nicer evening. I also attend many of the cultural functions."

"I imagine your friends do like mine, play cupid all the time. Everybody seems to have an available sister or a friend of his girlfriend who needs a date, and you're a third or fifth wheel for the evening if you refuse to escort her." He turned on to Stevens Creek Road. "Heaven spare us from countless good intentions, more blind dates, and those required companions for social and business occasions."

"It sounds as if you've had experiences similar to mine. I suppose it's because it's a couple's world after one reaches a certain age."

He crossed Riverwatch Parkway. "Don't you think the dating game gets harder as you get older or after you've been out of circulation?"

"Definitely. Times and conduct can change hugely but certain people— like me— have a tendency to remain much the same in our thinking. It's like diving into muddy water where everything gets obscured. You don't quite know where you fit into the big picture anymore."

He glanced at her. "That describes our predicament perfectly; you're good with drawing word pictures. Maybe you should consider getting into advertising or promotions; sounds as if you'd be a whiz at them. Actually, I think you'd be successful at anything you decided to do. You're easy to talk to and be with and you're a real lady, Rachel."

"Those are very nice compliments and I appreciate them."

Soon, Quentin pulled into her driveway. At her door, he said, "Good night, Rachel; thanks for another wonderful day. I'll see you at six tomorrow evening. Diet at breakfast and lunch so you can indulge at supper."

She laughed and asked, "Are you sure there isn't anything you want me to do?"

"Nope, just be here and be yourself. Good night."

Rachel watched him walk to the car, get inside, and start the engine. She waved, closed the door, and leaned against it to take a deep breath to steady her trembling. "Oh, my, three dates in three days," Rachel murmured, "and you didn't even kiss me goodnight, Quentin. Are you being wary or only trying not to press me too soon? At least we're getting better acquainted before we get intimate, and without deceptions this time, maybe. I want to trust you, but I feel as if you're hiding something from me. I wonder how you'll behave tomorrow night when we're alone. Lordy, woman, how are you going to act if he gets romantic?"

Six

At Formosa's Chinese Restaurant on Wednesday, Becky coaxed, "Tell us everything, Rach; you hardly gave us a clue on the phone."

Since no one was sitting in the booths on either side of them, Rachel said, "That's because you both were with your husbands. I hope you two haven't told them about us so they won't tease me when I see them."

Jen tapped her lips and said, "We've kept mum so far, but it won't be a secret for much longer if you keep dating him every day and night."

"This will be only the third time I've seen him since the reunion."

"But this makes three days in a row; that's promising, Rach."

"We're only friends."

"Friends first, then . . . who knows? You're having dinner alone tonight; things could get cozy. He sounds terrific; go for it, Rach."

"I doubt he's looking for romance or a commitment at this point in his life. He's been burned twice and he's in the midst of a career upheaval. You know men don't think about romance when they're under pressure or distracted. Besides, he's years younger than I am, and he'll want children when he settles down. As far as I know, he doesn't have any, and I can't."

To cleverly point out her friend wasn't interested in other men, only in Quentin, Becky said, "Well, you still have lots of choices around here."

"Not any good ones, at least for a serious relationship."

"I hope you aren't giving up on men and marriage."

"No, Jen, just waiting around for good ones."

"If Quentin's still in town, and I bet he will be, bring him to my party with you on Saturday. Let him get to know your friends. We surely want a closer look at him to see if he's good enough for you."

"Imagine everyone's reaction if I showed up with Quentin as my date, especially after he was with Carrie Simmons at the reunion. That doesn't bother me and I have nothing against her, but some of the others appear to still think badly of her. Gossip will fly."

"No one would dare talk about you at my house, Rach."

"They would the moment they left; rumors would spread like crazy. Janet and others would be calling me and asking all kinds of questions. I don't want to be put on the hot seat over nothing. After Janet worked on him at the party, he would run just to avoid that bitch and her wicked tongue. Or he'd tell her off and move me higher on her blacklist; she gives me enough fits as it is."

"Don't let Janet and her kind spoil this chance for happiness. Besides, she and Cliff will be out of town from Saturday morning until Tuesday, so they aren't coming; and Dianne hasn't RSVP'd yet, so maybe she and Greg won't be there. If they are, she'll behave without Janet's influence. I had no choice except to invite them, but don't let them spoil your relationship."

"We aren't having a relationship; we're only friends." *This time.*

"You could be more if you put your mind and energy to work on it. For heaven's sake, Rach, how often does a fine specimen like him come along? He's the first, and maybe the last, man since Daniel to give you a nice jolt. Don't tell me he doesn't send tingles up your spine because it won't be true. You like him and you're attracted to him; I can tell."

"I admit you're right about being charmed by him, and I'm positive that most women are. But even if he suited me perfectly, this is too soon and too sudden. I don't want to get too close too fast, in case he isn't interested in me. Quentin and I are having fun together, but it isn't serious and he'll be gone soon."

"Maybe and maybe not. He certainly seems interested, so don't panic and scare him off. Even if nothing serious does come from it, you can have a lot of fun with him. Bring him along,

Rach, please. The boys will have a great time talking with him; they all love football."

"I'm not sure Quentin wants to discuss his career; it's rocky right now. He also might not want to be included in a sort of meet-my-family gathering. I don't want it to look as if I'm chasing him."

"Just think about inviting him. Okay?"

"I will. I'll let you know if he's coming. Satisfied?"

Becky grinned and nodded. "Positively."

As they ate their lunches, they discussed their bridge and club meetings the following day and more collections for the Georgia flood victims.

Afterward, while standing at the cashier's counter, Janet and other women arrived, but Dianne wasn't with them.

"Well, well, what do we have here?" the redhead murmured. "I thought you were too busy with your projects to have leisure time, Rachel."

Rachel smiled and quipped in an innocently playful tone, "It was difficult, Janet; but I stole an hour from my hectic schedule to eat so I would have the energy to work this afternoon."

Becky laughed and fibbed, "We had to drag her away from the house and force her to take a break; she's earned one. Rachel is just too generous and determined to help others, and she gets herself overbooked."

"She didn't have any trouble turning down the woman's club dire need of her. Dianne and I explained our dilemma and practically begged her to help us with our new project, but she refused."

"Only this one time, Janet, and I explained why I couldn't do it."

Jen noticeably checked her watch and assisted her friend out of a tight spot. "Don't forget you're expecting a call at two, Rachel, so we have to hustle to get you home as promised. We'll see you all tomorrow. 'Bye."

Farewells were exchanged and the three friends left the restaurant. After Rachel thanked Becky and Jen for their fibs, they had a delightful time running errands together until four o'clock.

Rachel glanced around the house; thanks to Martha's visit today, it was spotless and smelled fresh. She was wearing a green shorts outfit and sandals so she'd be cool outside while cooking on the grill; and she didn't want to appear to be overdressed for a simple meal at home. When the doorbell chimed, she let Quentin inside the extended foyer which was lighted by an ornate Italian hanging fixture. "This way, Chef Rawls." She smiled and directed him ahead as he carried two grocery sacks.

Quentin was impressed by a wide Florida tiled walkway that divided two sitting areas of an enormous oblong room into a formal one with a fireplace to his right and a casual one to his left. Interested in the way she lived, he paid close attention to details. The furnishings were a blend of traditional and neoclassical; the casual sofa and chair were in shades of turquoise, mauve, tan, cream, blue, and green; the formal sofa was tan with turquoise fringe, and one chair was a Louis IV with an antiqued white finish. Loose swag drapes were floral on a white background and laced through architectural brackets below radius fanlight windows. The twelve-foot ceiling was accented by thick and deep moldings.

On either side of the huge arch into the hallway were topiaries on a salmon-colored wall: trompe l'oeil handpaintings. He saw silk trees and flowers in decorative urns and bowls, several glass-topped tables with beveled edges, and well-chosen art pieces. He noticed that double French doors opened into a large formal dining room on the right side. In the hallway, he walked on a shiny pickled hardwood floor. To his right, there was another French door leading into the dining room for serving meals, perfectly positioned as it was across from the kitchen door on the left. The daylight was sufficient enough that he could make out wisteria wallpaper with matching swags over white rods with floral-tipped finials in lavender and green. The contemporary furniture was in burled walnut wood. The room was decorated splendidly. Before entering the kitchen, he looked up a staircase, one with a faux marbleized handrailing that led to the second story.

Quentin set his packages on a white counter in an immaculate room that gave him the feeling of airy spaciousness. No small appliances or foods were in view, only decorative objects here and there before white tiles with handpainted flowers, dragonflies, and butterflies. The large appliances were white, as was the woodwork; the floor tile was rose bisque with matching grout. Through a square opening with a row of small windows over it was the breakfast area, a lovely and uncluttered room with a garden theme. To its left and through French doors with paned windows beside and above them was a Florida room with four tall windows on all three sides for lovely views of her front, side, and back yards. "You have good taste, Rachel," he commented following his appraisal, "this is lovely and looks comfortable."

"Thank you, Quentin; I enjoy it. The problem is, with the children gone, it seems awfully big for one person."

"To clean, to manage, to afford or just to roam around in?"

Rachel laughed as she unpacked his purchases. "All of those things."

"Do you keep it this spotless or do you have a hidden maid?"

"I have a housekeeper once a week; she's been with me for twenty years. I thought I mentioned Martha and her son, my gardener, to you."

"You did. Some people have maids every day and still can't keep their homes clean and neat. Messy surroundings don't appeal to me."

"It's easy when you live by yourself; impossible with young children around. If you give them the time they need, they can be full-time jobs."

"I would imagine so; I guess that's something I'll learn someday. After I get these chops to marinating and get the grill to heating, you can show me around. Maybe I'll get some ideas to use at my place. I'm beginning to renovate and redecorate before Christmas."

"I don't envy you; those are big and frustrating tasks."

"That's why I'm hoping to get the work done while I'm away on road trips. I've heard it can be hellish if you're at home."

"Two friends of mine would agree with you. Looking around for ideas is the best way to decide what you might want. Now, what can I get for you?"

"A deep, square dish and a fork, for starters. I'll wash up first."

"Wonderful, a man with good habits; I see that your mother trained you well." He grinned and nodded. "The soap dispenser is on the sink; paper towels are there under the top cabinet to the right." She put out the requested items and asked, "What else?"

"You can put the wine in the refrigerator. I need a large bowl and a knife for the broccoli, and aluminum foil for the potatoes. Set the oven for four hundred degrees, bake. Do you have a steamer for that microwave?"

Rachel nodded, set the oven to preheat, and retrieved the item he requested. She held out an apron to protect his clothing. "What else?"

As he tied on the apron, he said, "That's everything for now."

"Surely there's something more I can do to help."

Quentin smiled. "Just keep me company." He prepared the meat and set the dish in the refrigerator. He rinsed the broccoli and placed it on a paper towel to drain while he washed the potatoes and wrapped them.

Rachel leaned against the center island and watched him work skillfully. He was wearing casual brown slacks, brown shoes, and a brown-and-white striped golf shirt. He was so masculine and attractive that she warmed from head to feet. His back was broad, his waist was narrow, and his legs were long on his over six-foot frame. As if sensing her study, he glanced at her and grinned.

His blue eyes almost twinkled with mischief. "Did you think I was kidding about treating you tonight and knowing how to do this?"

"No, I believed you. It truly *is* a treat to have somebody pamper you. I like a man who knows his way around a kitchen, around a house. It's amazing in these days that so many men don't, and won't try to learn."

He sent her a smile, which she returned. "A woman like you deserves to be pampered; I'll enjoy being the one to do it tonight."

"Thanks." *Don't get cozy yet; I need to know more about you.* "I forgot during our tours that you're originally from Georgia. I hope I didn't bore you chattering on about our state like you're a stranger to it."

"I lived a long way from here and I'm not familiar with this area. Too, I've been gone since I left for college in '74, except for visits home. I enjoyed learning about the . . . CSRA, wasn't it?"

"That's right; you're a good listener. So you live in Texas now."

"Yep, southwest of Dallas, on a small but working ranch."

"Tell me about your hometown and family. You already know about mine. I've never been to Colquitt or spent any time in that area of Georgia."

"History and geography were two of my best subjects, so you're in luck," he said with a grin. "Colquitt has a population of about two thousand; Miller County has around sixty-three hundred; it's the only town in the entire county. It's small, rural, old, and nice; everybody knows everybody and most of 'em are friends. It's kind of coincidental that our county was named for Andrew Jackson Miller of Augusta; he was a state representative and a senator. At his death, he was President of the Medical College, City Attorney, and Director of Georgia Railroad Bank all here in Augusta. How about those facts, Mrs. Gaines?"

"That's interesting, quite a connection between our towns." *But I doubt your liking of history and geography and that coincidence explains your unusual interest in Augusta.* "Are there lots of Rawlses there?"

"W. H. Rawls was a Colquitt councilman and

our mayor in the fifties, but he isn't any kin to my family. The rest of our kinfolk live in Kentucky. We have family reunions every few years; I missed the last two, but I hope to make the next one in '96. If I don't, my parents will chase me down with a switch. You remember those, right? Switches, not family reunions."

Rachel laughed at his comical face. "Of course not, I was always a good girl. Besides, I didn't have any siblings to get me into trouble, and there were few neighbors around us with children, and none my age. We lived in the country and farmed, too, so I behaved myself on the long bus ride to and from school and in class. Actually, I think I would have preferred a spanking to my father's disciplinary talks; he was good at them. I would have to explain to him what I did, why I did it, and why I shouldn't do it again. Reasoning out misbehavior was tough and educational."

He glanced at her. "Is that the method you used with your children?"

"Yes, and it worked beautifully. But I must say, my girls got along very well together, especially after they became teenagers, then young women. They never got into any serious trouble, that I learned about anyway. I'm very proud of them and very fortunate; they've given me a lot of happy times."

"I have some friends who should hire you to train theirs how to behave. I've seen some terrors and whiners. I would never allow my child to act like that or rule my house; that isn't how I was raised."

"Did your parents practice the old saying about being seen not heard?"

"Nope, they're just honest, hardworking people, and good parents. Our family was close, is close. Back to Colquitt: we're known as the Mayhaw Capital of the World. You know what those are?"

Rachel shook her head. She noticed he left the family topic fast and mused if it was because of his brother, a troubled man according to tabloids.

"Mayhaws are cranberry-size applelike berries used for jelly; once you smell them cooking, you never forget that delightful aroma; it fills the house and makes your mouth water. I'll get Mother to send you some. We have the Mayhaw Festival in April; maybe you can go down and take it in one year. We have a famous folk-life play during October called *Swamp Gravy*. It's performed by a cast and crew of about one hundred locals; Mother said they've been asked to give performances during the '96 Olympics in Atlanta; that should put Colquitt's dot darker on the map."

He halted while he slid the potatoes into the oven and set the timer for one hour. He went to work preparing the broccoli to be steamed. "We're small and country, but we're close to big cities for entertainment and shopping. Albany is forty-five miles northeast; Tallahassee, Florida, is about sixty miles south; Dothan, Alabama, is forty-five miles west. For recreation— much of ours is watersports and camping, too— we have the Chattahoochee River, Lake Seminole, and the Flint River not far away."

"The Flint River, that's the one that flooded so badly last week."

"Yep, but Miller County and my family survived it, thank God. Other counties weren't as lucky; it did awful damage to our neighbors, Mitchell and Decatur counties, and those northeast of Miller. Some farmers were wiped out; plenty of families and towns, too."

"I'm glad your family was all right and my heart goes out to those who weren't and to those who lost everything. The people of Augusta have been sending food, bottled water, clothing, and other necessary items to the worst areas. Our people are understanding and generous because we've suffered several bad floods here, but none like that one. The news reports showed horrible devastation and suffering. It will take them a long time to recover from such losses. I read in the newspaper that Augusta and neighboring counties are going to help fill peanut orders that usually go to South Georgia growers who lost their crops. That's a terrible way to improve our local economy."

"That crazy flood, atop the harsh drought of '93, was devastating to farmers on the other side of the state. Daddy told me that when the river crested, three hundred thousand acres were underwater; one hundred fifty thousand of those were planted in peanuts, and peanuts can't take such abuse. He told me there was a hundred million dollars in crop damages."

"When you were young, did you help your family grow peanuts?"

"Yep, on rented land back then. I bought the farm for them in '85 while I was with the 49ers and having a great season." *Gave Casey hysterics over the amount I paid for it, money she couldn't spend on furthering her modeling career.* "Miller County is the number-two producer of peanuts. They generate about twenty-five-million dollars in our county alone. Fifty percent of all peanuts grown in the U.S. are within a fifty-mile radius of southwest Georgia." He chuckled. "Daddy keeps me informed on facts and figures. I'm sure you remember President Carter was a peanut grower. It's big business, but it's hard and you have to know a lot of things."

What kind of childhood did you have? "Such as?" she prompted.

His gaze met hers. "You want a quick education on them?"

"Why not?" *It involves you and your family.* "I'm sure it's fascinating, and it's important to Georgia. I shouldn't be ignorant about one of our leading crops." *Who knows when I can use such facts in my writing?*

He set the steamer with broccoli florets and tender stems aside for cooking later. "Let's go light the grill while I give you a crash course. I never thought about being a teacher but having you as a student may be fun. I bet you're a quick and easy learner."

Rachel guided him out the back door and to a brick barbecue on a stone patio, the one she had cleaned earlier while Martha worked inside the house. Henry had been there today, so everything was in perfect condition. The shrubs were trimmed and healthy. Recently weeded beds were in bloom with colorful summer flowers. Sunlight sparkled off the clear blue pool water. The outdoor furniture that was placed in several areas was shiny clean, as was the gazebo where ivy grew in and out of its latticework on three sides. Nearby in a pebbled area was a three-tiered fountain of ever-enlarging basins; a fish statue connected to the top one spewed a stream of water from its mouth which cascaded from level to level. Rosebushes flanked it. The cabana had been painted two months ago and cleaned by her last week. The high brick wall around the large yard and tall trees beyond it gave them total privacy from curious neighbors.

Quentin complimented her on the tranquil setting, which greatly impressed him. He arranged charcoal briquettes and lit several. While he waited to make certain the fire didn't go out, he began enlightening her on growing peanuts.

She was impressed by the depth of his knowledge, and enjoyed his enthusiasm for his topic. It was a pleasure just listening to his voice. "You sound so interested in the business," she commented as she accompanied him back to the kitchen so he could turn the chops in the refrigerator so the other side would be able to marinate. "Why don't you want to raise them with your family after you retire from football?"

"I just don't care for farming as a career, but I do like ranching. My sister and her husband live on the farm and work with my parents."

"I remember my father planting peanuts, but only enough for our consumption. He would toss them atop the shed to dry. Sometimes I would sneak up there and eat them green. Oh, what a bellyache they can give you."

He chuckled. "I remember; I've done the same thing, eaten them out of the field before they were dried and cured. Ouch!"

"It sounds as if you love your family and get along well with them."

"I do, we do. My parents own a four-hundred-fifty-acre farm. Daddy rotates four crops— peanuts, corn, millet, and pasture grasses— on hundred-acre tracts. The other fifty are taken up with their home, barns, sheds, vegetable garden, animal pens, stock pastures, my sister— Mary— and her family's home, and one worker's house and grounds. I also have a younger brother— Frank— but he doesn't live in Colquitt. He works at a car dealership in Dothan, used to live in Atlanta. Years ago, he got in with the wrong crowd and got into trouble, spent some time in prison for drugs. I've tried to help straighten him out, but it's something he has to want and do for himself. If the media would leave him alone, maybe he could. Sometimes they use his problems to write badly about me, sort of like they did with Billy Carter when Jimmy was in office. Now let's take that tour of your house before I put on the chops," he suggested, wanting to get off a touchy subject. "Maybe I'll pick up some clever ideas to use on mine."

Rachel showed him the Florida room with rose bisque floor and walls, white woodwork, and an assortment of silk trees and hanging baskets. "Henry has a green thumb, but I don't, so this is the only way I can have plants inside," she said with a laugh. She saw him glance at the wicker sofa and chair with plush cushions, a square wicker end table with a lamp, and a white television set on a wicker stand. Overhead was a brass ceiling fan to stir the air during overly warm periods. She motioned to a glass-topped eating table with a mushroom-styled base and four chairs which were covered to match the other cushions and the shirred balloon curtains over soft shades, all in a tropical forest pattern. "The girls enjoyed eating and doing their homework and visiting with their friends in this room. I spend a lot of time here now because it's so open and light and relaxing." She nodded toward a treadmill and a stationary bicycle. "Keeping those handy are the best way to make sure I exercise; with Augusta being so hot and humid in the summer and with pollen and insects and animals outside to worry about, it's more comfortable and safer to do it inside, unless I use the pool."

"It's nice to have a beautiful view and a fan while you're working up a sweat. I've surely spent plenty of hours outside in all kinds of weather; we play in rain, sleet, snow, high winds, and sweltering heat. A game isn't called unless there's lightning or a blizzard strikes. I suppose that TV keeps you from getting bored while you're exercising." She smiled and nodded. "Maybe you can catch a few of our games this winter. I like the aquarium," he remarked, changing the personal subject as he leaned over to see what kinds of fish she had in it.

Rachel's fingers drifted across the edge of the tank that was positioned atop a wrought-iron stand. As she watched the fish swim about, she said, "I bought it for the girls after Daniel's death; I thought it would be soothing and distracting. Karen was twelve and Evelyn was ten when the plane crash occurred. They never asked for cats or dogs, thank goodness, because I'm a big-dog person— like boxers and collies— who like plenty of space to romp in, not a small and landscaped yard. I had both when I was young."

"I had a collie, too, named Ranger. You're right, and kind; they have a hard time living in a fancy subdivision where they have to be cooped up. They're like cowboys; they prefer big, open spaces and running free. I plan to get another dog, after I start ranching. Kids love 'em 'cause they're so gentle and affectionate."

There you go mentioning children again. "Come this way."

She guided him through the hallway to a large laundry room and walk-in pantry with shelves almost to the ceiling. "It's nice to have plenty of work space and a fan to cool you off while you're washing and folding clothes," Rachel explained. "As for the extra-large pantry, without one, you can never have enough storage space or keep things in easy reach and view. I keep holiday decorations in here so I don't have to haul them back and forth upstairs. My children always loved decorating for every season: Easter, July Fourth, Halloween, Thanksgiving, and Christmas: I have things for all of them. In fact, they still like getting an Easter basket and a plastic pumpkin filled with treats."

As Quentin eyed the items, he said, "It sounds as if you were a good mother, Rachel; I'm sure it was hard raising two kids alone."

"It was at times, but one-parent families are common these days. Now let me show you the dining room; you'll probably be doing a lot of entertaining and my decorator did some wonderful things in there."

Quentin sensed she was escaping a painful topic, as he had done earlier. He looked at a fancy half-bath for guests before they toured the striking dining room where he did collect several ideas.

"If you have time before you leave town and you're interested, you may want to talk with Scott Cooper for suggestions," Rachel offered as he nodded appreciatively. "He's the husband of one of my best friends. He's in construction and he's done several projects like this."

"That might be smart of me to make time to see him."

Rachel realized that gave her a good excuse

for asking him to go to Becky and Scott's pool party on Saturday. Besides, Scott was one of the best builders in town and could be helpful to him. Perhaps she'd invite him. . . .

Quentin looked in the living room again, paying close attention to the faux-marble fireplace and recessed lighting, before he followed her upstairs where four bedrooms and baths were located. The girls' rooms were almost as they left them— Rachel told him— for return visits: Karen's was in blues, white, and greens, and Evelyn's was in mauves, blues, and greens, colors and patterns the girls had chosen. Childhood and teenage keepsakes were scattered about the bed, floor, walls, and dresser in each.

Those mementos told Quentin a great deal about the girls' interests and the Gaineses' lifestyle. "I didn't see a piano anywhere." Quentin was puzzled, since there were programs from piano recitals among the items. "Did you get rid of it?"

"Evelyn took it with her when she moved to Ohio; she still plays, and she hopes her daughter, Ashley, will when she's older. She's three and her son, Alex, is one. I'm biased, but they're precious children."

"I bet you miss having them live nearby; I would."

Rachel saw him pause to look at pictures with Daniel in them as she responded, but tried not to brag about her family. After peeking into a lovely guest room, she led him to Daniel's old office which she used as a project and writing room, though her private work was kept out of sight.

Quentin smiled as he strolled around the masculine area with a cognac leather sofa and matching bergere chair with ottoman. There was a kidney-shaped table in warm and shiny burled walnut, the same as was the desk, credenza, and file cabinet. One wall was comprised of shelves with books and decorative items. Most of the pictures and paintings were outdoor scenes, several of them were of the Augusta National Golf Course and Master's Golf Tournament. He noticed two pieces of crystal, an apple and a bird, which he recalled her purchasing at the glass factory near Caracas. He forced himself not to stare at them or to let his mind linger on that wonderful day. The windows were covered by Roman shades in various colors, one matching the walls and carpet, the same fabric covering two cushions on the sofa. "I like this room, Rachel," he said with genuine enthusiasm. "A person could do great work in here. I wish I had my camera with me so I could take pictures of things you've done."

"Thanks for the compliment; I have to admit I love this house; moving would be difficult. I'm sorry I don't have any film for my camera. If you brought yours with you to Augusta, you can take pictures another day; I don't mind at all; in fact, I'm flattered you see things you'd like to use."

Yes, he had brought a camera and a camcorder for business reasons. "It's at the hotel, so

I'll do that before I leave, if you're sure it's okay."

Rachel knew that gave her another chance to see him alone and was glad. "It is. Of course, some of the credit goes to my decorator and builder. But I did what you're doing now, looked around for ideas and used them."

Quentin gazed at her, smiled, and said, "Always knew you were an intelligent woman; that's a good quality to have, Rachel. You have plenty of them. I really enjoy spending time with you."

Don't stare into those incredible blue eyes or listen to that mellow voice or you'll lose those wits he's complimenting you on! Darn you, Quentin, why must you be so irresistible? "Thanks. I have fun with you, too." *Change the subject and mood fast!* "One thing you might like to include if you don't already have one is a wall or floor safe for jewelry, valuable papers, and irreplaceable keepsakes like old family pictures. We— I have one buried in the garage cement; a burglar would have to dynamite or jackhammer it out to steal it. Scott also installs them in walls between steel beams to prevent removal. In case Mother Nature or misfortune strikes your home, valuables are saved." Rachel decided not to show it to him unless he asked to see it, as pictures and mementos of their cruise were locked away in it, protected from discovery by the wrong person and safe from harm.

Quentin nodded his approval. "I have one behind a painting, but I suppose it would be easy for almost anyone to axe it out and steal it; I surely don't want to lose my Superbowl and Championship rings and personal papers. That's another good idea."

Rachel knew he had at least four Superbowl rings for being on the winning teams in '82, '85, '93, and '94. He was wearing the one from '85 when he was with the San Francisco 49ers where he played the last quarter in terrible pain from an injured knee. She wondered what drove such men to risk permanent damage just to stay in the game. Had he done it for glory, out of ignorance of how badly he was hurt, from a sense of responsibility and loyalty to teammates, for sheer love of the sport, or the misconception he was invincible or irreplaceable?

In her bedroom, Quentin grinned, nodded, and complimented her taste once more, admiring the light and dark lavender sponged walls, white woodwork with superbly crafted moldings, a trey ceiling with ivy and roses wallpaper, a green marble fireplace with a Victorian scene painting above it, a cozy sitting area with a wicker sofa and round table near the hearth, and an entertainment unit in a pickled wood finish to make it look antiqued. She pointed out furniture placements that might be of interest to him, and various objets d'art that she treasured. A ceiling fan— as in almost every room of the house— was suspended near the foot of the king-size bed. Ivory softshades and antique lace panels gave privacy to the windows where curtains were draped over leafy verdigris rods. The room and aura hinted of romance, beauty, serenity, and femininity, the Victorian period.

Quentin strolled into a large bathroom with a corner shower which had cherubs and fleur-de-lis sprays etched into frosted glass. A matching Jacuzzi was situated in another corner, with decorative items placed along a tiled shelf surrounding it: three different bottles of bath oil with dried flowers floating inside, a cherub soap dish, and a square glass container of Passion bath oil beads. He noticed a collection of Passion body powder, lotion, and perfume placed among other decorative and feminine items on a white marble-topped vanity. It was the scent she was wearing, the one his mother also favored. It was a good choice for her, a woman of great passion he remembered too well . . . He forced his mind from the memory and pointed to the white ceiling fan. "I like that idea; it can get mighty hot when you're bathing and dressing in a hurry." *Or doing other things.*

"It keeps makeup from sliding off faster than you can get it on in the summer, and Augusta can have sweltering summers," she said and laughed.

"A heat lamp to warm you in winter," *when you're naked and alone.*

"It prevents having to turn up the heat system just to bathe and dress." *But if you were here with me like in that shower, I wouldn't need it.*

"I like what you've done with your bedroom suite; this is beautiful and comfortable. May I peek?'' he asked and she nodded. After he opened the door, his eyes widened and he chuckled. "This is what I call a woman's closet. It must be twenty by eight feet." She grinned and nodded when he glanced at her. "Wow! Hanging rods of different heights for long and short clothes, even a tall one for gowns, I guess. Shoe racks. Lots of shelves, and to the ceiling so there's no wasted space, very smart. A built-in dresser, cubby holes for items you can fold. My, even jewelry pegs and tiny cribs. My closet and drawers stay in shambles most of the time because I pack and leave or unpack to repack in a rush. Half the time I can't find what I need, and I don't like being messy, leftover training from Mom. You're a clever woman, looks as if you thought of everything."

As he continued studying the area, Rachel quipped, "My friends often tease me about not wanting to sleep in the same room with my clothes. To me, this is just practical and time saving." She leaned against the doorjamb for support, as her knees were feeling weak and her body was trembling at their close proximity. She fantasized about him pulling her into his arms and then the both of them slowly sinking to the carpeted floor and making passionate love. She ached for his touch, his kiss, his embrace. She didn't know how she would react if he made such an overture. Would she try to postpone it or surrender in a flash? Though they had spent only two weeks together twelve years ago and a few days recently, she didn't fear him. She did not doubt he was a gentleman and her safety wasn't at risk, only her emotions. Yet, she wanted to get to know him better this time before any intimacy occurred, if it did.

Quentin felt her attention on him and it was arousing, but it was too soon to act on his physical urges. First, there were some things to be settled between them, after he was assured she was the woman he hoped she was. "Even a full-length mirror to check out your stunning appearance. I'll have to steal this closet idea, if you don't mind."

"Of course not. But be prepared to take teasing from the workers. When I told them what I wanted, they chuckled and thought it was frivolous. I had to meet with the person doing the job to measure and draw out what I had in mind; she was a female, so she understood. I love it, too."

"Your ideas should be in home building and decorating magazines."

"The house was featured in several right after we moved in, mainly as favors to the builder and interior decorator. But I didn't let them use our name and location in the articles to maintain our privacy and security."

He moved toward the doorway and she retreated, almost in a rush as if to avoid being too close. *Don't press her; she's wary of you and your intentions.* "I certainly know about those things, and they can be hard to come by. Now I'd better get those chops to cooking before we get too hungry." *And I don't mean for food. As soon as we've eaten and relaxed, we're having a serious talk, woman, even if it's our last one and you refuse to see me again.*

Seven

Quentin retrieved the meat from the refrigerator and went outside to place it on the barbecue grill. He checked his watch for timing it.

"What can I do to help?" she asked after he returned.

"Check the potatoes and wrap the rolls in aluminum foil for heating. We'll set the table and steam the broccoli while the chops are cooking. We could sip wine while we're working."

"And talk. Most of our conversations have been about me and Augusta. You haven't told me much about yourself or about your football career," she hinted to see if that last topic was a taboo or painful subject, which would determine if she extended Becky's party invitation where it was sure to come up among the men. She took glasses from a cabinet and handed him a corkscrew.

While Quentin opened the wine and poured it, Rachel did the tasks he had mentioned. She got out dishes, utensils, placemats, napkins, salt and pepper, and other condiments. She began to set the table in the breakfast room, as the dining room seemed too formal for the occasion.

As Rachel worked, Quentin sipped his wine, observed her with keen interest and pleasure, and talked. "I was born and raised in Colquitt, played football in high school, and worked on my father's peanut farm. My parents are Matthew and Inez Rawls. I have a younger brother, Frank, divorced, no kids, in the car-selling business. I have a younger sister, Mary, who's married to Steve; they have two children and live and work on the farm with our parents. We're Baptist, maybe because we have only Baptist and Methodists in Miller County. My best friends are football players, most of them on my team. I've been married twice: the first time to Casey Niles, a model, for two years; the second time to a secretary named Belinda Jacobs for a year, an old friend's sister. We called it quits in '89. I don't have any children and I don't have any contact with my ex-wives or support them. Nor do I have any emotional ties to them, or any other woman."

Rachel glanced at him, but he was gazing out the kitchen window over the sink. *Good, divorced for a long time and no current girlfriend.* Yet, she was surprised he was so open and direct about those relationships. Maybe he would tell her later why those two marriages failed.

"After Georgia, Florida, and Alabama refused to take me, I earned a walk-on football scholarship to the University of Oklahoma and played for them and Barry Switzer from '74 to '78. We won the National Championships in '74 and '75. I lost the Heisman Trophy to Billy Sims in '78;

he played for the Sooners at the same time I did
and deserved the award. That's where I earned
the nickname of the Man with the Golden
Arm." His gaze never left the window. "Well,
now we best go outside so I can keep an eye on
those chops."

At the barbecue, he took up where he left off
as he turned the meat. "I was drafted by the
San Francisco 49ers in '78. I played for them for
seven years, mostly behind Joe Montana. I was
in two Superbowls, three Pro Bowls, and picked
up six awards for quarterbacking. I injured my
throwing shoulder in the '82 Superbowl and my
right knee in the '85 bowl. I was traded to the
Dallas Cowboys in August of '85. Been there
nine years, played in two Superbowls and two
Pro Bowls and picked up one award. I reinjured
my left shoulder in Superbowl twenty-seven in
'93. Seems like those Superbowl games are bad
luck for me, but I surely would love to play in
one more before I'm out for good," he admitted
with a wry laugh.

"I had to sit out most of the '93-94 season
due to surgeries and therapy, but came back in
time to play in the last Superbowl. If the Cowboys win the next one, it'll be three championships in a row; that would be some kind of high
for me and them, one I don't want to miss. Plus,
this is the seventy-fifth anniversary for football,
so it's a special year. I've done sports commen-
tating, product endorsements, and commercials;
there's big bucks to be made in them. When I
have time, I visit kids in hospitals and schools,

and sometimes help coach kids' teams in Dallas.''

"You like children a lot, don't you?" *And you
want your own one day*.

"Yep, my sister has good kids, a boy five and
a girl eight, and wants more. Who knows, maybe
I'll give them some cousins to play with one
day?"

Not with me. "You love football; it's evident in
your eyes and voice when you talk about it. How
long do you men play?" She noticed a tiny frown
for a moment until he shrugged and masked it.

"Once it's in your blood, you don't go out
until you have to, then it's kicking and yelling
all the way to the exit for most guys." He looked
at his watch as if to check the cooking schedule
to give himself time to decide what to tell her.
"Age doesn't matter much as long as you stay
healthy and talented. But teams can have only
fifty-three men on their rosters, so they want the
best in each position. With the number of teams
and men limited, a lot of great college players
never get a chance to show what they can do,
and some veterans get cut too soon after they're
injured.'' Maybe his reason for being in
Augusta, he mused, would change that for a lot
of those men. He couldn't tell yet because he
had more facts to gather first.

"Besides, having an injured man on the bench
costs the team because he still counts against
their salary cap when he's useless. If he's drawing a big paycheck, it's too tempting for owners
and management to sign up somebody who's

cheaper and healthier. I've played in downpours where the ball was so slick that no amount of skill helped you or the receiver, in freezing cold where your fingers wouldn't work right if your life depended on them, in snow so thick you could hardly see the receiver or lines, and on days so hot you could hardly breathe and you're drenched in sweat and almost passing out from rapid dehydration. It's also hard to show your stuff when you aren't the starting quarterback and he stays healthy and in the game, especially when you have to play behind some of the greats. We were 12/4/0 last season; Troy Aikman has a sixty-nine percent completions record; he led the NFL in '93; he'll remain our starter, and Jason Garrett's his first backup." *Now, they have Rodney Peete, so where and how will I fit in? They surely don't need four quarterbacks.*

Rachel saw him grimace at some unwanted thought. She kept silent and alert to learn more.

"One of the best times in my career was being coached by Tom Landry; now, I'm getting Switzer back. The problem is, the team roster has to be cut to fifty-three players, and injured men aren't valuable. I hate getting out when we've got so many advantages and incentives now: Free Agency and new game rules this year, some excellent protection for quarterbacks. I could have used them years ago when I took late hits and got hurt. It cost the other teams penalties, but it cost me more, much more." *Too much! But don't sound like a whiner to her.*

"What new rules?" Rachel prompted to keep him talking if he would.

"They've gotten stricter about moves and plays that protect the team members. Most guys don't try to intentionally hurt you, but accidents happen when you're tensed up and trying hard to win. Your emotions are so keyed up that you sometimes do things without thinking. Drug testing is near mandatory considering the trouble with cocaine, steroids, and such over the years; that isn't a problem for me; I was never in to that scene; it's stupid and dangerous. Besides, pro ball players are in a position to influence young kids."

"I'm glad you feel a responsibility in that serious area. I hope you get to play football as long as you want too."

"Thanks. I'd like to be there when Emmitt Smith makes history; he's one of the best rushers and running backs to ever play the game. I guess what I want most is one more season, a great one, to go out in style and glory." He smiled wryly after making that confession. "I just can't see myself cooped up like a chicken in an office and wearing a suit and tie. If I make the cut, I'll have to prove myself again, show I still have what it takes. Coming off serious injuries is almost like starting from scratch and everybody is watching, and some are waiting and eager for you to fail. I have to prove I still have courage, consistency, cunning, and accuracy." *If I don't retire rather than risk being cut or traded. I'd rather get out than force Coach Switzer into making that tough decision.*

Rachel had rented and purchased sports videos to watch him play and to learn more about him and football. A barrage of images flashed through her mind: the bruising sacks, interceptions, late hits, injuries. He had awesome odds against succeeding, as did she with her writing, so empathy filled her. "You also have to keep from getting reinjured."

"Yep, but permanent damage is always a risk when you do anything of value." *We'll both find that out very soon.* "The media is calling us 'every team's target.' As I told you, with the salary cap in force, injured players burden a team with an empty position, and there's no money in the budget, or a slot available to replace him. I do have one advantage: experienced backup quarterbacks are important because a starter can get wiped out at any time; that might be helpful to me if I can make it through and shine during preseason." *If I can pass the physical, get a chance to play, and play well.* "I did some of my best and longest quarterbacking when Montana hurt his elbow while I was with the 49ers."

"Do you have any plans for what you'll do after retirement?" She noted that he hesitated before responding.

"I haven't decided. Maybe I'll ranch or do something else."

Change the subject; he's bled enough today. "You're lucky to have a brother and sister and nephew and niece, and your parents still living.

I miss mine, and I miss my daughters and grandchildren."

"I imagine so; family is special. Well, why don't you steam the broccoli and warm the rolls? I should be ready out here about the same time you finish."

Rachel followed his requests. Afterward, she peeked out the window and saw Quentin gazing around her yard at the pool, gazebo, and cabana. She wondered what his ranch and lifestyle were like in Texas. Perhaps he was like her in the sense that she was lonely and unfulfilled when it came to emotional bonds with the opposite sex. Or maybe at this difficult point in his life he just needed somebody whom he could trust to talk and relax with. She saw him place the chops on the dish and head her way.

"Smells wonderful," she told him as they sat down to eat.

"It's my mother's recipe; she's a super cook, so is my sister."

While they ate, they chatted easily. Quentin asked about her charity, volunteer, church, and club work.

"After I married and moved here, I was pulled into most of them by the Gaineses because they're a prominent family with many business and social connections. But I like helping the unfortunate, so I do it as much as possible. I've discovered that most people will contribute money and donate items for sales for worthy causes, but few will give up their time and energy to do the actual work needed. I suppose it's hard to do with families and busy work schedules. I have extra time, so it isn't difficult for me. My biggest problem is learning to say no to everyone's pleas for help. Some think that because I don't have a husband and children at home, I'm loaded with time and energy, so they make any refusal sound like a crime. I'm sure it's the same with you concerning public appearances and interviews." His mouth full, he nodded. "As soon as I finish the projects I'm doing now, I plan to slow down and refocus parts of my life, start a career. For example, tomorrow, I have my bridge club, a luncheon, a woman's club meeting, and another meeting. Afterward, I have to get some work done on a project that's due soon."

Before sipping his wine, Quentin said, "I suppose you've used up a lot of time with me this week."

"Yes, but it's been fun and," she said after a laugh, "sorely needed. I've purposely kept myself busy since my children left on their trips, so I was tired and needed a change."

"If your schedule isn't too tight and you need another relaxing evening out after your hectic day tomorrow, how about having dinner with me on Friday night?"

"Sounds wonderful; I accept. Say about seven o'clock?"

"Perfect. We can have a fancy dessert then because I didn't bring one tonight. I don't eat many sweets so it never entered my mind to buy something."

What I want for dessert is you, Quentin Rawls.

Should I mention what happened years ago and risk spoiling our evening or let it slide like you're doing? Maybe you're waiting for me to do so and wondering why I haven't. It might stand between us until I handle it, but how do I explain why I ran like a rabbit without scaring you off? Not yet, Rachel. She took an easier plunge. "There's a pool party on Saturday at Becky Cooper's house if you'd like to go with me. It would give you a chance to meet Scott and discuss your renovation ideas with him. You met so many people at the reunion that you might not remember him. They're terrific people and she's one of my two best friends. I think you'd like them. It's from two until six o'clock."

"Sounds both fun and profitable to me. I'll pick you up at one-thirty, okay?" To him, she looked surprised that he accepted without hesitation.

"Perfect," she echoed his earlier agreement.

After they finished eating, they cleared the table, put dishes in the dishwasher, and cleaned up the kitchen.

"Would you like to get some fresh air and a little exercise out back?" Quentin asked.

"Let's go."

Without talking, they strolled around the pool, admired the lovely view, and enjoyed the serenity of the evening and each other's company.

Quentin halted by the fountain to listen to its soothing ripples before he entered the ivy-covered gazebo and leaned against its archway.

He watched the reflections of clouds on the pool's surface as they drifted across the sky. He inhaled fragrant smells of flowers, recently mowed grass, and trimmed shrubs— and the scent of the woman who passed him and took a seat behind him. He heard dogs barking in the distance, nocturnal birds and insects singing, and soft music coming from a neighbor's house. As the wind picked up, tree limbs and vegetation swayed. He could smell moisture in the air. He half turned and propped his back against the arch post. Light filtered through lattice openings and danced across his companion's face and body. She was looking at him in a mixture of hesitation, wariness, and— oddly— contentment.

Quentin joined her on the bench. "Don't you think it's time we talk about us, Rachel, about what happened twelve years ago? You left without saying good-bye or exchanging addresses. I thought we had something good and special going. Did I misread how you felt about me and our relationship?"

When Rachel started to rise to pace while she explained, he grasped her hand and asked her to stay and respond. "I will," she assured him, "but it will be easier if I can move around and not be distracted by your closeness."

He released his hold and she stood. "I distract you?"

Rachel faced him at a short distance. "More than you can imagine."

He forced himself to remain seated. "Is that good or bad?"

"I don't know; that's partly why I fled you like a coward; I didn't understand how you could affect me so strongly and quickly. Even though we were . . . intimate, we never talked about our feelings. We never made promises or mentioned a commitment or even seeing each other again. In all honesty, I didn't think our paths would cross after that cruise."

"Are you sorry they did?"

"No, of course not. I've never done anything like that before or since meeting you. It happened so quickly and so easily that it scared me. I told myself it was one of those summer shipboard romances and nothing would come of it because our lives and ages are so different. I thought and hoped you cared for me, but that didn't mean you wanted more from me than what we shared, and you didn't say or imply otherwise. I just wanted to spare us both a difficult parting. I didn't know what to say or how to behave under such circumstances, and I didn't want to end it with lies or excuses, or to cheapen it."

"You never gave me the chance to tell you how I felt or to tell you I wanted and needed to see you again," Quentin refuted. "I tried to locate you, but you'd given me your maiden name and hometown, which were dead ends. I even hired a private detective to locate you, but he lost his license before he could start the job." He noted her look of astonishment at that news. "Soon, I got caught up in surgery and then therapy for my shoulder and trying to make a comeback. Almost everybody, especially the media, was watching me like a hawk to see if I failed, ready to pounce on me if I did. By the time things settled down, it seemed as if too much time had passed to try again. You were special to me, Rachel; you were one of the few women who seemed to like me for myself. I could totally relax with you, and I did." He took a deep breath before continuing.

"I finally told myself that maybe you didn't feel the same way or you'd contact me; I figured I'd be easy to find. Then it occurred to me you would realize I had given you a false name while I was trying to avoid the media and get my head straight, so you'd think I'd been conning you, just out for a good time."

Rachel revealed how she had discovered his identity. "I was shocked and confused, but— in a way— I misled you, too. I was afraid I would wind up in one of those celebrity tell-all books or become a locker-room joke."

"I would never do such a terrible thing to any woman."

"I didn't believe you would; it was just my imagination running wild."

"I can understand, given the playboy reputation those tabloids have given me; I'm not, Rachel, honest. All I have to do is be seen with a female on any occasion and they write crazy reports about me. Anyway, when I didn't hear from you, I tried to forget you. I made two bad marriages looking for what we had, or could have had, given more time together. But those divorces weren't all my fault; I wasn't what they needed, either, so none of us got hurt in the process, thank goodness. You and I have a lot in common, Rachel, and we seem good for each other. Why don't we start fresh, take it slow and easy, and see what happens between us?"

Don't rush it! "We do have a wonderful time together, Quentin, but our lives are so different, and I'm nine years older than you. My family is grown and gone when you're just getting ready to begin one. You have problems with your career, and I'm just starting a new one."

"What if we don't try and never know we're perfect for each other?"

What if we're not and I get hurt? "How can we test our feelings and compatibility when you're about to . . . 'hit the road' as you said?"

"I'll be here for another two weeks; that should give us time to see how we feel and get along. Don't decide tonight. Think about it while we spend time together; then we'll talk again. Deal?"

"I can't make you any promises tonight, Quentin." *Not because I don't trust you, but because I don't trust myself to have a clear head.*

He joined her under the entry arch. "Don't, just relax and have fun with me for a while. We won't rush anything, I will promise you that. We're too mature for playing games and we don't want to hurt each other. I've made two mistakes in the past, so I don't want to make another one; and I'm sure you don't want to create problems in your life. Another thing, I don't want the media, especially those tabloids, to get wind of our relationship and cause trouble while we're testing our feelings. But we owe it to ourselves to learn the truth, don't we?"

Rachel felt weak with longing, trembly with desire. It was a struggle not to fling herself into Quentin's arms and coax him to make rapturous love to her and damn any consequences. Yet, from somewhere deep within her mind, a hesitation came, one she had not experienced— or perhaps heeded— the last time, a weakness that had brought about twelve years of yearning and denial. "I suppose so."

Quentin grasped her chin and lifted her head. He smiled into her uncertain gaze and said, "Trust me, Rachel, I know so." He leaned over and gave her a brief kiss and an encouraging hug. "It's getting late; I should leave. I'll see you Friday at six-thirty."

"Slow and easy, get to know each other first this time, right?"

"No pressure, I promise. We'll know when and if it's right between us to move onward. It has to be a mutual decision. But no matter what happens, we'll remain friends."

"That suits me. Good night, Quentin, and thanks."

After Quentin left, Rachel went to the floor safe and took out two snapshot packets from their cruise. She had not shown the mementos to anyone, but had viewed them many times. Most were of scenery and some were of the two of them— taken by genial tourists on the ship and during stops at exotic ports. She recalled every location, who snapped each picture for them, what they did before and after each pose, and what they said that day or night. Those details were imprinted in her mind, and would remain there forever.

Quentin was right, she admitted, about them being compatible and attracted to each other. But, Rachel mused, were rapport and splendid sex enough to outweigh and overcome their differences? If she confessed she couldn't have— and didn't want— more children, would that discourage him? Or would he say it didn't matter, when later it might? Did he love her or was she just the best choice he had found so far? Did it matter what her daughters, his family, their friends, strangers— and even the harsh media— would say about them? How would she feel about having their romance— and their past if discovered— plastered over the front pages of those horrible tabloids? Would every area of their lives be invaded and reported to the world? How would she look and feel when she was sixty and seventy and he was only fifty-one and sixty-one, as men usually aged so much better than women? Was a nine-year span that important to either of them? Would the media make it seem so, appear cheap?

Time and privacy were what they needed, but would they have them? Was there a real chance for happiness and a future with him? Would she be risking a broken heart if she searched for them? *Wait and see, Rachel.*

* * *

After Quentin returned to his suite at ten, two reporters phoned him: Todd Hardy of a local magazine and Pete Starns from a local television station. He brushed off Pete nicely, but Todd was persistent in wanting an interview right then or in person tomorrow and had to be dealt with firmly. He was tired of answering the same old questions for months about his injuries and plans. How the hell *should* he feel, he scoffed to himself, about having half of his heart cut out? How could he talk about his future when he didn't know what it held at this moment? His physical exam, impending practice, and preseason games would determine his decision, and the team management's. He didn't want to think or talk about maybes with probing reporters; he wanted to concentrate on succeeding with one last season, on his work here, and on Rachel.

Quentin realized he hadn't told her what he was doing the next day or asked her to go with him; it was too late to phone and enlighten her. Besides, the media— including the offensive Todd Hardy— would be there with eagle eyes and ears and sharpened pencils. He also hadn't mentioned his commitment on Sunday, which would be announced in the media this week and would receive coverage during the event. He should phone her in the morning before she heard about them from another source.

Quentin reminded himself he had to call his agent and business contact on Friday afternoon to report what he had learned. Saturday before the Coopers' party, he would call his parents and best friend to chat.

Things were going well between us years ago and until now, but we'll have to see just how much I mean to you. There's a chance you won't be interested in pulling up roots and moving to Texas to live on a secluded ranch, not as busy as you stay with your social life and volunteer work.

Thursday evening, Rachel worked on two projects at her desk after playing bridge that morning, having lunch with friends, and attending a club meeting afterward. By seven-thirty, both Becky and Jen had called to tell her about seeing Quentin Rawls on the six o'clock news!

"I was busy making calls for Heart Fund donations and for the church bake and attic sale, so I didn't see it," Rachel admitted.

Becky clicked her tongue playfully. "Heavens, Rach, how could you forget to tune in to see your man in action?"

"Because I didn't know about it until Jen called earlier. I suppose he forgot to mention it to me last night. I'll stay up to watch the eleven o'clock news; I'm sure they'll run it again."

"He looked wonderful, Rach. And it was nice of him to take time to visit the MCG Children's Medical Center and the shelter for abused children. I bet those kids were thrilled to meet him. It's also generous of him to do that charity appearance at the mall on Sunday to benefit both places. Anybody can have a picture made with

him and he'll autograph it for a five-dollar donation. Scott says he's very popular, and he has
a great personality, so I'm sure the mall will be
packed and he'll be swamped for hours. Are you
going with him?"

"He hasn't asked me to go."

"I'm sure he will. After all, he's coming to
my party with you."

"He wants to meet and talk with Scott about
some renovation ideas."

"That's just an excuse to spend time with you
and to meet everybody to see what your friends
are like."

"He doesn't need an excuse to ask me for a
date. We're getting along fine, but I am curious
about why he didn't mention those two appearances."

"Probably an oversight. I'm sure you two were
busy with other things."

Rachel told her about their evening. "We did
have a wonderful time and we agreed to keep
seeing each other."

"See, I told you so; he likes you a lot. You
like him, too, right?"

"Yes, but it's too soon to think about hiring
the preacher."

Becky laughed. "Maybe not."

They chatted for a while longer, then ended
their call.

Rachel finished her tasks in a near distracted
state and put away her things. She showered,
changed into a nightgown, and went to bed. She

propped herself up on several pillows and waited for the news, worried and baffled.

After she saw his interview with Pete Starns and clips from his two visits to the children's centers, she pressed the off button. She glanced at the phone and murmured, "Why haven't you called today? Why didn't you tell me about your plans? Are you hiding me from public attention or didn't you want to be in an uncomfortable situation? Let's see if you've changed your mind and cancel tomorrow night. I hope you weren't deceiving me last night for spite or for an easy conquest. I can hardly wait to hear your reason for such secretiveness."

Eight

Friday while en route to La Maison for dinner, Quentin explained his oversight. "A doctor from that class reunion saw me Tuesday at the gas station after I left your house and asked if I'd visit the kids at the medical center and abuse shelter yesterday, and I agreed. By the time I realized I had forgotten to tell you about those plans Wednesday night, it was too late to phone. I suppose it was because I had other things on my mind, such as talking about us. I tried several times to reach you on Thursday, but you were either out and your answering machine was off, or the line was busy. After those visits and doing interviews, I got caught up in a dinner with members of the local Sports Council and their friends that ran late."

Quentin frowned as he said, "I didn't realize the good doctor was planning to alert the media and have them in the way while I was trying to talk with the kids; it annoys me when special things like that appear as if they're publicity stunts on my part. Sick and frightened kids can't enjoy a visit from anybody with cameras, blinding lights, microphones, and strange men crowding them. It's as if those reporters don't comprehend why I'm there; it's a push-and-shove contest to see which one can get the closest to me and ask the most questions while I'm trying to ignore them and focus on the children. They make it hard to stay calm and be polite to them so the kids won't get upset. I suppose it'll be another media circus on Sunday at the mall while I'm doing pictures and autographs."

"Do you sign them even if someone can't afford to make a donation?"

"Yep, because I don't believe in discriminating against the unfortunate. We were poor when I was a kid, so I know how denial feels. They won't get a picture because there's a charge for the photographer and film that will be taken out of the donation, the only expense to be deducted. I'm doing this event for free, just to raise funds for the center and shelter. It's a hassle but it feels good to be able to help two worthy causes at once."

"You're a kind and generous person, Quentin Rawls. I'm proud and pleased to know you and be your friend."

Her remarks touched him deeply, as did her favorable opinion of him. "Thanks, so are you. Did you catch my TV interview?"

"At eleven. Becky Cooper and Jennifer Brimsford— my two best friends, you'll meet them tomorrow— they phoned to see if I had watched you on the six o'clock news. I told them at the reunion picnic that we met on a cruise twelve years ago and were tablemates, and I told them earlier in the week we're seeing each other while you're in town. I hope that was okay."

At a red traffic light, he looked at her. "Were they surprised to learn those facts about us? Is that why Becky let you invite me to her pool party?"

"Yes, but the three of us weren't best friends until three years ago, so there was no reason to mention you until you came to the reunion. I didn't reveal we were . . . close years ago; that's between us." She almost rushed onward to reveal to him how sorry she was that her answering machine was off and she had missed his calls; she had forgotten to reset it after she collected her messages and didn't notice it until this morning when the phone kept ringing so long while she was on the treadmill; she never stopped for anything during her exercise.

After she told him when to turn right, he asked, "Were you worried about me not telling you beforehand?"

Rachel smiled. "A little, more confused than anything."

"Thanks for being honest, and I'm sorry it slipped my mind and I couldn't reach you later to explain."

"It's fine, really. Now look, that's where we're going, the big house on the corner," she said, and pointed to it. "This area is called Olde Town, part of the historic district. It's beautiful in the spring when dogwoods and azaleas are in bloom, surrounded by oaks and magnolias. Fortunately many of the original homes were saved years ago when the restoration project began. Some were turned into doctors', lawyers', and business offices, and some into quaint restaurants like this one."

Quentin parked, helped her out of the car, and guided her inside where they were seated within minutes in a cozy upstairs room. The large house had wonderful atmosphere with its creative blend of past and present decor. Easy-listening music was low, and lighting— overhead and table candle— was soft, as were voices and laughter coming from patrons on both floors. So far, only one couple had been seated in their room, but on its far side; and the twentyish duo had eyes only for each other.

The night's menu was given orally by a waiter. After they'd made their choices and selected a wine, they chatted about Quentin's appearances. Then, Rachel almost winced as Janet and Clifford Hollis paused at the table while being led to their own not far away.

"Why, Rachel dear," Janet cooed falsely, "it's surprising to see you getting out so often with your busy schedule. You look . . . very presentable tonight. I see you took my advice and tossed out that horrible lipstick."

Without conceit, Rachel thought she looked good in a slate-colored dress with a mottled design. Its silk fabric flowed over her figure and flattered it, as did three skirt tiers with graduated lengths that halted just above her knees. A twenty-four inch strand of Brazilian Hematite beads and matching earrings were perfect accessories, as were slate shoes and silk pantyhose. Too, she had made certain her cosmetics were not overdone tonight, and Dawn had coiffed her hair and manicured her nails today. She chose to ignore Janet's snide remarks. "Quentin, this is Clifford and Janet Hollis. Cliff is my banker— and financial advisor on occasion— and Janet is in several organizations with me; they also attend my church and live on the same street that I do. Cliff, I'm sure you remember Quentin Rawls; he's a quarterback for the Dallas Cowboys." She watched him rise to shake hands with a smiling Cliff and nod to a staring Janet.

"I certainly do," Cliff said with enthusiasm, "and I've enjoyed watching you play over the years. It's a pleasure to meet you, and I hope you enjoyed our high school reunion."

"Yes, I did, and it's a pleasure to meet you, too."

"Is playing with a ball your only job?" Janet asked.

"Practice, games, and public appearances take up most of my year." Quentin's tone was curt. He remained standing, but hoped their visit would be brief. Already he disliked this woman who had addressed Rachel in such an impolite manner and who craftily insulted him and his career.

Janet dismissed the hostess after telling the woman they would take their seats soon. "What are you doing in Augusta, Mr. Rawls?"

Quentin was surprised at the bold question but it didn't show as he smiled. "Vacationing. This is a lovely and quiet town, very historical."

"We saw you on the news last night," Cliff said. "That was a nice thing you did for the children here. I'm sure you'll raise lots of money on Sunday."

Rachel noted that Janet did not give Quentin time to reply, just as she noted Quentin's manners and restraint.

"You were at our class reunion with Carrie Simmons, wasn't it?"

"Yes, she's the sister of an old and close friend."

Their appetizers arrived and Quentin sat down, but Janet lingered despite Cliff's urging to leave and allow the couple privacy to eat.

"We remember Donnie, don't we, Cliff? He left Augusta right after graduation, so did Carrie. I suppose she prefers living in another town."

"Larger cites have more to offer in her line of work."

"What line of . . . work is that, Mr. Rawls?"

Quentin sipped wine as he studied the obnoxious woman. "Fashion merchandising, I believe it's called. She lives in New York City and works in the apparel industry, if I remember correctly."

"Oh, I didn't realize she was into high fashion."

Quentin's voice was icy as he said, "She's quite successful at it. Perhaps we can chat another time when our food isn't getting cold. It was nice to meet you two. Good night."

All three noticed that Janet looked stunned at being dismissed like an errant child or a nobody.

Janet refused to take the cue. "How long do you plan to . . . vacation here, Mr. Rawls?"

"It depends on how much I like the town and its people. So far, *most* of the folks I've met have been cordial and gracious."

"That's nice, but I hope you don't take up too much of Rachel's time; she's a very busy woman. Isn't that right, Rachel dear?"

"I always take time off for friends," Rachel said with a sly smile.

"Friends? Are you old friends or did you meet at the reunion?"

Quentin's patience was ebbing. "I hope you don't mind if we start on our appetizers before they chill, Mrs. Hollis."

Cliff grasped Janet's elbow. "Let's go, honey, so they can eat. It was nice to meet you, Quentin, and good to see you, Rachel."

Quentin thanked him, then placed a crab stuffed-mushroom in his mouth. He said, ignoring Janet's continued presence, "Taste yours, Rachel; the chef has cooked them to perfection. They won't be good cold. They're delicious, Cliff; you should order them, too."

An embarrassed Cliff insisted, "Come along, Janet. Our table and waiter are ready. Nice seeing you, Rachel; you, too, Quentin," he repeated almost apologetically.

"Same here," Quentin replied pleasantly, then sipped his wine.

"Thanks for stopping by to chat; I'll see you later," Rachel added.

Janet turned and departed without saying

good-bye and Cliff followed like an obedient puppy, his discomfiture obvious to all of them.

With her back to the Hollises, Rachel whispered, "I'm sorry about that, Quentin; she can be most difficult at times."

"I hope I didn't embarrass you with my behavior. I've seen her type before: snoopy, arrogant, insolent."

Rachel explained who Janet was and why she got away with her actions, and related the meaning behind Janet's remarks to her. "At least she won't be at Becky's party; they're going out of town in the morning."

Quentin grinned. "Good; that means we'll have fun."

"You handled her with great skill. Thanks for being so understanding and patient. She's a pain in the rear, but we endure her for everybody's sake and to keep the peace in our social circle."

"That's because you and others have real class. You're right about it being best to ignore her, unless she gets too nasty. I know from experience, if you're forced to get tough with certain people, you can come off appearing the heavy, make yourself look bad instead of them."

Their empty dishes were collected and the main course was served.

As they ate and chatted, Quentin said, "If you want to come with me on Sunday, I'll take you, but it could be a rough ordeal with the media there, especially if you aren't used to dealing with them. If they see us together, they'll start asking you questions about me and about us, and some can be real clever and persistent, like Janet. On top of that, they often misquote you. A few have been calling my room and pestering me for extra interviews. Ever hear of or meet Todd Hardy from a local magazine?"

"Yes, but I rarely read his articles; he seems too cold and biased."

"That's the same opinion I got of him. He phoned the other night and was at the center and shelter. He's about as pushy as Janet. To put him off, I promised him a long interview before I leave town if he gets off my back while I'm resting and having fun. I've gotten pretty good at thwarting and eluding his kind, but my methods don't always work. Sometimes they shadow you, sneak pictures, and eavesdrop. I just don't like for them to intrude on private moments or lie about them in the press, which they will without giving their actions a second thought."

"I have church that morning and lunch afterward at the club with friends; you're welcome to go to either or both with me. As for the charity event, it will be crowded and hectic and you'll be busy, so I think it's best if I wait for you at home, if you want to come by afterward for dinner."

"Sounds perfect to me."

Quentin wondered if he should risk subjecting Rachel to close and perhaps vicious scrutiny; he wasn't "old news" yet and some reporters were certain to begin following, digging, and writing about them as a couple. Bringing down the famous or infamous was like a bloodthirsty sport to them. He recalled how his brother, Frank, had been chewed up by the cruel media after troubles with drugs, jail, and a bad marriage, all of which had also created embarrassing moments and bad publicity for Quentin. He wanted and needed to learn if Rachel Gaines was the right woman for him and, if so, he had to win her. His goal could be hard or impossible to obtain if her privacy was invaded. Somehow he must prevent that from happening.

Later as she was leaving the ladies' room, Rachel was vexed to find Janet waiting outside the door. She suspected the woman had followed her just to pry and be spiteful. She smiled and attempted to escape, but an unmoving Janet blocked her exit.

"You seem to be having fun with your famous guest, Rachel."

"Quentin is good company and an interesting conversationalist."

"How long have you known him?"

"Twelve years. I have to get back to the table. See you later." *Get out of the way, you hateful bitch.*

"Twelve years? So, you didn't meet at the reunion?"

"No, as I said, we've known each other for a long time. Quentin is from Georgia." *Don't you dare ask when, where, and how we met!*

"Why on earth did he go to the reunion with that Carrie Simmons creature instead of with a socially acceptable person? You came alone, but

I saw you dancing and chatting with him for a long time."

"He told you earlier that he's a friend of her brother's, so he escorted Carrie as a favor to Donnie so she wouldn't have to come alone." *And face vultures like you.*

"Did he know you were going to be present?"

"No, we haven't seen each other in years, and I'm not a classmate. He lives in Texas now. If you'll excuse me, Janet, I really need to get back to our table."

"Surely you aren't interested in somebody like him?"

Rachel was miffed. "What do you mean by 'somebody like him'?"

"Surely you've heard and read the awful gossip about him."

Rachel knew Janet was about to fill her ears with garbage if she didn't silence her. "It's my belief that vicious gossip can't be trusted, so I avoid listening to it; and I certainly don't spread malicious rumors."

"These are undeniable facts, Rachel dear. His brother has been in all kinds of trouble with the authorities. Surely you know that Quentin has been through two wives and countless other women."

"Plenty of men are divorced these days, including your brother several times." *You did it now, Rachel; she looks as if you slapped her face.*

"Rachel Gaines, you know my brother is nothing like Quentin Rawls and his kind; shame on you for even putting them in the same sentence."

You're right for a change; that was an awful insult to Quentin.

"Lordy, he came to our reunion with that low-class tramp, so no one of quality and good breeding could have a high opinion of him. Surely a woman of your standing doesn't want to socialize with a man like that."

"You're a smart woman, Janet, so I'm certain your opinion of him would be different if you knew him. Quentin is kind, well mannered, and generous. He frequently donates his time, efforts, and money to worthy causes; he even did so this week while he's on vacation. As to those other matters you mentioned, I prefer to do as the Bible and our pastor say, not to judge people by past mistakes. Now, if you'll excuse me, I must rejoin Quentin. I'll see you next week. I hope you enjoy your weekend trip," she said, and wiggled past Janet. She mentally dared the woman to pause at their table again.

After he assisted with Rachel's chair, Quentin asked, "Did she corner you in the bathroom? She was on your tail in a flash the moment you left."

"She was nervy and annoying, but I brushed her off and escaped. Maybe I should take evasion lessons from you."

They laughed, then refused dessert and coffee so they could leave before the Hollises finished their meal and approached them again.

At Rachel's house, they sat in the casual area of the living room and chatted for a while as they sipped amaretto. Each was positioned slightly sideways and only a short distance apart, their gazes often meeting and lingering as they spoke. Quentin's right arm rested along the back of the sofa and his left hand held his glass. His fingers brushed the silky material of her dress as he told her how lovely she looked.

Rachel knew why she felt warm and quivery, and nervous. "Thank you, a woman my age needs all the compliments she can get."

Quentin chuckled; he wanted to touch her, feel her, taste her. "Forty-seven isn't old, Rachel; you're an attractive and vital woman. I feel happy around you, and optimistic about almost everything."

You're so tempting, Quentin Rawls; you drive me wild with need. "Thanks. I enjoy your company, too, more than any man's."

Quentin's blue gaze roamed her face and savored the appreciative glow on it. "We seem much alike in many ways; that's good. I think friendship and respect for the other person are important to a lasting relationship. Maybe that's why my first two marriages failed; we didn't have those things. Frankly, I don't know why Casey and I got married. I suppose it was because so many people— and the press— shoved us together. It seems as if the world functions around couples and families; loners stand out like sore thumbs. Southern boys are usually hitched by twenty-eight, so I figured I should settle down and Casey was an all right girl. But she cared more about herself, modeling, fame, and money than about me or our marriage; and I admit I cared more about myself and my football career. After two years, we called it quits; rather, she did and I agreed. It was about the same with Belinda; we married for the wrong reasons. At thirty-two, I figured I'd better make another try before I got too old for children, and the choices were slimming down fast. She was there, the relationship was going pretty well, so we drifted into a marriage. It didn't take long, a year to be exact, for us to realize it wasn't going to work. Fortunately, both Casey and Belinda married again and are happy this time. As for me, I realized I wouldn't seek a third marriage until I had my priorities straight and the right woman came along; it isn't worth changing your life if you're going to be miserable."

"I know what you mean; that's why I'm still single after so many years of widowhood. My friends are determined to get me remarried and some of the men I've dated are eager to settle down, but— as in your case— too often it's for the wrong reasons. When it comes time to make a commitment, it has to be done carefully. Life is too short to be unhappy."

"Were you and Daniel happy, if you don't mind me asking?"

"We had a good marriage, but I'm not grieving over his loss anymore. His family gave me a hard time and still do, but I'd rather tell you about that another time. I don't want to spoil a pleasant evening."

"I don't either, and I'm finished talking about

my mistakes. I just wanted you to know I have no hangups about my ex-wives. But I do want to explain something else: I used 'James Rawlings' on the cruise to guard my privacy. Reporters were hounding me like crazy after my injury, so I had to escape them for a while; that was one kind of intrusion I wasn't familiar with and it frightened me. I had worked my way to the top, then suddenly I realize I might not be able to ever play again. It was scary and frustrating, and it made me angry. Spending time with you was like a dose of good medicine. I'll always be grateful to you for helping me get through that rough period."

He smiled and caressed her cheek. "My full name is Quentin James Rawls, so I just doctored it a little to mislead people. I was living in San Francisco when we met, but I was in the process of purchasing the ranch so that claim about Texas being my home wasn't a total fib. I didn't tell you the truth during our relationship because I wanted you to get to know me as a regular person, not as a celebrity; I was afraid that revelation might color your opinion of me. I did plan to confess my deceit on the last day of the cruise."

"But I never gave you the opportunity, right?" He nodded. "I'm sorry; it was cowardly of me to just take off like I did."

"Maybe it was for the best. Maybe we both had to get our lives straight." He cleared his throat abruptly. "Well, I best be going. We have a busy weekend ahead."

Heavens, what a change! "Would you like to watch the eleven o'clock news before you go to see if they mention your appearance on Sunday?"

"No thanks." *I should leave while I can still keep my promise not to rush you into my bed. You're far too tempting tonight and my blood is boiling to spill-over level.* "You said the Hollises live close by. After meeting Janet, it wouldn't surprise me if she rode or walked by just to see how long I stay." *Or if some nosy reporter like Todd Hardy did the same.* "We have to protect your reputation." He set his glass on a coaster and stood up to go. "I'll pick you up at one-thirty for the party."

Rachel put hers aside and rose to walk him to the door. Before she opened it, she allowed him to pull her into his arms and kiss her. She had been thinking about kissing him all evening; no, since she saw him again. The kiss was long and enticing, but his hands did not rove her body. There was no arguing that she desired him and would— if she lost her wits— guide him upstairs to her bedroom and surrender to rapturous passion. If she did so, it would alter things too fast, and she had to be sure about him this time. It required all of her willpower not to entice him to kiss her again or stay.

As his fingers stroked her rosy cheek and he looked into her softened green gaze, Quentin grasped her warring emotions and was pleased. He murmured, "You excite me now even more than you did years ago, woman, and that was plenty." He took a deep breath to restore his lagging control. "I couldn't get you off my mind after we parted. It's amazing we spent so much time together but learned so little about each other. I guess we were denying how strongly we were attracted to each other. We were too damn cautious and kept our feelings hidden." *Maybe that cost us twelve good years together.* "I care a lot about you, Rachel Gaines, and I'd like for our relationship to work. Please give it a chance."

She flattened her palms against his broad chest and detected his swift heartbeat. "We'll see how it goes. I don't think either of us was prepared for what happened between us years ago. It was wonderful and unforgettable, but— as you said earlier— we both had living and changing to do; a commitment just wasn't possible back then, not one that would have worked. I believe we both knew that fact on some level and that's why we didn't press each other. I had two preteen children to raise; you had troubling injuries and a skyrocketing career and were traveling back and forth across the country. I was thirty-five and you were twenty-six. Our lives were so different, and our priorities didn't match. We became deeply and intimately involved so fast that it was scary, at least for me. You're the only man I've . . . been with except my husband. I guess I'm still trapped by my upbringing and old-fashioned values; I can't just carry on a casual affair, and I can hardly believe I did such a thing with a stranger. I suppose we caught each other at vulnerable moments. I don't want it to be that casual way again: I want us to really know each other first this time. I do care a great deal about you, Quentin, but I want to make certain I think with my head as well as my heart and body." She couldn't stop herself from asking how long he would be in town.

"I have to leave on the twenty-seventh to head for practice."

Eleven short and swift days. . . . Heavens, is that enough time for us to make such a serious decision? Can I risk all, anything, for love?

"I may have some business to do here before I leave. I'll know after I speak with my agent and another man tomorrow. As soon as they give me an answer, I'll explain everything to you."

They shared another kiss before he smiled and left. As Rachel leaned against the closed door and sighed dreamily, she recalled what he had said. So, she mused, he did have an unknown reason for being in Augusta, just as she had suspected. She wondered what it was and if it was the real motive behind his arrival and lengthy stay. *Don't get crazy, Rachel; wait and see.*

Saturday, while the other guests were talking near the pool, Rachel and Jen helped Becky prepare the buffet inside.

"So far, so good," Becky remarked as she glanced out the window at Quentin as he chatted and laughed and mingled. "He seems to be getting along splendidly with everyone, and everybody is impressed to the hilt with him. The boys promised not to get nosy about his injuries and career."

"That's good, but he's been frank and mostly relaxed when he mentioned them while we're together."

Jen eyed Quentin for a moment. "He's so handsome and sexy, Rachel. Those blue eyes must make you melt when he looks at you. Whew, and that mellow voice. Doesn't he make your heart beat like crazy?"

"I must confess that he does, Jen. He's such good company."

Becky grinned and asked, "Is he a great kisser?"

"Becky Cooper, you snoop," Rachel jested with a merry laugh.

The woman halted her task and pressed, "Well, is he?"

"Yes, but we've only kissed twice, last night."

"Did he make your knees weak?"

"Naturally. While we're alone, let me tell you what happened at the restaurant." Rachel related the intrusive incident at their table with the Hollises and at the ladies' room with Janet.

Becky was horrified when Rachel finished her story and said, "That brazen witch, how rude! Thank heaven she couldn't come today. She had better watch out if you two team up against her."

"If our actions don't backfire on us, more precisely on me. I mean, I practically told her to shut up, with a sweet smile and tone, of course."

"It sounds as if she deserved it; I'm glad you

didn't let her spoil your evening, and I'm glad Quentin didn't run for cover after meeting her."

"So am I, but he'll be leaving in eleven days."

"If you don't find a way to persuade him to hang around longer."

"I can't; he has preseason practice; then, football goes on for months. Once he leaves, there's no guessing when I'll see him again."

"You could attend some of his games. Dallas isn't far away by plane."

"He hasn't invited me to any of them."

"He will. If not before he leaves, then as soon as he's lonely for you."

"*If* he gets lonely for me."

"He will, I'm sure of it. I've seen the way he looked at you today."

"Then you've noticed more than I have. No doubt Dianne will give Janet a full report when she returns on Tuesday. He's coming to church with me in the morning, so I imagine that will spark some curiosity. I bet Janet is at wit's end about not being here to spy on us and ask questions."

"I'm sure she is, but let's forget about her and just have fun. No doubt that's easy with Quentin Rawls at your side. Rach, have you told the girls about him?"

"Not yet; there's nothing to tell. I received a letter from Karen on Thursday and one from Evelyn this morning; they're both fine. Evelyn said she was phoning next Saturday. Karen is phoning on the twenty-eighth during her next break. If anything serious develops between us before then, I'll mention him when they call me."

They chatted about their children for a while until Becky said, "The food's ready! Let's call everyone inside to serve themselves."

The guests were summoned to select their choices, to be eaten at tables with umbrellas that surrounded the pool.

Quentin eyed the buffet of barbecued chipped pork, tenderloin, hash, rice, potato salad, cole-slaw, rolls, pickles, ribs, potato chips, iced tea, and peppermints. "This looks and smells delicious," he told Rachel.

"It's from Sconyers; their barbecue, hash, and ribs are world famous; they've catered it to the White House in the past. It's the best anywhere."

When their plates were filled, Rachel and Quentin took seats with Becky and Scott. While they ate and drank, the men discussed Quentin's impending home renovations, with Scott giving him numerous good suggestions.

"Do you ever contract jobs outside of Augusta?" Quentin asked him.

"I haven't in the past; I get enough work here to keep me busy."

"If you decide you want to take on my job, let me know by next week. Since you understand what I want, you're the ideal contractor for me."

Before he started on another juicy rib, Scott responded, "That's nice of you to say, Quentin, and I'll think about it. Of course, it would be more expensive to use me and my workers because of travel and lodging costs. And the men would need to make visits home every two weeks while the work was being done; the project should take about two to three months."

"I understand; families and happy workers are important. I know it would cost more to get you and your team, but you know what I want. Maybe Becky and Rachel could come along or fly over for a visit or two while you're there; Dallas is a great place for shopping and sight-seeing. If it's during the season, I can get you all tickets to a Cowboys game."

Scott grinned. "That's what I call an enticing perk. I'll put a pencil to paper on Monday and get an estimate ready for you. I'll also need to check my schedule for a starting date; I think it would be September."

"That's perfect. Games will be played on the eleventh and eighteenth; we're idle on the twenty-fifth. If I'm not playing this year, we can go as spectators. I'll know where I stand after preseason in August."

Scott put down his iced tea. "I hope you're standing on the field because I've enjoyed watching you over the years."

"Thanks. We'll see."

As they ate, Rachel warmed at how Quentin had handled that touchy subject and moment. He appeared at ease around her friends, and sent her occasional smiles as if to tell her that fact. His nearness and attention were arousing. He looked appealing in his knee-length shorts and golf shirt, his legs long and sleek, his arms

muscled, his waist narrow, his chest broad, and
his hands large and skilled. She remembered
how it felt to have those deft fingers drifting
over her flesh, urging her to cast aside any inhibitions. She felt a rush of heat over her body,
her nipples tingled and hardened, and she
hoped they didn't stick out noticeably from her
T-shirt. She was unaccustomed to raging desire
burning her alive in public and prayed she
didn't start squirming in her chair. She was
eager to hear his secret and to learn how— or
if— it would affect their romantic relationship.
As soon as she knew that answer, she would—

"You want me to bring you anything? I'm going back for seconds."

Rachel's gaze met his beneath the shade of the
large umbrella and partially concealed by sunglasses. "No thanks, Quentin; I'm stuffed." *But,
Lordy, you would be an excellent dessert. I could lick
you up one side and down the other. I would be putty
in those marvelous hands if I knew things could work
out between us.*

"I'll go with you," Scott told him, and the
men left the table.

Becky leaned toward Rachel, "He's wonderful, woman; grab him."

"I'm glad you didn't invite Keith Haywood
today."

Becky laughed. "You sidestepped that question with skill."

"I didn't realize you asked me a question,"
Rachel quipped.

"A sly one, I thought. Well, are you going after him?"

"I haven't decided; it depends on him and what happens next."

"Doesn't that partly depend upon you, Rach?" Becky whispered.

Rachel noticed Dianne watching them, smiled at the woman, and replied to Becky as Dianne jerked her gaze away from them, "I suppose so, but I don't want to be rash, and sorry later."

"Somehow I don't think you will; he appears smitten by you. But if it doesn't work out, Keith is still available and he's a dreamboat."

"Hold it, Becky; I can handle only one man at a time."

"Then, start handling him, Rach, before he's out of reach, and I do mean, *handling* him. Do like Scarlett, go after what you want."

"If there's enough time. He'll be gone soon."

"Have you already forgotten he invited us to Texas? Wasn't that a clue about his feelings toward you?"

"Maybe, but I don't want to dupe myself with false hopes."

"Do you want me to encourage Scott to take on his job?"

"No, let's wait and see if they work out a deal on their own."

They stopped talking when the men returned. For the remainder of the afternoon, they talked, swam, snacked, and sipped beer or wine. Rachel appreciated the way Quentin restrained himself from making improperly romantic gestures toward her in front of her friends, but he did whisper how stunning she looked in a black one-piece swimsuit that flattered her curves. As for him in his trunks, he was tantalizing to her senses. She wanted to stroke his bare chest, float in his embrace, press her body against his, strip off their garments, and interlock their bodies in blissful delight.

When a huge thundercloud moved overhead about five and threatened an imminent downpour, everyone hurried to change clothes and to help Becky clear the area so they could depart before it arrived.

Rachel and Quentin told everyone good-bye, spoke final words with the Brimsfords, and thanked the Coopers for a lovely time and delicious meal. Scott told Quentin to phone him Monday evening to set up a meeting to discuss their possible project. The men shook hands, the women exchanged hugs and kisses, and everyone took their leave.

At Rachel's home a few blocks away, Quentin walked her to the door and said, "I'd better get moving before that storm strikes; it looks like a bad one. I'll pick you up at ten for church and lunch. Thanks for inviting me to the barbecue; I don't get to partake in many fun and relaxing events. You have some nice friends."

"Thanks. You can come in for coffee, if you want."

"I best not do that tonight. The Blackwells have driven around the block twice to see how long I'm staying," he remarked with a grin.

"You did say Dianne is Janet's best friend, so I doubt she'll go home before I do."

"I'm sorry, Quentin; it's just that those two women are so nosy."

"You are a beautiful woman, and single."

"And you're a handsome man, and single, *and* a celebrity."

"We'll have more time and privacy tomorrow night and Monday. We can talk then. How about if you leave the garage door open for me?"

"A sly trick to fool our little spies?" she teased.

Quentin liked the way her green eyes sparkled with playfulness. "Yep. See you soon, Rachel. Sleep well."

"Good night, Quentin. I had a wonderful time."

Rachel watched him return to the rented car, wave, and start the motor. She noted with annoyance the Blackwells drive by again, then went upstairs and soaked in a bubble bath as she reflected on how Quentin had gazed at her before his departure, as if he wanted to yank her into his arms and cover her with kisses and caresses. His voice had been husky, and her receptive body had ignited with passion.

Soon, Quentin, because— right or wrong— I can't resist you much longer. Lordy, I don't want to resist you. Sharing a life with you sounds so wonderful. Is it possible to win you, Quentin Rawls, despite our differences? Do you truly want me and care about me, or am I only duping myself?

Rachel turned on the Jacuzzi. *Should I tell Karen*

and Evelyn about you when I write them tonight? No, not yet, not when there's nothing concrete to report. If things get serious between us, will they be upset with me if I marry a younger man? I'm their mother, so they probably don't think about me having such flaming desires. Oh, my, if you girls only knew the truth. I just can't allow my name to be blackened, and Janet and Dianne would certainly do their best to smear me if they caught you staying the night. Those witches are probably watching me like a hawk, ready to spread gossip the instant they suspect we're sleeping together.

Sleeping together. . . . Are you planning my seduction tomorrow? Is that why you want to hide your car from their sneaky eyes? Heaven forgive me, I surely hope so. I have to know if we're still magic in bed, my love, and if sex is the only thing you want from me this time.

At the Bradberry Suites, Quentin called his best friend Vance and then his parents. He mentioned Rachel during both conversations, and exposed his surprising reason for coming to Augusta. His mother was delighted by the hint of a new romance for her son, but Vance cautioned him to take it slow and easy, a course of action which Rachel made difficult and time made impossible.

As he snacked on a pizza and diet drink from room service, he reflected on talks that morning with his agent about his precarious career, with the businessman who had sent him there, and with his other two closest friends— Ryan and

Perry— who had filled him in on team rumors about cuts and trades on the Dallas Cowboys and other teams. But, he knew, if he didn't pass the physical, he wouldn't even make it to preseason games. If he did make it but didn't shine like a shooting star, he was out for good.

What, Quentin mused, would he do with himself and his time if he didn't play football, at least for one more year? The wild idea which had brought him to Augusta just didn't sound or feel right for him, even if it meant keeping him close to Rachel. On the other hand, her life was here and she might not want to leave it, even for him. He had changed over the years and carried a lot of heavy baggage from two failed marriages, so she would be wary about leaning in his direction too fast, if ever.

At ten, while he was in the steam shower to soothe his shoulder and knee, he missed Todd Hardy's call. He left a message he would call back later if he didn't hear from Quentin by eleven. Quentin told the hotel operator to tell the pesky reporter that was too late to talk tonight and he would see him tomorrow at the mall. Afterward, he instructed the operator not to put through any more calls unless the person asked for James Rawlings, and to change his name to that on their registry for his privacy. He made a mental note to tell Rachel about the change in case she tried to reach him.

At the thought of Rachel and James Rawlings, memories of their cruise filled his mind. He remembered how she felt in his arms and looked beneath her clothes. He knew how stimulating it was to make love to her in different places and different ways. He remembered how she had surrendered to him with such fiery need and total abandonment, how she took and gave and shared with him. They had talked about many things, except their personal lives and emotions. As if afraid to believe their own and each other's feelings were real and strong or to imagine a joint future was possible, they had concealed and denied them and had cast such a beautiful goal to the wind.

Afterward, believing it was nothing more than a wonderful shipboard romance, she had returned to her life in Augusta to rear her children alone. He had returned home to recapture his dream of a successful comeback, to heal his injuries, to become a bigger celebrity, and to enter two ill-fated marriages in search of what he had already found with Rachel Tims Gaines and didn't realize. Now, her life was settled; his was still in turmoil. Was it possible, he wondered, for them to make a new life together, for her to love him? Maybe all she wanted from him was friendship, nice evenings out, and a satisfying bed partner for a short time. Maybe she was holding back because she was afraid he would want more, or believed he couldn't fit into her lifestyle.

Quentin decided it was time to reveal to her and the local public why he had come to town, and it was time to see if she was receptive to him. If not, he should get his rear out of town pronto before he got hurt.

* * *

Quentin didn't make it to Rachel's house for the evening. After his appearance at the mall on Sunday afternoon, he was coaxed into going to a dinner for young sportsmen and saying a few words of encouragement to the boys. During the speeches and meal, he found himself missing her presence and smile, and had made a hasty phone call to arrange to see her the following afternoon. He was grateful she had agreed and was understanding about the change in plans. He had enjoyed himself at church and at lunch with her friends, the Coopers and Brimsfords; and Saturday's party had been very nice. His presence at all three places had created stirs and stares, but it was with Rachel that he yearned to be, and alone. Very soon, he promised himself. *But if you don't give me a little encouragement, I'm outta here, woman.*

Quentin arrived shortly after Rachel returned home following her Daughters of The American Revolution meeting and lunch with several members. She waved him forward into the garage, where he parked next to her BMW.

"Your car will stay cooler in here, out of the July sun," Rachel told him. She pressed the control button to close the garage doors, which concealed his presence from inquisitive neighbors. "That was perfect timing. If you haven't eaten, I can prepare you a sandwich and drink."

"I had lunch earlier, but thanks," he said, as he followed her inside to the kitchen where she set down her packages and a grocery sack.

"Tell me about your appearance yesterday. From the news coverage, it looked as if you were swamped the entire time."

"It was a success, thank goodness; and I managed to get rid of Todd Hardy without too much fuss. I promised him an interview to get him off my back, but I think he's afraid I'll skip town without honoring my word. I haven't sighted him lurking in the bushes, but I have a feeling he's keeping a sharp eye on me." *And on anybody I socialize with, the snake.*

"Did you enjoy yourself with the kids last night?"

"It was nice spending time with the boys and their coaches, but I missed you. We need to talk, Rachel. Now."

At his serious tone, her gaze met his and her heart began to beat faster. *Am I about to be dumped?* "Talk about what, Quentin?"

"About us, and the real reason I came to Augusta."

Nine

"Why don't we go sit in the living room so we can relax while we talk?"

"That's fine with me, Quentin. Do you want something to drink?"

His gaze met hers and he sensed her uneasiness, though Rachel attempted to quell and conceal it with a smile. "Just some juice or water."

Rachel poured two glasses of tropical fruit juice and handed one to him. Quentin followed her into the casual area of the living room and sat down beside her, placing his glass on a coaster on the coffee table. She tried not to stare at him or to tremble noticeably as she watched him and waited to learn his news.

He took a deep breath and began his revelations. "As you probably know, all professional sports have only so many players and teams in their leagues. In football, the NFL and AFL have twenty-eight teams and fourteen hundred and eighty-four players. Because those numbers are limited, a lot of talented college players don't get chosen to play professional ball; and a lot of veterans get dumped for younger men with lower salaries, or when they get injured and don't play as well as they used to. There's a group of wealthy investors who are interested in forming a new league, a semi-pro one, that would allow some of those college stars an opportunity to play and those aging mainstays— as we're called in the media— a chance to play longer. They're thinking of setting twenty to thirty new teams around the country, mainly in large towns where support for them would be good. Like it is with baseball, those boys could move up to pro ball if they have the talent. The new league would mean more games for people to attend and ticket costs would be lower due to reduced salaries and expenses. Plus, people wouldn't have to travel so far to see a game if they had a local team to enjoy."

Quentin paused to sip his juice, but Rachel remained quiet and alert to prevent distracting him. Too, she couldn't surmise where this line of thought was going and if it had anything to do with her, with them.

"Augusta was selected by one of those investors— Bill Effingham— because the Falcons are in Atlanta and your town seemed the next best choice for locating a second team. Its position is excellent for drawing spectators from two states, maybe three with Florida only a few hours away. The Master's Golf Tournament and those other national and international events you mentioned pull in large crowds, so he's hoping the same would be true for a semipro football team. I guess you could call me an advance scout for the project. Bill asked me if I thought it was a good idea and could be profitable; I believe it is. Since I had to almost shove my way onto the playing field, I know what it's like to want to play and to have a difficult time getting accepted. Before he proceeded with his plans, Bill asked me if I would come to Augusta to look it over and test the waters for interest and support. That's why I needed to learn so much about the CSRA. I suppose you wondered why I was so curious about this area."

At Rachel's nod, he grinned and continued, "If Bill's going to be able to lure players here, in particular those with families, it has to be a nice place to live and to find work during off-season. Naturally their salaries will be lower than those of pro ball players, and especially in the beginning when things are just getting started. Local and state governments will have to help finance a stadium and approve the idea, so their cooperation is vital to success. The public must be eager and willing to support a team with steady attendance. From your expert tours, there seems to be plenty of land available for a building site and plenty of people to hire as workers on the construction and for the games. I already know the Augusta Eagles team didn't make it years ago and funds were denied for building an ice rink to lure in semi-pro hockey, but it might be different for football, and with a new league to support a local team. I also know that your mayor is trying to find funds to enlarge and improve Heaton Stadium for the Augusta Green Jackets baseball team. It might be possible to make Heaton into a joint baseball and football stadium; that way, it could be used almost year round."

"Are you thinking of playing on that team if it becomes a reality?"

"No," he said without hesitation, "when I leave the Cowboys, I'm hanging up my cleats for good. But Bill did ask me if I was interested in coaching the team. He'll need a good recruiter to select players, and he also suggested I might want to invest in the project. I doubt they'll put another team in Texas; we already have pro teams in Dallas and in Houston, the Cowboys and the Oilers. Right now, I'm not in the mood to decide on investing, but I'm fairly certain I don't want to coach *any* team, new or old. To be honest, I don't want to be that close to football if I'm not playing. Also, the salary wouldn't be that good, especially in the beginning."

Quentin didn't mention at that time that he had just lost his one remaining endorsement. He knew if he was cut from the Cowboys, his big salary was gone, money he wanted to replace retirement dollars lost in two soured investments, money to finance a new career, money to provide aid to his parents if needed, and money to renovate his home for Rachel's possible occupancy. He was financially secure, but the year's salary would prevent him from having to draw those large expenditures from his savings and retirement fund. Lordy, he thought as he sipped more juice, how he craved one last season and a chance to go out in a blaze of glory;

he yearned to play during the seventy-fifth anniversary season; and he longed to be in a final Superbowl if the Cowboys threepeated. He hated going out this way, a has-been. There was no way he was moving to another team; even if one wanted him, he'd most likely have to take a huge cut in salary and spend most of his time on the bench. The media would have a field day over his demotion; no doubt the public would pity him. Yet, he didn't know what kind of job, career, would replace his lost earnings and would support a new family. Sportscasting was out, as it would keep him on the road too much. Perhaps ranching was the best avenue to pursue.

Quentin set down the empty glass. "I need to meet with the mayor and council to see if they're receptive to Bill's idea. Who knows, it might not interest them at all. After I do that, the project will become public knowledge. Until my scouting was finished, Bill wanted this kept a secret; that's why I couldn't tell you and why I was pretending to be on vacation."

"I know the mayor and his secretary, I can probably arrange a meeting with him for you this week."

"Thanks. Do you know anyone on the Augusta Sports Council?"

"I'm afraid not; at least, I don't think so. I can get a list of names from the mayor's secretary when I phone her."

"Their help could be what swings the deal here. I need to check on land prices with a real estate company so I can give Bill and his group a cost estimate for comparison with other cities. The agent can tell me what's available close to town; a large tract will be required for a stadium and parking. The ideal solution could be to tie in football to Heaton Stadium, if there's sufficient space, if the location is acceptable to the investors, and if the local government approves the project and funding. I'll check with the mayor and the Richmond County Board of Commissioners on their feelings, and Bill will have his man follow up. As to builders, a contract this size is put out for bids to large companies; that angle will be handled by the investors. I'm not responsible for hashing out this kind of business deal. I'm just the fact gatherer and water tester because Bill figured I could get better results at this preliminary stage than a fancy suit could."

"He was clever to send you. Who better than a beloved sports star to interest the right men in their project? Those appearances you made must have shown local politicians how popular you— and football— are, and pointed out how good it would be to have our own team."

"I hadn't thought of that angle. Since this isn't in my regular field of expertise, any suggestions or help will be greatly appreciated."

Rachel was delighted that he wanted her involved. "I'll do whatever I can to assist."

"Thanks, Rachel, and you've been a big help already. We'll talk more about this business later. Right now, I want to talk about us."

Her gaze fused with his. "What about us, Quentin?"

He slid closer to her on the sofa and placed one arm along its back, making contact with her shoulders. His fingers toyed with the brown hair at her nape. "Do you think there's a chance for us to become more than friends? I don't want to pressure you into a romantic relationship you don't want or give myself false hopes about a possible future with you. The bad thing is, with the season starting soon, our time together is limited."

I know. "There's something important I should tell you, Quentin." She saw his expression turn apprehensive at her grave tone. "I can't have any more children and I don't think I would want another child at my age if it were possible. I know you love children; I can't give you an heir, but a younger woman could."

Quentin considered her unexpected words for a long moment. "I did want children when I finally settled down, but having you in my life means more to me."

Rachel closed her fingers around his hand on his knee. "Don't say that before you have time to give it long and serious thought. That sacrifice may not seem important to you now, but later it might be, and that could cause problems for us. I had to have a hysterectomy in '78, so it isn't something that can be fixed if you change your mind. I wouldn't want you to regret this decision. You would make an excellent father, Quentin, and I'm sure your parents want grandchildren."

He interlocked their fingers and gave hers a

gentle squeeze. "They have grandchildren, Rachel."

"Not yours. If Frank doesn't have a son, there's no one to carry on the family name. I'm sure that will disappoint them." *And maybe you one day.*

He chuckled to ease her tension, and was touched by her concerns for him and his parents. "It isn't the end of the world not to have kids these days; plenty of couples choose not to have them. Besides, I'm thirty-eight; that's getting up there to rear rambunctious kids."

"That's another point, our age difference; I'm forty-seven, nine years older than you, only eleven years younger than your mother."

"That doesn't matter to me and shouldn't matter to you. If we're suited to each other, shouldn't we spend the rest of our lives together? It's only a number, Rachel, and nine years isn't that wide a span." He smiled and gave her hand a playful shake. "Besides, you don't look your age. And who would know about that difference if we didn't tell them?"

"I'm sure those tabloids would reveal it to the world."

"As soon as I retire, they won't be interested in me anymore."

"Perhaps," *but our friends and families will know the truth.* "And another thing. You said you don't intend to become involved with the Augusta team if it becomes a reality. Somehow I don't think you would want to settle here. You live halfway across the country, and you'll be gone soon. How can we get to know each other well enough in nine days to make such a serious decision about our futures? You can't remain here and I can't traipse around the country following you from town to town; that would certainly give tabloids and gossips something to talk about. I can't do that to my children or to myself, Quentin."

"I know you can't, Rachel. To be honest, I don't want to live in Augusta. It's a nice town and I like most of the people I've met, but there isn't any kind of career for me here. I'll probably wind up ranching. Are you set against Texas?"

Are you proposing this soon? I haven't known you long enough to accept. Are you turning my world upside down and my feelings inside out? "I have friends and family here. Karen will be returning next June."

He perceived her hesitation and careful reply. "If I recall, you said she might not settle in Augusta; and Evelyn lives in Ohio. If you moved to Dallas, you could visit your friends and family any time you want. Did you have your fill of simple country life while growing up?"

"No, I love the country, and I'm sure Dallas is a wonderful place," *especially with you there.*

"Are you afraid your girls won't accept me in your life, in theirs? Are you worried about my reputation with women and my past mistakes?"

"My daughters love me and would accept my decision, if I convinced them you're what I want and need to make me happy. Actually, I think Karen and Evelyn and Eddie and my grandchildren would like you. As to your playboy image and past marriages, they don't worry me. But what about your parents and friends? How would they react to you marrying an older woman, if our relationship went that far one day?"

Her words and expressions were encouraging to him. "They'll adore you, woman, I'm certain of it. Am I in your game plan or still benched?"

Rachel laughed. "This isn't the time for you to be creating new problems and decisions for yourself; you have a career to concentrate on. Even if you retire, you'll have a new one to consider and establish."

"I'll know where I stand after my physical, and after practice, then preseason games in August. Why don't we see how our relationship goes while I'm here? If we aren't certain about our feelings, we can test ourselves during our separation until September first; that's five weeks of loneliness and thinking. If I make the team, I'll be playing from September through mid-January, to the end of January if we make the Superbowl. By then, we'll know what we want to do. Right?"

Rachel remained quiet and thoughtful, so Quentin added, "That's too long to go without seeing each other, so you'll have to come visit me."

"How? I know games are usually played on holidays."

"You can come when I'm idle; that means, our weeks off."

"How will that look to people, especially if we

don't get married later? I don't want to sneak around as if we're doing something wrong, but I don't want to risk staining my reputation. In the South, that old double standard still exists for women. And I know what those tabloids write about couples who . . . live together."

"We'll be careful, Rachel, but we can't ignore and avoid each other if we want to be together. Besides, there will probably be talk no matter what we say or do; some people just have dirty minds and loose tongues."

Like Janet. "Intimacy can be dangerous these days, Quentin."

He smiled and caressed her rosy cheek, her meaning clear to him. "I've always used protection, Rachel. Don't you remember?"

Her flush deepened, but she smiled and nodded.

"I don't take risks with women and I've never slept with any of those groupies who hang around ball teams. I also have regular physical exams and blood tests; they're a team regulation."

"I've never been with anyone except Daniel and you, and I've never taken drugs, or had a blood transfusion since my hysterectomy in '78. I should be safe, but I'll have a blood test if you prefer."

Quentin took her hand. "Since a test isn't necessary for either of us, does that mean we can get closer today?" he asked.

Rachel smiled and said, "Yes." She wanted him, if only for a short while. Though they could spend the rest of their lives together, she was far from sure that would come to pass. She was not convinced at this point that he could— or should— give up having children or that she could move to Texas, so far from at least one of her daughters. Too, she would miss her friends and her comfortable life here, and she didn't know how he would view her writing career, something she wanted deeply, something that would fulfill her in other ways. Nor did she know how a change in his career would affect him and his personality. A hasty commitment based on emotions alone could be a painful mistake, one she must avoid. Even so, her yearning for him must be sated.

Quentin drew her into his embrace and she went willingly. Their mouths fused in a series of kisses that began softly and tentatively but swiftly became heady and urgent as their passions were ignited into scorching surrender.

"Rachel, Rachel," he murmured against her delicious lips. "I want you like crazy."

"I want you, too, Quentin," she responded, almost breathless with raging desire and exquisite pleasure. It was wonderful to be with him like this again.

Their tongues explored in reckless abandon and their hands stroked each other's bodies, savoring the contact. He nestled his cheek against her silky hair and inhaled her sweet fragrance, needing to catch his breath for a moment. He wanted to move slowly but wondered if his rampant ardor would permit it.

Quentin's blue gaze engulfed her lovely face as his fingers stroked its surface. "I knew you were special when we met years ago, but I thought you were out of my life forever. I'm so glad I found you again. It's as if there never was a long separation, as if the present is the only reality, and all the years in between don't exist. I don't want to lose you again, woman."

Rachel's fingers wandered into his ebony hair and were concealed amidst its wavy strands. She felt more alive than she had in years, in twelve years. She felt desirable, carefree, adventurous, daring. "I know what you mean; it's strange, but it's as if we've been apart for only a short while. I feel just as at ease with you now as I was back then. You're much too disarming and captivating, Mr. Rawls."

Quentin chuckled and beamed. "You're the one who's captivating. I never could get you out of my mind and, Lordy, I tried hard."

"I couldn't forget you, either; that's why no man I dated after you suited me; you were always like a cunning shadow between us. I would compare them to you, and they would come up short, too short. Would you be surprised if I told you I've been a closet football fan since I learned your identity?" He grinned. "I even rented and purchased tapes of old games just to watch you and to learn more about you. I'm glad you're back in my life, Quentin, because I've missed you terribly. You're a tough act to follow."

"So are you, woman. I discovered you're irreplaceable."

Rachel laughed merrily as Quentin lifted her in his arms and hugged her. "Put me down before you hurt yourself," she protested.

He nibbled at her neck. "I won't, because you're as light as a feather."

She looped her arms around his neck as he carried her up the stairs, down the hall, and into her bedroom.

Quentin placed her feet on the floor and gazed into her upturned face. One of his greatest victories was within his grasp and joy suffused him at this triumph. He unbuttoned her tailored ivory jacket, slipped it off her shoulders, and laid it on the nightstand. He removed his golf shirt and dropped it to the carpet. As he trailed his fingers up her sleek arms and cupped her jawline between his hands, he said in a husky tone, "You're so beautiful and tempting. I'm lucky no man has snared you. I don't know what I would have done if I'd found you married at the reunion."

"Or if *you'd* been married when we met again."

"Fate is shining on us; we were meant for each other, I'm sure. It just took us twelve long years to get our heads straight."

Rachel smiled as she replied, "It does appear that way, doesn't it?"

"Yep, it does." He pulled her slip straps over her arms and let the undergarment dangle over a pleated ebony skirt. As his adoring gaze drifted over her supple flesh, he unfastened her lacy beige bra and discarded it. Quentin embraced her again with their warm skin in stirring contact as his mouth seemingly devoured hers.

Rachel experienced a flood of heat and tingles as her breasts pressed against his fuzzy chest. Her mouth slanted across his with eagerness to taste him and to take the pleasures he offered with tender generosity. Her body felt so responsive. In a burst of golden happiness, her heart yearned for what was to come, for she remembered well the delights he had given to her. She felt the evidence of his own desire pressing against her and took pleasure from the rapid beating of his heart. She was glad he shared her arousal. She noted how his fingers quivered as they worked their way down her back with sensual teasings to unbutton her skirt. Afterward, it and the slip snaked to the floor around her ankles; she stepped out of them and kicked them aside. He eased his hands inside her pantyhose and panties and grasped her buttocks, kneading them with gentleness as his mouth lavished attention on hers. She trembled when he teethed her earlobe and his hot breath teased her ear. His lips roamed her neck and shoulders from side to side as his hands traveled up her rib cage, covered her breasts and massaged them. She pressed kisses to his forehead and sighed dreamily as his thumbs toyed with her taut nipples. She liked the feel of his muscles as they rippled from intoxicating motions. She liked the smell of his cologne and the taste of juice on his breath. She loved the way he touched her with such talent and gentleness and appreciation of her figure. Though the room was well lighted by filtered sunshine, no modesty troubled her, for she was too enflamed to be hindered from her quest.

Quentin's mouth sought hers and claimed it feverishly. Soon, their legs were too weak to stand longer. He knelt and removed her hose and panties, after sliding off her low heels. He kissed both knees before rising to discard his shoes, pants, and briefs.

As he did so, Rachel grabbed the floral spread and flung it off the bottom of the bed, along with the many throw pillows. She yanked down the top sheet and reclined, eager for him to join her. As he did so, her gaze took in his superb form. His body was a thing of sculpted beauty. She lifted her arms in invitation and he was embraced by them.

After several heady kisses, Quentin's lips, tongue, and one hand teased and stimulated her breasts, causing their peaks to stand tall and rigid as if enticing him to linger. His other hand drifted down her stomach ever so slowly and provocatively and into the core of her womanhood; there, his eager fingers played in satiny folds. He found it arousing to excite her beyond will and thought, to realize she wanted him as intensely as he wanted her. He felt her hands teasing over his chest and back, and savored her touch. He leaned back his head and gazed into her green eyes, so full of desire for him and— if he wasn't mistaken and prayed he wasn't— glowing with love. His fingers below became bolder as they prepared her for complete lovemaking, which would come only after she was writhing with unrestrained passion.

Rachel pressed kisses to his nose, cheeks, and chin. She could hardly wait for him to enter her. She looked into his hungry blue gaze before he lowered his head to enthrall her breasts once more.

Rachel grasped his manhood and caressed it, bringing forth groans of pleasure from him. His body was strong and firm, sleek and appealing. He was in excellent physical condition and was almost sinfully handsome. His fingers were long and deft and drove her wild. She drifted her hands over his back, shoulders, arms, and sides.

"You're testing my self-control something fierce, woman."

"Mine was lost the moment you touched me. My body is like an oven."

Sensing she was ready to receive him, Quentin rolled to his side, retrieved a condom from the nightstand, and donned it. At first, he permitted only the head of his engorged organ to enter her, as the contact was almost staggering to his whirling senses. After sucking in a breath of barely calming air, he slowly sank deeper into her moist heat. It was as if electrical currents were racing within his body. Every fiber of his being— emotional and physical— craved her.

Rachel eagerly welcomed him inside her. She felt his every motion with heightened sensitivity and thrilled at the sensations he aroused as he thrust and retreated countless times, something within her loins began to wind and coil tighter than a mainspring.

Quentin could barely maintain his control as Rachel entreated him with caresses and movements. The fire within him blazed higher and hotter and his very essence begged to be unleashed. His muscles rippled and his hips labored as he drove onward in his quest to sate them.

Heat and tension mounted in Rachel's body with every passing second. His hands fondled and caressed her as she did the same to him. She returned each kiss with fervent ardor.

When the climactic moment arrived, which he sensed from her coaxing responses, he kissed her deeply and sought glorious fulfillment.

On the brink of release, Rachel gasped in delight and arched her back. Then, it happened. Her heart sang with happiness as she was swept away in the throes of rapture.

After her release began, he hastened his movements, raising and lowering himself upon her, and allowed himself to surrender as well as sheer ecstasy consumed him. Jolt after jolt of pleasure shot through him as his hard length throbbed and contracted in her loving receptacle.

They kissed and embraced tenderly, their hearts pounding as they gazed into each other's eyes and smiled. Each perceived how special and fulfilling their lovemaking had been and how attuned they were to each other.

He kissed her, caressed her cheek, and cradled her in his arms. He had enjoyed sex with other women, but never with the total satisfaction he received from this one. Yep, he decided serenely, they were as well matched as a pair of his handmade boots. He said, "Wonderful, Rachel. You're the best thing that's happened to me in and out of bed."

She smiled, nestled against his chest, and agreed. "I feel the same way." She was aglow with love, happiness, and contentment. "Your individual stats in today's game are excellent: completions for all attempts, no fumbles, and no penalties; a Superbowl performance, Quentin Rawls."

He chuckled at her comparison to his cherished sport. "I'd say this game was a tie, and a high scoring one, wouldn't you?"

Rachel's fingers drifted over his torso as she replied, "Absolutely, and I'm your biggest and best fan."

"My only fan, Rachel; that I promise you." *I love you, woman, but I'm afraid it's too soon to make that confession; it could scare you off or make you feel pressured to respond in like kind before you're ready. Surely that intelligent mind of yours can guess my feelings for you. I believe you love me, too, and I can hardly wait to hear those words escape your lips.*

The doorbell chimed several times, then a persistent knocking on the solid oak surface. Rachel tensed. Did someone know he was here? A neighbor? A friend? A stalking reporter?

Quentin lifted his head. "Are you expecting anyone?"

As the bell continued to chime and the knocking increased in volume and rapidity, Rachel fumed over the intrusion that spoiled the relaxing aftermath. "No, but somebody is determined I answer the door."

Quentin rolled to his side and looked at her. "Are you going to?"

"Dressed like this?" she jested to relieve her tension as her gaze motioned to her nakedness. *And perfumed with passion's unmistakable scent?* "I'll look through the peephole to make sure it isn't an emergency. I'll be back in a minute. Stay here; remain quiet and think about me."

Without donning a robe, Rachel left the room, almost tiptoeing so her footsteps couldn't be heard outside. She peered through the revealing device, then observed her brazen visitor's actions in anger and amazement.

Concealed by drapes and soft shades over windows covered by reflective sunshields, Rachel knew she could not be seen. Peeking around the edge of the breakfast-room arch, she watched Janet Hollis walk to the Florida room, wade through shrubs, and attempt to see inside the house! She observed as the nosy woman even leaned an ear close to the window. Since the only gate to the backyard was locked, the nervy woman could not get inside the area to pry, though she made that effort, and also tried to see into the garage, only to be thwarted by the window shades. Rachel hurried to the casual section of the living room, eased the shade aside only a smidgen, and saw Janet depart. Rachel lingered until she was certain the bold creature was gone, then rejoined Quentin who had tossed the top sheet over his hips and legs.

She slipped into a satin robe, the fury was clear in her voice as she disclosed her findings. "Would you believe that was Janet Hollis, Quentin, and that she snooped around outside. How dare she spy on me! I know that's what she was doing." She related all of the woman's actions to him as he stared at her in astonishment.

"You think she saw me arrive and park in the garage?"

"I don't know and I don't care, the little witch. She dislikes me and considers me an outsider, so she's dying to ruin me."

"I'm sorry if I've done anything to cause you embarrassment."

Rachel halted her movements, and smiled at him. "You haven't. This was the best afternoon I've spent in ages. Why don't we shower, dress, and go out to eat? It's dinnertime."

"That suits me."

"You take the shower and I'll take the tub; then we can be ready quickly."

"In case she returns?"

"No, because I'm starving— for food this time, Mexican food and perhaps a margarita. Maybe two," she joked with a grin.

"Let's get moving then, woman. I'm hungry, too."

The phone rang just then and Rachel glanced toward the white one on the bedside table. "I'm not answering it; I bet it's that sneaky Janet. On second thought, it could be one of my daughters or a friend. You jump in the shower while I go into the office and listen to the answering machine."

"Screening your calls, eh?"

"Today, yes." She hurried into the room down the hall as the machine clicked on.

"Rachel, this is Janet. I just came over to discuss a matter with you, but I suppose you were too busy to come to the door or to answer the phone. Have a nice time, and I'll talk to you about it later."

The moment Janet hung up and the machine clicked off, Rachel erased the annoying words and innuendo. She wondered if her neighbor was speculating about her lover's presence and their actions or knew the truth, had been spying and was certain she was home with the football hero. Janet was surely going to be a thorn in her side about Quentin in any case.

And what, she fretted, about that pesky reporter? Was Todd Hardy also lurking in the shadows and scribbling nasty notes about them to put into print for all to read? What damage could he and Janet do to her budding relationship with Quentin? Would wild rumors spread and stain her reputation? Would be she ostracized by her social circle? How could she live in a town and travel in a group that viewed her as trash, as they did poor Carrie Simmons? She asked herself if she was risking too much, everything, anything, for love?

Don't think about that complication tonight, just enjoy your time with Quentin. I'm going to take a chance with you, my darling, but we have to be careful and alert.

Ten

On Tuesday, Rachel hung up the receiver after phoning Janet. She was even more annoyed with the woman after Janet told her she could not remember what she wanted to discuss. Rachel was convinced now that Janet was being snoopy and intrusive. She told herself she was not going to allow Janet to aggravate her or to cause problems, but that was easier said than done. To work off her tension, Rachel exercised on the treadmill, then showered before sitting down to work on the celebrity auction to raise funds for the library extension.

Several times during that task, she halted to make notes on future chapters of her novel in progress, or to think about Quentin.

At six, Quentin arrived and parked his rental car in the garage.

Rachel smiled and caressed his cheek. "You look tired," she observed.

"I'm beat; that isn't my normal kind of work. Thanks for getting me in to see the mayor on such short notice; I liked him. He had a few of the councilmen with him. They appeared interested in the project, particularly liked the idea

244 *Janelle Taylor*

of possibly combining baseball and football at Heaton Stadium. They're going to talk it over and get back to me in a few days."

"That's great news, isn't it?"

"For Bill and his group of investors, if they decide on Augusta. What has me peeved is that Todd Hardy. He was hanging around outside the mayor's office today. I'd bet my Superbowl ring he's following me. In fact, he rode behind me for a long way after I left the building. I had to do some clever driving to lose him, but I finally did. That should tell him I'm on to him and, if he doesn't back off, he won't get that interview from me."

"Why don't you relax in the Jacuzzi with a glass of wine and some soft music?"

Quentin warmed to that provocative offer. He pulled her into his arms, kissed her, and murmured, "If you'll join me."

Rachel grinned and said, "Sounds like what I need to relax me. You pour the wine and bring it up while I get the Jacuzzi going."

Rachel handed him two plastic glasses from a past pool party. "There are several kinds of wine in the refrigerator, but I'll take the blush. Here's the corkscrew and two stoppers." She left him to do his task while she attended to hers.

As the Jacuzzi filled with water laced with Oriental-scented bubble bath, she took candles from a drawer, placed them around the large tub, and lit them. She laid out thick towels and washcloths, then turned on the CD player in the entertainment unit in the bedroom, already loaded with disks and the selector set on random picks of romantic songs. She didn't care if she was being wanton; she desired him wildly, and she remembered sharing another sensuous time long ago in a ship shower. Her body glowed and her spirit soared at the thought of being with him again. She could not imagine ever feeling reluctant to hop into bed with him when she knew the blazing and unrestrained lovemaking that was in store for her. She adored him. She felt so alive and carefree in his presence and arms, whether they were in bed or not. He made her feel desired, special, important. There was no denying they were well suited. There was no denying she loved him and wanted to marry him. She prayed that everything would work out for him in his career or in a new one; she prayed her children and friends would accept him in her life; she prayed outsiders would not intrude and spoil their chance for happiness. *Please be the man I think you are and be sincere with your feelings and words.*

Quentin joined her as she undressed and stepped into the water. He set down the wine-filled glasses, glanced around at the seductive setting, and smiled. He stripped and entered the tub, facing her and stretching out beside her, the lengths of their bodies touching. "Yep, just what I need," he said, as the silky fluid flowed around them.

Rachel pressed the control button and the Jaccuzzi began to swirl the water, coaxing more bubbles to life with its movements. She lifted her glass and sipped wine as her gaze roamed his handsome face and muscular torso. Locks of ebony hair toppled over his forehead and almost grazed his thick brows. When he grinned, creases halted just before making dimples in his cheeks, and his blue eyes seemed to sparkle with affection and delight. His angular jawline was beginning to reveal a slight five-o'clock shadow which made him look sexy and rugged. She noted the cords in his neck and the hollows near his collarbone. Her gaze drifted over the rises of his pectorals and the flat tautness of his abdomen. The arms which he rested along the tub's edge in separate directions were powerful—one, a legendary "golden" talent. She knew the heat on her flesh was from the encompassing water, but the flames within her were from rampant desire for the man nearby.

Over the sound of the Jacuzzi, they chatted about his meeting and her afternoon work while they allowed themselves to relax and the water's movement to quell their troubled moods. He offered to give her an autographed football to use in the auction; she was grateful and made a mental note to add it to her list. Her hand massaged his right calf and foot as his did the same to hers at the other end of the tub. A layer of fluffy white suds concealed her breasts, but her bare shoulders aroused him with the promise of her complete nakedness. When the tub was filled to the right level, Rachel pushed the brass handles to halt the flow.

The room darkened a little as sunset neared

on the far end of the house, but candlelight created a stirring atmosphere as it danced in a gentle breeze created by the overhead fan on low speed. The music was soft and romantic. The fragrance of exotic flowers reminded both of the tropical adventure they had shared. Wine and enslaving passion coursed through their veins. Yet, all they did for a time was gaze at each other and give little caresses, as if basking in the glorious wonder of being reunited again. They waited in mounting suspense until desires intoxicated them and incited steamy actions.

Quentin shifted his position to slip a foot between her thighs. With gentleness and caution, he used it to caress the triangle of hair at her groin. Soon, its smooth edge began to rub against silken pleats and the tiny nub that guarded the center of her need. As if of their own volition, the delicate folds parted to give him easier access to the throbbing peak. His toe accepted the invitation to rove that pinnacle of smoldering allure. He knew from the flush on her cheeks and upper chest and dreamy glaze in her green eyes that she was enjoying his titillation, and so was he.

Rachel lapped a smooth leg over his hairy one and sent her foot on an exploratory mission to seek out his concealed treasures. Her probing toes made careful contact with the softened hair around his manhood. The bottom of her foot teased back and forth over the responsive organ that rapidly rose to the occasion as his grin broadened. Her mischievous toes playfully toyed with the sack beneath it. The dreamy smile on his face told her those actions were appreciated; the swelling of his organ told her they were enticing. A mixture of feelings consumed her when he halted his stirring caresses to come closer to knead her breasts and to suckle their points to hardness.

Quentin's lips traveled up her neck and spread kisses over her face and ears before he fastened his starving mouth to hers. His tongue delved the tasty recess and delighted in her eager response. After many kisses he grasped her slippery body and lifted her to sit on the edge of the tub. His hands drifted down her rib cage and past her hips in deliberate leisure to stroke the inner surface of her bubble-splattered thighs. He rinsed the ivory suds from her womanhood, then made a trail of kisses from her knee to her groin.

Rachel leaned her head back and closed her eyes, absorbing the blissful sensations. His tongue and lips sent electrical shocks through her body as they worked their swift and rapturous magic. She quivered with anticipation when his fingers joined his task to give her immense pleasure. The tension built as her senses whirled faster than the agitated water. She moaned and writhed as she gave him free rein over her body and will. Soon, she could endure denial no longer and climaxed in a rush of splendor. Weak and shaky, she slid back into the water and embraced him, kissing and nibbling on his shoulder and neck as he fondled her breasts.

Rachel urged him backward and upward to
the ledge and knelt between his legs, which she
parted with her body. Her palms moved back
and forth along the hairy terrain of his thighs.
Her fingers tantalized, then firmly grasped his
slick erection. They massaged the full length of
the turgid member as he groaned with satisfaction and from heightened desire. Candlelight
flickered on the beads of water which trickled
down their bodies; the fan attempted in vain to
cool their sweltering heat. Her fingers circled
the sensitive tip countless times and felt its
smooth wet surface. Her hand encased the shaft
and fondled its interior to a rock-hard state with
a satiny exterior. Her head and mouth followed
that same erotic path, as she flicked her tongue
over the head, then closed her lips over it. She
teased him with her tongue and fingers until he
quivered and the arms bracing him on the tiled
shelf trembled.

"You're driving me crazy, woman; Lordy, that
feels better than good."

"Isn't turnabout fair play in your rule book,
Mr. Rawls?" she jested.

Quentin chuckled and said, "Yep, but this
game is coming to an end fast." He grasped her
by the shoulders and changed their positions
while he still had a little self-control left. Rachel
turned and bent forward, hands propped on the
tub edge and legs parted. He slipped his manhood within her and began to thrust rhythmically
after taking a deep breath. As he did so, his hands
closed around her breasts and massaged them,

stimulating the buds between his thumb and fore-finger on occasion. Soon, Quentin sent one hand to stroke the sensitive button at the core of her loins. He worked upon it until she was squirming again in rising hunger.

Rachel could hardly believe she was about to experience ecstasy for a second time in such a short while. Her heart pounded; her breathing was swift and ragged; her body was afire with the new flames he had ignited and was fanning with skill and speed. His loins ground and undulated against hers, her buttocks rubbing against his lower abdomen, as she coaxed him not to stop.

"Oh, Quentin, this is wonderful. Heavens, it feels so good."

"Lordy, I enjoy making love to you, woman. Show me no mercy."

"I won't. Now," Rachel told him when she felt her release starting, a different kind from the first one, but just as wonderful and staggering.

"Come with me, love," he murmured as he pressed kisses to her wet back and plunged repeatedly into her moist depths until both were sated and their legs were quivering in splendid weakness.

When the gripping aftershocks faded, they sank into the cooling water and cuddled for a few minutes. Their gazes fused and they exchanged smiles of contentment and love for each other.

Quentin propped his head on the tub and sighed, "Whew! You get to me, Rachel Gaines. We're well matched in every area."

"You certainly know how to whet a woman's appetite and feed it."

"I'd be more than happy and willing to nourish you every day."

"Maybe that can be arranged after you finish this season."

Quentin looked at her and said, "I hope so, Rachel, I hope so."

He looked and sounded so earnest that she could not doubt his claims or feelings, which matched her own. *Let nothing and no one come between us, my beloved, for I must have you in my life until death.*

As they bathed, she realized they had not used a condom, had not even thought about one in their urgent quest for each other.

The same realization struck Quentin and he apologized for his lapse. "I put one on the nightstand because I thought we'd bathe then head for the bed later. You got me so dazed and hot I couldn't think clearly."

"Nor could I. Since we're both certain we're no risk to each other, I'm sure it's safe."

"I swear I told you the truth about my past experiences and tests. There's no doubt it's better this way. Without the condom, the sensitivity and pleasure are greater. But I won't forget again if you prefer to use one."

"I don't think it's necessary since I can't . . . get pregnant." There, she had reminded him she could not give him a child. If that fact mattered to him, it did not show in his expression.

Quentin reached out his hand and caressed

her cheek. "We can have a good life together without kids, so don't worry about that. We can go and do whatever we please without a baby to control our schedule. I know from watching and listening to my friends and sister, children are a huge responsibility and it never ceases once they're born. It would be hard on us to start a family at this point in our lives. That's the truth, Rachel."

"Thanks, Quentin, and I agree with you. Now let's finish our bath and go downstairs to prepare something to eat."

"Seems as if I've worked up an appetite, so that sounds good to me," he jested as he lathered his body and she did the same.

Afterward, Rachel rinsed the tub and straightened the bathroom. She handed Quentin the empty glasses to take downstairs with him while she put away the candles, turned off the music system, and gathered the used linens into a pile. She pulled on shorts, a T-shirt, and sandals, then brushed her hair, touched up her makeup, and sprayed on fresh perfume. She was glad she had refurnished and redecorated the master suite after Daniel's death to prevent any ghostly reminders of her days and nights there with him. She had not removed everything that reflected his presence, though, and felt there was no need to do so for their daughters' sakes. Yet, she was convinced now that Daniel Gaines was part of her past. She knew in her heart it would not appear traitorous to Karen and Evelyn to replace their lost father with a new love. In fact, the girls often encouraged her to find someone and remarry. When she next wrote to them, she would mention Quentin Rawls. She lifted the towels and washcloths and went to join the man who ruled her heart.

After eating roasted chicken, a garden salad, hot rolls, and leftover green beans, they watched television for a while and chatted until eleven when Quentin kissed her several times and left for his hotel.

Wednesday, the housekeeper cleaned and hummed while Rachel chatted on the phone with Becky and Jen, who were excited and pleased about the steady progress of their friend's romance. Though Rachel was forthcoming about the many things she and Quentin had shared, certain intimate details she kept to herself.

Before dressing for her meeting with the library committee about the auction to be held on September third, Rachel checked with Martha to see if the woman needed anything. Martha had worked for her for twenty years, and they often talked about their families and problems; neither would ever breach the other's confidence. "Do you think I'm being foolish to date a younger man and risk gossip?" Rachel was eager to hear the older woman's opinion.

"You should follow your heart, Mrs. Gaines, and not listen to those old busybodies." Martha's words came from her heart. "They woulda had you married off to some doctor or lawyer or banker by now if they could run your business like they want, 'specially that Mrs. Hollis. She's a bitter pill if I ever saw one. Lordy me, some of them high society ladies are so snooty and finicky I couldn't even work for them for more than a week." Martha laid a hand on Rachel's arm and patted it. "Don't you go letting nothing they say or do change your mind if Mr. Rawls is the one who makes you happy. We both know good men are few and far between. If you love him, you take a chance with him. I'd be willing to say the Good Lord sent him into your life. Since he's been here, you been smiling and singing more than I seen you do in years. That twinkle in your eye and that glow on your cheeks, they tells me all I need to know about you doing the right thing for yourself."

"Thanks, Martha, that's what I needed to hear." She gave the woman a hug before going to dress for her one o'clock appointment.

Rachel wished her meeting had taken longer or she had run errands afterward so she would have missed the vexing call she received shortly after returning home. Hoping it was Quentin, she answered with a smile and a cheerful "Hello."

"Rachel, this is Dorothy."

Her smile vanished and she went on alert, as her mother-in-law wouldn't phone without a

motive she was certain to find irritating. "Hello,
Mrs. Gaines. How is everyone?"

"Fine." Then she minced no words and got
straight to the point. "Janet Hollis called this
morning to check on us and she mentioned
you're dating a young football player who's visiting town. Richard and I were wondering if this
matter is serious."

"I beg your pardon?" Rachel murmured, deciding to play ignorant of the woman's meaning.

"Janet said you two are seeing each other
steadily; she said you even took him to church
with you last Sunday. Is that true?"

Rachel knew, when someone took a date to
church in the South, it was viewed in the same
light as being introduced to one's parents. "Yes,
we attended church together; he's a Baptist."

"I see. Richard and I were wondering if
this . . . relationship is serious and there's a . . .
strong chance you'll be moving away from
Augusta. If so, we wanted to know if you're interested in selling Daniel's stock in *our* candy
company back to us. We certainly don't want our
son's holdings falling into the hands of . . . an
outsider, especially one who came to town with
that Simmons . . . girl. I must say, I'm surprised
at you, Rachel, for spending time with a man
like that. But if he's your . . . choice to replace
Daniel, that's your affair. We just don't want it
to give us problems with our business. I'm sure
you grasp my meaning."

Rachel caught the words Dorothy stressed after short pauses and her meaningful intona-

tions. "If you're referring to Quentin Rawls, Mrs. Gaines, yes, I have been seeing him. After the ARC class reunion, he asked me to show him around Augusta, and I agreed. We Southerners are known for our hospitality and good manners. We've become close friends, but our relationship has not progressed to the point you implied. Quentin is an enjoyable and interesting man, but he'll be leaving town soon. As to my stock," *not Daniel's, you hateful witch,* "I haven't given any thought to selling it. I'm sure you know that it's doing extremely well right now and I have no doubts it will continue to do so with the skilled way your husband and son-in-laws are running the company. It's my firm belief that Daniel would want his shares to go to his children and grandchildren to give them financial security, so I plan to hold on to them for that purpose. I will ask the girls to give you first option to purchase their shares if they ever decide to sell them."

"I see. Well, we do appreciate you selling that land and some of those rental properties back to us in March. We would have hated to have a stranger owning property in the midst of our holdings."

"It seemed the right thing to do and you paid fair market prices. As I told you, I needed the cash to help the children with their trips and now I plan to help Karen set up her medical practice when she returns home."

"That's nice. Well, if you have a change of

heart, I do hope you'll phone us. Good-bye, Rachel."

"Good-bye, Mrs. Gaines. Say hello to Richard and the others for me."

After the call was terminated, Rachel muttered, "You didn't even ask how I was doing or anything about the girls. You're so selfish and spiteful and nosy."

Martha asked from behind her, "Is there a problem, Mrs. Gaines?"

Rachel related details of the call from her mother-in-law. "She's never going to accept me, Martha, or forgive me for marrying her only son. She still behaves as if I'm to blame for his death and for not bearing a grandson to replace him. She can be so cruel and cold."

"Don't you go letting her upset you. One day the Lord will deal with her and the rest of her kind. You just do what makes you happy."

"Quentin makes me happy," she confessed. "I just hope things work out for us, but I can't imagine moving to Texas with him and leaving my children, friends, and you behind."

"Don't you worry none about us; we'll be fine. So will you, Mrs. Rachel," the genial housekeeper added, as if changing her name for her.

"You're one of the kindest people I know, Martha. I love you and appreciate everything you've done for me over the years."

"I love you, too, Mrs. Rachel. Now, you hustle yourself upstairs and take a long bath to relax you before Mr. Rawls comes calling tonight. I'll make you a nice cup of hot tea to soothe them nerves and bring it up soon."

"Thanks, Martha; you're wonderful."

Rachel greeted Quentin with a stimulating embrace and long, sensuous kiss.

As he held her in his arms and nuzzled her neck, he murmured, "I like this kind of welcome; I could get used to it as a daily occurrence fast."

Rachel decided not to spoil their evening by relating her talk with Dorothy Gaines; later she would explain matters, but not tonight. "So could I, Quentin; I love seeing you every day."

He thought it best not to pressure her about a commitment at the moment, so he forced his words to skirt the topic. "Carrie phoned today. She's getting married next Sunday. I told her we're seeing each other and having a wonderful time."

"I'm happy for her. It seems as if her trip here was successful. Right?"

As his blue gaze adored her and his fingers stroked her cheek, he said, "It was, but I didn't ask any personal questions."

"How did she know you were still in town?"

"She called my agent, told him who she was and that she needed to reach me, so Derek gave her my number."

"Was she surprised to learn about us?"

He grinned and shook his head. "Not really, not after the interest I showed in you at the reunion and how many questions I asked about you afterward."

"Did you confess we'd met long ago?"

"I saw no reason not to since you told others about it. Was that okay?"

Rachel's fingers toyed with his shirt collar but her gaze stayed locked with his. "That's fine; in fact, it's best that we're old friends."

"How so?"

"That explains to others how we got so close so fast this time."

"Are other people asking questions about us?"

"They will soon. We are practically insepara-ble."

"I hope we'll become totally inseparable by the end of January, but we'll discuss that later, and before I leave town."

Rachel hugged him as her response. "I have a roast and vegetables in the crockpot. How about if we eat early tonight?"

"Suits me; I ate an early lunch, so I'm ready. What can I do to help?"

They prepared dinner together as they talked, laughed, and teased each other with stolen touches and smoldering gazes. After they ate and cleaned up the kitchen, they went outside for a stroll in the backyard. The moon was al-most full and spread golden light around the landscaped area where flowers bloomed and gave off heady scents, as did freshly mowed grass. They walked to the gazebo and sat down on its bench. Light, natural and artificial, filtered through the designs in the latticework and played across their faces and bodies; it also reflected off the pool's surface. Water trickled in the fountain nearby, creating lovely and tranquilizing sounds. A gentle breeze wafted over them, the July night cooler than normal. Even the familiar heavy humidity was lower tonight and made the air less oppressive. It was as if they were in a secluded haven.

Within minutes, they were kissing and caressing each other. It did not take long for desires to mount.

Quentin pulled her onto his lap at the end of the center bench, her legs dangling over his. He lifted her T-shirt and unfastened the front catch of her bra so he could feast on her breasts. Rachel bent her head backward to allow him plenty of room for his stirring action; as she did so, her fingers danced merrily through his ebony locks. Her nipples thrilled to the flicks from his tongue and the pressure of his hot mouth. "I want you here and now, Quentin," she whispered in yearning.

"I want you, too, Rachel, and I need you." He stood, placing her feet on the floor for a minute, and lowered his trousers as she removed her shorts and panties in a hurry. He guided them to the wall, lifted her against a beam between two sections of latticework, and thrust himself within her. He was delighted that she was so aroused and eager she was moist and ready for him. His large hands gripped her buttocks and his strong arms held her in place for slow and shallow strokes, then swift and deep ones. At times, he just held her and rotated his hips.

Rachel's back was protected from scratches by her shirt and the finished surface of the wood. But even if she were being pricked by splinters, she wouldn't have cared. His lips drove her wild as they journeyed from one breast to the other, gently teething, licking, and sucking their taut points. Rachel kissed the top of his head and lavished attention on his earlobe, causing him to moan with rising need. When the core of her being burst into roaring flames and tingled, she murmured, "Now, Quentin, my love, now. Take me. Take me."

Quentin rode her with delight as her hands clutched his shoulders and she writhed upon his turgid manhood. He dashed aside his control and followed her lead with haste. When his ecstasy was spent, he lowered her feet to the floor but continued to hold her in his tender and possessive embrace, covering her face and lips with many kisses. He cupped her chin and gazed into her eyes. "I love you, Rachel Gaines, and I need you to be a permanent part of my life."

Her fingers trailed over his damp features as she replied, "I love you, too, Quentin, and I can't imagine being without you. Just give yourself time to get your life straightened out, then ask me to marry you. By then, it won't seem to everyone as if we're moving too fast and impulsively. It's not that I want to fool others, I just don't want gossip to interfere with our relationship."

"I know you care what people think and say about you, about us. I understand and agree. Lord knows I've been plagued more than enough by bad press and hateful talk to want to avoid it."

She hugged him and thanked him for his reaction. "Let's go take a shower, then enjoy a decadent dessert while we talk or watch TV."

Her words sounded to him like a family evening at home; he wanted countless more in the future. With all his heart and mind and soul, he knew she was the right woman for him, and Rachel had to realize by now they were meant for each other. He would not stop trying to win her until she was his wife. Whatever it took, he was willing and determined to make certain nothing and no one came between them.

Before their arts council meeting, Rachel had lunch with Becky and Jennifer. Amidst their shocked expressions and words, she revealed Janet's visit and call to her on Monday, and subsequent call to Dorothy Gaines.

"This is absolutely incredible, Rach. It's too much, even for Janet. What on earth possessed her to spy on you and to phone Mrs. Gaines?"

"The woman dislikes me and wants to hurt me, pure and simple. I bet she's already spreading vicious and nasty rumors about me."

"She hasn't said anything to me or asked me any questions. What about you, Jen?"

"Me, neither, and she better not."

"She will, just wait and see. She wants to cause me trouble over that supposed slight against her brother and for refusing to chair that committee. She must be miserable and she wants to make others miserable. Well, she had better not fool with me on this matter; I won't take it."

"That's the spirit, Rach, and I'll help you defeat her on this one."

"You can count on me, too, Rachel," Jen echoed. "Friends stick together."

"Thanks, I may need your support if she's out for my blood. Maybe I should have answered the door, but I just wasn't in the mood to banter with her. And, yes, Quentin was there, and I had to explain my behavior to him. Of course, he'd already had a foul taste of her at the restaurant last week. At least he has met her kind before; he understood and agreed with what I did."

"How are things going with Quentin?" Becky asked, grinning.

Rachel warmed all over as she sighed and said, "Wonderful."

"That's it?" Becky teased as she fluffed her short blond hair.

"I could use every descriptive word in the dictionary but I doubt they would explain how I feel and how marvelous he is."

"You love him, don't you?"

Rachel gave Becky a radiant smile. "Totally, helplessly, endlessly."

"Wow, I got three words out of you that time," Becky jested. "Do I hear wedding bells ringing in the near future?"

"Probably, if we can work everything out between us."

"Has he asked?" Jen questioned, delighted for her friend.

"Yes, but I'm not to give an answer until later. He doesn't want to pressure me for a commitment this soon. And please, both of you, don't tell anyone until we're ready to announce it."

Becky made a playful *X* across her heart. "You can trust us to keep mum, even to Scott and Adam; we promise. Just tell us as soon as you've accepted, no matter what time of day or night it is."

"You'll know right after Quentin does."

"How do you think the Gaineses will take the news?" Becky asked.

"From what Dorothy said on the phone, she sounds happy about getting rid of me. She never accepted me as Daniel's wife. She thought he should have married one of her friends' daughters, a local. She was most displeased when I inherited part of the family's holdings. She'd like nothing better than to retrieve them."

"They belong to your children and grandchildren, so don't give in to her demands," Jen said adamantly. "It's no secret Dorothy Gaines can be cold and manipulative. I remember when she kept several newcomers to the area out of the women's club because she considered them out-siders and social climbers. She said they didn't know or understand southern ways and tradi-tions, but that was only a crock to exclude them. Unfortunately, she had enough power and influ-ence to get her way with the other members. She can be a real snob. I caught hints of strain between you two over the years, but I didn't want to mention it and hurt you."

"I tried my best to get along with her, but she held me at arm's length. Frankly, I'm glad they moved to Charleston so I don't have to be around them much. Let's change the subject be-fore we lose our appetites."

"Suits us, right, Jen?"

"Right. What do you think about this new art-ist we're helping?"

The conversation drifted to their imminent meeting, talk about their children, the church bake sale for the homeless shelter next weekend, and their dinner plans for Saturday night.

After returning home, Rachel wrote long let-ters to her daughters and included special notes for her grandchildren. She revealed she was see-ing Quentin Rawls, told when and where they had met both times, and related a little personal information about him. She was eager to speak with the girls to get their reactions and would do so as they were scheduled to phone soon. Even if the air-mail letters reached them after-ward, they would realize she had not waited too long to reveal the news to them. She was sure they would be happy for her, and hoped they would like Quentin. Perhaps she should not marry him before they both returned next spring and had a chance to meet him. Her marriage to Daniel before meeting his family had caused trouble for her, and she didn't want to cause any resentment toward her new husband, the girls' stepfather. But time passed so fast at her age and she wanted to spend every minute possible with him. Too, until they were married, they would be risking a scandal with an affair that was certain to be noticed, perhaps by the wrong person.

Quentin picked her up and they drove to his hotel suite to drop off papers from his meeting with the real estate agent about suggested land locations and estimates. While there, they made deliciously slow and passionate love, then they showered, dressed, and went out to dinner.

As they did so, neither caught sight of Todd Hardy as he spied on them; this time, taking sly precautions to remain hidden from view as he made copious notes and snapped picture after picture.

Eleven

On Friday morning, Rachel exercised and ran errands, one of them to the grocery store to purchase items for a cookout that night with Quentin. Another was to the post office to send letters to her family, paying extra for express mail so they would get them faster.

She had told Quentin to bring along his trunks, and after their food settled, they decided to take a swim.

They sat on a long, submerged bench in the shallow end of the water, sitting close and touching while they chatted about his recent appointments, football and the impending season, his family and friends, her children and grandchildren, and her many charitable activities.

Rachel decided it was time to relate her problems with her in-laws, and did so, but kept the reason for her hasty marriage to Daniel private. Quentin listened sympathetically and was relieved she had no strong ties to the Gaineses so they couldn't make trouble between them.

"I promise you won't be treated that way by

my family," he assured her. "They'll love you and welcome you as a member. I'm biased, but they're good and kind people."

"They would have to be to raise a son like you."

"Thanks, and they'd appreciate that compliment. They'll be pleased with you, Rachel, because you bring out the best in me. They'll be happy I've found the right woman and they'll see how well we're suited. I want you to meet them as soon as our schedules allow, but I've already told them a lot about you. They think you're perfect for me."

"I hope I live up to their expectations."

"You will, have no doubts. Mom said my brother Frank is doing great in Dothan; he's even seeing a nice young woman. That's what he needs, somebody to love him and to help keep him straight."

"I hope things work out for him."

"They will, if the media will leave him be. I don't know why they keep tormenting him over his past mistakes and comparing him to me. Most articles about me mention him; that's downright cruel, keeps his wounds from healing. Once I'm out of the limelight, they shouldn't trouble him again." *Or us.*

"I know that's one aspect about your career you won't miss."

"Nope, not in the least. What I hate is having to leave you behind next Wednesday. Lordy, I'm gonna miss you." He cuddled her close to him. Rachel curled toward him, and nestled her head against his chest. "I'm going to miss you, too. Six months sounds like forever."

"We're not going to go that long without seeing each other, are we?"

"We'll work something out," she said, lifting her head to look at him. Light from a full moon revealed his features and expression. She gazed into his eyes and traced his lips with her forefinger.

Quentin's mouth enclosed it and his tongue played with it. He shifted her body to rest across his lap so they could kiss and caress each other freely. Warm water lapped at their bodies as movements created swirls. He undid the strap around her neck and lowered the top of her swimsuit. His hands fondled her breasts, and his cheek nuzzled them in serene delight.

Soon, their suits were discarded in rapturous abandon so they could tantalize bare flesh with eager fingers and seeking lips. Sounds from neighbors' homes did not dissuade them from taking a carefree swim in the nude or from uniting their bodies on the bench afterward. They knew they couldn't be seen inside the enclosed yard. The daring episode was romantic and erotic as their desires heightened and ultimately sated.

Relaxing in his arms ultimately Rachel said, "I love you so much, Quentin, and I love being with you."

He kissed her shoulder and neck as he held her in his lap, totally content. "I love you and love being with you. We'll have a good marriage and a wonderful life together. I just wish we could tie the knot sooner."

Rachel lifted her head and locked their gazes. "We don't want to rush things too much, but waiting will surely be hard."

"How can I concentrate on football when I'll be thinking about you?"

"You'll manage," she teased, "because you have to do a great job."

"If I'm given the chance."

"Will it bother you that much if you don't make it?" She watched him take a deep breath and saw the expression of longing in his eyes.

"I want this last season badly; it's a special one, and I don't want to go out on the bottom, but I'll accept what fate deals me. I won't have any choice, will I?"

It was clear that resentment chewed at him, yet, he seemed man enough to accept the inevitable. "I hope and pray you succeed, and I'll be waiting for you if you don't."

"That will make a defeat easier to take. Lordy, you're good for me."

She moved wet hair from his forehead and smiled. "And you're good for me, perfect for me. I love you."

"I've loved you since we met on the ship."

Rachel smiled again. "That's when you stole my heart, too."

"Promise you won't forget me while I'm gone."

"How can I when your memory stayed fresh for twelve years?"

"I know what you mean; the same is true for me. I wonder how it would have been for us if that detective hadn't lost his license and he'd found you for me years ago."

"I think it's best we were reunited when we were. We're stronger now, and closer than we might have been then. Our lives are almost settled, and our responsibilities are different. Marriage to somebody who's gone half the time would be difficult."

"Football is a demanding mistress."

"That's a colorful and amusing way of putting it, but accurate."

"I think that may be why so many marriages in my career fail, too many separations and for too long. Maybe it is good that we won't be taking that risk. Of course, retirement means I'll be underfoot more."

"Oh, I think I can take having you around most of the time."

"Can you now?" he jested and nibbled on her neck.

Rachel laughed and squirmed, then wiggled free to take a swim, coaxing him to follow her.

They enjoyed each other's company until eleven, when Quentin dressed, kissed her good night several times, and departed with noticeable reluctance.

As she locked the door and set the alarm system, Rachel smiled and murmured, "I wish you didn't have to leave. I think I could make love to you all night. But somebody might see you leave in the morning or realize you didn't leave tonight. If only I didn't care what people said and thought, but I do, and I should." They had spent twelve days together and made love for the last five in a row. She could hardly wait to see him Saturday afternoon.

Rachel was overjoyed when her youngest daughter phoned her early the next morning. She sat up in the bed and almost squealed in delight, "Evelyn! It's so good to hear your voice. I miss you terribly. It must be an awful hour to be up and on the phone."

The girl laughed. "It is, but I had to hear your voice, Mom, and I miss you something fierce. How are you? What's happening over there?"

"I'm doing fine, and things are going great, except for you and Karen and your family being so far away. How are Alex and Ashley doing, and Eddie and Barbara?"

"Everybody's fine and having fun. Eddie's working hard but he's enjoying himself and learning a lot. Barbara's been fantastic help; I'm glad she came with us; we're even picking up some Japanese. They all said to tell you hello; they've been in bed for hours. I was reading while I was waiting to call; I didn't want to get you up too early."

"Call any time, I don't mind, and collect is fine with me. I worry about phoning at ungodly hours and disturbing everyone's sleep or waking the children. Are you still planning on return-ing home in April?"

"Nothing's changed in our schedule so far. You are coming over at Christmas, aren't you? Do you have your passport ready?"

"I received it a few weeks ago and checked on everything I needed to do before I come. Karen's phoning next week during her break."

"How are my sister and her sweetheart doing?"

Rachel related the most current news from Karen and they talked about things Evelyn was doing in Japan. "I just mailed you a long letter yesterday. Express so it would reach you fast."

"Eddie said to thank you for the newspaper and *Parade* articles on the automotive industry. Things are looking up for both sides right now."

"For me, too. I met a man and we're seeing each other regularly."

"That's wonderful, Mom! Who is he? Do I know him or his family?"

Rachel revealed information about Quentin Rawls and their romance, then added, "He's younger than I am."

"That doesn't matter these days, but how much younger?"

"He's thirty-eight, nine years my junior."

"That's nothing to worry about, and you look thirty. Is it serious?"

"Yes, for both of us. He's wonderful, Evelyn. I hope you and Karen and the others like him."

"If you do, I'm sure we will. Is he handsome and sexy?"

Rachel laughed, and warmed as his image

filled her mind's eye. "Yes to both. You don't think I'm being silly or impulsive, do you?"

"If anyone has a head on straight, it's you, Mom."

Rachel told her about Dorothy's call and Janet's intrusive behavior.

"Don't you dare let Grandmother or Mrs. Hollis or *anyone* spoil this relationship. Tell them to keep their noses out of your business."

"I wish you were in the States so you could meet him soon; Karen, too. He's asked me to marry him."

"When?"

"January, or sooner if he retires from football."

"Has he given you an engagement ring?"

"No, we didn't want it to appear as if we're rushing things."

"I hope you can wait until we return to have the wedding so we can celebrate with you two. If not, go for it. Daddy's been gone for fifteen years, and you deserve this chance for happiness. You did a good job rearing me and Karen, and we're grateful. We both love you. This is so exciting; I bet I won't sleep a wink tonight. My mother getting married . . ."

"It is exciting and unexpected, isn't it?"

"Yes, but I'm thrilled for you. I bet he's fantastic."

"He is, and more, much more, Evelyn."

"It sounds as if you're head over heels in love, Mom."

"I am, and so is he. I'll write as soon as we make plans."

"Write, nothing; phone me the minute you set a date."

"I will, and thank you for being so supportive. I love you."

"I love you, too, Mom."

They talked for another five minutes, then Rachel lay on the bed unable to go back to sleep in her elated state. She wished Quentin were there to share this special moment with her, to hold her, to kiss her, to make passionate love to her. *You've spoiled me already, Mr. Rawls. Rachel Rawls . . . Mrs. Quentin James Rawls . . . Heavens, that name sounds good. Thank you, Lord, for bringing him back into my life and making me happy.*

As soon as Quentin finished making a video and taking pictures of some of the rooms in Rachel's house, he joined her in the laundry room where she was washing and folding clothes. He leaned against the counter and said, "That does it, I'm ready to plan my renovations. I'm meeting with Scott on Monday at his office. I think he's taking my job."

"That's wonderful, Quentin; I know you'll be pleased with his work."

"I think so, too; he certainly understands what I want. I just hope I can afford his price; construction out-of-state is expensive, he said. I'll know after our appointment. If we agree, we'll sign the papers."

"That's one matter almost settled."

"Yep, only two more to go: football and you."

"I didn't realize I was a problem to be resolved," she teased.

"Until my ring's on your finger and you're living in my home, our home, I won't be satisfied, woman. Maybe you'll be more compliant if I make your new surroundings more familiar; these ideas and Scott's skills should help accomplish that goal," he said, tapping the cameras.

Rachel laughed. "You don't have to change your house to suit me."

"Why not? You have some things here we'll enjoy. I know women require ample closet space, love cozy bedrooms and bathrooms, and like for things to look pretty and be comfortable."

"Any place I lived with you would be cozy and comfortable."

"Even in a sparse line shack without a bath on a ranch?" he jested.

"Well, maybe I wouldn't go that far," she quipped and grinned.

"You're in a sunny mood today after that call from Evelyn. I'm glad she reacted as she did to our news; that's another load off my mind. One daughter down and one to go."

"Karen will react the same way, so don't worry. I just hope your family does the same."

"They will," he stated matter-of-factly. "I called them this morning and they're eager to meet you. My friends are eager to meet you, too.

I'll be surprised if you don't like Perry, Vance, and Ryan; they're great guys. I also phoned Bill and told him the facts I've gathered. I Express mailed my report, brochures, maps, video, and pictures to him before I came over; he'll get them on Monday and can make a decision on the suitability of this location. If he needs for us to check on anything else for him before I leave, he'll call Monday night and we can handle it Tuesday. He said to thank you for your help." He pulled her into his arms and kissed her.

Rachel put aside the towel she was folding to embrace him and return his hot kisses and stirring caresses. "Is this how he said to show his appreciation?"

"He didn't say, so I'll use my imagination." Following several more passionate kisses, he murmured, "I wish I didn't have to leave Wednesday."

"I understand, but let's take full advantage of the four days we have left."

"How do you propose we do that?" he asked in a husky voice.

"Like this for starters," she murmured, and began to undress him.

Quentin's gaze softened and gleamed as Rachel used her hands and lips to lavish stimulating attention upon his body. Within fifteen minutes, it seemed as if only a few inches of his towering frame had not been tantalized and ignited and pleasured. "Great day, woman, that was dizzying, a real treat. Now, It's your turn." He stripped her and lay her on the counter so his deft fingers and talented tongue could give her supreme ecstasy, which they did in record time in her highly aroused state.

Rachel writhed and moaned as he carried her to the brink of bliss, held her there for a while in exquisite delight, and then toppled her over its enticing edge. He didn't stop his titillating actions until every spasm ceased and she relaxed on the hard surface, deliciously weak and satisfied. She sat up and hugged him, unmindful of her nudity. "You're a dream come true, Quentin Rawls."

"So are you, Rachel Gaines, and I love your reality. I love you. I've never been more relaxed or happy in my life, and I have you to thank for it. Yesiree, retirement is looking real good to me with you sharing it. You don't mind if I help you with the laundry again, do you?"

Rachel fingercombed his black hair and caressed his face. "I'll consider it a slight and a loss of interest if you don't."

As he kissed the peaks of her breasts, Rachel sighed dreamily and began to warm anew. "We'd better go take cold showers and get dressed or we'll have the Coopers and Brimsfords wondering where we are."

"Ah, yes, dinner at the country club and a movie with our friends."

"You do like them, don't you?"

"Yep, both couples. You have good friends and excellent taste."

"I do like things with a superior flavor," she said, licking her lips.

"So do I, and yours is tops. Get up and get moving or we'll be late. You're much too provocative like that."

"So are you. Oh, well, duty calls."

Quentin pulled into Rachel's driveway at eleven forty-five and walked her to the door. "I can see even more why you like the Coopers and Brimsfords and why you'll miss Becky and Jen; they're nice people. I enjoyed myself."

She noted his strange mood. "Aren't you coming in for a while?"

"It's late and we have church in the morning. You need your sleep; for rest, not for beauty. Lordy, if you looked any better, I couldn't take it. I'd be fighting men off you with a stick, a big one."

"Thanks for the compliment, but I have the only man I want. We could have a glass of wine and talk for a while."

"Trying to coax me into your silky web, woman?"

"Why not, when I know how you behave there?"

"I'll be with you all day tomorrow. I should go. It's almost midnight."

"If you're worried about neighbors seeing you leave later, don't."

"We have to care, Rachel; you'll be here for months while I'm gone."

"You're right; I'm being foolish and greedy."

"Stay that way until tomorrow afternoon, okay?"

"I will. Good night, Quentin. I love you."

"I love you, too. Good night. Pick you up at ten-fifteen sharp."

"I'll be ready and waiting. Drive carefully and lock your car doors."

"I will. Now, you get inside and do the same."

Rachel entered the foyer, smiled, and closed the door. She sensed something was bothering him and wondered why he didn't disclose it. He almost seemed in a rush to leave, and hadn't even kissed her good-bye. She then told herself *she* was being silly and insecure. She shrugged, went upstairs, and got into bed, longing for him to be lying beside her.

As Quentin drove off, he scowled in annoyance. He saw the car that was parked up the street from her house follow him at an assumed safe distance to avoid being noticed. He had recognized it in passing and knew the concealed driver was Todd Hardy. Obviously the irritating reporter forgot he had a giveaway license plate. He hadn't wanted to spoil a wonderful evening by telling Rachel they were being watched by the pesky reporter; that would worry and upset her. He would deal with the nuisance on Monday.

After church on Sunday, Janet approached Rachel and Quentin before they could escape. "You look nice, Rachel, glowing like a bright candle."

"Thank you, Janet; that's very kind of you." *I know you're trying to put me off guard, make me relax, so you can plunge a knife in my back.*

She turned her attention to Quentin. "Mr. Rawls, I'm surprised to see you still in town. You must be having an exceptionally wonderful visit with our Rachel to hang around for such a long time. She must be getting terribly behind with her many projects."

"I try not to interfere with her schedule, but Rachel's a kind and generous person, as you must know. And how are you today, Cliff?"

Before her husband could respond, Janet murmured, "Things must be getting serious between you two if you'd bring him to church with you again." Janet laughed. "Next, you'll be introducing him to your parents. Oh, I forgot, they're deceased. But I'm sure you're anxious for your girls to meet him. And how are Karen and Evelyn doing?"

"They're both fine and happy; thank you for asking about them."

The offensive woman eyed Rachel in her stylish turquoise suit with black braid outlines, a Nehru collar, and matte golden buttons. "Rachel looks good for a woman with grown daughters and two grandchildren, doesn't she, Mr. Rawls?"

Quentin glanced at his companion and smiled. "I'm sure women of any age would do anything to look as gorgeous as Rachel does. I would imagine she's mistaken more for her daughters' sister than their mother."

"Too bad they're away and you can't meet them to test your theory."

"I've seen lots of pictures of them. They're lucky they favor Rachel."

"You two must be spending a great deal of time together. Am I right?"

Rachel waved and said in a faked cheerful tone, "There's Jen. I need to ask her a question about the homeless shelter project. Excuse us, Janet, I need to catch her before she leaves. It was good to see you, Cliff."

The couple departed before Janet could detain them further.

Following embraces and cheek kisses and while Quentin chatted with Adam to one side, Rachel whispered details of the incident to her friend.

"What a little witch. Obviously she didn't learn anything from the minister's sermon this morning. Why do we have anything to do with her?"

"If Cliff wasn't my banker, advisor, and a good friend, I wouldn't."

"You may have to find another banker if matters get worse."

"I can't; that would cause hard feelings. Besides, Cliff is sweet and smart, so I'll ignore her ridiculous antics as long as possible."

After they left church, they stopped by Rachel's house and then Quentin's room to change into sports clothes, picked up chicken at Wife-Saver, and went to Clarks Hill Dam for a picnic and stroll.

When they finished their outing, they sneaked

to Quentin's suite to relax, talk, and make love away from any prying eyes.

When Quentin arrived at Rachel's house mid-afternoon on Monday, he told her about Todd's spying on them Saturday night and how he threatened the pesky reporter with a refusal to interview him if he didn't halt his actions. He said Todd was miffed and tried to act innocent, but realized how vexed Quentin was and promised not to shadow him again. Of course, Quentin did not trust the sneaky man and would take precautions to elude him.

He rushed to change the subject. "So, my love, what have you been doing today? Catching up on those projects Janet said I was keeping you from?"

Rachel laughed to calm her tension over his initial news. "No, I've been writing for most of the day. When you asked if I had a career in mind, I didn't tell you I was trying to become an author. I was keeping it a secret. Maybe I should write a murder mystery with a villainess and victim like Janet."

Quentin chuckled. "Sounds fun and interesting to me."

Rachel observed his reaction as she asked, "You don't think it's silly I want to write books at my age and without professional training?"

"Nope, it's a great idea, and I bet you can do it. A clever southern murder mystery should become a best seller. I have a friend who's an editor at a big publishing house. He's been after me for years to co-write my life story.''

''Why don't you?''

''I'm not old enough or done enough living and learning yet to make a good tale,'' he jested. ''Seriously, I'm not interested in doing a tell-all and that's the only thing that would sell with my name on it. I value my privacy and peace too much, what little of them I'm allowed.''

''Lots of guys would be delighted to read about a football hero who came from a small town and made it big.''

Quentin caressed her cheek. ''I have a better idea: you do your story and I'll give it to my friend to read.''

''What if he hates it but is too nice to say so?''

''Friendship never overrides a business decision with a smart man. If it needs work, he'll tell you. If it's rotten, he'll be honest. If it's good, he'll buy it. All I can do is get your foot in his door; walking inside and staying will be up to you. Look at me, I'm still playing football at thirty-eight, and I'll be starting a new career soon. I'll retire only when I'm forced to quit. Lots of people think I'm silly and too old but it doesn't faze me. We can't live by other people's ideas or we'll miss out on great opportunities and things which would make us happy. We can't let others tell us what to say and do, how to live.''

''That's easy for you to say. Most men have always been able to do and say what they please in public or in private with few if any repercussions. When a woman tries that freedom, she's labeled an aggressive bitch and is viewed as being unladylike and unfeminine. That old double standard still exists no matter who says it doesn't. Women can't get away with the same things men do. You rarely see a man's reputation injured when he makes a mistake; but let a woman do the same, and she's trashed."

"Unless you're in the limelight and the media pounces on you. I was trashed for having two bad marriages and for dating what the public viewed as a lot of different women. I was linked as a couple to anyone I saw more than once. There were plenty of times I just needed an escort for certain functions; but to hear the media tell it, a hot romance was in force."

Rachel had to ask, "Has the media ever ruined a promising relationship by dogging you?" *Like Todd's doing to us?*

"No, and I'll be careful they don't intrude on our relationship."

"I'm almost fortunate I became a widow rather than a divorcee, because so many women in that category are slighted. As I told you, my in-laws didn't approve of Daniel's choice and never accepted me into their family."

"Did Daniel get along with his parents?"

"Yes and no. They were and are domineering; they always want everything to go their way, but he usually stood his ground. I didn't give them a male heir to the Gaines bloodline, so I'm a failure in their eyes. Would you like to have a glass of wine?"

Quentin realized she was dropping the painful subjects of her miscarriages, her baby's death, and troublesome in-laws. "Suits me. You would have plenty of peace and privacy to write at the ranch; I could get Scott to build you an office. You could even write my life story; that way, I know the book would be in my favor and be accurate. If you marry me, woman, it can include a beautiful romance and a happy ending."

"You're right, maybe we'll do it together."

As they gazed into each other's eyes, they knew there was something else they wanted to do together at that moment . . .

As Quentin undressed near the bed, Rachel's body came to life and a fiery flush teased over it from head to feet, spreading through every inch of her receptive frame, lying naked within his reach. Suspense and eagerness washed over her, cleansing her of all thoughts except of him and what was in store. Anticipation mounted as he joined her and cuddled her in his embrace, just as a violent storm broke overhead and a deluge of rain began.

As when they were in the tropics long ago, Quentin wanted to bask in the radiant glow of her being, to share another sultry and passionate adventure with her. There was never a dull moment when she was present, and he missed her when she wasn't. His quivering fingers trailed over her arms, and his hand closed over her breast as his mouth claimed hers. At first, he kissed her tenderly and slowly, then with swiftness and hunger.

Their tongues touched, teased, savored. They clung together as his seeking mouth wandered down the silky column of her neck, and her fingers traced the path of his spine. His teeth gently nibbled at her collarbone and his tongue danced in the hollow of her throat before his quest continued. It was a provocative and stimulating journey which Rachel enjoyed and encouraged. He was skilled and generous in his lovemaking. She moaned as he fondled the firm mounds of her breasts and deftly thumbed their peaks. With desires increased and passion's flames heightened, their limbs entangled as they stroked and pleasured each other.

Soon, Quentin's fingers sought the peak hidden in the core of her feminine domain. She parted her thighs as if in invitation for his explorers to invade that area, and he massaged the hot bud until it burst into bloom like a summer flower. He worked her into a frenzy of yearning that matched his.

Rachel hardly noticed the booming thunder and flashes of lightning beyond the cozy room. Her heart pounded from excitement and exertion. Her mind was dazed by feverish ardor. "You're driving me wild, Quentin; I need you inside me."

He was thrilled by her intense need of him as he moved atop her and into a glorious paradise that stole his breath for a moment.

Rachel adored everything he did to her, for

her, each caress, each kiss, each fulfillment of an unspoken promise to delight her. Her hands roamed his shoulders and she matched the pattern of his rhythmic thrusts. She savored the contradictory tension and relaxation that assailed her. It was like a rollercoaster ride. Her nipples reacted blissfully to his fingers and lips. The core of her being tingled and pulsed, and she coaxed him to continue his actions.

Quentin restrained himself until he could hardly wait any longer to possess her to the fullest. When she stiffened, inhaled sharply, arched upward, and moaned "Oh, oh, oh," he knew control was unnecessary and cast it aside. Within a few minutes, his erection was spilling forth with speed and joy into her receptive body. "Lordy, I love you," he said in a ragged voice as he breathed heavily and thrust wildly until he was totally spent.

They nestled in the bed, darkness surrounding them except for occasional lightning and the soft glow from nightlights in the hall and bathroom. They kissed and caressed and sighed dreamily as they relaxed and relished their contentment and satisfaction.

"That's some storm out there," Quentin murmured. "Almost as powerful as the one in here a while ago. I can't imagine our sex life ever being dull."

"It will be nonexistent soon; you're leaving Wednesday."

Quentin hugged her and took a deep breath

of resignation. "Don't remind me. Lordy, I'm going to miss you."

"Maybe Bill Effingham will need you to hang around a little longer."

"Even if that was true, I couldn't. I have to face the music Thursday."

"Your physical?" She knew he was dreading that first step to learning the truth about his impending fate.

"That's right. If I don't pass it, I won't be going to practice."

"You will, because you're in excellent condition. Your stamina and strength are superb, Mr. Rawls; I can vouch for them."

He chuckled. "Too bad the team doctor and coach wouldn't value your opinion."

"I know how badly you want this last season."

"It just seems as if I don't play and do well, it's unfinished business."

Like I was unfinished business after I seemingly dumped you? Now, Rachel, don't go getting insecure because he's leaving soon. "You will, Quentin, so don't worry." *And come back for me.*

Twelve

Rachel cancelled an historical society meeting for noon on Tuesday in order to spend every available minute with Quentin until his departure the next day.

Quentin came over around ten after making a stop at a local sporting goods store to purchase a football to donate to one of Rachel's projects: the celebrity auction for the library extension. While in the store, he agreed to sign several collector's cards, two footballs for a promotional giveaway soon, and autographs for ecstatic customers. He only chatted for a short time because he was eager to get to Rachel's.

She thanked him for his kindness and generosity. He also gave her names and addresses of several entertainment stars who were friends who would send her something useful if she used his name when contacting them.

As it stormed for most of the day, they talked and planned and ate lunch, each aware of how swiftly their separation was coming and how lonely they would be.

While clearing the table, she said, "You're a

good person, Quentin Rawls, and I love you for being that way. I'm going to miss you terribly."

"Just promise you won't believe any trash you read about me in those tabloids; you know they print lies and innuendos and half-truths. I won't go flirting with any Cowboy cheerleaders, either. I won't be fooling around no matter what they say or how any sneaky pictures might look. I'll never cheat on you, Rachel, I swear."

"I know, Quentin, and I won't cheat on you. I'll— " The phone rang and sliced into her sentence. "Just a minute," she told him, and put aside the dish cloth to lift the receiver.

"Rachel, this is Janet. Are you ill today?"

"No, why?"

"You missed the society meeting, and that isn't like you."

"Thanks for being concerned, but I had a schedule conflict."

"Since I missed you there, I wanted to call to tell you I'm worried about you and so are some of your other good friends."

You're no "good" friend of mine or concerned about me and we both know it. "Really? I can't imagine why." *Quentin's car is in the garage and you were gone, so how do you know he's here, and I bet you do?*

"I thought I should give you some obviously needed advice: you really shouldn't be getting so serious so fast with this . . . football player. It really isn't safe or ladylike to be carrying on with him. He could break your heart and ruin your reputation. I think you should— "

"I'm sorry to rush you, Janet, but I'm busy. I have company and can't talk right now. I'll see you at the Heart Fund meeting on Thursday and we'll chat there. 'Bye." Rachel hung up the receiver with Janet still talking. She frowned in annoyance.

"What's wrong, love? What did she say this time?"

Rachel related the brief talk and frowned again.

"That woman is a conniving and nosy bitch, but let's not think about her when our time together is so short. If she comes over, we won't answer the door."

Quentin grinned and nuzzled her neck. "I know what we need."

Rachel leaned against him and looped her arms around his neck. She looked up into his fiery blue gaze. "I know what *I* need: you."

"That's an easy request to fill. Why don't we lower the A/C to freezing, turn on the gas logs and throw a blanket on the floor in the bedroom, put on some romantic music, open that bottle of champagne, shuck these clothes, and pretend we're in a secluded cabin in the mountains in the dead of winter?"

"That sounds enticing, Mr. Rawls. How about a hot shower first so we'll be squeaky clean for anything that comes up?" she ventured in a sexy tone as she caressed the sudden rise in his pants.

Quentin needed to have Rachel completely before the time came for him to leave. He needed to be as close to her as possible, to lie beside her, to hold her, to be within her, to unite their hearts and bodies. He cupped her face and kissed her, and she clung to him as if she experienced those same deep yearnings. His senses spun at her nearness, and her ardent response. For today, nothing and no one existed except them and their needs. His tongue explored the tasty recess of her mouth, his teeth nibbling at her soft lips. He felt her tremble with longing, as did he.

Rachel clasped his head between her hands and held it while she almost ravished his mouth. She tingled when his lips brushed her shoulder, bared to his quest after he removed her shirt. His mouth roved her neck and upper chest as his hands wandered along the same path. He unfastened her bra and kneaded her breasts. "Whew, you're heating me up to boiling level. If we don't stop now, we won't get to that shower."

"Let's go, woman; my appetite for you is increasing by the minute."

"You go first while I get things ready. If we share another bath, we'll never make it to a blanket by the fire."

"Don't be long," he murmured in a husky tone, then went upstairs.

While he showered, Rachel put the open bottle of champagne in an ice bucket, then carried it along with two glasses to her bedroom. She turned the air-conditioning system on full blast to chill the area, spread a blanket on the floor before the fireplace, and turned on the gas logs.

After she started the CD unit to playing romantic music, she lowered the shades and loosened the drapes to darken the room, and lit many candles to give it a seductive glow. To prevent an intrusion, she set the alarm system control panel near the bedroom door; a light on the outside switch on the front porch would make it appear she was gone if anyone dropped by to visit. The answering machine was readied and the office door closed so any message being taken would not be heard and distract them. The ringer on the phone nearby was turned off. Last, she stripped and went to bathe, just as he was finishing.

"Everything's prepared for your conquest, Mr. Rawls," she jested as her gaze swept over his impressive physique and provocative nudity. "Except for me, and I will be soon. Pour the champagne and relax."

"Relax?" he teased with a chuckle. "How can I when I know what's in store for me, for both of us, this afternoon?"

"*All* afternoon, too. I hope your stamina is at its peak," she told him as she took the damp towel from his grasp and finished drying his torso. She knelt to wipe trickling water from his long legs and feet, and, before rising, placed mischievous kisses on his hardening member. She tossed him the towel, instructing him to dry his hair before he got cold, and slipped into the frosted-glass shower, evading the hands which reached for her as she laughed merrily.

"That isn't fair, woman; I'm crying foul; that's a stiff penalty."

"Just so it isn't the only stiff thing around today," she quipped as she adjusted the water's temperature and flow.

"It won't be, not with you around and in this splendid mood. Lordy, woman, I stay half aroused most of the time. All you have to do is look at me and I come to attention."

"Excellent. The blow dryer is lying on the counter. I'll be quick."

They ceased their playful banter as he dried his jet-black hair and combed it. As he did so, his gaze kept wandering to her strikingly sensual form, part of it unobscured through the clear designs etched onto the glass door and side panels. He could hardly wait to have them touching and loving.

Quentin went to lie on the soft blanket and wait for her. The setting was cozy: the air chilly; the flames' heat relaxing. He poured the champagne when he heard her spray on Passion perfume, her finishing touch. She closed the bathroom door to shut off light coming through the half-round window above the Jacuzzi, then she came to sit down beside him.

Quentin smiled and passed her the bubbling pale-gold liquid. He tapped his glass to hers and said in an emotion-hoarsened voice, "To Rachel Gaines, the woman I love, the woman I've loved and wanted for twelve years, may you become Rachel Rawls by the end of January."

"To Quentin Rawls, the man I love," she responded, "the man I've loved and wanted for twelve years, my best friend, my future husband."

Their tender gazes remained locked over the rims of their upturned glasses as they sipped from their glasses after the stirring toasts. Bubbles tickled their noses, fire and candle lights danced over their faces and naked bodies. Exotic aromas filled the air from the scented candles and dreamy strains of music floated around them. The only noises from outside were the deluge of rain and an occasional rumble of thunder; inside, only the humming of the air conditioner and their breathing as sweet tension claimed them. Until they finished their drinks, they watched each other without touching or speaking; they simply savored being together and arousing each other with sensual looks of increasing anticipation.

He placed his empty glass on the hearth. "You're utterly intoxicating."

She put hers aside. "It's the champagne going to your head."

"No, it's you, Rachel. I enjoy every minute I'm with you and miss you every minute I'm not."

"The same is true for me, Quentin." Rachel's entire being responded to every inch of him, to the way he enthralled her, the rippling of his muscles as he reached for her. He had won more than her physical submission; he owned her heart, soul, and body forever. Long, deep, purposeful kisses heightened her blazing desires.

Quentin's lips paused at the pulse point in her throat, which told him how aroused she was. He guided them to a prone position. He kissed the rise of her collarbone and drifted into the cleft between her breasts. Ever so lightly, his chin passed over their protruding peaks before his mouth encased them in turn, eliciting moans from her. He was amazed by the hardness of her nipples in contrast to the satiny softness of her mounds. He stroked familiar planes and curves as his fingers trekked over her supple flesh, stimulating, teasing, pleasuring, always traveling downward toward the apex of her thighs. Her dark curls were incredibly silky. His fingers parted the pleats of skin which were warm and damp to his touch. He massaged her with care and joy. "Lordy, you're enchanting, woman. Every inch of you is perfect. I love you and want you. I can't ever have enough of you."

His words and actions caused Rachel to squirm with anticipation and intense delight. As he titillated the hardened bud in her delicate folds, she kissed and stroked him as far as her lips and fingers could reach. Her nails gently raked over his back, shoulders, and firm buttocks. She was charged with eagerness and energy. She was burning with pervasive heat. She offered herself to him without modesty or inhibition, and in near feverish abandon.

They stimulated each other in a variety of ways, as nothing seemed forbidden or reckless to them today. They took their time and gathered multiple delights as their hands and lips traveled each other's terrain and explored every facet of sensuous foreplay and lovemaking.

Finally, swollen and throbbing with urgent hunger, Quentin entered her with tormenting slowness. It was as if they were teetering on the precipice of triumph from the instant they fused their loins. He thrust and retreated time and again as he delved into her steamy recess. Without breaking their contact, he held her securely, rolled to his back, and sat up with her across his lap.

Rachel's legs surrounded his hips and she rocked back and forth upon his erection, tantalizing their most sensitive regions. "I love you, Quentin; I love you." She rested her head against his as her breathing became swift and ragged. She moaned as his lips worked on her neck, shoulders, and breasts. Heat and tension mounted in her groin from enthralling friction. Lovemaking was never dull or routine with him. Her thoughts never drifted, her interest never waned, her body never cooled. The man in her arms and the blissful fusion of their bodies were too emotionally, mentally, and physically consuming for any of those things to happen. Every occasion was unique, marvelous, vitalizing, satisfying to the fullest.

"I'm all yours, Rachel," he gasped between ragged breaths, "we'll never be parted again. We belong together."

"Yes, we do," she concurred in happiness.

As if by cue, their joined bodies sank to the blanket and he moved atop her, with Rachel's legs imprisoning him there. Love's beautiful music echoed through their veins as their hearts sang. They were locked so tightly together that even hot air from the gas fire or cold air from the air-conditioning system could not find space between them. They reveled in their snug contact and the rapturous sensations filling them. When their desires were at last spent, they nestled to savor the golden aftermath. In spite of the air-conditioning, the room was warm, but would have been sweltering if not for that foresight. Their bodies glistened with perspiration from the heat of the fire, their exertions, and the champagne they had consumed. Even so, neither wanted to end the special moment by sitting up to turn off the gas control, not yet anyway.

"Don't ever forget me or leave me, Rachel."

"I couldn't, even if I wanted to and tried. I love you and desire you as I have no other man. You're stuck with me now."

Her first sentence relieved him, her second thrilled him, and her last amused him. "I can't imagine a more enjoyable condition."

"Neither can I." She halted herself before adding, Who better to capture me than the Man with the Golden Arm? It could be tarnished now and she didn't want to remind him of unpleasant matters today.

They snuggled and fell asleep for an hour. After they awakened, they cooled off the bedroom and picked up scattered items, exchanging playful words and caresses as they did so. They revived themselves in the Jacuzzi, lathering each other until they were compelled to make love again . . .

The storm had diminished in force during their nap, but they decided to eat dinner inside and stay off the slick streets. They talked about many things as they prepared the meal, ate it, and cleaned up afterward.

"I wanted to take you out for a romantic meal for our last evening together. I didn't want you to have to cook and do chores tonight."

"You're helping, and I don't mind. Besides, we probably have more privacy here than we would in any restaurant."

"You're right, especially since word has leaked about Bill's project. It was mentioned on the news and in the paper yesterday."

"That was expected after your various meetings, wasn't it?"

"Yep, that's why I worked in secret for a while; I didn't want anybody trying to influence me in one direction or another."

"What's your opinion about locating one of the new teams here?"

"Frankly, I don't think it would be profitable, and they are businessmen looking to make money on the deal. I don't believe the population is high enough to give it the financial support needed. There are too many pro, college, high school, and semipro teams already drawing from this area to make bringing in a new one feasible. Jacksonville is getting a team soon, and that isn't far away. Besides, the Georgia Thrashers already playing, and the Augusta Eagles didn't make a go of it. I advised against this location for a variety of reasons; I hope you and other locals don't take offense."

"Of course not, particularly since you aren't interested in coaching the team."

"You're right, but I'm not interested in coaching *any* team *any* place. Playing is my love, not teaching others to do it." His change of subject was abrupt. "I hope you get plenty of writing done while I'm gone."

"I will, and I hope I'm as good at it as you are at football."

"I'm sure you'll do great, woman, and I'm proud of you for trying. Follow your heart and chase that dream, and you'll be glad you did. Just don't get too engrossed in it that you don't think about me," he joked.

"Nothing could be that distracting, Mr. Rawls," she quipped.

He held her and kissed her several times. "I wish I could stay all night, Rachel, but we shouldn't take chances the day before I leave. Let Janet think she chased me off; it doesn't matter. I'll be here for breakfast at seven. We don't have to leave for the airport until nine-fifteen. That will give me time to return the car and check in before my ten o'clock flight."

As she snuggled in his embrace, Rachel murmured, "Heavens, I miss you already. Call whenever you can; it will be easier for you to reach me since I don't know your playing schedule."

"I'll keep you informed of everything. The

Cowboys are playing against Houston in the American Bowl in Mexico City on August fifteenth; then, the Broncos in Denver on the twenty-first and the Saints in New Orleans on the twenty-fifth. Once the cuts and trades are made, we open with the Steelers in Pittsburgh on September fourth. I'll write them down for you so you can watch on TV, if I'm playing."

"Have faith, Quentin; I'm sure things will work out for the best."

"I'd better get moving now so we can get some sleep. I'll see you early."

She kissed him good night before she opened the front door. She didn't close and lock it until he left her driveway. He was leaving tomorrow, probably for months, long and lonely months. She was grateful she had her writing and other projects and activities to comfort her during his absence. She couldn't decide if it was smart or unwise to reveal their relationship to others until his return. Rachel thought Quentin might be afraid that if they exposed the extent of it, reporters would pester her, perhaps hound her for personal information and write unfavorably about them. She prayed the media, in particular the tabloids, would give Quentin the time and privacy he needed for making a difficult decision or for accepting enforced retirement.

Rachel went upstairs and went to bed, to be rested for a trying day.

* * *

At the airport, Todd Hardy intruded on Rachel and Quentin's remaining time together. The astonished couple watched him almost stalk toward their position in a far corner away from the other people. Quentin glared at the approaching reporter, but his hostile expression did not discourage Todd from joining them.

Todd's voice was surly, his words demanding. "You promised me an in-depth interview before you left town."

Quentin narrowed and chilled his gaze and iced his tone. "I promised you one if you'd leave me in peace during my vacation, which you didn't. You've been phoning and lurking in the shadows and spying on me."

"Because I didn't trust you to keep your word, and I was right."

"You're the one who didn't honor his word, Hardy; that's why you'll get nothing from me. No comment, so leave us be."

"Is Mrs. Gaines going with you? Are you two a hot item?"

"That's none of your business."

"Right now, everything and anything about you is hot news. You think you'll make the cut this year at your age and with your injuries? They've really slowed you down and damaged your throwing ability. Right?"

Quentin tensed in vexation. "I told you, no comment, so get lost."

"Your fans want to know it all; you owe them the facts for supporting you for so many years."

"They'll read or hear about them in the news as soon as I know them."

"*I* am the news, Mr. Rawls. I—"

"No," Quentin interrupted, "you're a sneaky and annoying leech who tries to inflict wounds and suck the blood from people."

Todd shrugged. "Think what you will, and I've been called worse."

"I'm sure you have, and justly so."

"Mr. Rawls, you can wait for departure aboard the plane if you like," the gate attendant told Quentin. "Your guest can join you until we're ready to seal the door and taxi," he added.

Quentin realized the smiling man was offering assistance and escape. He smiled and thanked him. "Let's go, Rachel."

"Wait a minute!" Todd commanded. "You haven't answered my questions."

"And I'm not going to."

Rachel and Quentin knew that Todd was drilling his frigid gaze into their backs as they headed for the walkway to the plane. They also knew other passengers had been observing the embarrassing scene. They were glad they had enjoyed a serene morning at Rachel's house where they had said their farewells in private and made slow, passionate love, knowing they would have to wait a while for their next union.

Rachel sensed Quentin's anger and frustration, and she was proud of him for keeping a clear head and being as well mannered as possible. She was grateful to the Delta employee for rescuing them and thanked him.

Quentin realized now that he should have advised Rachel to remain at home. He didn't like putting her in this kind of situation or having Hardy know about her existence. He imagined how the snake could slither after her following his departure, just as others had done to his brother Frank. He believed their bond was too strong to be damaged by nasty news stories. Still, there was always the chance such an invasion of her privacy could cause Rachel distress and cause her to back away from him. He didn't want her to ever be sorry she had been reunited with him.

They sat down in the first class section and, after politely refusing a drink, chatted in soft voices until the remaining passengers began to come aboard, many slowing to look at them, most aware of who he was.

"I should leave before the person who has this seat arrives," she whispered. "Phone me as soon as you can."

"I will. Good-bye, Rachel. I'll call you and see you soon. Take good care of yourself and don't worry about anything."

"The same to you. Good-bye and good luck tomorrow."

"Thanks, I'll need it."

Their gazes fused, exchanged heart-felt messages, and she left the plane.

Rachel intended to stay until the flight left, but changed her mind when she found Todd Hardy lingering in the waiting area. She tried to push past him but he grasped her arm to delay her. "Let go of me, Mr. Hardy, and leave me alone or I'll report your offensive behavior to the magazine."

"I just want to ask you a few simple questions. Don't be so rude and touchy. You don't have anything to hide, do you?"

Rachel detested the smug and insulting look in the man's eyes and the crudely suggestive tone in his voice. She had done newspaper, television, and radio interviews in the past, but they had been concerning her projects and worthy causes, not focused on her personally. She didn't like being in the spotlight. She understood how Quentin— and other celebrities— grew tired of being shadowed and harassed and having everything about them and their lives exposed to public scrutiny.

The guard at the check-in point asked, "Anything wrong, ma'am?"

Rachel had noticed the officer's approach and waited for it in silence as she glared at Todd. "Yes, sir, this man is bothering me."

"I'm Todd Hardy from *Augusta Now* magazine. I'm only trying to interview Mrs. Gaines about Quentin Rawls."

"I told him I have nothing to say to him and to release my arm."

"Well, sir, the lady doesn't want to be interviewed. If you don't leave her alone, I'll have to escort you out. You don't want to create a nasty scene, so why not leave quietly and stop pestering her?"

"This is absurd! You can't throw me off public

property when I'm only doing my job and I haven't caused any trouble."

Rachel yanked her arm from his loosened grasp. "Yes, you have."

"You want me to call the sheriff's office and let them handle you?"

"They can't arrest me for asking questions!"

"They can prevent you from harassing this lady, which is what you are doing. Go along, ma'am, and I'll take care of Mr. Hardy."

Rachel thanked the guard and hurried out the door while the two men were arguing. She heard Todd try to end the exchange and follow her, but the guard persisted, apparently to give her time to depart. She rushed to her car, locked the door, and cranked the engine. As she drove away she saw Todd running toward her. She prayed Todd would forget about her. If the reporter harassed her again, she would have Newton Thomas, her lawyer, dissuade him. Leaving the airport, she noticed Quentin's plane taking off in the same direction in which she was heading for home, and hoped their separation would pass swiftly.

Rachel returned to her house to freshen up and to calm down before she went to pick up several senior citizens, members of her church, to carry them to doctors' appointments, the bank, and the grocery store. That deed was part of her volunteer work for a six-month span. Later, she decided as she grabbed a sandwich and milk, she would write to her daughters and phone her friends.

* * *

At midnight, one hour later than Texas time, Rachel gave up waiting for Quentin to call her this evening as promised. From a fear of losing another love to a plane crash, she had watched the six and eleven o'clock news programs and had phoned the airline to see if the flight had landed on time and safely, then sighed in relief after making certain it had.

Yet, she could not imagine why she hadn't heard from him by now. She reasoned he might be busy with any number of personal or professional matters. She realized he had not given her his phone number, and learned it was unlisted from the information operator when she decided she would call him or leave him a message.

Don't get crazy and insecure in less than a day alone. He'll explain when he phones. There must be a good reason why he couldn't call.

Thirteen

Early Wednesday morning as she sipped coffee and read the paper, Rachel answered the ringing phone and hoped it was Quentin.

"Hi, Mom, it's me. I hope you're not still asleep."

"Karen! Oh, honey, it's so good to hear from you. I'm up, but it wouldn't matter. Call any time you get the chance. How are you doing? How is David? Are you safe and well? Is everything all right there?"

"Whew, that's a lot of questions," Karen jested amidst laughter. "I'm fine and so is David. In fact, we're absolutely terrific. Please don't get upset or be disappointed, but we got married yesterday."

"Married?"

"We couldn't wait any longer, Mom. The ship captain performed the ceremony. We can have a celebration party after our return."

"Congratulations, honey; I'm so happy for you, and I understand. I realize you two want to be together every minute possible and December is a long way off. I bet it was romantic, wasn't it?"

"Yes, very," Karen said, and described the ceremony aboard the ship. "We realized we would be busy setting up our joint practice after our return, so planning a big wedding would have been too hectic."

"You're right. We'll have a large party next June, and I'll send out announcements as soon as I can get them printed and addressed."

"I was hoping you'd offer; thanks."

"I'll call David's mother and get a list of their family and friends so I can include them. This is such a wonderful surprise, Dr. Phillips. I'll have to get used to your new name. David is a lucky man."

"I'm lucky to have him. He's doing fine to answer your earlier question. Our work is going great; we're helping so many children. You wouldn't believe the awful living conditions and lack of medical facilities and doctors and medicine in some of the places we visit. They really need our help, and the people are so nice and grateful to us."

"I'm proud of you and David for being a part of such a worthy cause; not many people would take a year out of their lives and endure such hardships to do something like this. Just be careful."

"We're not taking any risks that would expose us to catching anything. And our ship, vehicles, tents, and jackets are well marked to identify us as a medical team. We haven't had any trouble and don't expect any. Besides, David watches over me like a hawk, so don't worry."

"That's good to hear, but I'll still worry until you two are home again."

"I know. I really appreciate the care packages you send; some things are difficult or impossible to buy over here. I miss you and my friends. How are Evelyn and her family doing in Japan?"

"She called last Saturday. She's going to be so excited about your marriage." Rachel related the news from Evelyn and the others. "As far as I know, I'll be going over to visit during the Christmas holidays."

"That should be fun; I know Evelyn and the kids will enjoy seeing you. I bet Alex and Ashley are growing like spring weeds. I can hardly wait until we have our practice well established and we can have our first child."

"You and David will be wonderful parents. I love you and miss you."

"I love you and miss you, too, Mom. What's been going on with you?"

Rachel told Karen about her various projects and activities, about local happenings, and about people they both knew. She took a deep breath before revealing the big news. "I met somebody special at the ARC class reunion last month and we were seeing each other regularly until he left town yesterday. Actually, we met on that cruise I took twelve years ago." Rachel related information about Quentin and their romance, and was delighted by her oldest daughter's reaction.

"He sounds marvelous, perfect for you. Don't worry about the age difference, not in these days and times. If you decide to marry him before Evelyn and I get home next year, do it; time's valuable; you know that from what happened to Daddy."

"Thanks, honey, and I'll let you know what we decide after Quentin gets his career problems straightened out."

"David's a big football fan, so I bet he knows who Quentin Rawls is. He'll be delighted by your news; I am. I can hardly wait to meet him. If you love him, he has to be wonderful. Go for it, Mom, and don't let anyone interfere."

"I won't, but it's hard dating such a celebrity." Rachel told Karen about the incidents with Todd Hardy, Janet Hollis, and Dorothy Gaines.

"Just ignore them; they're all troublemakers. I bet Grandmother and Grandfather will be astonished to hear about me and David. She'll probably scold us for not waiting and having a big church wedding and lots of parties."

"I'm sure she will, but don't let her bother you. Besides, your husband is David Phillips, and she won't have many naughty things to say, since he is from one of the oldest, wealthiest, and most prominent families here; that will please her; you know how Dorothy is about status and lineages."

"Grandmother is a snob, pure and simple; so is Janet Raburn Hollis. I mean it, Mom, don't allow them to make you miserable. Just be happy."

They chatted for another five minutes before Karen said she had to get off the phone so others could make their calls. She wasn't sure when she could phone again but promised to write often. "I love you, Mom, and tell Evelyn my good news. 'Bye."

"I love you, too, honey. Good-bye, and congratulate David for me."

Rachel hung up the receiver and smiled. Both of her daughters were married to wonderful men and were happy. She was overjoyed by those blessings, and must send Evelyn the news by Express Mail today. Now, if only Quentin would call soon so she could share it with him.

Rachel cleaned up the kitchen and went to shower for her Heart Fund luncheon and meeting. She was glad Jen and Becky would be there, but so would Janet and she wasn't looking forward to seeing that nosy woman. At least, she thought, Todd Hardy hadn't phoned or come by to see her, which was slightly surprising, given his aggressive actions at the airport.

While she was taking her bath, Quentin left a message saying he would phone again that night and had wonderful news. He said he hadn't called the previous night because lightning from the recent storms had knocked out some of his electrical equipment including three of his telephones. He was leaving the house for an appointment in town so he wouldn't be there for her to return his call. He teased her about taking off so early in the day to enjoy her freedom since his departure.

Rachel warmed as she listened to the message several times, ecstatic with his vow of love. She rushed to dress to get her tasks finished to be home to speak with him later.

Before her arrival at the meeting, Janet pulled Becky and Jen aside to voice her opinions about Quentin and their relationship. "I, for one, am glad he's gone; you should be, too. Rachel was behaving foolishly with him. You would have thought, as long as she's been around the Gaineses and people like us, she would have absorbed more class. The truth is, she wouldn't be in our social circle if she hadn't snared Daniel; and she should have found a proper husband to replace him years ago. Heavens, to go traipsing around with a younger man, a football jock, is indecent and silly. And he's a known womanizer, twice divorced. What could she possibly see in a man who came from near poverty and with a brother who's into drugs and no telling what else, including jail? Quentin is probably just like him; brothers aren't usually very different. Well, I hope Rachel has come to her senses now that he's gone. Her reputation is already in question. Her daughters would have fits if they knew how she was carrying on; if Karen and Evelyn were here, Rachel would behave herself."

Becky was provoked to say, "You aren't being fair, Janet. Quentin is a nice man, and he really likes her. I think they could be happy together."

"Surely you jest, Rebecca Hartly Cooper! Then again, they might have more in common than any of us realize; their backgrounds are similar. I just hope she hasn't gotten herself in trouble with him."

"What do you mean?" Jen asked as she seethed inside.

"Pregnant, silly. Surely you realize they've been sleeping together. I mean, she wouldn't answer the door when I went over to visit, and he was there all hours of the day and half the night. I doubt they were only talking."

"That's a wicked thing to say about our best friend."

"Don't be naive or let her kind fool you, Jennifer. In fact, if Rachel continues along this ridiculous course, you two should think hard about your friendship with her; you don't want her troubles to rub off on you."

"Here comes Rachel now. Why don't you talk to her about it?"

Janet looked suddenly flustered. "The meeting's about to begin. I'll see you two later."

Becky watched Janet hurry away and was surprised the woman didn't hang around to interrogate Rachel. She smiled at her friend and said, "Perfect timing; Janet was irritating us to no end."

"Thank goodness she left before I arrived. I didn't want to tangle with her today. Wait until you hear the wonderful news."

"About Quentin?"

"About Karen and David; they got married on the ship yesterday," Rachel began, then related the facts and Quentin's call before it was time to sit down to eat and discuss the future gala and collections.

Not wanting to spoil Rachel's good mood, Becky and Jen didn't tell her what Janet had said earlier. Later, they would, as they thought Rachel should be aware of the woman's feelings and actions.

When Quentin called, Rachel told him she had been working on her novel and was pleased with her progress. Again, he gave her encouragement and offered to connect her with his publishing friend. She related Karen's news and they chatted about the newlyweds, their work abroad, and the future party for them.

"So, what's your good news?" she asked, suspense chewing on her.

"I passed my physical and I'll be starting practice. If I get through it without another injury and play well, I'll make it to the preseason games. That will be my final hurdle to stay on the team this year."

"That's wonderful, Quentin; I'm so happy for you and proud of you. I told you not to worry, that you're in excellent condition."

"Thank God, you were right and I'll try to relax. I'm sorry I couldn't reach you Wednesday night. I hope you didn't worry about me."

"Of course, I worried. I love you."

Recalling how Daniel had died, he realized how dismayed she must have been at not hearing from him as promised. "I should have driven to a pay phone and called so you wouldn't worry. My housekeeper had the repair men here when I reached home and I got tied up with them. Did you try to call and discovered the problem?"

"I tried to phone but couldn't get your number; it's unlisted."

"Grab a pencil and paper right now so I can give it to you. I picked up a new answering machine today, so you can leave a message if I'm not home."

"Ready," Rachel said, and jotted down his number.

"So, what else have you been doing since I left?"

Rachel told him about her confrontation at the airport with Todd.

"That sorry snake! I should've known he'd pull a stunt like that and warned you. Next time, you won't go to the airport with me and be subjected to such abuse. I'm sorry, Rachel."

"Is it always like that; I mean, with reporters?"

"Not always. Most of them are nice and cooperative. It's those tabloid reporters you have to worry about; they're all like Todd Hardy. They'll pounce on you anywhere and everywhere. I've even had one try to corner me in the men's room and another one in a store's dressing room while I was wearing only my briefs and socks. I've had them go through my trash at home and in hotels. If it happens to you again, just push past him and keep saying, No comment. And speaking of cunning snakes, how is Janet?" He chuckled.

"As awful as usual, but I'm not letting her bother me much."

"After we marry and we're living here, we won't have to deal with the Todds and Janets of the world anymore."

"That sounds marvelous, Quentin."

"Which part?"

"All of it, but especially the marrying and living together. I love you and miss you so much. It seems as if you've been gone for ages."

"I love you and miss you, too. When can you come to visit me?"

"Not for a while. You have practice and I have to finish my projects and commitments. Besides, you have to concentrate on practice and the pre-season games; you'll need all of your strength and stamina for them. I don't mind; this is important to you, so it's important to me. We'll have the rest of our lives to spend together."

"I'm happy you see it that way, Rachel. You're the kindest, most generous, understanding, and thoughtful person I know. Lordy, I'm lucky. I guess we'll have to settle for phone calls until September."

"Hearing your voice isn't as good as seeing you, but it helps."

"Would it help if I gave you a ring and we made an announcement about our future plans? Or do you think that would call too much attention to you while we're separated? I don't want those media dogs sniffing at your door and trying to get information about me."

"I think it's best to wait until your situation

is settled. And it won't be much longer. By staying busy, six months will pass quickly. Have you spoken to Bill about your trip here?"

"Yes, and he and his group have dropped Augusta as a possible site. To prevent offending anyone, he's sent explanations and thank yous to the people I met with and who helped me gather the information. He's even sending you a surprise."

"That's nice of him but unnecessary. I had fun working with you."

"I had more than fun working with you. I'm glad he asked me to do the scouting there for him or we wouldn't have been reunited. I'm the one who should be sending him a gift of gratitude instead of cashing his check. Speaking of earning money, a collector's company has offered me a contract for selling autographs and signed items. Some of the baseball players have earned big bucks selling autographs, so I figured, why not cash in on my name and fame while they're still worth something?"

"Congratulations, Quentin; that's exciting and well deserved; you are a star, a living legend. I want to get one of everything to save for Alex."

"I'll make sure you do. If it goes well, it should pay for the house renovations. I spoke with Scott this afternoon and everything is on go for late September. You are coming with him, aren't you? Becky, too."

"Sounds wonderful to me. Of course, we won't have much privacy with a friend along," she hinted in a suggestive tone.

"We'll figure out some way to elude the Coopers when necessary."

"Ah, yes, I had forgotten you're skilled in that area. And in others."

"Don't you go getting me hot and bothered this far away from you."

Rachel laughed again. "I hope I always have that effect on you, near or far. That's what you do to me if I only think about you or see your picture."

"In that case, I should have wallpapered your house with my pictures so you'd think about me constantly."

"You don't have to worry about me having a drifting eye."

"Me, either. Well, I best let you go; it's getting late, and I have to rest up for what's ahead. It's gonna be tough."

"You take care of yourself and don't get hurt. I'll talk to you soon."

"Tomorrow night?"

"I'm going to the opera with the Coopers and Brimsfords at seven."

"And I'll be out most of the day, so I'll call you on Saturday."

"I have the church bake and attic sale from one to five, but I'll be home before and after it."

"Always busy and helping others. You're a wonder, Rachel Gaines. I'll call you Saturday evening. I love you. 'Bye."

"I love you. Good night."

* * *

On Friday, Rachel ran errands during the morning, including a trip to the printers to select and order announcements of Karen and David's marriage.

That afternoon she worked on her novel and she became so engrossed that she had to rush to get ready for her evening at the opera and dinner with her friends. After noticing the time, she showered, donned an ivory lace dress with a matching silk slip underdress, and did a swift grooming and makeup.

When the Coopers arrived to pick her up, she learned that the Brimsfords were joining them at Bell Auditorium and that Keith Haywood was with Becky and Scott.

Becky came inside for a minute to explain the situation. "I'm sorry about surprising you like this, Rach, but you didn't answer the phone when I tried to call to warn you. Keith was going with the Zimmermans but they had to cancel on him today because of family illness. Scott saw him at the club this afternoon and asked Keith to go with us. I didn't know about it until Scott came home at five. I hope you don't mind and, honestly, we aren't setting you up with him tonight."

"Don't worry, as long as Keith knows we aren't on a date. I don't want him to get the wrong idea."

"Scott explained to him that you're seeing somebody regularly who's out of town, so it's only a friendly evening." Becky's gaze swept over Rachel's appearance. "You look terrific; I love that outfit, very classy and flattering. Well, we'd better go or we'll be late."

Keith had gotten out of the BMW to meet Rachel and assist the two women with car doors.

"It's a pleasure to meet you, Rachel," he said sincerely. "Scott and Becky speak highly of you. It was kind of him to rescue and include me tonight."

"It's nice to meet you, Keith, and I'm glad we could be helpful. It would have been a shame to miss the opera or to go alone."

En route, the four got better acquainted. They talked about Keith's move to Augusta and partnership in Newton Thomas's law firm. They talked about their children— he had two by a previous marriage that ended four years ago— and about local happenings.

As they chatted, Rachel noticed Keith's reaction to her. During their introductions, the tall man's green gaze had glowed with interest and his mellow voice had revealed interest. Becky had not exaggerated the newcomer's looks: Keith was handsome, and well-built, with good manners and an outgoing personality. He appeared to be younger than his forty-nine years, and not a hair on his brown head was gray. He had a fantastic tan from participating in many outdoor sports, which were mentioned during their conversation, and it enhanced his white teeth and a sexy smile. The lawyer, she knew, was from a prominent Macon family and old money, but he was not conceited about his status, or wealth. He was genial and charming without being forward or flirtatious. It was doubtful Keith Haywood had any trouble snaring women's interest or getting dates; that made her curious about why he had planned to go to the opera without a companion tonight. Perhaps, she reasoned, he only wanted to relax without having to entertain a date.

As the evening progressed into dinner at Michael's Restaurant after the opera, Rachel and the others were unaware of the man observing them in stealth and taking furtive pictures and notes.

When they reached Rachel's house, Keith walked her to the door, shook her hand, and said, "I had a wonderful time tonight, the best since I arrived in Augusta; in fact, the best in a long time. Thank you, Rachel, for a relaxing and fun evening. If you . . . part ways with the man you're currently seeing, please give me a call; I'd like to see you again."

"Thank you, Keith; that's very nice and flattering. I enjoyed myself, too, but I *am* committed elsewhere and happy about it."

"He's lucky he found you first. Good night and thanks again."

Rachel went inside, touched by the man's words and respectful behavior. She was relieved she hadn't met the lawyer and started seeing him before Quentin's return, as Keith was appealing and charming. She had no doubt Quentin would have stolen her heart again, but she might have hurt Keith by dropping him for the quarterback, or refused to see Quentin to avoid being cruel to Keith. She was glad things had worked out as they had, and hoped Keith found a good woman.

Saturday following the combination church bake and attic sale for the homeless shelter, Rachel returned to work on her novel.

When Quentin phoned later, she didn't tell him about Janet's sly remarks about what a nice-looking couple she and Keith made and how Rachel should grab the excellent prospect fast, but she did tell him about her day's tasks and her evening out last night.

"I forgot to tell you I'm a jealous man," he jested. "I wish I were there to protect my interest and I'm glad you discouraged his."

"You don't have to worry, because your interest is well guarded and safe. I love and want only you, Quentin Rawls. But," she added, "it is flattering to know you're jealous. You make certain my interest is just as safe out there, on and off the playing field."

"I can assure you that nothing and no one will come between us and I'll take good care of myself for our honeymoon."

"An excellent precaution, Mr. Rawls, because you'll need all the strength, stamina, and health you can muster to take care of me later. I'm working up a tremendous appetite."

"So am I, and we won't be disappointed. What's on your agenda for this week?"

"Changing the subject so you won't get aroused so far away from me?"

He chuckled. "Of course. Don't forget, I'm skilled in self-defense."

"Is it working?"

"Nope, but I'll keep trying until I see you again."

"So will I, but it's a difficult task. As to my schedule, I have to take flowers to our church's shut-ins tomorrow afternoon, but I'll be home by five. Monday, Jen, Becky, and I are having lunch. We're going to a bridal shower for a friend's daughter that night. Wednesday, I have my Community Outreach meeting, and that woman's club sale is still on for the Civic Center on Saturday from ten to five."

"I take it Janet and Dianne found somebody to handle it for them."

"Yes, but they're still annoyed with me for refusing to take charge. Actually, I hope everything goes well; it's for a good cause. I only wish their hearts were in the right place."

"I doubt either of them will ever change. Are you making progress on the book?"

"The first draft is almost finished. Then I'll have to polish it. Submission is the scary part."

"Let me know when you're ready for me to connect you with Jim."

"I will, and I'm glad you're so supportive."

"You'll succeed, so don't worry. We'll all be proud of you for trying, whether you get published or not; but you will, I'm sure."

"Thanks for the vote of confidence; I'll try my best. So, what's on your agenda next week?"

"Practice, practice, and more practice, tormenting the old body."

"That's fine, as long as you don't damage— shall we say?— vital parts."

They shared laughter and chatted another twenty minutes.

"I love you, Rachel. I'll call tomorrow night."

"Good-bye, Quentin, and I love *you*."

Rachel talked with Quentin on Friday, as she had done almost every night that week. She told him about receiving a gold bracelet from Bill Effingham in appreciation for her help on his project. She related news of additional collections for the Georgia flood victims who were still recovering from their devastating losses last month. She told him she had spoken to Evelyn and the grandchildren that morning.

"I'm turning in early tonight to rest up for tomorrow. It's going to be a long and busy day." Hopefully too hectic for Janet to harass me.

"Don't exhaust yourself, woman; take plenty of breaks."

"I will," she agreed.

When Becky arrived at eight o'clock Saturday morning, Rachel said, "You're early; I thought you said you'd pick me up at nine, but I'm almost ready. Uh, oh, I know that look; you're angry. What's wrong?"

"Have you seen or heard about this, Rach?" she asked, shaking a copy of *Augusta Now* magazine. "I picked it up yesterday while I was shopping, but I didn't read it until last night, too late to phone you. How could that lowlife print such trash or the magazine allow it?"

"What are you talking about?"

Becky flipped open the magazine and held it out to Rachel, who took it and gaped at the pictures. "Sit down and read it. I'll keep quiet until you finish. In fact, I'll grab a cup of coffee."

Rachel walked to the sofa while Becky headed for the kitchen. She looked at pictures of her and Quentin on dates, and pictures of her with Keith last Friday night. The article talked about Quentin's recent trip to Augusta and the reason for his visit. It said the deal was off because the town wasn't considered a good location for a new team. It was written in such a manner as to suggest Augusta was viewed unworthy and inferior to Quentin Rawls and the investment group he had scouted for last month. The words used implied that the town had lost a wonderful opportunity because of Quentin's dislike and disrespect for it.

The article went on to include information about what had seemed to be a promising romance between Rachel and the quarterback, but one that couldn't survive Quentin's absence. "It appears to this writer as if the widow of Daniel

Gaines isn't suffering over their separation since she has been seen around town with handsome bachelor and lawyer, Keith Haywood." Beside those remarks were two pictures of her and Keith, smiling and talking at the opera and at the restaurant. Worse, Todd Hardy's following comments were: "Let's hope the Dallas Cowboys don't dump Rawls as quickly and easily as it appears Mrs. Gaines has done or he'll be recovering from two additional injuries in the coming months." Todd had mentioned Rachel's charity work and reminded readers of the Gaines family stature. He revealed she had been Quentin's "tour guide and research assistant," but apparently "she was unable to persuade him and his group of investors to locate a team here," though he was "certain Mrs. Gaines gave it her best and untiring efforts during their many days and nights together."

"You sorry and devious bastard!" Rachel shrieked.

"Can you believe they would print such bull?" Becky asked.

"I thought vicious material and surreptitious methods belonged to tabloids, not to small-town magazines. I knew Todd was hopping mad when Quentin and I refused to be interviewed by him, but I never expected him to retaliate like this. How could the magazine print such trash? Dorothy and Richard will have a fit if they see this article; it's an insult to all of us."

"Do you think you should call and warn them?"

"No, that would give the matter too much importance. I'm going to ignore it. To say or do anything might make it look as if those implications are true."

"What if Quentin sees it?" Becky asked.

"He'll be mad, but he's used to invasion of his privacy. I'm not. Of course, I'll tell him about it when he phones later. Darnit, Becky, Todd shouldn't have even *mentioned* me in an article about Quentin. To tell such lies or to imply them as facts is outrageous. I just hope Janet hasn't seen it. If she has, she'll be all over me today with cutting remarks. And Keith will be so embarrassed, he'll wish he'd never met me."

"It isn't your fault, Rach. I'm sure Keith will understand; he has a good sense of humor so he'll probably find the matter amusing. If not, he's a lawyer."

"He wasn't maligned so there's nothing he can do. I just hope it doesn't cause him to think badly of me."

"It won't; he's a smart man. Relax, Rach, nobody who knows you will believe this nonsense about you, and *anybody* who reads the magazine knows about his slanted style of journalism."

"If Janet or others dare to harass me today, I won't stay at the sale."

"If anything bothers you, just come and get me and we'll leave."

"I'd better go finish dressing. I won't take long. Thanks for warning me about this so I won't be caught off guard, which is what Janet will hope."

* * *

When Rachel returned home at six, she was simmering with anger. She paced the kitchen floor and sipped wine to calm herself while she reasoned on what to do about a startling and infuriating matter. Janet had pulled her aside after the sale ended and spoken of her deep concern over the malicious and misleading article. She went on to say how it could destroy her new relationship with Keith Haywood, "that is, if you've gotten over your foolish infatuation with that young football player." But that wasn't the main thing that vexed Rachel, and Janet had gone too far this time.

Fourteen

Rachel did not attend church on Sunday and Becky took over her duties with the shut-ins for the afternoon because she did not want to see anyone so soon after the magazine's release on Friday. Nor was she ready to confront the Hollises following Janet's stunning behavior and the exposure of Cliff's treachery, at least not in a public place and certainly not at church. In her current state of mind, Rachel was unsure of what she might be provoked to do or say if Cliff or Janet— or *both* Hollises— approached her particularly if the brazen woman dared to make further comments about Rachel's private life. Never had she been so close to completely losing her temper.

After much soul-searching and prayer, Rachel decided she had done nothing wrong and would not go into hiding as if she had. If anyone asked questions at the woman's club luncheon tomorrow, she would deflect them with a woe-is-me smile and an "it's so ridiculous I don't even want to discuss it." But if the inquisitor was the daring Janet Raburn Hollis, she vowed, the woman was a total fool and was in for an astonishing surprise!

Yet, it was Rachel who received a stunning shock that afternoon.

On Monday morning, after she had taken time the previous night to calm down and plan a course of action, Rachel went to the bank to meet with Clifford Hollis who helped her manage her estate and make business decisions. She closed his office door, sat down before his desk, and stared at him.

Cliff noted her strange action and chilly expression. "Good morning, Rachel; I thought our meeting was set for this afternoon after the woman's club luncheon. I'll phone Dick Matheny and see if he's available to come over. I— "

"There won't be a meeting between us, Cliff, not after what you did. Of all the people I thought was trustworthy and was a friend, it was you." She saw confusion and dismay fill his gaze as he straightened in his chair.

"What are you talking about, Rachel?"

"My business with you is supposed to be strictly confidential." Rachel watched his gaze widen in surprise and heard his chair squeak as he leaned forward and propped his arms on the desk.

"It is; I would never discuss your affairs with anyone else without your permission. I haven't shown your financial statement and my recommendations to Dick, not yet. Have you replaced your accountant?"

"No, but I am withdrawing my funds from your bank. Our business relationship is terminated as of today. As to our friendship, that remains to be seen if I can forgive your recent actions. Even if your behavior was unintentional, it is inexcusable and distressing to me." Again, she saw confusion and anxiety flood his small hazel eyes.

"Why? I don't understand. Have I offended you in some way? If so, I'm deeply sorry and I apologize. Please, explain everything to me."

"Why did you reveal my private business matters to your wife?"

"Reveal them to Janet? What do you mean? I didn't show or tell Janet anything about your financial affairs. I would never do anything like that to any of my clients."

"Then how does she know my net worth, list of holdings, and my plan to sell some of them and turn the money over to my daughters?"

"What?" he murmured in astonishment.

"After the charity sale on Saturday, she mentioned things to me that she could know only if she read my records or was told about my affairs. You, my girls, my accountant, and the income tax office are the only ones with that knowledge; I'm sure none of them told her. That leaves only one source: her husband, you."

"I can assure you I'm totally blameless. Why didn't you phone me about this? There must be some kind of misunderstanding."

"I waited until this morning to handle the situation because I was so taken by surprise that I've been too upset and furious to do so earlier. I can assure you, Cliff, there is no misunderstanding; Janet made herself totally clear. She knew I was planning to divest myself of the Gaines candy stock and my real estate holdings and give the girls the value of the shares they would have inherited upon my death. She said it was a smart idea, if I was foolishly planning to marry Quentin Rawls in the near future, better than a prenuptial agreement since some clever lawyers find ways to break those agreements, and I would probably die before him since he's so much younger than I am. She said my idea would prevent him from getting his hands on my money and wasting it before I could leave it to the girls. She knew I have a large estate, and she knew the exact figure. Where did she get her facts, if not from you? Certainly not from the Gaineses, who don't know the figures."

"That's impossible because Janet has no access to bank records." As he pondered the troubling situation for a while, he suddenly paled and grimaced. "My God, she wouldn't! Lord have mercy, she must have. I took your file home on Friday to make notes over the weekend for our meeting today. Janet must have looked in my briefcase and read it while I was out playing golf. I can't believe she would do something like that," he murmured.

"Well, if you didn't breach my confidence, she obviously did snoop."

"I'm sorry, Rachel; I would never do anything like this. I had no idea she would go through my confidential files. This is horrible. I can assure you I will deal with her and this won't happen again, ever."

Rachel was relieved that Cliff had not betrayed her; she was certain he hadn't, because she saw how upset, furious, and embarrassed he was. "I can see that you've done nothing wrong, Cliff, and I apologize for my accusation. I'm sure you can understand how dismayed I was. Please reschedule our meeting with my accountant Mr. Matheny for next week. I'm still too unsettled to think clearly or to make any serious decisions on the sales. And please tell Janet not to sic our pastor on me again like she did yesterday."

When Cliff looked bewildered, Rachel explained, "She told him I was confused and behaving immorally and needed him to come over and pray with me and give me advice. He said she was worried about me because she believed I was going to sell my holdings here so I could go to Texas to live with Quentin. I have no intention of moving in with Quentin unless I marry him. Next, if she hasn't already done it, she'll be phoning the Gaineses to expose my plans and make more nasty innuendos. I was so shocked after her disclosures that I just stared at her, then went home without giving her a piece of my mind and warning her to stay out of my business. I will soon."

Cliff stood, as she had risen to depart. "Again, Rachel, let me apologize for this outrage and assure you this will never happen again."

Rachel smiled and shook his hand. "I believe you, Cliff. Thanks for all you've done for me in the past, and I'm sorry I had to be the one to bring you such disturbing and painful news."

"Goodbye, Rachel, and I'll call Mr. Matheny promptly."

As she left the bank, Rachel did not grasp how furious Cliff was or imagine what the man intended to do within the hour as his fury increased.

Before the women's club luncheon meeting began and after most of the members were seated at tables and chatting with friends, Cliff arrived at the Pinnacle Club and located his wife in the President's Room. He told Janet he needed to talk with her immediately. Cliff practically yanked his curious wife into a smaller dining room, as his seething anger would not allow the matter to go unchallenged until they were at home.

Rachel, Becky, and Jennifer were leaving the ladies' room— when Cliff almost stalked past them to find Janet. Since Rachel had related the terrible situation to her friends earlier, they were unable to resist the temptation to eavesdrop and learn the truth. They sneaked to a concealed corner of the hallway and listened. They overheard Janet scold her husband for his "ridiculous behavior."

"I'm being ridiculous? How dare you sneak into my briefcase and read confidential information about my clients and then reveal it! I'll tell you now, Janet, it's against the law to steal people's banking records and divulge those facts; and what you did is theft, pure and simple," he fabricated to scare her. "This is unforgivable and outrageous, woman. How could you do something wicked and criminal."

"What on earth are you jabbering about? Stop insulting me and keep your voice down before everybody hears you making an idiot of yourself and humiliating both of us. This isn't the time or place for such an absurd discussion. We'll talk about it at home tonight."

"No, we won't; we're finished. And you know exactly what I'm talking about: You could have gotten me fired, cost us our friends and social status, bankrupted us. You could have had us both facing criminal charges and multiple lawsuits. Talk about humiliation, that would be a huge and costly scandal, all because of your stupid antics. This was the last straw, Janet; I'm fed up with you and so is everybody else. You're rude, spiteful, conniving, crude, and hateful. The only reason anybody tolerates you and endures your despicable behavior is because you're my wife and the Raburns' daughter. I hope they all dump you like I'm going to do this very day."

"What do you mean?"

"It's over between us, Janet; I'm getting a divorce. In fact, I'm seeing a lawyer today at three. I'll pack and leave this evening."

"You can't! You wouldn't dare! What about the children, our families, our friends?"

"They'll understand and agree; they know what you're like. Why do you think our kids live so far away and rarely visit or phone or write? I'll tell you why, because you make them as miserable as you are with your intrusions and cutting remarks. With you out of my life, I can be the kind of father and grandfather I should have been for years, the kind I want to be. You're a cold, bitter, and destructive woman who shouldn't be inflicted upon other people, especially your family. I should have left you long ago."

"It's that bitch's fault, isn't it? You're taking her word over your own wife's. She's never been one of us, and this proves it. She's trash; she screwed around with that football jock and probably with Keith. She's— "

"Be careful, Janet, or you'll be facing slander charges. The fact you know the client's identity tells me you're guilty, because I never mentioned her name or sex. She's a nice person and doesn't deserve the garbage you've piled on her; nobody does. If you know what's good for you, back off and leave her alone, or she'll be provoked into ending the matter in a way I doubt you'll like. I can assure you, woman, she's reached her limit with you; so have I. You'll hear from my lawyer. Good-bye, and good riddance."

"Don't you dare speak to me this way!"

"I'll speak to you any way I damn well please and it feels great. Hell, it's cleansing just to get this off my chest and get you out of my life. I'm no longer your doormat, Janet, and I doubt anybody else will continue to let you step on them."

"Don't you dare turn your back and walk out on me. You'll be sorry. I'll take you for every cent you have, you miserable worm. You're lucky I even married you and stayed with you so many years."

"No, Janet, *you* were lucky I suffered in silence for too many years, and damn lucky everybody else did the same. You're coldhearted and mean, Janet, and you're blind and stupid if you think people don't realize you intentionally try to hurt and humiliate others. If you don't wise up and change your ways, you'll be ostracized, totally alone. Thank the Lord, I'll soon be free of you. I'll be out of the house before bedtime."

"Don't you leave me, Clifford Hollis, or you'll be sorry."

"It's over, Janet, so accept it. See a shrink and solve your problems. Find out why you act this despicable and disgusting way and stop it for everybody's sake, including yours. Good-bye."

Rachel, Becky, and Jen watched Cliff vanish around the corner, smiling and whistling as he waited for the elevator. They saw the double doors close to the room where Janet was; the woman was lingering there, they concluded, to collect her wits or to hide in embarrassment until the luncheon was over and she could retrieve her purse and escape.

"Can you believe it?" Becky whispered to her two friends. "Her comeuppance wasn't from a stranger or provoked victim; it came from a fed-up husband who finally found his backbone. Lordy, it was difficult not to congratulate and praise him. Surely you don't feel sorry for her?" she asked Rachel, whose expression implied she did.

"I suppose I'm too tenderhearted, but I do pity her. I know she brought it on herself, but she has to have deep-seated problems to act as she does. Maybe this episode will make her see the light and get help. Holding grudges takes too much energy and does emotional damage. Besides, it isn't the Christian way to be unforgiving and cruel and spiteful. If she leaves me alone, I'll just ignore her and avoid her as much as possible."

"You're right, Rach, and we'll try to do the same."

"You know Cliff was exaggerating about her sneaky deed being illegal," Rachel remarked, "at least, I think he was. He probably wanted to scare her and punish her for hurting and humiliating him, and to stop her from repeating the confidential information she gathered. I'm sure he could get into plenty of trouble for taking records home and giving somebody the opportunity to read them, but I'm just as certain it was an innocent mistake on his part. Now let's go eat, and pretend we heard nothing."

During the luncheon, a waitress retrieved Janet's purse for her, and she left the building, too ashamed to face the group again. Those near the door had overheard parts of the argument when the couple's voices were raised, and they whispered about it frequently during the meal and subsequent meeting. Fortunately for Rachel, the words about her had not reached their ears, sparing her from speculative involvement.

"Well," Quentin asked when he called that evening, "did you see Cliff today?"

Rachel related her conversation with Cliff and the man's subsequent confrontation with Janet. "If his phony threats worked, she'll be out of my hair for good."

"If not, and don't count too heavily on it with her, you won't have to endure her offensive behavior much longer, January at the latest."

"I know, but I hate to leave town with a cloud over my head, and I could if Janet and I come to verbal blows and a nasty scene. I also don't want her calling the Gaineses and causing me more trouble with them; that's exactly the type of thing she would do for spite and meanness, especially if she believes I'm to blame for her split with Cliff and that embarrassing scene at the Pinnacle Club. I'm certain she won't hold herself responsible, so she might make me her scapegoat. Of course, Dorothy and Richard should be delighted when they get Daniel's stock back. I'm definitely going to sell it to them, at fair market price. Those rental properties, too, if they want them. If not, to somebody else. After I leave Augusta, I don't want any business dealings here. I'll offer it to them first as an overture of peace."

"Maybe that will soften their feelings toward you."

"I doubt it; they've disliked me since the beginning and it's unlikely those ill feelings will ever change. But it might soothe matters between them and the girls; Dorothy and Richard are their grandparents and I hate for too many more years to pass in conflict because of me. It's sad and destructive to have such a long family rift."

"That isn't your fault, Rachel; you can't control their feelings and actions any more than you can Janet's. They have to decide they want peace; they have to change, not you."

"At least I know I've done everything I can to appease them."

"I can guarantee you'll love my parents and they'll love you, and we'll all get along beautifully. Every time I mention you to them, they get more excited about meeting you and us marrying. They're very happy for us."

"I'm glad, Quentin, and I'm eager to meet them."

They talked for a while about issues and details affecting both their lives, then Quentin said, "I handled that other nasty matter by phoning your local newspaper and Pete Starns at the TV station; I gave them interviews about the new league project and why Augusta didn't get cho-

sen and about Todd Hardy's motives. They were
most cooperative and professional. I got the feeling that Hardy and his type of journalism isn't
tolerated. Finding himself on the other side of
an exposé should shut him up. If not, my lawyer
will speak to the magazine editor about the repercussions of attacking you in print; I'm a public figure and have little— if any— protection
against such articles, but you should. Whatever
it takes, Rachel, I'll do my best to prevent your
exposure to further harassment. Hardy sent me
a copy of the magazine by Express Mail; he really tried to do a malicious number on us and
wanted to be sure I learned about it. I'm sorry,
Rachel."

"It wasn't your fault, Quentin. We'll forget
about Todd, the article, and Janet. Hopefully
they're out of our lives and hair."

"Maybe, but you can't ever tell about people
like them." He wouldn't be surprised if one of
the tabloids got wind of Hardy's article or was
sent a copy and reprinted parts of it, but he
surely hoped not. He didn't want anything or
anybody causing problems for them. "What's up
this week?"

Rachel realized he was moving on to a pleasant topic and was glad to reveal her activities.
"An arts council meeting tomorrow, a Heart
Fund meeting on Wednesday and a movie with
Becky and Jen that night, bridge on Thursday
morning, a meeting in the afternoon to discuss
our current project to benefit the child and wife
abuse centers, the art show on Friday, and the

symphony and dinner on Saturday night with the Coopers and Brimsfords."

"Are you going to the art show and symphony with Keith Haywood?"

"No, I don't think that would be a good idea. He's nice, a real gentleman, and good company, but I don't want him or others thinking we're a couple."

"In view of those pictures and implications, that's smart." *And I don't want to risk losing you to another man.* "I did get those autographed items for your celebrity auction; they're already in the mail to you."

"Thanks, and I'm sure they'll bring in good money. When do you leave for Mexico City to play in the American Bowl against Houston?"

"Friday, so we can rest and practice on Saturday and Sunday before we play on Monday. Since we'll be up to our necks in practices and interviews, I won't be able to call until I get back home on Tuesday. I'll give you my hotel number Thursday night, in case you need to reach me."

"Let's hope nothing happens to warrant it. You be careful down there; watch what you eat and drink. You don't want to be sidelined Monday with Montezuma's revenge. And don't be partying with those pretty senoritas."

He chuckled at her playful tone and words. "Don't worry, I'll behave, and I'll watch everything that passes my lips. The only things on my mind will be you and football. I promise I'll be careful, but I am going all out to prove myself to avoid being cut from the roster, if I get to play enough to accomplish that goal."

"Well, I'll be watching on TV. At least I'll get to see you; jump in front of the camera any time you can. Good luck, Quentin, I know this game is important to you."

"If anybody can understand my feelings for football and what it's like for me to give it up, it's you, Rachel. When I was playing in high school, I also had my family and studies and farm work to concentrate on. In college, I had my studies and other activities, a life off the field, outside the game. It's different in pro ball when it's your life's work. After I was drafted in '78, it became my driving force, my sole ambition was to be the best I could be, to rise to the top. Since then, I've practically eaten, drank, breathed, and slept football. My teammates are like family, some like brothers, the coach like a second father. It's a major part of my life. At times, it was the most important thing in my life, along with my family. It's full of challenges, rewards, and excitement. I love pushing myself to my limits and sometimes beyond them. My heart races and I get goosebumps and charged with energy when I hear a crowd roar my name, cheer a particular play, or see a monitor flicker my praises in bright lights. Winning tough games, earning championship and Superbowl rings, knowing my contribution was vital to a win, having my friends and coach pat me on the back after a cunning play, and setting records are tremendously satisfying. It's beyond description to relate how it feels to gain the respect and admiration of teammates, opponents, the media, and thousands of fans."

Rachel heard the longing and love in his voice as he exposed his feelings, probably as never told in such depth and earnestness to anyone else. Football was far more than a job to him, and she hated for him to lose it. But that day was coming, whether it be this year or the next. She hoped and prayed she was enough to fill the void it would leave in his heart and life, as he was enough to fill the one in hers.

"No quarterback or other player can win or lose a game alone, but it seems that way plenty of times. For sixteen years, my life has been centered around the sport: the practices, games, interviews, and even endorsements. I admit some of it has to do with the fame and fortune involved in making it to the top, but the main part is the sheer love of the sport and pitting yourself against such odds. To have to quit before I'm ready is like cutting off my arms and legs or cutting out my heart. I *am* my career, Rachel, or what it's made of me. It's hard and painful to imagine never playing again. But I don't want Troy or Rodney or Jason to get hurt just so I'm needed."

"That says a great deal about you as a person, Quentin. No matter what happens, I love you and I'm proud of you. When it's behind you, you'll know you did your best, and that's what counts the most."

"I do want to go out in style, not playing badly

and booted out. I desperately want this final season when a threepeat is at stake and the sport is celebrating its seventy-fifth year anniversary. But I'll retire before I shame myself, hurt the team's chances for victory, or get cut as a has-been."

"No one could ever say you're a has-been or a failure, so don't even think that way. You've won many awards, set records, not to mention that you've given pleasure to thousands of people worldwide, been a good influence on young sportsmen, supported many worthwhile causes, and become a wealthy and famous success. It isn't your fault or a weakness that you were injured twice and that might halt your career sooner than you desire. Think of all the good things that have come to you from playing pro football for sixteen years. And think how it affected us: if you hadn't been injured, you wouldn't have been on that cruise years ago when we met. If you hadn't been an excellent player, you wouldn't have been sent to Augusta to scout it for Bill so we could be united. Everything has a purpose in our lives, Quentin; good or bad, it pushes us to the next stage. We learn and grow from past experiences, or we're doomed to repeat mistakes. Whatever you decide to do after football, you'll succeed because you're smart, strong, resilient, determined, and brave, on and off the field."

"You're right, woman, and I'm glad you gave me that pep talk. You're an intelligent, kind, and generous person, Rachel Gaines. Have I told you today how much I love you and need you?"

Heat spread through her body and joy filled her heart. "No, so you're behind in your duty to me and our relationship."

"I promise, you and our marriage will be top priorities to me. Not even football could come between us. I love you with all my heart, Rachel, and I do need you; I need what you bring to me and my life— completion. Thanks for understanding my feelings and for giving me such good advice."

"We'll always be there for each other, Quentin, in good and bad times. I love you and need you, too. I miss you like crazy; it would be worse if you didn't call so often, but your phone bill is going to be sky high."

He laughed and said, "It's worth every cent to hear your voice."

"You were absolutely fantastic on Monday night, Quentin; I stayed glued to the television during the entire game. You got to play a lot, so I know you're ecstatic," she told him when he phoned on Wednesday.

"Thanks, it was wonderful, and I played well," he said in confidence, not boasting. "Coach Switzer knows Troy is great and didn't need testing and shouldn't risk an injury in a preseason game, so he gave me the chance to show what I've got left. Thank God, I didn't fumble or trip or throw an interception, and I put some points on the scoreboard. I only got sacked once, and that was because that big fellow broke through the line and nailed me. I saw him coming so I was prepared to take his hit and protected myself. My knee and shoulder are doing fine today, just a little sore and stiff. Lordy, it was exciting when I couldn't find a man open and had to run the ball on that last play in the third quarter, nothing between me and the end zone to stop me from crossing that line, thanks to great blocking. Do I ever love those guys, and they did a good job for me. I might be an aging mainstay and injury plagued, but I ignored any pain and went for the goal. Best run and six points of my career. What a rush."

Rachel was delighted by his elation and success. She loved the sound of his voice, so full of pride and joy and vitality. No matter what happened now, he had that glorious day to remember. "The articles in yesterday's newspaper raved about your skills, so did the sports announcers on TV."

"Yep, they were kind with their words. 'Course, everybody's still wondering if I'll make the cut or retire. Even if I did great on Monday, and I think I did, the Cowboys don't need four quarterbacks. It's rare for more than one to be put out of commission during a season. I won't fool myself, Rachel, I think Troy, Jason, and Rodney are more valuable to the team than I am with these injuries; and judgment calls for the final roster can't be based on friendship and loyalty to any player. It's no secret that my shoulder or knee could go out again at any time and leave them in a bind if they kept me signed up. Oh, well, the decision isn't mine to make, not yet. If I don't shine and shine brightly in the next two games, it's over for me."

"Do Switzer and the other coaches and the owner know you plan to choose retirement over dismissal?" *If you get that opportunity before they approach you, which I pray doesn't happen.*

Quentin was touched by the careful selection of her last word. "They probably suspect it, but we haven't discussed the situation. I don't want to make it appear to them as if my plans are set if they dump me; that could influence their decision, point them in the wrong direction if they believe I've already accepted the inevitable and won't be bothered. I'll just wait and see what happens in the next few weeks. Sorry I couldn't call last night but our afternoon flight back was delayed by bad weather. We didn't land until late last night and I didn't want to disturb your beauty sleep."

Rachel surmised he was terminating the earlier topic. "It's been awful here, too; we had almost four inches of rain yesterday. The meeting with Cliff and Mr. Matheny went off without a hitch; the sale is in motion. Or rather, the Gaineses will receive their notice tomorrow, and we expect them to snap it up immediately. I'll be glad to get that business out of the way. Janet wasn't at church or the meetings on Monday and Tuesday; she's taking a long trip, Cliff said. I haven't heard from Todd Hardy again, and no one else has made any snide remarks about his story."

"That's good news. Have you been working on your novel?"

"Yes, and it's going wonderfully; it gets easier and goes faster every day." Rachel laughed and added, "Except when I have to work by hand when it's storming, which has been frequent and unusual this summer; I can't risk lightning zapping my computer and eating my chapters."

"You do make a back-up copy, don't you? Daddy does for his crop records; a wipe-out would be terrible. Computers can be replaced, but facts are hard and sometimes impossible to recall."

"I make two, an extra in case one is in the machine when danger strikes. If I didn't, I could lose the original on the hard drive and the copy on the disk in one fell swoop. Of course, I print out everything I write that day before I shut down; that way, I have a hard copy; but it would take a lot of time and work to reenter it. And any work in progress that hasn't been saved or backed up can be lost forever; I've found that a scene is usually best the first time it leaps from my mind. The hardest part is trying to retrieve dialogue from memory. If I'm in to something heavy and the phone rings, I don't answer it; that's why I like to know when you're calling so I can be ready to stop."

"I understand what you're saying; concentration is important, crucial. After I take a hand-off from the center, I can't allow anything or anybody to distract me. If I do, their defense is all over me and I get sacked. Getting lost yards back can be difficult and sometimes impossible. Crowd noise, like a phone call, has to be ignored. You're learning a lot, woman."

"I'm trying to learn all I can about writing and getting published. I've started several files on how to do certain things, like submissions and research. I collect articles, and I've joined an author's organization; and after I'm published— see, I'm gaining confidence— I'll join two other groups that only accept published novelists. Most genres have conferences around the country so I think if I attended a few, I could meet other writers, editors, agents, and such. I wouldn't be as much in the dark as I am now."

"Don't worry, I'm sure you'll do fine. You are going to let me read it after it's finished?"

"Of course, and you have to be honest about its merits."

"All I can tell you is whether or not I like the story and characters. I'm not qualified to judge writing skills. My friend is, when you're ready."

Rachel's stomach seemed to do flip-flops. "Were you as scared when you played your first game as I am now?"

"Yep, but that's normal when we put ourselves on the line. Just believe in yourself and do the best job you can and you'll succeed. Trust me."

They talked for a while longer before he said, "I'd better go now so I can call Mom and Dad before it gets too late; farmers hit the sack early."

"Do ranchers?" she asked in a seductive and meaningful tone.

"Some do. I will if you're lying beside me. Heck, if you're there, I'll be ready to turn in at sundown, maybe earlier, maybe without supper. Lordy, I miss you. It seems like ages since I've seen you and touched you. I miss your smile and looking at you and touching you and kissing you."

Rachel tingled. "At least I got to see you on television, but I want and need more. I hope these next few months pass swiftly. I love you, Quentin. You take care of yourself. I know this is important to you, but please don't take any unnecessary risks."

"Don't want to spend our honeymoon standing or sitting beside my hospital bed with me in restrictive casts, eh?"

"You've got that right. I can imagine much nicer things to be doing."

"So can I, and it's heating me up just to think about them and you, so don't tantalize and tempt me without mercy, you sexy female. I love you, Rachel, and it won't be much longer before we're together again, for keeps."

"I love you, too, Quentin." *Please stay safe for me, for us.*

On Thursday, Rachel attended an historical society meeting, then wrote by hand for hours during a storm which dumped two inches of rain.

On Friday, she shopped for Karen's wedding and birthday gifts, then had a pleasant dinner with the Phillipses, who were friends in addition to being Karen's new in-laws.

On Saturday, she wrote her daughters with news about Quentin, the sales of the candy company stock and rental properties to the Gaineses, and the fact she was passing part of their financial inheritance to them soon.

That night, she went to a wedding and reception for the daughter and the son of two friends in her social circle. It was a happy and festive occasion and everyone appeared to be having a wonderful time, including Keith Haywood who was with Betty Burke's divorced sister. Becky had told her the two were seeing each other almost every night and a serious romance seemed possible. Rachel was delighted for both of them, as she had the man she loved and wanted, or would as soon as football season ended.

She enjoyed the evening immensely, talking and dancing and snacking on a variety of delicious foods; she even sampled the wedding cake and sipped champagne. She was relieved when those present had the good manners and kindness not to mention Todd Hardy's wicked article or to question her about Quentin Rawls. She realized the reason her secret lover was omitted as a topic: no one knew how serious their relationship was. Though she had a great deal of fun, she yearned for Quentin and wished he were there with her, wished that beautiful ceremony had been theirs, wished this reception was theirs, wished the impending honeymoon was theirs. She had missed out on those things with Daniel in their rush to get married before her ill-fated pregnancy began showing.

Rachel glanced around the large room and the splendidly attired guests. She didn't know if she wanted a large or a small wedding or if only she and Quentin would be present: that was something they would decide together. She smiled and nodded at friends she would be leaving soon. She would miss Becky and Jen most of all, but Dallas wasn't too far away for visits. And, there was the telephone and letters to keep them close. She would have Quentin and her writing there, and she would make new friends. Yes, they would be happy, deliriously happy, she decided, ensnared by love and fantasies of a glorious future together.

At eight o'clock on Sunday evening, July twenty-first, Rachel sat alone before her television in the casual area of her great room, eagerly awaiting Quentin's second preseason game and praying he played tonight so she could see him if only for a few minutes. The Dallas Cowboys and Denver Broncos ran onto the field, the starting line-ups in the lead and being introduced. She didn't care if it was storming outside and deluging Augusta with one-point-six inches of rain; the only points she was interested in were those which "The Man with the Golden Arm" put on the scoreboard.

A coin was tossed and strategy selections were made. The teams took their positions and players readied themselves to do their tasks. The clock started as the first ball was kicked and opponents ran toward each other as if to do fierce battle for the victory. The first quarter was underway.

Rachel watched in suspense, praying again for him to get to participate and to do it splendidly. Her tension mounted by the minute. Having learned facts about the sport, she found herself calling penalties and yardage won or lost before the officials announced them. Her heart leapt with joy and her body trembled with excitement when Quentin got to head up his team before the quarter ended. She smiled and cheered her lover on each time he was allowed to be in charge, and he played without errors and with enormous talent. She was elated when the sportscasters praised his skills.

Her gaze remained glued to the television, fearing for his safety while being awed by his movements. During camera close-ups, she saw his ebony hair peeking from beneath his helmet. She looked at the dark smudges under his blue eyes, there to prevent blinding reflections from the bright lights. He was so handsome that her breath caught in her throat. His body was sleek and muscular, sexually arousing, as the snug pants molded to his hips and thighs. She would love to touch him all over, have wild and wonderful sex with him again. She had become accustomed to their daily lovemaking and missed it terribly.

The hour grew late, but she didn't nod off a

single time. Quentin was on the field at least twice during every quarter and shone like the blazing star he was. After the game ended, he was interviewed in the locker room, and her gaze engulfed every sight of him, her ears, every word. When questioned about his plans if he didn't make the team, he flashed a sunny smile and said he would "think about that when and if it happens."

"Good night, my love." Rachel pressed the button to turn off the television, unaware of the tragedy looming ahead of him.

Fifteen

When Quentin phoned on Monday, Rachel laughed and asked, "Are you still soaring in the clouds or have your feet touched the ground again?"

"I guess I'm still on a high," he admitted, then chuckled. "That was some game; Lordy, I loved it. And I love you, woman. I think I'm doing this well because of you. Even if my career ends soon, it's been wonderful, and I have you and the ranch waiting for me."

Though he was sincere and elated, Rachel heard the yearning in his tone to finish the season and to do an exceptional job, to go out in pride and on his terms. She hoped and prayed he would be given that opportunity and would triumph, and do so without suffering permanent damage to his body. She knew that was a frightful possibility given his vulnerable right knee and left shoulder, his legendary throwing arm. "I'm glad to hear you talking like this. You sound so happy, relaxed, and confident."

"Thanks to you and to my last two showings. I'll accept the inevitable; I have no choice, but I'm aching to play the whole season."

She wanted to give him reassurance and faith but not false hopes. "I know, and you're on the right track; you're doing splendidly. I wish I could do as well in tennis as you do in football. I played with Betty Burke today after her partner canceled on her at the last minute. It's been a long time since I was on a court and I was rusty, but we had fun; she didn't go for my blood like so many sports lovers do to their opponents."

Quentin realized she changed the subject, knew why, and cherished her for it. "You didn't get too exhausted to work on your book, did you?"

"No, I put in five hours on it today and plan to do the same tomorrow. Before I forget, I won't be home Wednesday night. Scott is out of town on business, so I'm staying with Becky so we can work on the papers for the celebrity auction next Saturday. We have to get them finished and to the printers by Thursday. We were waiting until the last minute because items are still coming in that need to be included on the list. If you need to reach me, you have Scott's number."

"I'll call tomorrow night, then again on Friday. We leave Wednesday afternoon for New Orleans. Thursday's battle with the Saints is the last preseason game. Final cuts and assignments will be made afterward. That will be it, Rachel, my moment of truth. I can't afford a single error; if my hands and wits fail me, I'm done for, gone."

"Good luck, Quentin, but you don't need it; you'll be fine, I'm sure."

"It's going down to the wire on some selections, but I can't imagine Coach Switzer choosing me over any of the other three quarterbacks."

"From what I've seen, you're giving all three a run for their money. You have skills and experience two of them don't."

"Even so, they're young and healthy, not a risk like I am."

"Any or all of them could be injured on or off the field at any moment. You guys take these preseason games seriously."

"Our jobs depend on how we look during them. I want this badly, Rachel, but it won't kill me if I don't get it, now that I have you. If I didn't have something important waiting for me, I'd be crazed about now."

"I'm happy I mean so much to you."

"Soon, you'll be my life, my world, my career. Why don't you come to Dallas on September eleventh when we play Houston?" *If I'm still a Cowboy.* "The first game of the season is in Pittsburgh on the fourth, but I'd rather you come here so you can see the ranch and decide if you have any ideas for Scott before he begins his work. Since you'll be living and writing here, you should see if you want to make any changes. I think a nice home office is just what you need for creating your stories. I promise, no interruptions when the work lamp is burning."

"That sounds wonderful and thoughtful to

me. I miss you and I'm more than ready for a visit."

"After twenty-seven days of separation, so am I. Lordy, that's three more weeks until you're with me."

"All the better to work up a large appetite for me, Mr. Big Bad Wolf."

Quentin chuckled at her playful words, and his loins reacted to her sensuous voice and mood. "Extra time isn't needed, Little Red Riding Hood; I'm ravenous for you now. I'll probably devour your treats in five minutes."

"Oh, please, make our next meal last longer than that."

"Without exercise and practice in that area, my stamina is low and my skills are rusty."

"Good, but don't worry; I'll help you improve and repair them."

"That's an offer I won't pass up."

"I take it to mean I'm hired for that glorious and coveted job?"

"Only for the rest of our lives, beyond it if possible. I love you, woman, and I need you. Maybe we should get married while you're out here; then, you can stay. That would give you three weeks to get things done there. We play in Dallas again on the nineteenth and we're idle on the twenty-fifth, so that's three straight weeks in town."

Rachel was thrilled by his suggestion, but a clear head and unselfish heart prevailed over her desires. With so much at stake, she had to reason, "That isn't wise; you don't want the coaches and owner to think your mind and loyalty are elsewhere and you'd just as soon be home with a new bride than on a muddy or snowy field getting soaked or frozen and risking injuries. Right?"

"I hadn't thought of it like that, but you're right. They could view that as a major distraction, and it would be, you would be. Thanks for helping me see the light and for being so understanding and generous. Lordy, I love you, Rachel Gaines, and I'm a lucky man to have you."

"We're both lucky, Quentin. It won't be much longer before we are together for the rest of our lives. Do what you have to do, and I'll see you in Dallas next month. Whatever happens, I love you and I'm proud of you."

"I'm so happy for you and Mr. Rawls, Mrs. Rachel," Martha the housekeeper said on Wednesday, noting her employer's smile at the change in her name after twenty years of calling her Mrs. Gaines.

Rachel glowed as she said, "So am I, Martha. I hoped I would find a man like him one day and marry again, but I was doubtful. I certainly never expected to be moving away from Augusta, Karen, and my friends. I'm going to miss you and I doubt I'll find anyone like you. If there's anything you need besides a reference, just ask; I owe you so much."

"You stop worrying about me, 'cause I can find another house to do on Wednesdays after you're gone. My years with you have been good ones; you're the best person I've worked for. You go with him and be happy."

"I can hardly wait for the football season to be over so I can join him. It seems like ages since he left. As soon as he finishes his season and returns, we'll announce our engagement and get married. You're one of the few people who knows about our plans."

"I'm glad you trust me so much, Mrs. Rachel. I'll do whatever needs doing to help you get ready to move; we don't want you getting overworked afore your honeymoon. If you want, I can come over on days others cancel out on me and help you sort through stuff, like that attic and garage; those are big jobs. Have you figured out what to do about the house?"

"Not yet; I want to speak with the girls before I decide about selling it. Evelyn and Eddie won't be moving back here, but Karen might want it. She loves this house and it's perfect for her and David and their family. If Karen moves in, I'm sure she'll want you to keep working here, if you like."

"I would love working for her, Mrs. Rachel. I watched that girl grow up into a fine lady, and Mr. David is nice, too. With them working and afore the kids come, they'll need somebody to take care of things for them. If she don't want the house, I'll help you get it spic-n-span to sell."

"Thank you, Martha; you're a treasure and I love you dearly."

* * *

On Wednesday, Rachel and Becky decided to spend the night at Rachel's home instead of at the Coopers' because Rachel's computer was needed and just arrived items for the celebrity auction had to be marked and stored in her garage. As soon as they finished eating dinner, they went to the upstairs office and set to work on the project, laughing and chatting as they did so.

During one break, Becky asked, "How is the book coming along? Do you have much time to work on it between all of your projects?"

"I've been making the time because I want to finish it before Quentin and I marry and I'm busy with the move and a new husband."

Becky smiled and giggled. "If he's as sexy and attentive in bed as he is out of it, you won't have any free time, for a while at least."

Rachel laughed and murmured, "I hope not. He's so wonderful, and very supportive about my writing. I told you he wants to make me an office at the ranch. He even understands about the privacy required during the creative process. I'm not looking forward to packing up this computer and setting it up again; they can be so complicated. I suppose it would be best to have a professional disconnect the units and cords here, then hire another one in Dallas to reconnect everything."

Becky lowered her glass of diet cola. "That sounds smart to me, Rach. Jen hated to miss out on the fun tonight but this dinner with Adam's insurance client is important to him. The things we southern wives have to do sometimes to help out our husband's careers," she quipped and laughed.

"I remember. I'm going to miss you two terribly. I'm so glad you're coming over with Scott next month. Maybe you and Jen can visit later and check out the renovations. I'm confident Scott will do a fabulous job. I'm eager to see Quentin's home and 'spread' as he called it; I've never visited a ranch before, so I don't know what to expect."

"Without even closing my eyes, I can picture you dressed in cowgirl jeans, chaps, boots, and a Stetson, riding the range beside your handsome cowboy. It's a good thing all of us took those riding lessons years ago. He'll be surprised, impressed, and pleased that you know how to sit a horse and control one. You might want to start visiting Kelly's Stables to refresh those skills; at least get your body in condition. Mercy, remember in the beginning how we bruised, ached, and couldn't walk straight for days afterward?" Rachel nodded with a playful grimace. "Oh, Rach, I'm so happy for you and Quentin; you're perfect for each other. I just hate for you to move away."

"I thought my daughters would be the ones to live elsewhere, not me. And I never imagined he would walk into my life again. I don't want to sound silly, but I love him and he drives me wild with desire."

366 Janelle Taylor

They talked and laughed and reminisced as they worked and during other breaks, ignorant of the tragedy in Texas that afternoon.

Thursday morning, Becky departed at nine to take the celebrity auction list to the printer to make copies for the attendees. Rachel left shortly afterward to pick up a group of senior citizens to take them on errands and to appointments. Again, she missed an important call from Texas at eleven, but her answering machine took a message.

Rachel returned home at six, tired from the lengthy day's activities and sweaty from the late August heat. She took a long and soothing bubble bath and ate her dinner so she would be ready to watch the football game at eight o'clock on ESPN. She was eager for even a glimpse of her lover, and prayed it would be another glorious night for him.

She chatted with Becky and Jen before settling herself on the sofa, a glass of diet cola and the remote control within reach and her bare feet propped on an ottoman. Minutes before the game started, Rachel realized she had not checked the answering machine this evening. She decided to wait until an official time-out with lots of commercials to go upstairs to the office to do so. She had spoken with her two friends, and her daughters and Quentin weren't expected to call today. Anyone else, she reasoned, could wait until she was certain she wouldn't miss a single sight of or a precious word about the man she loved and missed terribly.

The sportscasters began talking about the Cowboys and Saints, and shook Rachel to her core with one revelation. She sat up straight, gaped at the screen, paled, trembled, and listened to their words in sheer terror.

"Tonight is a sad time in the history of football as the sport loses one of its all-time great quarterbacks: Quentin Rawls. It's a real shame Rawls won't be playing for the Cowboys tonight or in the future. In the last two games, 'the man with the golden arm' proved he was still at the top and deserved to be there. For a while, it looked as if Coach Switzer would have trouble deciding which three quarterbacks to keep on the roster. That accident which took place in Texas yesterday afternoon when Rawls was en route to the airport to join his team and fly here for tonight's game was a real tragedy. He's going to be sorely missed in this sport he loved. He gave a lot of people countless thrills and joys over the years. If anybody can be called a hero on and off the field, it's Quentin Rawls."

"You're right. To pull three trapped people from a wrecked car before it exploded when he was injured badly himself took courage and mettle, and he showed both. Thanks to Rawls, a woman and her two small children are alive today. The truck driver who jackknifed, struck both vehicles, and sent one over that steep embankment died in the crash."

"From news reports, he'd already gotten several speeding tickets and two traffic citations for drunk driving. The coin's being tossed, so we'll tell you more about Rawls and his career later."

Rachel felt weak, nauseous, faint. If Quentin was safe, she worried, he would have phoned by now so she wouldn't hear this shocking discovery on the news and panic. She leapt to her feet and almost tripped several times as she raced up the stairs to check the answering machine. Sure enough, the red light was on to indicate a call had come in. She extended her hand, then yanked it back in fear of learning who had phoned and why.

With trepidation chewing at her, she sat down at the desk, her legs too shaky for standing. What would she do if he was . . . "Don't even think such a horrible thing! Please, God, don't take him away from me. Let him be alive and unharmed." It had been terrible to lose Daniel in that plane crash fifteen years ago, but it would be far worse, she admitted, to lose Quentin to death. She loved, needed, and wanted him more so than she had Daniel. She couldn't imagine her life without him in it, She dreaded listening to the message, but had to see if it was about him. Again, she prayed for his survival, more than his survival, for him to be uninjured. Yet, she knew from what the two announcers had said that he was hurt or . . .

Her heart pounded. Her chest felt as if it were

constricted by a steel band. Her breathing was shallow and rapid. Her lips, mouth, and throat went dry. Her stomach felt as if it was in knots. Her anguished gaze was locked on the device that might hold news of her beloved and their future. Rachel's reluctant forefinger pressed the blue button to hear the message. She began to cry in relief and happiness when his recorded voice filled the room. She let the cleansing tears flow and thanked God even as she listened to Quentin's enlightening words. She pressed the repeat button to hear them again.

"Rachel, don't worry about me when you hear the news about that accident yesterday. I'm okay. I'll call again tonight and explain everything."

At that moment, the phone rang and Rachel snatched up the receiver.

"Rachel, it's me, love."

"Quentin! Thank God you're alive! Where are you? What happened? I've been crazy with worry," she told him amidst ragged sobs.

"Stop crying, love, I'm in the hospital, but I'm fine. Well, almost fine. I've got some problems, but the doctors are taking care of them. I tried to call you at Becky's after they brought me here but I didn't get an answer before they knocked me out for the night. I tried again this morning before they hauled me off to operate on my knee and shoulder. I've been in and out all day, catching up on my beauty sleep," he jested to calm her.

"Becky and I spent the night over here because we needed to use my computer. I heard about the accident when the game started to-night. They scared the life out of me until I listened to your message just now."

"I was watching, too, but I had to wait until the nurse finished taking my blood pressure and tem-perature before I could call again. From what those guys said, anybody who hasn't heard what happened yesterday probably thinks I'm dead. I hope they set the record straight before the game ends. I've already talked to my parents so they wouldn't get caught off guard like you did. I'm sorry they frightened you."

"I'm just thankful you're all right. How are you *really* doing? Tell me the truth, Quentin Rawls."

"Sore, but fine, honestly. I can't say the same for my Dodge pickup; it's a crisp. The other car went over a steep embankment, turned over sev-eral times, and landed upside down against a tree. A woman and her two kids were trapped inside by their seat belts, and the mother was unconscious. The gas tank was ruptured and fuel was pouring out; I was afraid the car would explode before help arrived, so I had to get them out and away from danger fast. The doors were crunched and jammed shut, so I used a rock to break windows to reach them. I got some cuts removing them, a bad one on my throwing arm, and I put my shoulder and knee out of commission again carrying them up that slip-pery embankment. I knew I was hurt and dam-aging them worse in my rush, but I had no choice; I couldn't let them die. The surgeon worked on that cut tendon last night, and two others repaired my knee and shoulder today. They told me I was out for the season and might not be able to ever play again, so I had my agent tell Coach Switzer I was retiring. He's a good man, and that lets him off the hook about deciding my future with the team."

"The announcers were right; you're a real hero and I'm proud of you. I'm sorry about your injuries, Quentin; I know you didn't want your career to end this way."

"It's all right, love; in fact, it probably gave me a good way out, too. I'm more than ready to enjoy this extra time I was given."

"Maybe this is why God kept you on the team this long; He needed for you to be at that scene yesterday to save those people's lives."

"Could be. At least He allowed me to go out in pride and glory. The doctors said I would be released on Sunday, but I'll have to get therapy and other treatments after Labor Day. It's a madhouse here with the media, and the staff is taking excellent care of me, so why don't you wait for me there? I'll fly in on Monday. You know what this means, don't you?"

"What?" she asked, wanting to fly to his side immediately.

"We can get married as soon as we get things settled and I'm patched up enough for our honeymoon. Say within the next few weeks?"

"That sounds wonderful, perfect. I love you."

"I love you, too. I hope you don't mind, but

I've already mentioned you and our future plans to the media."

"Of course I don't mind; that makes it official."

"Yep, and it is. Soon, we can get down to planning and enjoying our marriage. For a minute there, I thought it was over for me. Lordy, it was scary watching that big truck sliding toward me and I not being able to do anything to get out of his path; that woman couldn't, either. She and those kids are doing fine, too, mostly cuts and bruises. Her husband came to see me and it was a real emotional visit; he credits me with saving their lives. We're all lucky to be alive, and lucky our injuries aren't any worse than they are. I'm sorry that trucker was killed, but he should've had his seat belt on and shouldn't have been driving in that condition. Oh, no, here's the nurse with another shot; she's planning to put out my lights again so I have to go. I'll call tomorrow. Don't worry; I'm fine."

"I bet you were scared out of your wits," Becky told Rachel when her friend called and explained what had happened.

"The minutes between those announcers' words and listening to his message on the answering machine were the longest and most tormenting ones of my life. It still frightens me to realize how close I came to losing him. I couldn't have endured that loss, Becky, I couldn't have."

"I know, Rach, and I'm thankful he's alive. He was unselfish and brave to rescue those other people. You must be so proud of him."

"I am, and that's the kind of man he is, why I love him so much, why I need him to be a part of my life."

Becky was glad to share Rachel's joy.

"I know you'll be ecstatic to see him on Monday."

"Blissfully happy. I wish I could see him now, but he's right about me staying here. All I could do is sit by his bed and get in the way. I'm sure his room and the hall are flooded with people. I just hope they don't overtire him and he has a relapse. Heavens, I miss him."

"He'll be with you soon, and he said he's doing fine. Don't worry."

"I will worry until I see that fact for myself."

"You should drink some brandy to settle your nerves and to help you get a good night's sleep. I'm sure you're still tense. Do you want me to come over and sit with you for a while or spend the night?"

"Thanks, but I'll be fine now that I've talked with him."

"I'm sorry about my answering machine being turned off last night. Scott usually handles the messages. After I checked it, I forgot to reset it before we went over to your house. I'm glad Scott didn't get to his hotel until it was too late to phone or he would have been worried about me."

"I'm sure he would have called me or Jen to

locate you. The only reason Quentin didn't call here Wednesday night was because I told him I would be at your house. When he couldn't reach me there, he assumed we were out eating or running late errands before they sedated him. Will you phone Jen and tell her what happened? I'm too emotionally exhausted and keyed up for another chat; but if she and Adam hear about it during the football game or on the late news, she'll be frantic with concern about me."

"You just relax and I'll take care of it, Rach."

"Thanks for being there for me tonight, Becky."

Rachel was overjoyed to hear from Quentin Friday afternoon. He sounded wonderful; his voice, clearer; his mood, calm and reassuring.

"You're all over the newspapers and on every newscast. I saw pictures of the truck, your pickup and the woman's car on TV. It was awful, Quentin. If they had shown them before I talked with you, I would have been crazed with panic. It's hard to believe anybody walked away from that accident."

"God was watching over us; luck had nothing to do with it. You wouldn't believe how many interviews I've given when the doctors allowed visitors and I'm awake. Cards, flowers, gifts, calls, and telegrams are pouring in; it makes me feel great to know so many people care about me and wish me well. I got your flowers, too and they're the best ones I received. That wa:

clever of you to send tropical ones to remind me of when we met and wicked of you to start me to fantasizing about those days and nights together, not to mention future ones. I'm aching to see you, Rachel Gaines."

"If you aren't released on Sunday or you can't come here on Monday, I'm flying over there."

"I'll book your flight myself if they don't release me or say I can't travel; but don't worry, that won't happen. Vance is driving me to the airport and loading me on the plane. Half the team's already been by to see me and most of the others are coming by later or tomorrow. Perry and Ryan brought me the game ball. And the team owner decided to retire my jersey number; that's quite an honor. One of the major networks called my agent and wants to do a program about my life and career. *Time, Newsweek, US, People, Sports Illustrated,* and several football and other magazines are featuring me on their next covers. This was a tough way to become a big news item, but it's nice of them to consider me worthy of such praise and attention. And that trucking firm's insurance company has already contacted me about a settlement, a big one, Rachel; they're worried about me suing them and causing bad publicity. The firm knows they were negligent in keeping that driver on and they know the accident ended my career, so they're being very generous and quick to resolve the matter. I'm sure they'll do the same with the Carter family."

"That's wonderful, Quentin; they were at fault

and should be held accountable. You're a hero, so you fully deserve all of this attention. I'll buy a copy of each magazine and start a family scrap-book. How are Mrs. Carter and the children? I also saw their pictures in the newspaper and on TV; they're a nice-looking family."

"The kids were treated and released, and she should be out soon. They're holding her for ob-servation for a head injury; she slammed it hard against the window during the roll-overs. It was fortunate she had those kids strapped in securely or they would have been injured badly. Of course, you saw that her car is a burned wreck just like my truck. She and her husband dropped by to visit me for a few minutes; I don't have to tell you how grateful they are to me. I've even gotten thank-you gifts from both of their families and some of their friends. Now, let's talk about you. What's on your agenda until I get there?"

"First, how are the knee, arm, and shoulder?"

"Sore and bruised, but the doctor says I should heal nicely. He did stress I can't play football again or I'd risk permanent disability; that's why the insurance company and trucking firm were so nervous and were swift with a set-tlement offer. Would you believe, the firm is a Cowboy's sponsor and they've used several team members in their commercials? They even tried to sweeten my deal with a lucrative endorsement contract, but I doubt I'll accept that. My amateur acting days are over. I'm ready and eager to head in another direction, with you and ranch-ing."

Rachel recalled how complicated and frightful insurance settlements could be, in particular when a double indemnity clause was involved for an accidental death as in Daniel's case. It was thanks to her intelligent lawyer and agent, Scott's father, that she had fared well and avoided problems with another company who tried to lower her claim with charges of negligence against the crashed jet. "You are going to let your lawyer and insurance adjuster advise you on the matter before you sign a release, right?"

"I've already spoken to both of them and they'll study the papers as soon as they're ready. Back to you, woman. Tell me more."

"We're ready for the celebrity auction next Saturday. If you feel up to it, you can go with me and give the audience a thrill, but decide after you get here. I've been working on my novel. I hoped to complete it before you finished the season; now that things have changed, I can do that at the ranch, in my new office. I'm already typing resignation letters for my organizations, clubs, and boards. I'll get friends to take over any unfinished projects before I leave town. Jen, Adam, Becky, and Scott said to tell you hello and to get well soon; they're all looking forward to seeing you. If you're up to it, we'll have dinner with them at the country club after you arrive here and get some rest."

"Dinner with our friends and the auction suit me fine. Those other matters sound terrific; I'm glad you're getting things settled so you can move soon. Anything else new?"

"I spoke with the Dorothy and Richard Gaines this morning."

"I hope they didn't upset you," he said before she explained.

"Actually, they were nice to me for a change. They were surprised and delighted to recover their candy stock and rental properties. I think they believed I was holding on to them or might sell them to somebody else for spite. It seems as if I scored big points with them. That isn't important to me anymore, but it might improve their relationship with my girls. That would be nice for Karen and Evelyn and their families. It should also ease any tension between the girls and their aunts, uncles, and cousins. It's a shame Cynthia and Suzannah, their families, and my children were caught in the middle of that unpleasant situation for years. Now that I'm not viewed as the arch enemy, perhaps things will be different, better, for everybody."

"I hope so, Rachel, for your daughters' sakes; it's terrible to have a rift between them and their grandparents. Families should be close. I'm glad your Evelyn and Karen have accepted me in your life and I'm eager to meet them next year. Speaking of families, if you don't have anything scheduled for next week, would you like to drive down to Colquitt and meet my family? Say Tuesday through Thursday? That would get you back in time to rest Friday for the weekend auction."

"That suits me fine, Quentin, if you're up to it."

"I will be, and Mom will take good care of us. I have to hang up now; company is arriving in a drove; the Cowboys are galloping in," he chuckled. "I'll call you tomorrow."

Later, Rachel phoned her daughters and was fortunate to reach them without difficulty, as Evelyn was at home in Japan and Karen was aboard the ship doing medical tests. She related the news about Quentin and chatted with each for almost an hour. The girls were relieved to hear about Quentin's escape from near death and advised their mother not to wait until they returned, but to marry him as soon as possible to begin a new life of happiness. They were delighted to hear the good news about their grandparents and hoped aloud that peace would now reign in the family.

Rachel snuggled in her bed on Sunday night after talking with Quentin. She was almost too excited to sleep. He was supposed to come tomorrow and she prayed nothing would happen to prevent his arrival.

Sixteen

"Considering what you've been through, you look wonderful," Rachel told Quentin after hugging and kissing him. She noticed the bandage on his left forearm where a cut tendon had been repaired. She could detect another bandage under his shirt at his left shoulder where surgery had been done. His knee was in a brace to hold it straight during the healing process, so his movements were restricted. There were other scrapes and bruises on his handsome face and on both arms from his accident and from his rescue of the Carter family.

"Believe me, I've looked worse after being sacked a few times or from slipping and sliding up and down a muddy field for hours. You should have seen me the day I was tackled and thrown into a sideline camera; my helmet was knocked off and I broke my nose and had fifteen stitches in my head. I was a bloody mess. As for you, woman, you look ravishing."

Rachel hugged and kissed him again, being careful not to aggravate his recent injuries. "Heavens, it's good to see you. It seems like years. I just want to look at you, make sure you're all right." Her gaze drifted over his face as if examining every inch of it.

"I'm going to be fine as soon as I'm healed and I finish my therapy."

"You should have called and told me you got an earlier flight so I could pick you up at the airport."

"I wanted to surprise you; it was no trouble getting a taxi and the driver took care of my luggage; he's a big fan of mine. How's that for luck?"

"Everybody should be a fan of yours after what you've done. Heavens, I've got you standing at the door when you should be off that leg. Let me help you inside; then I'll get your luggage. You're staying here with me so I can take care of you, and I don't care what anyone says about it. Playing doctor will be fun."

"I like that twinkle in your eye, woman. I promise to be a perfect patient. Just tell me what to do and I'll follow orders."

"Let's sit you on the sofa and I'll prop up that leg."

"I would prefer to relax in the sunroom if you don't mind."

Rachel assisted him to the wicker sofa in the Florida room, put his foot on a chair, and asked if he needed anything else.

"A cold drink and some paper towel to mop this sweat would be great. It's hot today."

After Rachel satisfied his wishes, she collected his luggage from the front porch and placed it in the foyer, to carry upstairs later. Right now, she needed to spend time with him. She returned to find Quentin grinning. "What's that sly look about?" she asked.

As he put aside the wad of wet towels, he said, "I was wondering why you turned that diver upside down in the aquarium. He's trapped a fish. If he stays tangled, he'll drown or starve."

Rachel walked to the oblong tank and leaned over to check the problem. Her green gaze widened and her heart fluttered for a moment. Quentin's grin had broadened and his blue eyes sparkled like sapphires in sunlight. "What's that?"

"A sunken treasure for my beautiful treasure."

Rachel put her hand in the water and recovered the diamond ring he had nestled in the plastic treasure chest. She absently dried her dripping hand and arm on her T-shirt and went to sit beside him, holding the ring between her thumb and forefinger and gazing at it in awe. "This was your second sneaky trick today, Mr. Rawls. It's stunning, and the stone is so large."

Quentin chuckled as he took it from her and slipped it on her finger. "Now we're officially engaged, if you agree. I can't get down on my knee to propose in style, but you will marry me, won't you?"

"Yes, a thousand times yes. I love you so much, Quentin. This is such a huge surprise. How did you shop for this beauty in your condition? When? You just got out of the hospital yesterday and that was a Sunday, and you caught a plane early this morning. Did you buy it before the accident?"

"No. A friend of mine in the jewelry business brought a selection to the ranch last night so I could choose one. Vance, Perry, and Ryan acted as security guards to and from his store; I doubted any robber would challenge three big guys like them."

"Not one with any intelligence," she jested.

Quentin pulled Rachel into his embrace and their lips met. They shared a long, deep, and tender kiss that sealed their commitment to each other. After their lips parted, they gazed into each other's eyes as they mutely expressed their love and desires.

Rachel's hand stroked his strong jawline, and her thumb trailed over his full mouth. She laced her fingers through his ebony hair and savored the way the dark strands surrounded them. She pulled his head downward to seal their lips once more. She loved kissing him. He could make her go wild with hunger and weak with longing, quiver with anticipation, flame with suspense. He opened his mouth just the right amount and slanted his head to perfection. He knew how much pressure to use for a gentle kiss and for an intense and passionate one. His tongue was deft and magical, exploring, stimulating. His taste was delicious. Her lips tugged on his lower one while his suckled on her upper one. His hands wandered her torso, enticing, titillating, pleasuring. He was splendid and intoxicating, totally disarming and irresistible. She was elated to have him there with her, to have him alive, to make him her future. "I love you and need you so much."

"I love you and need you, Rachel. I get aroused just looking at you, touching you, thinking about you."

"So do I, my darling. Do you think I can get these pants off without hurting your knee? I would love to sit across your lap."

Quentin smiled and said, "Sounds excellent to me." He watched her squat to remove his left shoe. After she unfastened a waist button and slid down the zipper, he lifted his buttocks so she could ease the tan pants and light-blue briefs off his hips and left leg. She allowed both items to remain on the right one, which she propped on a low stool because of the rigid brace. She unbuttoned his shirt, gingerly peeled it off his injured shoulder, and tossed it to the tiled floor. He watched her strip off her shorts, panties, T-shirt, and bra. His gaze adored her striking figure as it traveled her nude body. He soon closed his eyes and moaned in rapture as her generous hands and talented lips worked his eager and responsive organ into a slick and hard erection, upon which she slowly lowered herself until he was sheathed within her sweetness.

They kissed and stroked each other to exquisite enchantment and blazing desire, hands and mouths journeying to any spot they could reach without disturbing their erotic contact. He surrendered most of the control to her, as his leg and movements were restricted by his injury and their position. Her knees were buried in the cushions beside his hips as she lifted and lowered herself in rhythmic joy, undulating up and down on his fiery manhood. She reveled in her freedom to do as she pleased, feeling no modesty or inhibitions with the man she loved and would soon marry. When she rested for a minute, Quentin spread kisses over her neck and chest. She leaned her head back as he fondled and feasted upon her firm mounds. His tongue swirled around their points and flicked them into greater hardness. He playfully nibbled at the buds with cautious teeth between ardent suckles. Unable to sit still, she writhed on his engorged member, bringing them both to a feverish peak. It had been so long since their last union and he so enflamed her that she required little stimulation and only a short time to reach the brink of ecstasy. She relished that level of pleasure until she could endure the sweet torment no longer. She allowed herself to topple over passion's precipice, tingling and warming as the splendid and powerful climax was achieved. Her mouth almost plundered his as their tongues danced in delight and she clung to him during the wild and wonderful ride to supreme victory.

Quentin's body seemed afire, his veins coursing with molten desire, as he reached a glorious release and savored it to the end. He held Rachel in a possessive embrace as his breathing calmed and his taut muscles relaxed. "Lordy woman, I've surely died and gone to heaven.

That was fantastic and sorely needed. I love you with every breath I take and with every beat of my heart, if the sucker doesn't burst out of my chest," he joked and chuckled. "I only thought I was in good condition. That lazing around in bed for days zapped my stamina and strength. As soon as I'm healed, I'll work you over from head to feet. You'll be shouting Uncle, before I'm finished with you."

Rachel used the damp paper towel to absorb perspiration on his face and neck. She realized why he had asked for it earlier, to dry water from his hand and arm after he placed her engagement ring in the fish tank. "That's a promise I'll hold you to, and I can hardly wait to collect it."

"It's one I'll gladly keep; and it shouldn't be long in coming. I certainly wasn't sluggish after you got a hold on me. Whew, that was great. I owe you big, and I always pay my debts."

"I'm glad you're an honest man, among your other countless good qualities and superior traits. Wait here and I'll get you repaired, just in case we have visitors. No," she said with a laugh, "not Janet; she's been on an extended vacation since her showdown with Cliff. If we're all lucky, she'll be changed enormously when she returns."

"That would be nice for everybody, and a huge shock."

"Right, but it isn't impossible, nothing is. We were reunited after twelve years, you survived a terrible accident, and we're together again."

"And we'll always be together, thanks to our guardian angel."

Rachel smiled and nodded before fetching a washcloth from the hall bathroom. She washed away the moisture of their union from his softened member. She replaced his briefs, slacks, shoe, and shirt. She smiled as she fingercombed his black hair. "Almost as good as new. That should hold you until I bathe you later. Relax and drink your cola. I'll be back in a minute." She went to the bathroom to wash herself and to re-dress.

"Now that we've gotten rid of our tension, how about some lunch?"

"Suits me; I'm starving. Been hours since breakfast."

"That's right, you ate in a different time zone. Food coming up."

As they ate at the table nearby, they discussed their impending plans, dating the wedding for September the eleventh, less than two weeks away.

Tuesday afternoon, they reached Miller County and the small town of Colquitt, Georgia. Rachel followed Quentin's directions to his parents' home. She was excited and nervous about meeting his family. She drove her silver BMW into the Rawlses' driveway and parked it. Almost instantly, his parents and his sister Mary and her family rushed out to greet them.

A beaming Quentin exchanged hugs and

kisses with his mother and sister, then embraced his father and shook his brother-in-law's hand. He introduced his fiancée to them, "Mom, Daddy, this beautiful woman is Rachel Gaines, whom I'm lucky enough to be marrying on the eleventh of next month. Rachel, my parents, Matthew and Inez Rawls."

With misty eyes and a glowing smile, Inez embraced her and gave her a kiss on the cheek. "It's so nice to meet you, Rachel, and have you visit for a few days. Quent has told us so many wonderful things about you. I want to thank you for making my son so happy."

"He makes me happy, Mrs. Rawls, and it's a pleasure to meet you. You, too, sir," she said to his father as they shook hands and smiled. She noticed that Quentin favored his father and got his height and part of his athletic build from the man. If Matthew had any gray amidst his coal-black hair, it wasn't visible; and if there was any shading difference between their blue eyes, she couldn't find it. Matthew was tall and muscular, the body of a man who worked hard and long hours. He smiled easily and often, his teeth white against the dark tan from countless days under the sun. The few wrinkles that etched his face appeared to be a result of squinting and smiling rather than from aging. She warmed to Quentin's father, who gave her the impression he was gentle, honest, and dependable.

"Quent, you did good for yourself, boy; she's lovely and nice. We want to welcome you to our family, Rachel. I'm sure you'll make Quent a fine wife and us a sweet daughter-in-law. I guess I'm biased, but I think my son deserves the best woman around, and looks to me as if he found her."

"Thank you, sir. I know I'm happy and lucky I found him."

Quentin also thanked his father. "Rachel, this is my sister, Mary, her husband, Steve, and their children, Bobby and Kelly."

"Down you wild bucks," Mary told the active children in a gentle tone. "Uncle Quent is hurt and he can't roughhouse with you this time. I want you both to be careful with his knee and shoulder."

"Momma said a big truck hit your pickup," Bobby remarked.

"And tore up another car," Kelly added, her gaze filled with wonder.

As Quentin ruffled the boy's brown hair and playfully tugged on the girl's pony tail, he said, "Yep, but we're all fine, just banged up a little. Soon as I'm healed, we'll play some chase and ball."

"We saw you play football, Uncle Quent," Bobby said. "Papa let us stay up late. He says you ain't gonna play no more."

"He said you aren't going to play anymore," his mother corrected.

"Yes, ma'am, that's right."

Rachel noted how well behaved the children were and how vivacious; that said a great deal about how their parents were rearing them. She and Quentin talked with the children for a few minutes.

"Why don't we go in the house and get out of this heat? I have some cold lemonade ready. Quent loves my lemonade, Rachel."

"I'm sure I will, too, Mrs. Rawls."

"Please, dear, call me Inez, and he's Matt," she pointed to Quentin's father. "You're among friends, make that *family*, and we're so pleased about your news."

"Thank you, Inez, Matt, for allowing me to visit with Quentin. I've been looking forward to meeting you all. It warms my heart to see such a close family."

"Rachel is very close to her daughters, Karen and Evelyn," Quentin told his parents. "Her parents are deceased and she has no brothers or sisters."

"Well, you do now, Rachel," Mary said with a sunny smile as she tucked a strayed curl behind her ear.

"Did you bring us anything, Uncle Quent?"

"Sorry, Kelly, but I couldn't shop in this condition. But I promise to bring you something real nice next time."

"Kids, behave yourselves. Quent came to visit, not bring presents."

"But, Momma, he always brings presents. Don't you, Uncle Quent?"

"I certainly do, Bobby, and I won't forget again."

"That's all right, since you're hurt."

"I appreciate your understanding and generosity," Quentin teased as the children, still keyed up from their second day in school, raced off to return to their game, one interrupted by the visitors' arrival.

"Still a handful, eh, Sis?"

"Always. You'll find out soon enough."

Quentin just smiled, feeling it unnecessary to reveal their inability to have any children; that could wait until another and better time. "How about that lemonade, Mom; it's as hot as Hades today."

The group went into a tri-level ranch-style brick home and sat down in a den with comfortable furniture and a huge fireplace. Pictures of the children and grandchildren were everywhere, as were keepsakes, many of them having to do with their celebrity son. The clean house was decorated with a country flair. Pieces of lovely embroidery and crochet were under lamps, frames, and various objects. A brown sofa and two chairs were large and inviting. A LA-Z-Boy in shades of blue sat near the hearth, Mr. Rawls's relaxing spot. Sports and farming magazines lay on one end table, a Bible and newspaper on another. A thirty-five-inch-screen TV was at the opposite end of the long room from the fireplace, visible from every seat and no doubt a gift from Quentin. A piano was positioned not far from it, with music books and a Baptist hymnal on its rack. A few toys were scattered about, as was expected with two grandchildren living on the property.

"Here, Rachel dear, you sit with Quent on

the sofa. You prop that leg up, Son," Inez said as she shoved an ottoman within reach.

Quentin grasped his leg and placed it there. "Thanks, Mom. So, what's everybody been doing lately?"

"Besides pest control and waiting for harvest?" his father jested.

"It is about that time. How is the crop doing this year?"

"Fine, Son, since that flood didn't attack us. Ruined a lot of farmers north and northeast of Miller County. Praise the Lord for His goodness in sparing us. Looks like we'll have a bumper crop this season. We've been blessed with no pest problems, and all of the machinery is working fine. Steve's a big help and he's learned all I know about growing peanuts."

"That's because you're a good teacher, Matt," his son-in-law affirmed, "and I love my job."

As the men chatted about peanuts and the flood, Inez and Mary prepared beverages and homemade cookies. When the women returned, Inez gently scolded, "You boys can talk farming another time; we have a guest, a very special guest."

"I don't mind, Inez; it's very interesting. I grew up on a farm outside of Athens. My parents raised vegetables, but my father usually planted a few peanuts for us. Quentin tried to educate me one day about growing peanuts; it sounds like a complicated crop. You have a remarkable son; you must be very proud of him."

"We are," Matt concurred. "You did a fine

and brave thing rescuing that woman and her kids, Son. We saw reports on the TV, and the papers carried several stories about it and your good deed. Makes me happy just to think on it, and plenty grateful you're alive. Your mother and I were sorry to hear you got hurt and can't play anymore. We know how much you wanted this last season, but you have a new life and challenge standing before you."

"It doesn't matter now, Daddy, not since I found Rachel to share my life. At least, being retired means I won't get hurt again."

"That pleases me to no end, Son," Inez said. "I never liked having those big mountains fall all over you. I cringed every time I saw it. At the school here, Rachel, they have a glass case with Quent's jersey and lots of pictures of him. Game balls and trophies are in there, too. If you have time, maybe he can take you over there to see them. A lot of folks would be glad to see you, Son, but I know your time is tight. Around here, Rachel, he's a big celebrity, a real star. After his first Superbowl victory, they held a parade for him around the town square and gave him a key to the city."

"It was well deserved," Rachel remarked. She took to the likable and unpretentious Inez with ease, as she did to Mary Mills, who favored her mother, except she was shorter and had a sprinkling of freckles.

"Will you two be living in Texas?" Inez asked.

"Yep, I'm going to ranch and Rachel is going

to write books. She's working on her first one now."

"I bet it will be wonderful," Mary said. "I can hardly wait to read it. This is so exciting; we'll have two celebrities in the family."

"Hold on, Sis; she has to get it finished and published first. That takes a long time. But knowing Rachel, I have no doubt she'll succeed; she's a smart and persistent woman."

"She must be; she snared you, big brother."

"Oh, I didn't put up a fight, gave her no resistance at all."

Rachel loved him for his response which implied *when* she was published, not *if.* She savored the way he joked with his sister. She liked these down-to-earth people who were warm and kind, hardworking, strong, and brave; they had to be those things to have reared Quentin as they did and to survive an arduous and unpredictable farming life. She detected no bitterness or resentment in Quentin's tone as he spoke about football and retirement; he appeared happy, relaxed, glad to be alive, pleased to be home, and thrilled to be marrying her soon. As they snacked and chatted and got acquainted, she observed Quentin's interaction with his family. It was obvious he loved and respected each of them, and the family was as close-knit as he had claimed.

"Frankie is driving over from Dothan tomorrow to visit. He'll be glad to see you, Quent. I believe that boy's about to get himself straight."

"That's good news, Daddy; I surely hope you're right."

"You've done a lot to help him and us, Quent, and we're grateful. I don't know if Quent told you, Rachel, but he bought this farm and most of the equipment to run it for us. That boy has a heart of gold, not a selfish bone in his body. We're real lucky to have a son like him."

"And I'm lucky to be getting a husband like him."

As the three women talked while they prepared dinner, Rachel learned many things about Quentin's family and Colquitt. She told them a lot about herself, the people in her life, now and in the past, and her various interests and activities. She also mentioned her hysterectomy so they would know children with Quentin wasn't possible; they took that news with kindness and politeness, and dropped the subject.

Rachel enjoyed working with Inez and Mary in the nearby well-stocked pantry. While fetching things from it, Inez gave her several jars of mayhaw jelly and related the fruit's history. She liked learning more about peanut farming and the family's lifestyle, which revolved around agriculture. The location was quiet and peaceful, green from irrigation. Their lives were busy and mostly routine, with early mornings and long days for chores and early-to-bed evenings. She warmed to the hardworking family, and was pleased by their devoted and cheerful attitudes.

Often, she heard laughter coming from the sitting room where the three men were chatting and relaxing, with two children playing nearby. It touched her deeply to observe the ex-quarterback sharing details of his life with his family. Yes, she told herself again, she had made a perfect choice in him.

Quentin showed Rachel to the room she would use for three nights, as they naturally would not share one in his parents' home. "I'll be next door if you need anything, besides me," he added with a sexy grin and wink. "Mom and Daddy's room is across the hall and the bath is there," he said as he pointed toward it. "Get a good night's sleep, and I'll see you in the morning. They have early chores, so you don't have to get up when you hear stirrings around at the crack of dawn. I'll be up about seven, and there's a clock in the guest room. I love you, Rachel, and I'm glad you're here with us. I promise we're going to be happy."

"I'm certain of it. I really like your family. I don't have to tell you how different they are from the Gaineses. I'm going to enjoy being a part of the Rawls clan."

"I'd better steal my good-night kiss fast so we won't get hot and bothered while sleeping alone."

They shared a stirring and tender kiss, gazed into each other's eyes for a minute, smiled, and went to their rooms to retire.

As she lay in bed, Rachel thanked God for giving her such a bright future with Quentin.

She could hardly wait for her daughters to meet Quentin's family so everybody could get acquainted. She would suggest one for June of next year after Karen and David's return to Georgia; Evelyn and her family would be back in Ohio in April. Thanks to the hefty insurance settlement for his accident and her recent sales of holdings and the estate left to her by Daniel, the couple would have no money problems.

Frank drove over for a few hours late Wednesday morning, arriving shortly after their return from touring the farm. The rapport and affection between the brothers was evident to Rachel. It was as if Frank had to inspect Quentin to make sure he really was all right. Quentin was delighted to see how well Frank looked and sounded, and to hear his brother was doing great in Dothan.

Rachel listened as Frank spoke to her in a heavy blend of country and southern accents. The younger man lacked Quentin's fantastic looks and many charms, but she liked Frank and found him funny and friendly. He even playfully warned her to be careful of the intrusive media, but she realized he was serious beneath his smile and genial mood, as he had been tormented by several tabloids over the years. She hoped the media would leave all of them alone, or be kind with their stories. Frank, and well as the other Rawlses, was coming to Augusta next month for the wedding and reception. She was touched when Frank told Quentin how proud of him he was, and how glad he was that Quentin had not been hurt— or worse— in the accident. She watched them embrace, then gave them privacy for a while as she helped Inez prepare lunch for noon as was their custom.

After lunch and Frank's departure, she and Quentin rode into town to pick up some things for his mother at the grocery store and for his father at the seed-and-feed and the hardware stores. Everybody they encountered was elated to see Quentin, to be given the chance to congratulate him and to praise his brave deed. They took time to visit the local newspaper so Quentin could give them a short interview and have his picture taken to accompany the article. A second one was taken of them to go along with an engagement notice. It was obvious to her that the townfolk loved, admired, and respected their local hero; just as it was apparent that Quentin had come from a fine southern community which had helped mold him into the splendid man he was today.

The remainder of Wednesday and Thursday passed swiftly and in great pleasure. When time came to leave Friday morning, hugs and kisses were exchanged and plans were made.

"You get us reservations at a hotel, Son; we won't hear of intruding on newlyweds Sunday night," his father insisted after Rachel invited

Quentin's parents and his sister and her family to stay at her house Saturday and Sunday nights. "We appreciate your offer of hospitality, Rachel, but that will be a busy and private time for you. We'll be just fine in a hotel, so don't worry about us."

Inez concurred with her husband and also thanked Rachel. She gave the couple tasty treats to take home with them. "Good-bye, Quent, Rachel, we'll see you next Saturday."

More hugs and kisses were shared, and the couple departed.

After reaching Augusta, Rachel assisted Quentin into the house and to the sofa, then unloaded the car. She freshened up before preparing their plates with food from Wife-Saver which she had picked up while en route home to save time and energy in the kitchen following the long drive.

As she was cleaning up after their meal, Quentin was watching TV in the casual area of the living room. After he switched to a local channel, he called out, "Rachel, honey, come quick and listen!"

Rachel grabbed a dish towel and dried her wet hands as she rushed to join him. She was astonished to hear a report that Todd Hardy had been arrested the previous night for breaking into a politician's office to steal information about an alleged crime for an exposé he planned to write. The announcer said that an investigation was in progress, with Hardy sitting in jail awaiting his day in court. "Can you imagine that?" Rachel murmured, looking at Quentin wide-eyed.

"Yep, after what he did to us and to others. I doubt he'll be able to worm his way out of this sleazy trap, and it serves him right for trying to hurt so many people. Even if what he claims is true, he can't break the law to get a scoop; he should have handed any clues he had over to the authorities. I hope they keep him in jail."

"At least other people won't get hurt while he's in jail, unless that magazine allows him to write in his cell and prints his articles. But at least he's out of our hair, my love."

"Thank goodness, and I hope he stays out. Do you need anything before I finish in the kitchen?"

He stroked her cheek as his gaze roamed her lovely features. "The only thing I need and want is you, woman, all the time."

Rachel nestled against him and stroked his chest. "You have me."

"And you have *me*. Lordy, we're in for a happy life together."

"Yes, my darling, we are," she said before sealing their mouths.

One meshing of their lips led to numerous kisses and embraces until they were feverish with desire and making love on the sofa.

* * *

On Saturday afternoon, Quentin went to the celebrity auction with Rachel. He received a standing ovation when his jersey and auto-graphed football were put up for bids. The two items brought in big money for the library exten-sion fund. The intense reaction brought shiny moisture to Quentin's eyes. Following the event, he posed for pictures with the two buyers and thanked them. Then he gave Pete Starns a short interview for a local television station.

After they freshened up at her house, Rachel and Quentin went out to dinner at the country club with the Coopers and Brimsfords, where a delightful meal and good time were had by all.

Sunday at four o'clock, Quentin and Rachel relaxed on the sofa and cuddled while they watched the Dallas Cowboys play the Pittsburgh Steelers in the season's first game. Several times, the sportscasters talked about Quentin and his past career, the accident which provoked his re-tirement, and his impending marriage to Rachel Gaines of Augusta, Georgia. The announcers praised his talents, courage, and contributions to the sport. They mentioned that Quentin was to be present and honored on September nine-teenth in Dallas during the Cowboys game with the Detroit Lions and that his jersey number was being retired on that team as a tribute to him.

"If you're watching, Quentin, congratulations and best wishes on your marriage and good luck in your new career, ranching we're told," one sportscaster said at the end of half-time. "You'll be sorely missed. Thanks for the many pleasures you've given to us and to your fans. You are and will remain one of football's greatest legends, a man who stands and walks tall, a man with a true golden arm that was extended on more than the playing field."

Quentin looked at Rachel and asked, "Whew, what can I say after being painted like that?"

"That you're going out in style and glory. I'm so proud of you, Quentin, and I love you so much."

After several kisses, he drew a deep breath and said, "If we keep this up, we'll miss the second half. 'Course, it'll be worth that sacrifice."

"Why don't we whet our appetites while we watch the rest of the game and feed them afterward for hours?"

"A woman after my own heart."

They cooked out on the grill on Labor Day, then spent part of the afternoon making passionate love. It was as if they couldn't get enough of each other following their long separation, a near permanent one.

On Tuesday morning, they got their blood tests and marriage license before Rachel put Quentin on a plane to return to Dallas for his doctor's appointment and preliminary treatments before he began therapy. Though people were watching, they kissed and hugged good-bye. Rachel waited until the plane took off before she left the airport, missing him already, as he missed her and watched clouds hide the ground.

Later, she finished typing letters of resignation to her clubs, boards, and organizations. She called the friends who had agreed to take over her unfinished projects and told them she would deliver those files tomorrow and thanked them again for their kindness. She learned from Becky that Janet Hollis had not returned to town. She hoped, if the woman had not had a change of heart and behavior, that Janet would not come back before her departure and try to cause trouble. It was calming to know that Janet and Todd Hardy were occupied elsewhere and fate was dealing with them.

The remainder of the week was filled with hours of shopping and appointments concerning the wedding and reception. She spoke with her daughters again and told them about her visit with the Rawlses, the special occasion on Sunday which they would miss, and the joint party for her and Quentin and Karen and David next June— which amazingly was being given by Dorothy and Richard Gaines who phoned on Wednesday to make peace and to insist on hosting the celebration of the two marriages. Rachel hoped they were being sincere; it had seemed that way to her during the talk. After so many years of difficulty, a truce would be marvelous and welcomed.

She also told the girls about the financial arrangements she had made with her accountant and banker. Karen and David were thrilled to get the house and a nice amount of money from Rachel's recent business dealings. Evelyn was to receive a sum equivalent to the value of the house and any furnishings that Rachel did not take to Texas. Martha had agreed to come over every week to clean and check the house until Karen's return, and Henry would continue to tend the yard and pool. Neighbors and friends agreed to keep an eye on the property during the period between Rachel's departure and Karen's arrival.

On Wednesday, with Martha's help and using boxes Henry had brought over in his truck, Rachel went through the house, garage, and attic and packed things she would need at the ranch. On Thursday, her two best friends assisted with that lengthy task, the three laughing, joking, and reminiscing as they did so. Yet, there were many possessions only she could sort through. She would decide if she needed other items after viewing her new home, as space and styles must be considered; then, Martha, Becky, and Jen would have them packaged and transported to her. Some things she wanted to give to Evelyn or leave for Karen, and made a list of them. Items none of them could use would be sold, but only after the girls were given first choice.

In one box, she placed the many magazines and newspapers that had featured recent sto-

ries— most with pictures— about Quentin, some
including her. She added the pictures from their
cruise and the celebrity auction to be placed in
their scrapbook and family album.

A man came to disconnect and pack her computer system. She would get back to work on
her novel as soon as she was settled. With
Quentin at her side and giving her confidence
and encouragement, she believed she would succeed as an author.

As she rested at each day's end, she looked
through pictures, papers, and keepsakes and reflected on her life.

Rachel lay in bed on Friday night after talking
with Quentin and thought about how busy and
glorious the next few days would be with her
lover's return tomorrow, a bridal shower that
night, their wedding on Sunday, and their departure for their new home on Monday. Life and
love were blessings, and she would never take
them for granted. Her future was sunny and she
almost was too excited to sleep. She was close
to having her dreams come true. Nothing and
no one, she reasoned, could interfere with them
now that past troublemakers were off her back.

Seventeen

On September eleventh at four o'clock, as soon as the soloist finished singing "Whither Thou Goest," the organist played the traditional wedding march and Rachel began her walk down the red-carpeted aisle on Scott Cooper's arm as he led her toward the man she loved. She was grateful to the church's wedding committee for accommodating them today between the two Sunday services.

As a gift to Rachel, a close friend in the florist business whose services she had used during many projects had decorated the church in romantic splendor. Ivy was draped like a thick lacy cloak over the white waist-high partition between the choir loft and altar platform. Flames flickered on multi-branched candelabrums on the raised dais; they also were wrapped in ivy and accented with white bows. A large floral arrangement sat on a pedestal behind where they would stand for the ceremony, which would create a lovely backdrop. On the ends of the first four pews, he had attached hurricane globes with candles, greenery, and white bows. The chandelier bulbs and numerous recessed lights were dimmed, except for the ones under which they would stand so the minister could see to read Biblical passages. Many family members and friends were turned sideways to watch Rachel approach. Quentin— handsome in a black tuxedo and fancy white shirt— awaited her at the front with the First Baptist pastor and Matthew Rawls, his best man. Becky, attired in a robin's-egg-blue tea-length dress, had preceded her down the aisle as her matron of honor.

The bouquet of sweetheart roses in Rachel's grasp quivered from excitement and happiness, not great tension or anxiety, though she *was* a little nervous, which was natural for brides. A photographer snapped pictures to place in the album that Becky and Jen had given her yesterday at the bridal shower. She knew two video cameras, as the Sunday morning service was sent out over a local television channel, were recording the blissful event, as she had asked for a tape to be made.

Rachel smiled and nodded at friends as her jubilant mind sang, *A real wedding, a beautiful wedding, with all of the trimmings this time. How lucky and blessed you are, Rachel Gaines.*

Yet, she wished her daughters, son-in-laws, and grandchildren could be there; the girls had sent telegrams yesterday to give their enthusiastic approval and to say how glad they were that the occasion had not been delayed for months. Gifts and cards had poured in this week from distant friends of Quentin and Rachel; even a silver-engraved serving tray had arrived from the Gaineses. The media was huddled outside, waiting to take pictures later and perhaps get a few quotes from the famous groom who was major news following the traffic accident, his courageous deed, and his retirement from football.

I'm almost there, my love, her mind told him.

Before Rachel began her graceful walk toward him, Quentin had glanced at his teary-eyed mother whose expression was one of sheer joy, one which said she agreed with his choice this time and believed this marriage was forever. His sister's gaze also was misty and her smile sunny. Mary was leaning close to her husband, both in a romantic mood. Bobby and Kelly were behaving to perfection, their gazes wide and shiny. His brother was grinning in delight, his disguise removed, a precaution Frank took to avoid problems with any nasty reporters. Quentin smiled at each member of his family as his gaze traveled down the pew where they sat together. He looked at his father who was standing beside him, and they exchanged smiles. A glow of pride and love was evident in Matthew's expression. But when the wedding march sounded, he could not take his adoring gaze from his future wife. She looked radiant and stunning in an ivory lace dress with long sleeves, fitted waistline, Victorian neckline, and V-shaped bodice. Her brown hair was positioned like leafy curls atop her head, with tiny pearls entwined, a gift from her longtime beautician and friend. Her soft mauve lips were smiling at him. Her arresting green eyes captivated him. Soon, they would be joined as one forever.

Blazes, she was breathtaking, and he loved her! She was the most wonderful thing that had happened to him and he vowed to do everything he could to make her happy.

Rachel's heart swelled with pride and anticipation, as she reached Quentin's side and took his hand. While Scott was seating himself with Jen and Adam and two surprise guests were sneaking to their places, she and Quentin mounted the dais to stand before the pastor. Matthew assisted his son up the steps, as Quentin's knee brace was restrictive. Becky joined them, awaiting the moment she could hold Rachel's bouquet.

The minister smiled and said, "Family and friends, we are gathered today in the sight of God and these witnesses to join this man and woman in the bond of holy matrimony. Rachel is a longtime member of our church and a fine lady, and Quentin has visited with us on several occasions, a man whose good character and deeds are well known to those present. It is an honor and pleasure to perform this marriage ceremony."

After the pastor read Scriptures from Ephesians and the Book of Ruth and spoke about them to the attentive couple, he asked, "Do you, Quentin James Rawls, take this woman to be your lawful and wedded wife?"

In a voice heavy with joyful emotion, the groom replied, "I do."

"Do you, Quentin, promise to love, honor, protect, support, guide, and cherish her in sickness and in health, in rich and in poor, in good times and in bad, and forsaking all others until death do you part?"

"I will." *After twelve long and lonely years, you'll be mine soon.*

The minister focused on her. "Do you, Rachel Marie Tims Gaines, take this man to be your lawful and wedded husband?"

She looked at her beaming love and vowed, "I do."

"Do you, Rachel, promise to love, honor, and cherish him in sickness and in health, in rich and in poor, in good times and in bad, and forsaking all others until death do you part?"

"I will." *And I promise there will be only golden days ahead for us.*

"May I have the ring please?" he asked Quentin, who passed it to him while Becky took charge of Rachel's bouquet. "A ring is a perfect circle to symbolize a never-ending bond of love and marriage. May your union always be as shiny and precious as the gold herein. This will be a sign unto you both and to the world of your commitments to each other. Place this ring on her finger and repeat after me, with this ring I thee wed."

Quentin slipped the gold band on her finger and repeated those precious words, his gaze lifting to join hers as he did so.

Following the pastor's instructions, Rachel repeated the same words as she slipped a gold band onto Quentin's finger, their gazes fusing once more and the contact of their hands rapturous.

"With the power invested to me by the church and this state, I now pronounce you man and wife. As Matthew chapter six says, 'Wherefore they are no more twain, but one flesh. What therefore God hath joined together, let no man put asunder.' Let us pray and bless this union." Afterward, he said with a smile, "You may kiss your bride."

Rachel and Quentin faced each other, smiled, embraced, and kissed. Before they parted, each whispered, "I love you."

The minister concluded with, "Congratulations and may you live long and happy lives together. Face the audience, please. Family and friends, I have the honor and pleasure of introducing to you, Mr. and Mrs. Quentin James Rawls. You are cordially invited to join the newlyweds at Westlake Country Club for a reception. Please feel free to go on over and enjoy yourselves; the bride and groom will join you as soon as pictures are taken."

As the pastor spoke and Rachel's eyes drifted over those gathered to share in this glorious occasion, her emerald gaze came to an abrupt halt and widened in astonishment. Joy flooded her as she saw Karen and Evelyn sitting among the guests, smiling and beaming with love and happiness. She could not imagine how she had missed sighting them earlier during her stroll down the aisle.

Noting her reaction, Quentin leaned toward

her and murmured, "I couldn't think of a better wedding gift than bringing the girls over today. They sneaked in after your back was turned."

Their gazes locked for a moment, and she smiled. She hugged him and said, "I love you, and it's the best surprise I've ever had. Thank you."

The elated girls hurried forward and embraced and kissed their mother, with all eyes misting.

"It was beautiful, Mom, and you look fantastic," Karen told her.

"Absolutely radiant," Evelyn added. "We're so happy for you. We've missed you like crazy. Eddie, Barbara, and the kids send their love. He couldn't come, and the trip was too long and fast for Alex and Ashley."

"I'm so glad you two made it, and I'm still in shock to see you here. As for you, Dr. Karen Phillips, congratulations on your marriage to David. You two are perfect for each other."

"Thanks, Mom, and we're deliriously happy. David sends his love and best wishes. It was too difficult for him to come with me, but he's very excited and pleased to have Quentin Rawls join our family circle."

"I can hardly believe my daughters are here," Rachel murmured, her gaze studying each in turn as if searching for any changes in them.

Karen laughed and hinted, "This must be Quentin, our new stepfather." She introduced herself, and then her sister Evelyn. "We're delighted to meet you, Quentin. You couldn't have done a nicer thing for us and Mom. She's told us so much about you, all good things, I might add. Now, we can see why you stole her heart. Welcome to our family." She gave him a hug and a kiss on the cheek, noting how handsome he was and mentally praising her mother's taste and victory.

"Thank you, Karen; she's made me the happiest man alive. I'm glad you two could come; I've looked forward to meeting you. I promise to take very good care of your mother."

"I know you two are perfect for each other," Evelyn said. "I'm so excited to be here, thanks to you, Quentin." She also gave him a hug and a kiss on the cheek.

Quentin noticed that both daughters favored Rachel and were lovely young women: vivacious, charming, polite. He looked forward to meeting their husbands and Evelyn's children next year. It was clear to him they were a close and loving family.

"How did you manage this enormous surprise?" Rachel asked him.

"Quentin contacted us last Wednesday after we talked on the phone and asked if we'd come," Karen responded. "He made the arrangements and paid for everything. I arrived early this morning. Evelyn got here late last night. But we both have flights out in the morning. It's been months and we hate to rush off, but David's covering for me, and Barbara is keeping the children for Evelyn, so we have to get back pronto. Besides, you have a new groom to concentrate on and a move coming up.

Quentin said you'll honeymoon later, after he completes his physical therapy."

"Why didn't you stay at home last night?" Rachel asked Evelyn.

"And spoil the surprise?" the youngest daughter teased. "That look on your face when you spotted us was worth a million bucks."

"I didn't see you when I came down the aisle."

"Because we were hiding in the back and sneaked down after you were up here," Karen explained. "We didn't want to distract you or make you nervous and tongue-tied. I take it you didn't suspect a thing?"

"I didn't have an inkling of a clue. And those cunning telegrams yesterday fooled me completely. If Quentin is this sneaky, I'd better keep a close eye on him," the bride jested, and he chuckled.

"Mr. and Mrs. Rawls, I'm ready to begin," the photographer said.

Pictures were taken of the newlyweds with all the members of both sides of the family, and with the minister and Scott and Becky.

As soon as he finished and was packing up to head for the reception, Rachel's daughters, Quentin's parents and the Mills family were introduced to each other. The group laughed and chatted for a few minutes before Quentin said they needed to leave for the reception. Too, the florist and janitor needed to put the church back in order for the evening service.

The elated couple paused outside to pose for

the media's cameras and for Quentin to answer a few questions, then were whisked away in the limo he had hired, Karen and Evelyn riding with them to the country club. The newlyweds were grateful to a thoughtful and sly Frank for disguising himself on their special day and for sneaking in and out the side door to elude any sleazy tabloid reporters, but none were there. Those present from the media couldn't have been nicer and kinder to the couple.

As Rachel and Quentin Rawls entered the large room at the country club, the guests applauded them and many came forward to speak with them; others waited for the crowd to thin out around them. Embraces, kisses, and handshakes were exchanged as they received congratulations and humorous words of advice. During the commotion, the girls stood with the Coopers and Brimsfords; the six laughed, reminisced, and caught up on personal news. Karen was congratulated on her recent marriage to David Phillips, whom they all knew and liked and whose parents were present today.

Rachel was introduced to Quentin's sports agent, Derek Hodges, who had flown in for the wedding. She knew that his friends on the Cowboys team could not attend, as they had a game with the Houston Oilers this afternoon; but they would see them in Dallas this weekend at a party those men were giving for the newlyweds on Friday night.

Rachel and Quentin conversed with friends, nibbled on ample hors d'oeuvres, sipped cham-

pagne, and ate wedding cake after they cut it and
fed each other a piece for a picture. The club chef
had done a marvelous job with the food, and the
servers worked unobtrusively. The florist had
placed hurricane globes with flowers, greenery,
and ribbons on each table; candelabrums and
large arrangements of flowers were on the re-
freshment tables; and potted palms had been set
in various locations in the already lovely surroundings. Romantic music on low volume filtered into the room through the club's sound
system.

Everyone appeared to be having a wonderful
and relaxing time. Gifts and cards lay on a table
near the door, alongside a guest registry, a present from Betty Burke at the shower. The couple
was pleased that many of Quentin's old friends
from his first pro team— the San Francisco
49ers— had sent cards, telegrams, and gifts to
Quentin while he was in the hospital and to Rachel's home this week as wedding congratulations. The same was true of some people from
the media and from companies for which
Quentin had done past product endorsements,
from the Carters and their families, and from
countless fans across the country. She was
thrilled that so many people held her love in
such high esteem and deep affection.

Rachel thanked Becky and Jen once more for
the bridal shower they had given her the previous night while Scott and Adam kept Quentin
company. The three friends talked about past
times, future plans, and the wedding. It was de-

cided that Jen also would come to visit when Scott and Becky came to begin renovations on the ranch house later this month.

"I miss you two already and I haven't even left town."

"We'll miss you, too, Rach. I doubt anyone will ever be able to replace you in our little group."

"We're so thrilled for you, Rachel; you deserve this happiness."

"Thank you, Jen, and I love you both."

"We love you, too, Rach," Becky said, and hugged her. "Any time you get lonesome, just pick up the phone and call us, but *I* doubt you'll have those feelings with Quentin around." The blonde grinned.

"He is wonderful, isn't he?" Rachel murmured with a glowing smile.

"Yes, and it was nice of him to bring the girls over for the wedding. You're lucky, Rach, and smart. You said you would wait for Mr. Right to come along, and you found him. The girls have taken to him quickly."

"Yes, and I'm glad, but I knew they would."

"His family is nice, too, and they seem crazy about you and your marriage to Quentin; I know you're ecstatic about that."

Rachel grasped Becky's allusion to past problems with her first in-laws. "You're right, but things appear to be better between me and the Gaineses; that's especially good where the girls are concerned."

Jen and Becky nodded agreement.

"I want to thank you two for taking care of the presents today. It's so thoughtful of you to pack them up and send them to Dallas with the movers."

"That's what are friends for," Becky remarked.

"And you two are the best friends anyone could have. Mercy, I'm going to miss you." Rachel hugged them again before she said, "I'd better mingle for a while. I'll talk with you two later."

At one point, Clifford Hollis whispered to Rachel that Janet had returned, had agreed to seek therapy and to attend counseling with their pastor, and they might get back together if she changed. Rachel was stunned when her banker and neighbor told her that Janet sent her an apology for past mistreatments. She told him she hoped everything worked out for the best for them, and her generous heart was sincere.

In the ladies' room later, Rachel spoke privately with her daughters for a few minutes. The girls were relieved and delighted by their grandparents' surprising change of heart and behavior. Karen was pleased that a party would be given for both couples next June. The Gaineses and their daughters had apologized for being unable to attend the wedding, as they had left on their annual family vacation on Friday, to Hawaii for two weeks this time. In a way, Rachel, Karen, and Evelyn were relieved the Gaines family couldn't come, as it prevented reminders of Rachel's marriage to Daniel and his tragic death which could dampen spirits today. Yet, they knew, if the reservations hadn't been made long ago, Daniel's family would be present. At least they had an excellent excuse for the Gaines' absence for appearance's sake, as their trip had been planned long before the wedding.

Rachel went over the early inheritance gifts for Karen and Evelyn, and mentioned the large settlement Quentin was to receive for his accident and future earnings from a deal with a collector's items company. "I hate to talk about business matters here and so fast, but you're leaving tomorrow and I didn't want to go over them by phone or letter. Quentin and I have discussed money and wills; he wanted mine set up so everything I have will be divided equally between you two upon my death. Newton has taken care of it for me, and a copy is in the safe at home. Is there anything else you can think of we need to discuss quickly?"

"No, Mom, and we're most appreciative of what you've done and to Quentin for being so considerate," Karen told her.

Both girls hugged and kissed Rachel in love and gratitude.

"Are you sure you two don't want to sleep at home tonight? Honestly, we don't mind; we have a lifetime to spend together."

"Heavens, no, Mom, we wouldn't dare intrude on your wedding night. You just focus on that handsome hunk who's crazy about you. After we eat dinner with David's parents, Evelyn and I will catch up on our news at the hotel; Quentin rented us a two-bedroom suite. He even had champagne and a fruit-and-cheese basket delivered, and hired a limo to bring us to the church. He did invite us to have breakfast with you two before we fly out tomorrow, in case he's forgotten to mention it in the excitement, and we're all on the same plane to Atlanta. I think his family is joining us, too, before they drive home."

"That man thinks of everything. I'm so lucky to have him and to have wonderful daughters like you two. Lordy, I love you and I've missed you."

"The feeling is mutual, Mom, and we're so happy for you. He's terrific, and we're already crazy about him. His family, too. Right, Evelyn?"

"Absolutely, Mom. You did great. We're proud of you."

"Thanks for being such wonderful and caring daughters. I'm very lucky to have you both and to have Quentin. I know you and David will be just as happy as we are," Rachel told Karen. "Don't forget to tell him how delighted I am about your marriage." To Evelyn, she said, "Thank Barbara for keeping the children so you could come. Give Alex and Ashley and Eddie hugs and kisses for me and tell them we'll visit in April after your return."

"I will, Mom, and don't forget to send pictures to show them."

"As soon as the photographer sends me the proofs and we make our choices, I'll have albums made up for each of you and send them along. Well, we should get back to our guests and party. After Karen returns home, Evelyn, you and I can fly to Augusta and we'll have a hen party."

As they left the ladies' room, Evelyn quipped, "Considering the abundant number of gifts and favors friends and even strangers have sent and done for you two, you'll be writing thank you notes for weeks."

"I know, and isn't it wonderful that people are so nice and kind?"

"That's the only way anyone could be to you and Quentin," Karen said.

Rachel and Quentin Rawls snuggled in the king-size bed at her house, candlelight glowing In the room and flickering over their nude bodies and tranquil faces. They talked about their lovely wedding and reception, their families, friends, and future together. They kissed and caressed as they relaxed after the busy and exhilarating day, glad to be alone at last. A special aura of intimacy and closeness was heavy in the air and between them tonight.

He stared at her face with its serene expression and murmured, "Lordy, I love you, woman. You're beautiful, especially ravishing today. I wanted to hug you and kiss you every minute."

His husky tone and the seductive gleam in his gaze enflamed her from head to feet. He had a way of making her feel like the most desirable female alive. "We're complete and strong together, two halves of the same whole."

"You're right, we're a perfect match, and we're so lucky, so blessed."

Her entranced gaze meshed with his enticing blue one. "Yes, we are, and I love you. I couldn't be happier than I am at this moment."

"Neither could I," he agreed as he stroked her mussed brown hair and emotion-flushed cheek. He adored and enjoyed everything about her. He was indeed fortunate he met her years ago and found her again. Without a doubt, she was his destiny, his soulmate, his consummate partner in all things.

Her fingers trailed over his neck and collarbone, then she drifted them over his broad chest as they admired and stroked that hairy and strong terrain. She teased them over his rib cage and laughed when he wiggled at the ticklish sensations. They paused at his waistline. He was firm and supple, so magnificent and arousing. She felt as if she could do, be, or say anything she wanted with him; he was good for her and good to her. Yes, her dreamy mind concluded, their powerful physical and emotional attractions, easy rapport, and total compatibility made them perfect for each other.

Quentin's fingers roamed her silky flesh; they traveled along the rises of her spine, past her slim waist, across her firm buttocks, and down her taut thighs. He wanted to tantalize every inch of her to unbridled yearning, and tried to do so. Never had a woman given him such exquisite longing, evoked such hunger, and sated him with such supreme satisfaction. He heard her sigh with pleasure as he fondled her breasts and noticed how responsive they were to his touch. He noted the textures and contrasts of her sensuous frame. He craved to be within her, but he proceeded with deliberate leisure, drawing out his skilled foreplay for as long as possible.

Rachel inhaled and savored his manly scent. When they kissed, her tongue danced playfully with his to a sweet melody heard inside their heads. When his lips journeyed down her throat and wandered through the canyon between her mounds before climbing their peaks, she writhed and moaned in rapture. The points hardened even more as his tongue flicked over them rapidly or circled them slowly, provocatively.

Quentin guided one hand down her warm flesh to the triangle of hair between her thighs, its feel downy soft and the mist of her arousal dampening it. His fingers roved the satiny folds and entreating pinnacle, massaging the hot bud until she quivered and squirmed and moaned. He teethed her nipples, then his mouth returned to hers for several kisses before nibbling at her earlobe. He decided she was as near to flawless in looks and personality as a woman could be. She seemed to cover him like a warm and cozy blanket on a freezing day. She whet his appetite, then appeased it with generosity. He had come to know her so well that he could grasp her signals and messages without her speaking them aloud. His craving for her was huge and fervent, and his manhood pulsed with suspense and eagerness to enter her inviting portal.

Pleasure— blissful and titillating— enthralled them. They stroked and enflamed each other without restraints; they yielded and enslaved each other's senses. Their wits were spinning wildly; yet, clear. They were visiting an erotic and steamy paradise, reveling in their love.

Deep within her womanhood, sensations mounted and deepened. A wonderful ache chewed at her. Her need for him was large and urgent. He was everything she wanted and needed in a man, in a husband. She adored being his quest, his goal, his wife, his forever. Her head thrashed upon the pillow as she savored each sensation and begged for more with words muffled by her lips against his right shoulder.

Quentin was elated that he could so arouse and satisfy her. He was coaxed onward by her uninhibited responses and enormous need. His senses reeled in wild and free abandonment. She was his heart, his soul, his future. She gave to him willingly, eagerly. Carnal flames engulfed him in a blazing inferno that only fulfillment could douse. No love could be stronger or deeper than theirs. No fiery passion could burn brighter or fiercer. No union could be more perfectly paired than theirs.

Rachel rolled to her side and Quentin glued himself to her back like two spoons stuck together. He guided his swollen erection into her moistness pausing for a minute to summon self-control. Despite the restrictive knee brace he thrust into her with ease as she undulated against him. They labored thus for a while; then, she shifted to her back and placed her right leg over his hips, her left one resting between his sleek thighs, his tumescent organ buried deep in her core. They seemed to move and to moan in unison as their needs reached a feverish pitch.

One of Rachel's hands stroked his muscled thigh and the other grasped his uninjured shoulder to cling to him. Her inner recess throbbed, contracted, and climaxed wildly as jolt after jolt of a glorious and potent release seized her and swept over her. She felt almost euphoric, enjoying every instant and movement of the torrid experience, even beyond the fading of the tiny aftershocks when she was limp with contentment.

Quentin delved inside her, plunging into her now slick depths, retreating slightly, almost reluctantly, before thrusting again and again as the intensity of his desire built. Every fiber of his being was aware of her, aware of the enormous thrill of his release when he seemingly exploded with rapturous vitality and supreme satisfaction.

"Whew, that was wonderful. How can it keep getting better and better?" he asked, almost breathless and still quivering from the experience.

Amazed, she said, "I don't know, but it does. Incredible, isn't it?"

"Yep. I loved playing football, but I love playing with you far more," the ex-quarterback murmured in honesty. His mouth covered hers with tenderness and great love, and she responded in like kind.

As they rested and nestled, caressed and kissed, both knew that was only the first time they would unite their bodies this evening as they had united their hearts long ago and united their lives today.

As the jet took off on Monday morning, Rachel held hands with Quentin and cuddled her left shoulder against his right one. Her daughters sat across the aisle, chatting continuously; in Atlanta, they would take separate flights to rejoin their families in Japan and aboard the medical ship. Breakfast with the girls, the Rawlses, and the Millses had been a joyous occasion for all; and Quentin's family was en route home to Colquitt to prepare for their peanut harvest soon.

Rachel looked out the window and watched the town of Augusta as it vanished in the distance. Her existence there was fading from view and into the past, and a bright future with her new husband was before her in Texas. She wondered what life on a ranch would be like, but knew anything would be wonderful at Quentin's side. Of course, they would be returning to Augusta next June for the Gaineses' party for them and for Karen and David. No matter how terrible her in-laws had been in the past, she was grateful they had softened and prayed they would continue to mellow even more.

As her mind raced with plans, she thought it would be fun to write in that location, and probably inspirational to her creative juices. She was eager to see where she would be living and working, and hoped the impending renovations went smoothly for them, in light of horror stories she had heard about such projects. Yet, with Scott Cooper and his crew handling the job, she did not expect any problems.

Becky and Jen would be arriving at the end of the month with Scott and his workers, to stay for several days. Her two best friends were taking care of the movers tomorrow at her former home. On Wednesday, the trucking firm would deliver the things she was taking to Dallas with her, which would allow her and Quentin to settle in on Tuesday and to make room for those items, in particular her computer system.

She looked forward to the party on Friday and to meeting his friends and teammates. She was delighted about attending the Cowboys and Detroit Lions game next Monday in Dallas where Quentin would be honored at half-time. His injuries were healing nicely and shouldn't, according to the recent tests and doctors' opinions, give him trouble after therapy was completed in a few months, if he was careful not to reinjure those sites again. She was grateful he was alive and would be fully recovered soon, and the Carters, too, who had sent a wedding gift, as had their families, out of affection and gratitude. During this past week, she had visited the graves of her infant son and Daniel, side by side in the cemetery. She had told them good-bye and had made sure their burial site would receive perpetual care and flowers on certain dates.

She mentally said another prayer of thanks for being given a second chance at powerful love and passionate romance. She had thanked Becky and Jen for insisting she go to their high school reunion that night in July when fate had thrown her and Quentin together again. Twice she had been tempted by the unique man beside her and twice she had succumbed to his charms, and she would never regret either passion-ruled decision. It was as if she were riding off into a glorious sunset with her handsome and sexy Cowboy, heading for a splendid future as his wife and partner.

Rachel fused her gaze to his, smiled, and whispered, "I love you."

Quentin smiled and murmured, "I love you, too, Mrs. Rawls, and we're going to be so happy you can't think or see straight."

Rachel smiled again, never once doubting those beautiful words. She had risked everything for love and had come out a rapturous winner.

Author's Note

The Dallas Cowboys name, team members, and sports record were used only to provide my hero with fictional membership on a championship football team. The same is true for the use of— my husband's alma mater— Richmond Academy class of 1964 high school reunion for my heroine. It was fun to research my husband's hometown of Augusta, near which we live, and to feature it as my setting. However, feelings and opinions expressed about the setting and Old South traditions are those of the characters, not of the author who is a born and bred true Southerner and proud Georgian.

If you would like to receive a Janelle Taylor Newsletter, book list, and bookmark, send a self-addressed stamped envelope (long size best) to:
Janelle Taylor Newsletter
P.O. Box 211646
Martinez, Georgia 30917-1646